I0699851

After
THE
RAIN
AMBER PALMER

Complete Editing Services performed by Heather Nix

Cover Design: Forensics and Flowers

For Heather -
My Glinda. My platonic soulmate. My lifeline. Thank you for giving this
anxiety queen a safe place to run to.

For the eldest daughters who work themselves to the bone just to be
seen... You're not alone.

playlist

For the full playlist, scan the QR code!

Red Dirt Road (with Cody Johnson) - Brooks & Dunn
Duet (feat. Stephanie Briggs) - Penny and Sparrow
Cover Me Up - Jason Isbell
Red (Taylor's Version) - Taylor Swift
Sun to Me - Zach Bryan
Iris - The Goo Goo Dolls
Somewhere Only We Know - Keane
Rest (with Sasha Alex Sloan) - Dean Lewis
Till There's Nothing Left - Cam

content warning

While this book is sweet and swoony, there are a few matters that may be sensitive to readers.

- Alcohol Use / Abuse
- Death of a parent (cancer)
- Domestic violence (physical and verbal, on page)
- Issues of grief and loss
- Mental Health: Depression, PTSD, on-page therapy sessions
- Infertility, mention of miscarriage

cleo

. . .

"JUST BREATHE, Cleo. You're safe here." I closed my eyes, unable to stare at the tiny video screen on my computer anymore. My hand wrapped desperately around the stress ball my therapist sent me years ago after our first session. Once upon a time, it'd been a pristine white and yellow daisy—one of my favorite flowers. Now, it was split and faded after easing me through yet another therapy session.

"We're getting a divorce. Thomas is staying in Montana with his brother, or at least that's what he told me. I don't know, and I don't care. He can rot in hell."

Memories of last night hadn't stopped haunting me since I retreated to my childhood bedroom in the early hours of the morning and cried. Announcing my divorce at the dinner table might have seemed out of left field to my entire family, but it'd been a long time coming.

I wanted to say it lifted a weight off my shoulders, but that wasn't true. If anything, I felt heavier—like the truth only added to the burden of shame I constantly carried around. It was one more thing I'd failed at. One more thing for people to pity me for when they passed me on the street.

Ashwood, Texas was your quintessential small town—complete with a picturesque town square filled with local businesses, two barely passable dive bars, and a population of busybody gossips who made it their mission to stick their noses in everyone's personal lives.

I'd been back in town for six months, and I was still pelted with questions in the produce aisle. The interrogators fell into one of two categories—catty mean girls I went to high school with or little old ladies who'd known me since I was born. It was why I never went shopping alone anymore if I could help it. Getting asked why I moved home or when my soon-to-be ex husband would be joining me wasn't my favorite topic of conversation. I thought if I kept my answers simple, people would ignore me and move on, but it only added to the intrigue.

It was why, after months of near silence about my unexpected return, I decided to blurt it out at the dinner table. I think on some level, my sisters, Josie and Lennox, already knew something had happened between Thomas and me. Other than a random question here or there, they knew I was a private person and respected that. Even my dad had bitten his tongue when it came to the whole surprise return thing.

My mom, bless her, was the opposite. The moment she smelled something sour, she was determined to find the source. I had a bit of a reprieve at the beginning of summer when she'd gone out of town for a month, but since she'd been back, she'd subjected me to an inquisition nearly every week.

"How long are you staying?"

"When is Thomas joining you?"

"Why hasn't he called or come to visit?"

I don't know, Mom. Maybe because he is an abusive piece of shit who gambled away his inheritance and drained our savings before taking out his frustrations on me?

"This isn't working," I said through gritted teeth. "It feels like I can't squeeze hard enough to take the edge off."

I could hear Laura, my saint of a therapist, rustling papers on her desk. "Then throw it at something."

"What?" I stopped mid-squeeze, cracking open an eye. "Throw it at something?"

She shrugged. "Why not?"

"What if I break something?"

I looked around my room at my parents' house. It hadn't changed much over the past seventeen years, but it never really had to. Other than the cheesy boy-band posters that'd been promptly removed the first summer after college, my style hadn't evolved much. The walls had always been a pale shade of powder blue—still one of my favorite colors—and I'd bought a white linen comforter set when I'd moved back in. There were two bookcases on the wall opposite my bed, filled to the brim with shelf trophies of my favorite books.

"What if you do?" Laura asked, bringing my focus back to the computer. "What would happen?"

"You know, sometimes I feel like you don't know me at all," I said, dropping the stress ball onto the table with a sigh.

Her laugh was soft, like tinkling bells. "You and I both know that isn't true. Perhaps it upsets you that I know you better than most."

Laura and I hadn't known each other long, but she already knew more about me than most others. The only exception was my best friend Rachel.

Back in college, our dorm rooms were right across from one another, and we'd often found ourselves locked out on the weekends when our roommates brought "friends" over to spend the night. After the first few weeks of camping in the hallway, we decided to form a two-person study group in the common area instead, and the rest was history.

After we graduated, we went our separate ways like most do. We'd checked in on one another through social media from time to time, but never stayed in touch past that. It wasn't until I saw she'd opened her own psychology practice that I decided to reach out.

Making the first call had felt like hitting rock bottom. I wasn't used to asking for help of any kind. In fact, it was the first time I'd done something just for me in years. The thought of adding my issues to someone else's plate nearly broke me out in hives, but I did it anyway.

It turned out to be the best thing I'd ever done. While Rachel couldn't take me on as a client, she was able to refer me to Laura. There were a lot of things I needed to work through, but my progress had been great. Looking back, I knew I wasn't the same person I was when I started. But just because I could admit the therapy was working didn't mean I always liked it. In fact, sometimes I ended the session hating Laura just a little and wishing I'd never reached out.

It was almost comical how processing trauma in a healthy way could be more painful than locking up the vault of memories and throwing away the key.

Almost.

"What're you scared of, Cleo?" she asked, gently prodding me. "Talk to me. That's the point of these sessions."

I rubbed my temple. "I don't want to break something."

Laura nodded, urging me to get to the point. "And why is that?"

I grabbed the daisy, staring at it in the palm of my hand. There'd be no fixing it. No amount of cleaning could undo the damage I'd done to it. It'd be easier to get a new one. Maybe I should. Maybe it didn't work anymore because it was broken and—

"Cleo."

I forced myself to meet Laura's gaze through the screen. "Sometimes broken things can't be fixed," I admitted quietly, looking back down at the stress ball. "Sometimes they stay broken."

That was how I'd felt lately.

Broken.

I loved being home, but sometimes it brought out a side of me I didn't care for. The moment I crossed the property line of Black Springs Ranch, my dad's pride and joy, I reverted to my role as the eldest daughter just as I'd always done.

It scared me how easily I fell into the swing of things again. Even though I'd been gone for years, it was almost like I'd never left. I loved spending time with my family, especially my sisters. There'd been too much of an age gap between us to bond when we were growing up, but it'd been different as adults.

Watching Josie and Lennox grow into themselves was strangely rewarding. I wasn't their parent, but the seven and nine-year age gaps between us meant I sometimes struggled to balance the relationship between sister and caregiver. We'd fought about it so many times. It was always the same. I tried, in my own way, to make them understand things about life I wished I'd known when I was their age, but it always turned into someone screaming at me that I wasn't their mother and couldn't tell them what to do.

I'd be a liar if I said I didn't feel a little pride at the strong young women they turned into, even if it meant I wasn't as close to them as they were to each other.

Knowing we were going to be together again as adults had been a bright spot in my otherwise gloomy life, but the one thing I wasn't prepared for was the reality that their lives were now more on track than my own.

Josie had recently fallen back in step with her five-night summer fling from last year. They were inseparable. Where one went, the other followed. Before they'd gotten together a few months ago, Josie had been dating the king of douchebags. No one liked Ellis, and for good reason, but Lincoln Carter was different.

Even though it hadn't been long, anyone with eyes could tell the man was helplessly in love with her. It bordered on obsessive, but Josie had deserved someone who would put her first every single time.

And Lennox? Oh, my baby sister hadn't so much as uttered a word about her love life, but I had a sneaking suspicion she and our ranch foreman weren't too far behind. Lennox and Bishop were always fighting and bickering, but there was this electrifying tension, too. They were probably the only two people who didn't clock it, choosing instead to live in oblivion.

Then there was me. Going through a messy divorce at thirty-five and living in my childhood bedroom. Clearly, I was thriving.

No matter where I looked, I was surrounded by people maddeningly in love, chasing the rush of euphoria they all seemed to be consumed by. When it was only my mom and dad's over-the-top public displays of affection, it was easy to shrug off. They were my parents; in a perfect world, that was how it was supposed to be, wasn't it?

They were the best role models I could've asked for—kind, patient, and loving. More importantly, though, they showed us what a healthy relationship looked like. And not just the good parts, either.

As we grew up, they made sure we knew life and love wasn't all sunshine and rainbows. Sometimes, it was going to be hard to put one foot in front of the other. Relationships of any kind were hard without proper nurturing, but it didn't matter because at the end of the day, the thought of living without your person was too much to bear.

Seeing my parents' devotion to one another filled me with the hope that maybe I could have that one day, too, but it wasn't their fault I let myself be duped by love.

I wanted to be blind with passion. I wanted to feel free, to soar through the sky like a bluebird spreading its wings. I wanted to know if I fell, someone would be there to help me back up again.

Honestly, I wanted a lot of things I knew weren't in the cards for me anymore.

I'd been close to having it all. Twice, actually—though I tried not to think about the first. Thomas and I met my freshman year of college. We shared a class together. After years of keeping my nose in textbooks instead of putting myself out there, he finally won out.

He'd been cute. Stupidly, so. I was charmed by his boyish good looks and those green eyes that promised mischief. The rest of our story? Well, it was much more complicated than I ever let anyone know.

When things were good between us, they were *good*. Great, even. The first six years were some of the happiest of my life. When things started going south, I told myself it was just a part of life we needed to get through. A storm to weather. I was more than willing to step up and be whoever he needed me to be if it took some of his stress away.

But Thomas saw my generosity as my being a doormat. It didn't take him long to wipe his dirty boots against my dignity, to dig in his heels and grind me down just to free himself of whatever debris clung to his soul.

It would've been easy to blame my parents for why I stayed in my marriage for so long—clinging to the hope I might someday have what they did. Or I could've looked at the men who still haunted me, laying the blame at their feet instead of my own. But pointing fingers at others never did any good. Especially considering I was the common denominator.

There were parts of me missing. Parts I still didn't know how to get back, even after intensive and continuous therapy. Some mornings, I didn't recognize who I was. The woman in the mirror was an empty shell of someone I once knew.

I normally kept it to myself. The only person I'd ever openly admitted everything to was Rachel, but that'd been after many tears and just as many vodka tonics. She encouraged me to talk to Laura, which I begrudgingly did. To this day, they were the only two people who knew every part of my story, even those secrets I'd kept close to my chest.

I guess it made sense my therapist needed to know these things.

There were days I dreaded my sessions because I knew Laura would want me to dig deep. Sometimes, I felt myself growing tense before we'd even begun. It was like my body was preparing for the inevitable crash that came after the screen went dark. The train of thought cast a dark cloud over my mood and no matter what, I couldn't shake it.

I knew today was going to be a heavy appointment. Laura had been encouraging me to tell my family about the divorce since I'd been back home, but I kept pushing it off. Last night, I'd finally snapped under the weight of my parents' curious questions. Spilling the beans before my dad's birthday bash—his words, not mine—hadn't been the best move.

Earlier in the year, my dad's health had given us a major scare. Apparently, not even the world's best dad was immune to a sick heart. Seeing him in a hospital bed was an image I'd never forget. It'd been a wake-up call—one we severely needed because we had never talked about what would happen after he was gone.

When Mom had told me the news, I'd slid down the wall and cried. I hated myself for the fleeting sense of relief I felt at my dad's expense. It was the out I'd been searching for, my reason for leaving Montana and never looking back.

"Do we need to take a break?" Laura asked, crossing her arms. "I can feel you shutting down."

"No, I'm good," I said, straightening my shoulders and forcing a smile. Her pursed lips told me she wasn't buying it. "I'm just thinking about all the things I need to do today. You know how it is."

"And now you're deflecting," she said, sitting back in her

chair. "Look, I want to make it clear how proud of you I am. Telling your family what happened with Thomas couldn't have been easy. I know we practiced the speech together, but I want to stress the importance of this achievement."

"Thank you——"

"But by rehashing the details of your relationship, I'm worried you might be slipping back into your self-imposed guilt."

"Well, no one can make me feel worse about myself than I can," I said, trying and failing to inject a dash of darker humor into our conversation. Sometimes it worked, and I'd successfully change topics, but today was not the day.

"Cleo—"

"It's fine. I'm fine," I said, holding up my hands. Then I grabbed my ball and gave it one long squeeze. "See? Just like the doctor ordered."

"You can thank Rachel for that one," she said, smiling slightly. "Let's stop here for the day. I know you said you're fine, but I don't want to push you too much. You've come so far. I hope you can see that."

"Cleo!" My name came from the hallway, and the sound of her barging through my door came seconds later.

I screamed as I heard Lennox's voice behind me. "You little shit," I said, turning around. "How'd you get in?"

"The master key?" Lennox asked, holding up a small silver key in her hand.

"Why do you have that?" I asked, trying to rein Lennox in.

She shrugged. "Yeah, I had it made years ago so I could break into Josie's room. Did you know she used to hide liquor at the back of her closet? Completely unrelated, of course." She plopped down on my bed.

Lennox was quiet for a second before asking, "I already know the answer, but I feel it's my sisterly duty to ask if you want to talk about it."

Despite her loud and extroverted personality, there was no one who loved as fiercely as Lennox. She'd fight a fence post if she thought it'd wronged you somehow.

I pushed from my chair, going over and laying my hand on top of hers. I wasn't big on physical contact, but she was. "No, I'm good. Thank you, though."

She nodded. "You know I'm always here, though, right?"

"I do." It was the first genuine smile I'd given in what felt like weeks. "And you know the same goes for me, right? If there's anything, or anyone"—I nudged her leg—"that you want to talk about..."

"Nope," she said, hopping down. "Not until there's something, or someone, for *you* to talk about." She gave me a pointed look, and I raised my hands. All I had to do was make it through a day without thinking of the first boy who broke my heart, which was easier said than done.

cleo

. . .

"DAMN, IT'S HOT FOR OCTOBER," Cook said as he leaned over the massive portable BBQ pit and grabbed a foiled baked potato. "Thought the news said it wasn't supposed to be so hot?"

I laughed, putting my hands on my hips and surveying the space. Cook was right. It was hotter than hell, but that didn't seem to stop people from showing up. Today was one big celebration and Dad's party was in full swing. Cars had been pulling through the Black Springs gate all day, and they were still coming.

Red and white tents filled the pasture, giving people a place to escape the sun and grab a drink to cool off. Lennox and Lincoln's carefully curated playlist played softly over speakers placed throughout the masses. Tonight, there'd be a live band playing, though no one knew who. Dad had kept that one a secret from everyone.

Knowing him, I wouldn't have been surprised if it was some drifter with a single guitar who only played Conway Twitty covers.

My dad loved to give back to the community and had invited

damn near everyone he knew, which meant most of the Ashwood population was going to be out at the ranch. Even our employees got the day off, thereby giving the Hayes family a busy morning attempting to pick up the slack.

After Lennox dragged me from my bedroom, I wandered over to Cook's tent to help with the food prep. Most of it had already been taken care of—he was a bit neurotic when it came to his craft—but there was still plenty of setup to account for.

I was the only one of my siblings working today, which was fine. I didn't mind. It gave me something to do instead of crashing out while watching cowboys wrestle steers. I looked toward the table where my family sat. Mom and Dad had come by multiple times, trying to get me to hang up my apron and join them. I made up some excuse, telling them I felt bad leaving everyone else to deal with Cook's wrath. It wasn't completely a lie.

For someone who listened to nothing but Hank Williams and spent his weekend fishing, you wouldn't think he'd be such a snob, but I'd seen Cook get worked up over the order of toppings on a burger. I could still remember the time he had the audacity to criticize my great-great-grandma's banana bread recipe in front of my mom. She didn't talk to him for at least two months because he remained steadfast in his opinion.

Honestly, it was still a hot-button topic. I didn't think they'd ever been the same.

"You know how Texas weather is," I said, refilling a roll of paper towels. "No one can predict what it's gonna do."

"It's days like this I wish I'd taken a job in a state that actually has seasons," Cook muttered. "This is bullshit."

I paused, turning over my shoulder to look at him. "And you've lived here how long again?"

His eyes darted to the side. "My whole life."

"That's what I thought," I laughed. "You had the chance to

leave, and you didn't. Just think about all the places you could've worked if you'd followed your food-loving heart."

"I couldn't give up fishing."

"You realize there are lakes and rivers in other states, right?"

Cook nodded. "Yeah, but your dad keeps y'all's stocked, so I don't have to worry about running out."

I shrugged. "I guess that's the price you pay." I picked up the case of sodas, ready to walk past him to refill one of the coolers, when my stomach let out a horribly embarrassing growl.

Before I knew it, the drinks had been plucked from my hands, and there was a very large, angry man standing in front of me. "When's the last time you ate?" he asked, narrowing his gaze.

"I've been busy," I said, shrugging him off and reaching for the case once more. He raised it above his head, looking down at me with an expression that screamed trouble.

For all his strong opinions—and believe me, there were many—nothing got Cook more fired up than people going hungry. When he wasn't on duty at the ranch, he was often volunteering, donating his time and talent to those in need of some help and a good meal.

"Get the hell outta here until you've gotten some food in your belly, girl. Anthony!" he called, looking over at one of the employees he'd taken under his wing.

The kid came running up. "Yes, sir?"

"Get Miss Hayes a plate. Load it up with everything, but make sure to put the BBQ sauce on the side," he said.

I couldn't help but smile. "You always take good care of me, Cook."

He huffed, but there was a flush on his cheeks. "I still remember you throwing knock-down, drag-out fits when your mom poured it all over your chicken. If I can avoid a mess, then I'm gonna do my best. I even made the spicy sauce you love so much."

It was true. I hated most condiments, but I was pickier about BBQ sauce. Most were too sweet. After a lot of hysterical moments and refusing to eat meals, my parents finally learned what worked and what didn't.

And Cook made one hell of a sauce.

Anthony came rushing back, plate laden with food. "Here ya go, Miss Cleo," he said, dipping his head.

I thanked him, taking the plate so he could get back to work. Cook gestured toward the table. "Now, you go sit down and enjoy all your hard work."

"I'll be back," I said, pointing in his direction. "You won't get rid of me that easily."

"You should be partying it up!" he called. "Not hanging out with me."

"You're not such bad company," I replied. He just waved me off and started barking orders at everyone else.

Now that I actually had food in my hand, my stomach was going crazy. Hunger hit me like a sharp knife to the gut. I surveyed the table, clocking an extra seat beside a pissed-off looking Bishop. The foreman constantly wore a scowl, but he was staring down Lincoln like he'd personally offended him.

I dropped into the empty space, groaning as the stress of the day began to show. I was running on adrenaline, denial, and an ungodly amount of coffee. "God, I'm starving," I said, immediately digging into the food before me. I groaned as the first taste of homemade mac and cheese hit my tongue. It was so good. Honestly, Cook should've been in some Michelin-star restaurant rather than working on our ranch.

"Remind me never to volunteer when Cook asks for help. I don't know how anyone keeps up with him and his standards. He's nuts!" It was only half-true. He could be a bit extreme, but I kind of enjoyed his company.

Bishop chuckled beside me. "Naw, I think you'll still help. That's just who you are."

For some reason, his comment took me off guard. I'd always felt like my niceties did more harm than good—at least when it came to my own well-being. Rachel and I had joked about oldest-sibling-syndrome in college, but it'd planted a seed in my mind that continued to grow.

Neither Mom nor Dad were exceedingly strict parents. There were basic expectations—manners, respect, and honesty were big in our house—but they didn't ask for anything they didn't give in return. They never pushed me to do something I didn't want to or told me I needed to improve at something I loved. I think it was just a matter of loving them so much I didn't want to disappoint them.

Rachel said I was a people-pleaser with a heightened sense of responsibility and crushing need for perfectionism, which was a fancy way of telling me I never said no and needed to learn how ASAP. In my defense, no one had taught me to be this way. It just kind of happened.

Without realizing it, the traits people had found endearing became something they expected from me. When I tried to break out of the habit, they pushed back, and guilt struck. Eventually, I found it was easier to just do what they wanted rather than live with their disappointment.

"Well, maybe I don't want to be that person anymore. Being nice doesn't get you anything," I grumbled, staring down at my plate.

I didn't know why I said it. Clearly, I was still in some kind of funk from my therapy this morning. I was too damn tired to care, though. Bishop was one of the few people I could speak to plainly.

He was a straight shooter and didn't entertain bullshit or offer comfort because it was the polite thing to do. What you saw was what you got, and there was something refreshing about that.

Not that I'd ever say that to him. I didn't think I'd survive the scowl he'd give me.

He didn't push the matter, instead turning the conversation toward complimenting my cooking skills and laughing about my mom's obsession with those stupid handheld vegetable choppers. We were still going by the time the woman in question wandered over to the table and dropped into the seat next to mine.

"What time does the band go on?" she asked, taking a sip of her wine. "I'm ready to hear some live music."

"Around seven, I think," Dad said, checking out the stage. I followed his gaze, noting two white vans peeking out from behind the structure. "I dunno. It was all a little last minute, so I think they're just making sure everything is good to go."

Josie leaned forward in her seat. "What do you mean, last minute? This thing has been planned for months."

Dad sighed. "The band I originally booked canceled a few days ago. Said they'd broken up. Guess our little shindig had gotten missed when they made their cancellations."

"That sucks. You seemed excited about them."

"Who'd you get instead?" Lennox asked.

I knew my family was excited, but I really couldn't care less about music, especially the live kind. On the off chance I let one of them drag me to a concert, I usually sat at the back with some kind of noise-cancelling headphones. Though, my reasoning had nothing to do with the decibel level, and everything to do with the memories attached to music in general.

Dad splayed his hands on the table. "Well, I guess the kid I spoke with was the singer. He seemed pretty confused about why I was even calling at first. I explained the situation, and he said he'd refund the full amount I paid and still do the set."

Goosebumps prickled across my skin as internal warning bells began ringing out. There was no way. There was absolutely no way. It was coincidence and nothing more. "That's nice of him, but how's he going to do that if the band's broken up?" I asked.

Dad shrugged. "I don't know. Guess he made some calls and they agreed to do one last show. Ain't that cool?"

Lennox's smile looked pained. I could feel her eyes scanning my face for a reaction, but I had nothing to give. I was frozen. Locked up on the spot and unable to think or breathe. "Sure is, Dad. Out of curiosity, what's the name of the band?"

No. No, it is very not cool, I wanted to scream. I couldn't, of course. Only my sisters knew a fraction of my history with the boy who became a country music star, and it needed to stay that way.

My mind was just being a dick. It was jumping to conclusions like it always did, because there was no way in fucking hell—

But then a tall figure blocked out the sun and cast a too-familiar shadow across our table. I looked up from beneath my lashes, hoping my heart would stop jumping in my chest.

"Lawson! How the hell are you?" my dad asked, rounding the table to shake my high-school ex-boyfriend's hand.

Fuck. Me.

cleo

. . .

JUST WHEN I thought this day couldn't get any worse, piercing blue eyes found my own, pinning me to the spot. I couldn't move, couldn't breathe, couldn't think. My hands fell to my lap, and I clutched them together, trying to stop the shaking.

How could my father—an exceedingly talented and sharp-witted businessman—manage to book the only person in the world I didn't want to be within one hundred feet of? We'd spent a good twelve years and thousands of miles apart, and I'd wanted to keep it that way for the rest of my life.

Seeing him here, in our hometown, for the second time in four months was putting a bit of a kink in my plan.

When Lennox had dragged me out to the Lonestar, one of the only bars in Ashwood, earlier in the summer, I hadn't fought her. As the baby of the family, she usually got what she wanted anyway. It would've been useless to argue. Plus, I wanted to have some fun. I couldn't remember the last time I'd gone out for a few drinks with anyone, let alone my sisters.

However, I should've known to ask a question or two before agreeing because my sister was too damn sneaky. She knew if she'd told me about the live music from the get-go, I would've stayed home. Not that I blamed her for what happened next. She didn't know Lawson Wilde, county music superstar, was the small-town boy with a different name who I swore I'd marry someday.

If it hadn't been for Lennox's running into him after the show, he wouldn't have even known I was there. I should've been able to slip out from under his radar, but that was too much to hope for. The moment he looked up and saw me standing mere feet away was like a lightning strike to my barely beating heart.

I thought I'd be fine. That our chance encounter was a one-time thing, and I'd never have to see him again. But now he was here, and there was nothing I could do, nowhere I could hide.

Had he taken the gig on purpose, or had it all been one massive cosmic 'fuck you' from the universe? Penance for some heinous atrocity I didn't know I'd committed in a previous life?

My leg bounced beneath the table; an uncontrollable tick that happened whenever my anxiety was racking up. I was hovering somewhere around a Defcon 2 status, which meant it was taking everything in me not to bolt and run for the hills.

"We've actually met before, Mr. Hayes," Grady said, rubbing the back of his neck. "Cleo and I went to high school together."

"Un-fucking-believable," I scoffed, rolling my eyes. Of course, he'd drop that little bomb before flitting back to his perfect life. Meanwhile, I'd get hounded by questions from my mom and sisters, the lot of them wondering why I never said anything before.

Maybe because it was none of their business.

If I wasn't so damn angry, maybe I'd be more hurt by his words. After all, we'd done a hell of a lot more than just go to school together. He'd been my first everything. First date, first kiss, first time, and then... first heartbreak. I hated that they all belonged to him. It hurt so much more remembering he was entwined with some of the most defining moments of my life.

Dad studied him. "Huh. I don't remember anyone with that name in Cleo's graduating class."

"Yeah, Lawson's a stage name. My agent thought it'd be a good idea, so I ran with it."

Mom snapped her fingers, smile faltering as she connected the dots. "You're Marsha Wilde's boy, aren't you? Grady?" He nodded, hiding the sting of a painful memory with a forced smile. "I was so sorry to hear about her passing. She was a good woman."

"Yes, ma'am, and thank you. She was something special." Grady rocked back on his heels, hands in his pockets. He always had this way of looking way too casual and cool. It was the first thing I noticed about him—like he was wholly unaffected by the world around him, just doing his own thing. His gaze found my own, waiting just for a beat too long. "I'd love to catch up if you have time—"

No, I couldn't do this. Not here. Not now. Not ever.

I pushed to my feet and grabbed my plate. Not that I was going to be able to finish it. My appetite had vanished. "Sorry, I'm busy."

He stepped forward, bumping into the table. "I can talk while you walk. You know, just wanted to say hi and—"

"And now you have," I said quickly, attempting to keep my voice even. The damn thing was trying to betray me. "I'm sure you have better things to do anyway."

"I don't." Grady smiled, nodding toward the stage. "The show doesn't start for another hour, and I'd love to catch up while we wait."

"I've got to get back to Cook. I told him I wouldn't be gone long." I paused, tapping my finger on the table before adding, "I'd say maybe next time, but I'm sure you'll be gone by morning."

Lennox mumbled, "Oh shit," beneath her breath and laughed. Josie quickly jabbed her in the ribs when I looked their way.

I'd barely taken a step when his next words stopped me dead. "Actually, I'm home for good. Now that the band's on a break, I thought it'd be a good idea to move back. I never got the chance to go through Mom's things when she passed, and there's a lot to do around her place."

You've got to be fucking kidding me. He was moving back?

"You're not leaving?" I whispered, closing my hand into a tight fist. I pretended I had a hold of my stress ball, that I could take away this burning hot flash of frustration. Just like this morning, no pressure was strong enough to take away the pain.

Grady couldn't stay. This was *my* town. *My* safe space. I'd come back to get away from my past mistakes, not run back to them. It was supposed to be my chance to reinvent myself, to clear my head of all the bullshit I'd had to face in my marriage and move on with my life.

"I'm not leaving," he said, softening his voice. It was almost like the voice in my memories, but it was deeper now. Melodic and soothing and ultimately so dangerous. It wouldn't take much for him to persuade me to say yes. Not if he kept talking to me like that. "So, if you can't catch up tonight, I understand, but I'd love to get together sometime—"

"DADDY!"

With one word, I felt my entire world collapse. A little girl, likely five or six, catapulted herself into his arms. He caught her easily, lifting her up and kissing her forehead.

Grady Wilde has a kid. He has a fucking kid.

Oh god, I was going to be sick.

I didn't know why I was surprised. He'd been married longer than I'd been to Thomas, so it made sense. Seeing their resemblance was almost more than I could take, though. It reminded me of long suppressed memories and broken promises between two kids who'd had no business dreaming of a future together.

"Hey baby girl, what're you doing here?" Grady's eyes briefly darted my direction. "I thought I told you to stay backstage."

"Well, Momma said Uncle Ben needed your help, and she asked me to go find you." The girl brought her finger to Grady's nose and tapped it once. "And so that's what I did!" She looked around at the table. Everyone had gone deathly still. "Daddy, who're they?"

I couldn't stop my hand from shaking, the plate I was holding nearly clattering to the ground. Lennox rushed around the table and took it from my grip before I dropped it.

"They own this ranch, honey. We're here to celebrate this gentleman's birthday." Grady motioned toward Dad, but I felt his attention linger on where I stood.

"I love birthdays!" she said, throwing her little arms in the air. "They're my favorite day!"

"You know what?" Dad chuckled. "Me too. Mine's been pretty good so far."

"Are you gonna listen to my daddy play?"

"I sure am."

"Yay! He's the best. My momma loves listening to him play, too. She says his music is pretty," she said. Even though she was young, there was such pride in her voice as she spoke about him.

It was like a trainwreck I couldn't look away from. Beautifully tragic in so many ways. He had everything I'd always wanted, everything we'd always talked about.

Just not with me.

"I like your dress. Blue is my favorite color."

I blinked, coming to myself and staring at her little face. I offered a brittle smile, hoping like hell it came across as genuine. I'd taught kids long enough to know how to fake emotion, but this was harder than the rest, and sometimes kids were too perceptive. "Thank you. It's mine, too."

"Mommy and Daddy did my whole room in blue," she said, looking back at Grady for only a second. "It's my favorite room ever."

I felt the tear slip down my cheek before I could stop it. Why did I care? Why did it hurt my heart so much that this precious girl loved the color blue? Why did I ache at the sight of him holding her so close?

I wiped my cheek before the moisture could reach my jaw. "You're so lucky to have them." My voice broke on the last word, and I quickly turned my face to hide it. "I don't mean to be rude, but I need to get back to work."

Bishop reached out, gently touching my arm. "You good?"

My bottom lip wobbled. "Yeah, it's just a lot."

He didn't know much about Grady or our history, but he dipped his chin. "It is. You know where to find me if you need me."

I reached out, placing my hand on his shoulder. I didn't consider myself the type of person who enjoyed or easily gave physical affection, but Bishop was the closest thing I had to a brother. He was family. Something about him spoke to a part of my soul. "Thank you," I whispered.

I wasn't sure if my family noticed I was heading in the opposite direction of Cook, but it didn't matter. I took off, making my way through the throng of people. Everyone was crowded around tables—talking, laughing, and having a great time. Their smiles were genuine, and I wanted to be able to enjoy the celebration too, but I couldn't.

All I could think about was him.

"I'm not leaving."

I didn't own Ashwood, but if I did, I would've made a rule that Grady Wilde was banned from coming within thirty miles of our town. I was being irrational, I could admit it, but all I could think about was the audacity it took for him to not only move back home, but to then agree to do a concert at *my* family's ranch.

That bastard knew I'd be here. He knew how much I loved my dad. I wouldn't miss his birthday for the world. What kind of game was Grady playing at? There was nothing for us to talk about as far as I was concerned. Anything that needed to be said had been long ago.

Even if there were anything new, I wasn't interested in hearing it.

God, Laura was going to have one hell of a time unwinding my twisted thoughts about everything that'd just happened.

I didn't realize how far I'd walked until I stumbled into the barn. People milled back and forth in the enclosed arena, watching the amateur rodeo events and betting on how long people would last on the back of a bucking bronc.

I looked around. It was too loud. There was nowhere to hide. I couldn't even climb up to my sister's renovated hayloft for peace because it didn't have any damn walls. Other than hiding in my parent's house, there was only one place I knew I could turn to.

One place no one knew to look.

grady

. . .

YOU GODDAMNED IDIOT. *You absolute fucking fool.*

My heavy boots thudded against the familiar pasture as I made my way back to the stage. I clung to Charlie as she rambled about the different toys she brought with her—blue pony, blue dolly, blue monster truck… She sure didn't need to. I already knew exactly what we brought. The only reason we'd avoided an absolute meltdown while packing is because we let her bring all her favorites.

My daughter hadn't been lying. Blue really was her favorite color. It was mine, too, but I liked a specific shade. One that was as deep as the ocean depths and as sweet as the wild blueberries that grew along the fence line of this ranch.

The one that matched Cleo's eyes.

I tried not to focus on that little detail. Because when I did, all I could think about was the hurt and confusion on her face that had deepened the moment she'd seen Charlie running up to me with open arms.

Had she not known I had a daughter? Charlie's mom and I had worked hard to keep her out of the media as much as possible. Having two parents with high-profile jobs meant we were under constant scrutiny. Our kid didn't deserve that. She didn't choose this life.

We never hid her, though. We were proud parents, and I thanked my family in every acknowledgement or speech I gave. It was important to me Charlie knew how much I loved her, and the way her birth had changed my life in ways I could never fully explain.

The band and I were coming up on nearly twelve years together. After the first ten, we'd been able to negotiate a yearly contract, which was convenient at the time. None of us were sure what we wanted to do. Life on the road was hard, and we weren't getting any younger. Most of us had families, and touring took us away for months on end with little time for much else.

When our contract was up for negotiations this year, we unanimously agreed it was time to take a hiatus. It wasn't a breakup by any means. We all wanted to get our asses back on the road eventually, but the thought of a year or two to ourselves was too good to pass up.

So much had changed since we'd first signed on the dotted line. The guys and I had come a long way from the scrawny nobodies we'd been before we signed with the label. None of us had known each other at first. We were brought together by desperation and a handful of dreams, which still rang true today. The break just gave us a chance to figure out what we wanted, write and record some new music, and prepare for our eventual return to the public to be better than ever.

There were downfalls to having so much time on our hands, though. For the first time in twelve years, I had time to overanalyze. The guys and I were at the height of our career, topping the charts left and right with every single we dropped. If we walked away now, would all of it still be waiting for us if we decided to come back? Would we even want it? It was all a guessing game.

No matter how exhausted I was, I was selfishly worried

about myself, too. Music was like therapy to me. It helped me through some of my darkest moments and allowed me to celebrate the highest points. But after tonight, there would be no work to fall back on. No screaming fans to drown out the incessant chatter in my head. No melodies to lose myself in. It was just going to be me, myself, and my thoughts, which had been a dangerous combination over the past few months.

Because no matter how hard I tried, those damn thoughts always drifted right back here to a beautiful blue-eyed blonde and Black Springs Ranch.

God, so much time had passed since the last time Cleo and I had seen one another. It felt like another lifetime, and I guess it was. We weren't the same people we used to be. Yet when I looked at her, I felt the same rush I did when I was young. Like we were still the same kids we were at sixteen—reckless and running through this very field to meet one another at our secret spot.

Only, back then, she would've greeted me with a smile and a kiss before asking me what took me so long rather than running for the hills like I was a monster. Which, in her story, I might've been.

Our history was long and complicated. There was fault on both sides. No one was perfect, but Cleo was damn close. When she'd been by my side, I'd felt invincible. Nothing and no one could bring me down. No one except, it seemed, myself. The day I'd let her slip through my fingers, prioritizing all the wrong things and heading down a wildly twisted path, was one of the worst of my life.

It was why thoughts of Cleo were easier handled with a bottle of tequila after dark. Memory lane was a bumpy ass road to walk by yourself. If I was gonna be forced to do it, it sure as shit wasn't going to be sober.

When the band and I had talked about where we would play our last show, our label pitched the idea of ending it where everything had begun. The decision was met with a bunch of cheers and pats on the back from our PR team and agents. They raved about the sentimentality of it, how it would look *so good* to bring revenue to a no-name, small town in Texas and pay tribute to my humble roots.

I'd smiled and nodded, pretending everything was fine, but it couldn't have been further from the truth. I hadn't stepped foot in my hometown since my mother passed, and I'd vowed to never do it again.

It wasn't that I didn't want to give credit where credit was due. The Lonestar was the birthplace of a wild dream. I owed a lot to my hometown bar. If I hadn't played my first acoustic show on that simple stage to a group of half-drunk old men, I wouldn't have had the courage to follow my heart and be standing here today.

But all those accolades and accomplishments were only possible because of one person. Cleo had been the only thing I saw during my first set. She watched me with nothing less than utter love and adoration, believing in me before I ever did in myself.

I'd felt every bit of it, too. Her excitement never felt like an obligation. There was never a roll of her eyes when I told her I wanted to play music for a living. She didn't balk when I deferred college to chase my newfound dreams or tell me I should have a back-up plan.

I tried like hell to convince our label that somewhere, *anywhere,* else would've been better for our final show. I worked with some of the best tour promoters in the world to come up with bold new ideas that should've had our label jumping up and down in their plush leather seats. Instead, they just nodded their heads and told me to save it for our comeback.

When we drove into town for the show four months ago, something had felt off. I couldn't explain what it was or why, but it was there all the same. It'd been enough to scare me off for good. I had every intention of playing the show and high-tailing it out of there so I could get back to Tennessee. There was no reason for me to stay. No reason for me to do anything but handle my business and leave as soon as possible.

Until I saw *her*.

Twelve years may have passed since the last time I'd seen her, but Cleo Hayes was just as beautiful as I remembered. Even inside the darkened bar, all it had taken was one look at her for my world to flip upside down. It'd felt like a fever dream at first. She wasn't supposed to be there. She was supposed to be in Montana with her husband, living out her dreams.

I knew because I'd checked.

Cleo may have blocked me on every social media site known to man, but the same couldn't be said for my band members. So, I did what I'd always done in the rare moments I found myself spiraling at three in the morning, curious about what she was doing—I stole one of their phones and looked her up.

My daughter jumped in my hold, pulling me from my thoughts. "Mommy! Mommy! Mommy!"

I looked forward, noticing my wife striding toward us. "Hi, baby girl!" Olivia said, holding out her arms to take our daughter. Charlie gave her a kiss on the cheek and nuzzled into her neck. "I see you found your daddy." Her eyes met mine as she mouthed the word 'sorry' behind our daughter's back.

I shook my head, stepping back to let them have their moment together. Charlie may have had me wrapped around her finger, but she was a momma's girl through and through. Neither Olivia nor I had planned on kids, so finding out she was pregnant had thrown our worlds topsy-turvy in the best way possible.

Watching them together was a special kind of joy. Their bond was magical. Our daughter idolized Olivia. She went on and on about how when she grew up, she wanted to be just like her mom.

Olivia Hart was country music royalty. Her grandfather, Franklin Hart, had started one of the biggest record labels in Nashville. She grew up in an entirely different world than I had —one of glitz and glamour and more money than I could ever fathom. The Hart name carried a lot of weight in the music business, and a lot of pressure to boot.

When her grandfather retired, the company had been passed down to Olivia's father. Just like Charlie, she'd revered the man, wanting nothing more than to be just like him when she grew up.

She'd only been fifteen when he passed away.

While the industry mourned, and the family was devastated, it hadn't taken long for her uncle, John, to step up to the plate, holding down the fort until Olivia was old enough to take the reins. She learned a lot from him before taking her role as CEO of the label. He was still on the board, helping her navigate the complexities of the job.

She and I had met by sheer luck and total coincidence the night Cleo had rightfully called it quits. Olivia hadn't wanted anything from me, nor I her. We became fast friends on a one-way track to something bigger than either of us anticipated.

My mom had always told me to marry my best friend, so that's what I'd done. There was no one who knew me quite as well as she did. Not even Cleo, as much as the thought killed me. We'd been good together until we weren't.

"Charlie said Ben needed me?" I asked, shoving my hands into my pockets. The gold band on my ring finger suddenly felt heavy. It felt wrong wearing it here, especially when it wasn't Cleo who'd put it there.

Olivia waved her hand. "He was looking for the setlist. I couldn't remember where you stashed it when we were packing, but Beau found it." She stepped closer, lowering her voice. "I'm so sorry, Grady. I know you were going to see her, and I swear I wasn't trying to be a cockblock—"

I barked out a laugh. "Uh, yeah. I don't think that's gonna be a problem since she couldn't get away from me fast enough."

She scrunched up her nose. "Oh, no."

"Yeah, it wasn't great. She looked like a deer caught in the headlights. I don't even think she knew I was going to be here, Liv. It was a disaster."

"Didn't her dad hire you?"

"He did," I said, rocking back on my heels. "But god knows what the fuck Doug was thinking."

Charlie gasped, covering her mouth with her little hand. "That's a bad word, Daddy."

I held my hands up. "You're right, baby girl. It is." She laid her head back down on Olivia's shoulder, satisfied with her scolding. "Anyway, it wasn't great. She ended up running off before I could try and stop her."

"How did she not know her dad hired you?" Olivia asked, running a hand up Charlie's back.

That was the part I was trying to figure out. When Douglas Hayes had called me about playing for his birthday celebration, I'd seen this as my chance to redeem myself. That maybe she'd had a hand in the hiring and was ready to talk things out.

Apparently, it was just my delusion talking.

After Cleo and I had awkwardly run into one another a few months ago, I lingered in Ashwood, surrounded by the ghosts of my past until I stumbled into a drunken depression. I was supposed to have stayed with my dad, but being in my childhood home brought back too many memories. It wasn't just Cleo, but my mom, too. I couldn't help but realize how much I'd missed by chasing my dreams. Suddenly, I found myself wondering if it was all worth it if I didn't have her.

After several missed calls, and my refusal to open the motel door when Dad knocked, Olivia had been forced to fly out. I'd been locked in that room for four days by the time she'd found me. There'd been no judgement as she surveyed the empty bottles of liquor perched on nearly every surface, or the trash littering the floor. She'd just sat down next to me while I clung to a tattered photograph and cried.

"I don't know," I answered honestly. "I thought so. I thought that was why Doug had reached out, but now I'm not too sure."

Olivia drew her lips together, rolling them tightly. It was her tell, something I'd learned early on meant she had thoughts about whatever was going on but that she wasn't going to voice them.

"Come on, Liv. Don't gimme that look," I groaned, tipping my head back.

She rolled her eyes at me before bending forward to set our daughter down. "Girl, you're getting too big!" she said, forcing a smile. "Who gave you permission to keep growing? I thought I said you weren't allowed."

Charlie giggled, looking down at the length of her small frame. "I gotta grow, Mommy. It's how I'm gonna be big like you one day."

"I know you do, baby." Olivia crouched in front of Charlie, tucking a piece of hair behind her ear. "Hey, why don't you go show Uncle Ben the stuffed animal we picked up yesterday?"

My guitarist was close enough I didn't need to grab his attention. He marched over at the sound of his name and put his hands on his hips. "You got another new toy? Mav is gonna be so jealous!"

He really wouldn't, but none of us were going to tell Charlie that. She adored Ben's son.

Maverick was the result of a one-night stand in Chicago ten years ago after Ben found out his wife had cheated on him. He'd had a rough go of it after that, but his son was the light of his life. It'd given him a reason to keep going when things got hard.

I can relate.

"Really?" Charlie asked, jumping up and down.

"Really, really," Ben said with a dip of his chin. "Wanna show me what it looks like so I can tell him?"

Charlie gripped Ben's hand and took off running in the direction of the parked vans we'd rented. Olivia and I both waited until they were gone before she spoke. "I hope you know what you're doing."

"What do you mean?" I crossed my arms and shifted on my feet.

She looked away, lowering her voice. "I don't want to see you like you were before. I don't want you to stay here and drink yourself—"

"Olivia—"

She whirled toward me, jabbing at the center of my chest. "No, you're going to listen to me, Grady Wilde. I won't be here to pull you out of the dark again. This time, Charlie will be with you. I need to know being here isn't going to send you back to that place again." Her chocolate eyes watered slightly, but she wouldn't let the tears fall. She never did.

"Liv, I won't—"

"Promise me," she said, meeting my gaze. "Promise me you know what you're doing for our daughter's sake."

I was reaching for her the second her lip wobbled, pulling her into my chest and wrapping my arms around her. I let my chin rest on top of her head and looked out over the pasture. As much as I wanted to say those words, I couldn't. Not yet anyway.

I wasn't going to break another promise to a woman I loved.

cleo

. . .

I ROUNDED the corner of the barn, following the footworn path through the pasture until I reached my destination. The sun was fading fast, but I didn't need light to know where I was going. It was a trek I'd made countless times growing up. I knew it by heart, even when I wished I didn't.

Since the moment I walked away from the table, my phone had been vibrating in my pocket. It was likely just Josie or Lennox, although I wondered how long it would take until one of them came searching for me. I shot off a single text, letting them both know I was okay but I needed space.

Grief was weird.

Up ahead, I saw my destination and felt the first sharp tug telling me to turn around. The little voice in my mind echoed the sentiment, telling me how bad an idea this was. What was I looking for? Peace? Solace? This place wouldn't make it any better. If anything, it would make it worse.

But did I listen? Nope. I guess I never did.

Hidden next to one of our holding pens was my old treehouse. Dad built it when I was about five so I could come out with him and the hands during the summer. Watching him work was one of my favorite things, but my attention span as a little kid wasn't the best. It was his way of compromising. I had a way to entertain myself and keep out of the sun while they were working. It sat high up in the tallest oak tree, surrounded by a cluster of orange and brown leaves. There was a tire swing hanging right below it, blowing softly with the wind.

I'd spent so many summers right here, daydreaming about my future. They were some of my best memories. Things had turned out so different from how I imagined them, but I'd been so young and full of hope. Idealistic, as my mom would call it. The woman I was today couldn't have been further from that girl.

I stood beneath the oak, one hand on the rung of the ladder. It felt sturdy enough. For years, Dad had made sure to maintain the structure because he'd told me he wanted his grandkids to be able to use it. One day, I hoped my sisters would make sure he got his wish. He really would make the best grandpa.

Slowly, I climbed up the tree, holding my breath that the hatch wouldn't be locked when I reached the top. Mom made Dad install it after I failed my first science test in fifth grade. I was so upset thinking I'd disappointed them that I left a note telling them I was running away.

Dad was the one to find me. When his head poked through the floor of the treehouse, I could see the relief on his face. My body tensed, waiting for the lecture to come, but it never did. Instead, he signaled for one of the ranch hands to let my mom know I was safe before climbing inside. I couldn't remember how long we stayed like that. All I knew was by the time we'd come down, the sky was pitch black and both my sisters were sound asleep.

"Here goes nothing," I whispered, pulling on the handle. It gave way, and I said a silent prayer before pulling myself up.

Except for a much-needed paint touch-up, the space looked the same. I took out my phone, turning on the flashlight and scanning the room. The toy box Dad had built was sitting in the corner next to a small bookshelf. He'd made sure I had my own little reading nook, complete with a window that looked out over the pen below.

I ran my fingers through the thick layer of dust along the top of the chest. As I grew up, I used it less for storage and more for hiding the things I knew I shouldn't have. I cleaned it out before I'd gone away for college, but I knew my sisters had used it after I did. There was no telling what they'd hidden in there and forgotten.

Reaching for the rusty bolt, I tugged it free and peered inside. I laughed as I saw a dusty bottle. There was a small, yellowed notecard attached to the neck with twine. I recognized the handwriting, smiling to myself.

For emergency use only - Dad

Dad used to drink like a fish, but he'd slowed down on the harder stuff over the past year. The man was notorious for hiding bottles of whiskey in random spots around the ranch. Sometimes when I came home from college on break, Bishop and I would see who could find the most—which wasn't always fair, since he had the upper hand by working with Dad every day.

Old habits, it seemed, died hard.

Carefully pulling out the bottle, I twisted the cap. The sharp tang of cheap whiskey filled the space, and I scrunched my nose. I wasn't sure how people enjoyed it, but I'd never been much of a drinker. When I did, though, I leaned toward the clear stuff.

I slid to the floor, letting my back rest against the chipped paint, and took a sip. My phone lie next to me, and I stared at the lit-up screen. The picture was of my sisters and me a few years ago at Christmas. Mom was adamant about making sure we took family pictures in front of the tree every single year. She went all out, buying us a new set of matching pajamas that were always ridiculously corny.

That year, right before the flash went off, Lennox had snuck up behind me and jumped on my back. Josie was beside me, head thrown back in laughter. It was still one of my favorite pictures, even though it brought back memories I wanted to leave behind. I seemed to have a lot of those. The image was cropped to focus on the three of us, but I could still see a hand resting on the floor next to my leg. My stomach churned as I zeroed in on the simple gold band on their ring finger.

No one had seen the fading bruises beneath my shirt, or the way I'd nearly curled into a ball at my sister's sudden touch. They hadn't noticed the thick layers of color-correcting concealer I'd applied around my right eye and down to my jawline. Not that I blamed them. By that point in Thomas and I's relationship, I'd perfected the art of pretending everything was fine.

It was just another day.

As soon as my screen went dark, it lit up again. Only this time, I didn't see a photo or a name I recognized. If it hadn't been for the goddamn Nashville area code, I wouldn't have known who it was.

But those three digits were a dead giveaway.

I wasn't sure how Grady had my number. I'd gotten rid of the one I had from high school when I filed for a restraining order against Thomas. My lawyer had suggested it would be a good idea, and Laura had agreed. Any conversations that needed to be had regarding the divorce could be done through our representation.

I was okay with that. I needed it, actually. When Thomas and I first separated, he would get wasted off his ass and call me over and over. Most nights, I was forced to turn the damn thing off to get a reprieve. I never knew what I'd find when I woke up, though.

Sometimes it would just be missed notifications. Others would be long, screaming voicemails and berating text messages. It didn't bother me at first because it made my lawyer's job easier. The case against him was practically building itself. But after so long, the threats and constant promise of danger wear you down. For my sanity, I had to put a stop to it.

The buzzing ceased, but the silence left behind felt heavier. I took another pull from the bottle and winced as the sharp liquor hit my tongue. "Oh my god, that's horrible," I muttered, tightening the cap and placing it beside me.

Yeah, I'll stick to my tequila, thank you very much.

I felt a single vibration and looked down. Out of the sea of missed calls from Josie and Lennox, there was one notification that stood out among the rest.

The Nashville number had left a voicemail.

I stared at it, unable to stop myself from reaching for the device with shaky hands. I should've answered the call, but I couldn't bring myself to face him so soon. All I needed to do was hide out here until he was off the property. It wasn't like he was going to come searching for me.

Did I even want him to, knowing his wife and child were with him? His wife, who seemed wonderful and lovely if the tabloids were to be believed. Did I trust myself not to do something stupid or reckless or desperate if he knocked on that stupid floor hatch and let himself up?

A steady rhythm shook the floorboards, signaling the start of the show. I could hear the faint shouts of the crowd as the intensity grew, and then everything went silent right before the rest of the band joined in. When Grady's voice joined the fray, I fought back a sob and hung my head in my hands.

God, I was such a mess. His music had once brought me solace, but now all I felt was pain.

I wasn't sure if I could do this. If he was serious about moving here, how was I supposed to put my emotions aside? And was everyone coming with him? Surely, they were. It would make no sense for him to come alone.

My dad used to watch those old western shows that ended up in a showdown–two men standing alone in the dust, fingers twitching at the trigger. They always muttered something dramatic about how the town wasn't big enough for the two of them before shots rang out, leaving only one standing.

That was how I felt right now. Ashwood's population was barely above six thousand. There was no way I could avoid Grady *and* his family. It was impossible. Every county fair and rodeo and round-up would have me looking over my shoulder, waiting for the moment I'd catch him pulling her close for a kiss or hear her laugh at one of his jokes.

That's all it'd take for my heart to shatter completely.

I wish there were two of me so I could snap myself out of this spiral. I wanted to shake myself, to scream at the poor, pathetic woman I was being and say, "My god, girl, get a grip! It's been twelve years. You've got to move on."

It didn't matter how many times I repeated the mantra in my head, it seemed lost on me. I was always destined to be a fool.

My twenties had been wasted thinking about him. How much I loved him, how much I hated him, how much he'd broken my heart. My relationship with Thomas had been driven by my need to move on from Grady, and that'd been a terrible disaster.

Maybe listening to the voicemail was a good start. That's what Rachel and Laura would say. "Just listen to whatever he has to say and move on for good this time. Let your heart rest for once."

I stared at the red circle until my eyes ached and my vision blurred. The sun had set, leaving me alone in the dark save for the glow of my screen. In the distance, I could just make out the silhouette of the party tents, lights from the stage flickering as they played a slow song.

"Just do it," I whispered. "Get it over with."

As I was about to press play, the music came to a screeching halt. Shouts rang out, but I couldn't tell what they were saying. I pushed to my feet and peeked out of the small window to see what was going on.

My instincts were to run toward the fray, to make sure neither Mom nor Dad had to worry about taking care of whatever had happened. I reached for the hatch, pulling it open and carefully climbing out. The moment I landed on my feet, I heard a familiar, gut-wrenching scream.

Lennox.

I didn't think. I just ran, pumping my arms and legs as fast as they would go. I rounded the corner of the fence, nearly falling on my ass as I took the turn too fast, but I caught myself before I landed fully.

My eyes scanned the crowd as I sought out the problem. Had someone gotten too drunk and rowdy? Had there been a fight? It wouldn't have been the first time fists were thrown at Black Springs Ranch, nor would it be the last. But there was no continued screaming, no shouting for help or the push-and-pull of people trying to separate two drunken idiots.

I caught conversational fragments as I pushed through the sea of sweaty bodies, but nothing made sense. As much as I wanted to turn and ask them what they meant, I only fought harder to get through the crowd. Whispered words became nothing but a dull roar in my ears as I made it to the center.

My eyes dropped to the ground where Lincoln was hunched over an unconscious body. His back was to me, concealing their identity, but I didn't need to see it to know. Somehow, I'd felt it in my bones the moment I heard my sister scream.

She was one of the toughest people I knew. Nothing ever rattled her. I'd seen her go toe-to-toe with a man twice her size because he called one of her friends a bitch, and she was ready to make him eat his words.

But there was one person who could make Lennox crumble. My youngest sister was the strongest out of all of us until it came to our father.

We were all close with him in one way or another, but each of our relationships looked different. Lennox, true to her birth order, was the baby. He looked at her like she was his entire world.

When we first found out about his health issues, Lennox had been a shell of the woman she normally was. She didn't come out of her room for days, refusing to eat at all. I had to force her to drink water so she didn't end up in the hospital for dehydration.

I was the only one around the day she broke. She'd laid her head on my lap and cried for hours. I let her, trying my best to create the safe space I'd never had so she could process her emotions in a healthy way. I wanted her to know that no matter what happened, I was there for her. I'd always be there.

That was what big sisters were for, after all.

So, I knew without a shadow of a doubt the only person who could make my sister scream like she was losing her entire world was our dad. Only this time, I didn't know how to fix it. I didn't know how to calm her fears or tell her it was going to be okay, because for the first time in my life, I didn't know if it would be.

My sisters both turned to me at the same time, their eyes red-rimmed and full of fear. Our mom clung to Josie like she was the only reason she was standing. She stared down at Lincoln as he performed CPR on our father. Her husband.

Oh god, I didn't know if she would survive if he didn't. He was the center of all of our worlds, and now he was lying unconscious and not breathing on the land he loved so much.

Lennox surged forward, breaking free of Bishop's hold. I

barely caught her, rubbing my hand up and down her back as she wailed. "Talk to me, Len."

"S-Someone's already called 911," she sniffed. "They said they were on their way, and I-I told them he had issues..." Her words trailed off as she pulled back and looked up at me. "Is he going to be okay?"

I swiped my thumbs beneath her eyes, but it only made her cry harder. My silence made things worse, her heart breaking more than it already was. "I don't know."

Bishop came up behind Lennox, his eyes wide with fear. "What can I do?"

"Get your truck," I said, pulling Lennox closer. "And have someone grab Lincoln's, too. We'll need two vehicles to head to the hospital."

"Alright," he mumbled, keeping his eyes on Lennox's back. "Yeah, I can do that."

He didn't move right away, his eyes lingered on my sister like he wanted to take her from my arms and bring her with him. With a shake of his head, he grabbed one of the workers and they headed toward the house.

I felt the eyes of our guests. Every partygoer stared helplessly as our world imploded, but none of them made a move to do anything. They just watched like this was a trainwreck they couldn't look away from.

The sound of a microphone flicking on came from the stage, garnering the crowd's momentary attention. "Alright, I know there's a lot going on, but we'd like to ask everyone to clear the area and give the Hayes family some room."

My gaze flicked up, seeing Grady pointing toward the other side of the pasture. His sweat-soaked hair clung to his forehead as he stared out at the crowd. No one had asked him to do that, but he did it anyway.

When people didn't move fast enough, his voice filtered back through the speakers. "We're all concerned for Doug, but I'm begging y'all to move and give them room. They don't need you gawking at them." Grady leaned over, talking to the people on stage with him. They nodded and jumped down, jogging our way. He scanned the crowd before following, making his way straight toward me.

"What can I do?" He raised his hand like he was going to touch me, but it fell to his side. I hated how much I ached for his touch. How much I wanted someone to comfort me in the way I was comforting others.

"I've got it," I said, sucking in a deep breath to stave away the tears. I didn't want to cry, especially not here when everyone was looking at me to hold them together. "Thanks."

"Cleo—" he began, but I shook my head.

"Please, don't. Not right now. I can't—" My voice broke, but I pushed forward. "My family needs me."

And I need you.

The words were right there, right on the tip of my tongue, but they never came. I forced them down, down, down until I could breathe again. Because even if I voiced them, it wouldn't change anything.

He had a wife. He had a kid. And me? I was on the verge of losing it all. It would've been selfish to drag him down with me. At least this way, even if I drowned, I'd drown alone.

Grady looked like he wanted to push things, but he didn't. Instead, he backed away and joined his bandmates in redirecting the crowd. I didn't want to watch him walk away again, but anything was better than focusing on Lincoln's quiet, muttered curses as he tried to keep Dad's heart beating.

As the faint sound of a siren wailed in the distance, I let a single tear fall before wiping it away, and did what I did best.

cleo

. . .

Nine Months Later

"OH MY GOD, can you drive any faster, gramps?" Lennox chimed from the front seat of Bishop's truck. "Josie will probably be released from the hospital by the time we get there."

Bishop sighed as the light in front of us turned red and he slowed to a full stop. "I can't make the light turn green, killer. It's luck of the draw."

"Yeah, but you could've pushed through the last three yellow ones," she grumbled, crossing her arms and pouting.

"Yellow means slow down."

"Well in this case it's a suggestion," she shot back. "This isn't one of our safe words. And given the circumstances, I think yellow warrants pressing down on the gas pedal instead of the brake. I'm an aunt! I need to meet my little mini-me."

"Christ, Lennox. Do you ever keep some thoughts to yourself?" he cursed.

I stared out the window, chuckling to myself as they softly bickered. Or rather, Bishop kept his voice at a normal, even tone while Lennox babbled incessantly about how long it was taking to get to the hospital and why it was no big deal I knew what they did in the bedroom.

Honestly, I didn't care, but I felt like I'd learned way more about my younger sisters' sex lives in the past year than I ever thought I would.

It was still dark outside, just after five in the morning, and all of us were running on zero sleep. The excitement over the newest addition to the Hayes family had kept us up way too late.

Last night, Lincoln texted the family group chat to tell us Josie's water had broken, and they were on the way to the hospital. Mom, Dad, and Lennox had immediately tried to follow them up there, but Bishop and I'd talked them down. The new family deserved time for themselves because there was no way they'd get it once they got back home. I'd be surprised if either our mother or Lennox didn't take turns sleeping on the couch for the first few months.

Even though visiting hours at the hospital didn't even start until six, I couldn't hold them back anymore. Or rather, I couldn't hold *Lennox* back anymore. She'd bolted up to the main house the moment Lincoln's message came through, ready to storm through the doors of Ashwood Memorial Hospital like she was the one giving birth.

I'd give it to her. She really was going to be the best aunt.

Mom and Dad followed behind us, their headlights reflected in the rearview mirror. They hated going to the hospital, and rightfully so, but even that couldn't put a damper on their spirits today. When I came into the kitchen this morning, Dad was already buzzing around, making sure everyone had cups of coffee ready to go.

Growing up, his coffee was notoriously terrible. It was almost comical how infamous it was around Ashwood. No one would ever accept a cup if he offered it, but lately it'd been better. Over Christmas, we'd all pitched in for one of those fancy machines and tossed his battered old one out in the trash.

He'd been so angry, ranting and raving about how it had been "seasoned," and we'd thrown out decades of hard work. It died down after Lennox made him a cup and forced him to take a sip. Now, it was his newest obsession. He spent most of his free time trying new recipes and flavors. At least he had something productive to do with his time.

After Dad's health scare on his birthday, his doctor had told him he had two choices. He could either continue with the long, stressful days that came with being a rancher and dig himself an early grave, or he could retire and double his chances.

For a split second, I'd held my breath. I had no idea which one he'd pick.

Since I was a kid, Dad had told me he didn't know who he was without the ranch. It was in his blood, a part of who he was. He said it gave him a sense of purpose, a way to give back all the knowledge and advice he'd been granted over the years and pass it on to another generation.

I understood that more than anyone, except my identity wasn't tied to the ranch itself, but the people on it.

For the next month and a half, I listened to Dad moan and groan about retirement and how horrible it was. Sometimes I'd find him staring out the window, watching the cowboys in the field or the cattle passing by. I worried he'd never get over losing that sense of purpose, but thankfully it didn't last long.

Everything changed the moment he found out about Josie's pregnancy. Suddenly, his newfound free time was filled with crafts and projects and plans. Pregnancy had been rough on my sister, so he took her to nearly every doctor's appointment Lincoln couldn't make it to. His doting was adorable. Except for the new father, I'd never seen a man so excited about a baby coming into this world. Dad had told the whole damn town he was going to be a grandpa, and they'd rallied together to make sure Josie had everything she needed.

"Finally!" Lennox said, bouncing in her seat as the hospital sign came into view. Bishop slowed and turned into the parking lot. "We might actually get to see the baby before they go off to college." She paused, putting her hand behind her ear. "Wait, is that the graduation march I hear playing in the background?"

Lennox didn't wait for a response. She threw open the door before her fiancé had even parked, practically sprinting to the hospital entrance.

Bishop let his head drop to the steering wheel and groaned. "Ya know, I've been wondering why more grey hairs have been popping up since we got together," he mumbled. "But now I fucking get it."

I clapped him on the shoulder. "That's your girl. You chose that one."

He straightened in his seat and turned off his ignition, staring out the window to where Lennox had disappeared. The corner of his lips kicked up a fraction. "For all my bitching, I wouldn't change it for the world. Even if she *is* the biggest pain in my ass."

My heart seized at the adoration on his face, but I didn't let it show. "I'm sure you wouldn't."

Dad popped up on the other side of the door and yelled, "Boo!"

I screamed as he and Bishop both laughed. "You assholes," I cursed, reaching forward to punch Bishop's arm. He dodged, barely sliding out before Dad opened my door and held out his hand.

"Well, come on now. We don't have all day. Your sister is probably in there terrorizing the staff for visitation."

I placed my palm in his, letting the warmth ground me. "You started this, old man."

"And I'm finishing it, too." He pressed his lips to my temple and pulled me close. "Come on. Let's go save the nurses."

AS IT TURNED OUT, Lennox's pestering didn't win us any favors with the hospital staff. We were all stuck in the waiting room for over forty-five minutes before Lincoln strolled over, hands in his pockets. There were deep circles beneath his eyes, and he was clearly exhausted, but there was a new sparkle there. I'd never seen a man happier to be running on fumes.

"I heard y'all were causing a fuss," he drawled. Mom handed him a cup of coffee, which he took with a grateful nod.

Our fingers pointed in Lennox's direction, who didn't even try to deny the accusations. "Excuse me if I'm excited to meet my niece," she grumbled, leaning back in the chair with a huff. "That's not a crime."

"It's not," I said, shaking my head. "But threatening a nurse is."

"I didn't *threaten* her. You're so dramatic. I just told her if she didn't stop blocking my path, then I'd push her aside."

"That's a threat, killer," Bishop said with a sigh.

Lennox just stuck her tongue out in response.

Lincoln laughed and held up his hands. "Listen, I have permission to bring y'all back if you don't start bullying the staff again."

"Fine, fine. I promise." She hopped up. "But now it's baby time?"

Lincoln nodded. "It's baby time. Come meet the newest member."

We fell in line, following Lincoln until we stood outside a big blue door. Mom and I made a pink and green wreath to hang on the outside that said 'Baby Hayes' in big, white cursive letters. Lennox added a little pair of sparkly cowgirl boots at the bottom because she said we hadn't added enough pizzazz.

Lincoln knocked once, and we heard a muffled, "Come in!" from the other side of the door. He peeked inside, smiling widely before letting us follow him.

Josie was sitting up in bed, cradling the sweetest little

bundle in her arms. "Everyone meet Stella Carter Hayes," she said. Her smile was wide, brimming with the newfound joy of motherhood. "Eight pounds, six ounces. Twenty-one inches long."

Lincoln and Bishop stood back as we inched closer. Stella was perfect. There was a dusting of dark hair across her head, something she'd likely inherited from both her parents. Her little pout already rivaled her aunt's. There was no way she wouldn't have every single person in this room wrapped around her tiny little finger before the end of the hour.

"I'm so proud of you," I said, coming around and pressing a kiss to Josie's forehead. "You did good, momma."

She passed the baby over to our mom, letting her and Dad fuss over Stella as Josie took my hand and squeezed. "That is the hardest thing I've ever done," she said, leaning back on her pillow. Her eyes never left her daughter's. "But my god, she is perfect."

"She really is," I agreed. "And she will be so, so loved."

Josie nodded, pulling her gaze away to give me a soft smile. "She's gonna need some cousins to run around with."

Every muscle in my body tightened on instinct, but I forced myself to relax. I needed my smile to stay bright and happy for the sake of everyone else around me, even if it didn't reflect how I felt on the inside.

"I think you'll have more luck with those two," I said, lifting my chin toward Lennox and Bishop. He'd left Lincoln's side and was standing behind our youngest sister, staring down at Stella like she hung the moon. There was so much awe in his gaze. So much wonder. Lennox stared at her fiancé, whispering something that had him pressing a kiss to her temple.

I knew the feeling well.

"Okay, fair point," she said with a chuckle. "But I'm still holding out for you."

I shook my head. "I know you're sleep deprived right now,

but need I remind you it takes two to tango and I don't have a dance partner?"

She shrugged. "Who knows what could happen? Maybe that hot ex of yours will come rolling through again."

I scrunched up my nose. "Way to ruin the moment."

Talking about Grady was the last thing I wanted.

Despite my feelings at the time, there'd been the tiniest spark of hope after speaking with him. I'd convinced myself I could hear him out, that it *might* be different than last time. He said he was staying, after all. He deserved that much.

But I was wrong.

After Dad's emergency, he'd packed up his van and high-tailed it out of Ashwood without so much as a goodbye. Not that he owed me anything, let alone an explanation. Still, the whiplash was hard to wrap my mind around.

That'd always been his problem. It was one of the many reasons we'd broken up in the first place. I'd lost count of how many times I'd made excuses for him. After a while, I didn't want to do it anymore. I couldn't.

Waiting alone in a restaurant on my birthday had been the final straw. The killing blow.

Maybe I should've gotten used to it, but it didn't make the knowledge of his leaving any easier. Even if I'd wanted him to stay, it didn't matter. He was married to a beautiful, talented woman, with a little girl who was the spitting image of her father.

And after everything we'd been through, I could never be his friend.

cleo

. . .

16 Years Old

"MOM, I'm going to the barn!" I called out over my shoulder.

"Okay, baby. Tell your dad lunch is ready. I didn't have time to make it this morning," she said as I stepped into the Texas summer heat.

It might've only been the beginning of June, but it was already nearly a hundred degrees at noon. How Dad and the cowboys did it, I would never understand. It was so dang hot. I was probably out of my mind for deciding to do my chores right now, but I couldn't stay in the house anymore.

This morning had been rough from the get-go. Josie woke the whole damn house up with her screaming. We all ran in to find her crying on her bed, staring at her arms and legs, which were covered in itchy red spots. It took Mom about thirty minutes to calm her down so she'd listen when we told her she wasn't going to die, and that chicken pox was normal.

After her bath, Mom had all but threatened to duct tape kitchen mittens to Josie's hands so she would stop itching, which only caused her to start crying again.

Meanwhile, I was trying to keep Lennox entertained, but it hadn't gone well. All that girl did was cause chaos. I started following her around and cleaning up messes so Mom didn't have to worry about it. Not that it ultimately mattered. Just like a tornado, Lennox swept back through and destroyed everything I touched.

"Will do!" I said, pulling the door closed. I fished my iPod out of my pocket, then stuck in my earbuds and hit play. Iris by The Goo Goo Dolls began filtering through, drowning out the outside noise. Sometimes, my mind felt like it would never slow down, but music seemed to help a little. The words and beats gave me something else to focus on. It made me feel hopeful and understood in a world where I sometimes felt invisible.

Being so much older than my sisters was hard. All they wanted to do was run around and play, but I had things to do. My days were spent finishing homework, cleaning stalls, and helping with dinner. Once that was done, I helped Mom and Dad with anything they needed. By the time my head hit the pillow, I should've been exhausted, but I wasn't. Not always.

Sometimes my mind raced, keeping me up until the early hours of the morning. It didn't happen all the time, but those nights were the worst. It didn't matter how little sleep I got, I still had to get up and start the day all over again.

My least favorite part was the ranch work. I didn't hate it, but it was never going to be my life's passion like it was for my parents. They lived and breathed this place, but I wanted something more. I didn't know what yet, but I was sure I'd figure it out before college. At least, I hoped I would.

A chorus of neighs and whinnies greeted me the moment I stepped inside. I made my way to the feed room to grab a handful of treats for the horses. There was no way they'd let me get any work done if I ignored them.

Technically, Dad said I wasn't supposed to spoil them by handing out sweets every day, but I couldn't help myself. Especially not as they poked their giant heads through the stall doors and looked at me the way they did. This lot was waiting for the vet to come by for their yearly inspection and new shoes. They were old horses who'd been retired after spending most of their lives working the ranch. Now, they spend most of their time in the pastures being fat and lazy.

I approached the end of the aisle where my horse stood proud in his stall, already causing a fuss before I even came to a stop. Houdini was a small American Quarter Horse my mom had rescued, aptly named because he seemed to escape from nearly every enclosure we tried to house him in.

My parents didn't talk about his history much. Just that his previous owners were horrible to him, and he needed a good home. There were scars along his flank from their angry strikes.

And he was all mine.

In some ways, I wished I were as free as he was. Not just physically, but mentally too. I couldn't imagine the horrors he'd been through, and yet he never let them break his spirit. He was mischievous and playful, always stealing bags and running away, so our hands had to try to catch him, but they were always too slow.

"Hey, boy," I cooed, scratching beneath his chin. "You ready to give 'em hell today?"

If there was one thing Houdini hated, it was the farrier. It wasn't because the guy was mean or anything, but my little escape artist hated his hooves being touched. He always kicked and bit and stomped anytime someone came near them.

He chuffed, throwing his head back in glee as he chewed happily on the peppermint in my hand.

The sound of truck tires on the gravel road drew my attention to the front of the barn. Two large trucks pulled up next to one another, each branded with a business name. Laughter filtered inside as the drivers hopped out and shook each other's hands. While they chatted, I pulled out my phone to call my dad. Fingers crossed he stayed close to the house since he knew we had company coming.

"Hey, sugar. Vet there already?" Dad asked before I could even get a word out.

"Yup. Looks like the farrier, too," I said, peering through the large double doors. There was someone else standing with them now. I thought it might have been one of our hands at first, but his t-shirt had the farrier's logo on the back of the shirt. I guess Mr. Riley had finally decided to hire help for those grueling summer months.

"Shit, alright." Dad sighed on the other side of the line. "We're about fifteen minutes out from the barn. One of those old asshats is always late, but I should've known the one time I thought we had extra time..."

I stopped hearing my dad's rambles as the young guy turned around, and I got a good look at his face.

Holy shit.

If you had told me the boy I'd had a crush on since junior high would be standing on my family's ranch in a pair of snug Wranglers and a sweat-soaked T-shirt, I'd have said you were delusional. Or maybe hallucinating. Was that what was happening right now?

I pinched myself just to make sure, rubbing over the sharp sting when I realized I was, in fact, awake.

Grady Wilde was the golden boy at school. Everyone, including the teachers, loved him. He was always the first to volunteer when our student council asked for help, and there was no short list of admirers who followed his lead. Most of the girls in our grade talked about how hot he was. I tended to keep my opinions to myself, but inside I wanted to scream about how right they were.

If they could see him now, I was pretty sure that obsession would only grow. His blond hair was tucked beneath a worn baseball cap, sporting a big "A" on the front for our high school athletics department. He'd let his facial hair grow over the summer. Just a dusting of scruff along his jawline that shouldn't have made him hotter, but it did.

"Cleo? Everything alright?"

"Y—Yeah, Daddy. Everything's great," I stammered, glancing away from the three men outside. "Want me to pull the list and show them who we're starting with?"

I could hear Dad's smile over the phone. "Don't know what I'd do without ya, sugar. That'd be great. Tell'em I'll be there as soon as I can."

I said goodbye, slipping the phone into my back pocket and discreetly wiping my sweaty palms against the denim. This was silly. Why was I nervous? It's not like talking to him was going to change my life or anything.

Even though I wish it would.

Most of the time, I didn't feel the pressure to do the things other kids my age did. Between my never-ending chores at the ranch and all my extracurricular activities at school, I didn't even have time. Plus, I was way too worried about getting caught sneaking out and being busted at a party. Honestly, my parents' disappointment would be the hardest thing to get past. The embarrassment alone might take me out, so it wasn't even worth it.

Unfortunately for me, being from a small town meant there wasn't much to do on the weekends other than get into trouble. We didn't have malls or big movie theaters. Hell, we didn't even have a skating rink or a bowling alley.

The only thing we had was land, and plenty of it. There was usually at least one party a weekend in a pasture or old hay barn. If someone's parents were out of town, they might move it inside, but that was rare. I didn't blame them because there was no way in hell I'd let a bunch of drunk classmates inside my house. What if they broke something that couldn't be fixed?

But as I've gotten older, I've started getting a little bit jealous that everyone around me is experiencing things I never have. I mean, I'd never even gone to one of those stupid parties or been on a date. Never been kissed, either, but most of my friends had.

I bet Grady had.

Nope. Wasn't going to think about that. Instead, I headed straight for my dad's office to grab the list he'd made last night. I could sit around and mope over my lack of a life—love or otherwise—in the privacy of my own bedroom.

Someone called my name as I stepped out with the clipboard tucked beneath my arm. I turned, expecting to find my dad or Bishop, but came face to face with Grady. His bright blue eyes swept over my face, lighting up when he smiled. God, I liked it when he did that. It made me feel all kinds of things I was sure I shouldn't.

"Whoa, sorry!" Grady said, laughing slightly. "I didn't scare ya, right?" He gestured behind me. "Sorry, I saw you duck into the office and didn't know if you knew where your dad was? I'm here with Riley Farrier, but the old men are too busy bullshit-ting to get the ball rolling."

I blinked up at him in surprise, suddenly unable to use my voice. He was talking to me like we were old friends when I couldn't even remember if we'd said anything other than hi to each other our entire lives.

"You good?" he asked, raising a brow.

"Uh, y—yeah," I stammered. There was a long silence before I continued. "Sorry, I'm being rude. I'm Cleo, Doug's daughter."

Grady stared down at my outstretched hand. He only paused for a beat before taking it and smirking. "Oh, I know who you are."

"You do?"

"Well, we've been in the same class since kindergarten, so it'd be pretty rude not to, right?"

His eyes darted down to where I was still clinging to his hand. I could feel the sweat along our palms, so I quickly let go and tucked a strand of loose hair behind my ear. "Right," I agreed. "Totally rude."

"Bet you don't know my name, though."

The laugh that came out of me was way too loud and not ladylike in any way, shape, or form, but I couldn't help myself. Was he serious? He was one of the most popular guys at school, and it had nothing to do with the balance in his family's bank account or the sports he played. He was just one of those people you were drawn to.

"Something funny?" he asked, leaning his shoulder on the wall beside me.

"Well, yeah. Everyone knows who you are," I said, clutching the clipboard tighter.

He lifted one shoulder. "I don't really care about what everyone thinks." Before I could respond, he changed the subject. "What's that you're clinging onto for dear life?"

"Oh," I said, pulling the board free and handing it over. "My dad's on his way. He thought y'all would be late and had a bit more time, but he wanted me to give you the list of horses y'all will be working on and what they need." Grady flipped through the papers as I spoke. "Their full history is on there—age, breed, vaccination records, last shoe fitting, and what needs to be done today."

He nodded. "Damn, this is great. Really helpful stuff."

I fought the urge to blush under his praise. If it'd been up to Dad, he would've just guessed at half the stuff on those pages instead of taking the time to look everything up. It wasn't because he was lazy; he was just swamped. That's where I came in. I'd spent hours on the list, color-coding and alphabetizing everyone so nothing was missed. I even drew a little map of the barn and put the names of the horses they'd find in each stall.

"Thanks," I said, looking down at my feet.

"You did this?"

I nodded. "Yeah, it wasn't too hard. Just had to go through some files and stuff. Organization and lists are kinda my thing."

He chuckled. It was so soft I nearly missed it. "I see nothing's changed since elementary school."

"What do you mean?" I asked, confused.

Grady glanced over the edge of the clipboard. "Yeah, I think it was second grade? Mrs. Evans' class. You went toe-to-toe with her when she insisted her roll sheet was alphabetical and it wasn't."

"Oh god," I groaned, covering my face with my hands. "I remember that. She called my parents and everything. Told them I was being disrespectful and disruptive in class. It was so embarrassing."

Mom and Dad knew it wasn't true. They said I didn't have a disrespectful bone in my body, and if I was acting that way, then there was a reason. It wasn't until the principal asked to see the sheet and told her I was, in fact, correct that she relented even a little. I couldn't be sure, but I was almost positive she graded all my homework harder than the other students in retaliation. To this day, it was the only class I'd ever gotten a B in.

"I didn't think so," Grady said earnestly. "I thought it was so cool you stood your ground. Most kids don't care enough."

I peeked between my fingers, gauging his reaction. There was no humor in his voice, but something else. Something I didn't really want to think about, because there was no way Grady Wilde was in awe of me.

"Well, she was wrong," I mumbled. The strand of hair I'd tucked behind my ear earlier came loose, and I moved to put it back. Grady tracked the movement, his eyes lingering on the spot my fingers last touched.

"There she is! You got that list, sugar?" I jumped back as my dad and Bishop came into view with the vet and farrier in tow, their faces sticky with sweat from the Texas heat. They stopped beside us, looking between Grady and me with curiosity. "Who's this?"

"Grady Wilde, sir. Pleased to meet you. Mr. Riley has told me a lot about Black Springs, and I gotta say... Y'all really do have one of the nicest places around." Grady stuck out his hand, the same one I'd gripped moments ago, for my dad to shake.

"Ah, is your momma Marsha?" Grady nodded, smiling. "Thought so. Ya look just like her. She could bake a mean cherry cobbler." He leaned toward me, dropping his voice to a stage whisper. "Don't tell *your* momma though. She'd kill me."

"Secrets' safe with me," I said, holding up my hands.

"And me," Grady added. "But thank you, sir. Honestly, there isn't anything my mom can't make. She makes staying in shape hard."

"Eh." Dad shrugged. "That's what we have ranch work for."

"Ya ain't wrong 'bout that," Mr. Harris, the vet, said, tapping his stomach. "Ever since I started slowin' down 'round the practice, I've been noticin' my pants fittin' a bit tighter. Told Missy she better be careful cookin' like that, or else she's gonna have to buy me a new wardrobe."

"Or maybe your ass just needs to move around more," Dad said, jabbing his elbow into the man's side. "Probably do you some good."

"I'm seventy-three for Christ's sake. Don't a man deserve some rest?"

Dad shook his head. "Naw. Speak for yourself, old man. I can rest when I'm dead."

"Probably after, too, you crazy bastard," Mr. Harris muttered. "Let's get this shit goin'. I'm already sick of this damn heat."

"You got the list, sugar?" Dad repeated, turning to me.

Grady stepped up. "I've got it right here, sir. Cleo was kind enough to bring it over."

He handed it over to Mr. Riley and Mr. Harris, who studied it closely. They flipped through the pages just like Grady had, their brows raising slightly in surprise. "Damn, this is good," the farrier murmured, side-eyeing my dad. "But I know your ass didn't do it."

Dad wrapped his arm around me, pulling me tight. "Naw. That's all my girl right here. I'd lose my head if it weren't for her."

I couldn't help but blush, but it wasn't from Dad's praise. I was used to that. No, this was because of the way Grady kept looking at me. Maybe I was reading too much into it, maybe it was my childhood crush coming back full force, or maybe I'd watched too many rom-coms lately, but I swore there was something more to it.

Two people who didn't know one another didn't stare the way he was, especially not how his gaze dropped to my mouth every time I spoke.

Dad gave me one last squeeze before letting me go. "You finished up in here?"

I shook my head. "No, I've gotta finish the stalls. I started at the front and have been working my way back, so y'all are good to grab the first batch."

"You need some help? Bishop can stay behind."

I looked at the guy standing beside my dad. He'd been with us for a few years now and had given everything he had to the ranch. Dad always said he didn't play favorites, but I knew Bishop was at the top of the list without question. He'd come to our Friday family dinners since Dad hired him, which was a huge honor. Those were for family only.

I shook my head. "No, I've got it. Y'all go ahead."

"Alright, sugar. Whatever you say." Dad kissed my temple before ushering the others outside.

Before heading out, Bishop bumped into my shoulder. "You couldn't have lied to get me outta this damn heat?"

"You're the one who wanted to be a cowboy," I said,

laughing and making sure Dad was out of earshot. "So, go do cowboy shit."

I didn't cuss much, especially not out loud, but Bishop was a horrible influence on me.

Bishop's shoulders slumped before mumbling goodbye and heading out the way Dad went. It was only then I realized Grady was still standing near the entrance of the barn. I lifted my hand, instantly feeling stupid as I waved.

Get it together, Cleo.

I turned around before the embarrassment could take me and quickly pulled my iPod out of my pocket, slipping my earbuds in and putting up my hair. There were still stalls to finish, a tack room to organize, and feed levels to check. The moment the music started, I let the beat carry me through the rest of my chores.

I wasn't sure how much time had passed when I felt a tap on my shoulder. I paused my iPod, trying not to get tangled in the cord as I pulled the ear buds free. Grady was standing in front of me, shifting on his feet. He'd taken his hat off, holding it with both hands in front of his body. "Hey, we're finishing up," he said, throwing a thumb over his shoulder where the adults were talking.

"Really? That was fast," I said, pulling out my phone to check the time. It hadn't taken me long to finish the stalls, but then I'd started reorganizing the tack room. I swore no one knew how to put things up where they were supposed to be.

"Yeah, Mr. Riley said it was record time. Helps that there weren't too many to get through. And that you were so organized."

I shrugged. "It's the least I could do." Grady nodded, and we lingered in an awkward silence for a beat longer. "I guess I'll see you in the fall at school, then?"

Grady chuckled nervously. "Well, to be honest, I was kinda hoping for sooner."

"Really?" I blurted, and Grady laughed.

Christ, Cleo, pull yourself together. If I could tell how desperate I sounded, I knew he could.

His fingers danced nervously across the bill of his hat. "I'm kinda starving after working all day." He gestured around the barn. "So, I wanted to see if you were hungry, too."

I blinked in surprise, wanting to look behind me to see if I was suddenly standing in the middle of his conversation with someone else. "You wanted to know if I'm hungry…" I echoed slowly, and he nodded. "Right now?"

He huffed, running his hand through his sweaty blond hair. "Yeah, I mean… If you don't already have plans or anything. I know it's last-minute and all, but I asked your dad—"

"You asked my dad?" I squeaked.

"Of course. Would've been rude to ask his daughter on a date without asking his permission," Grady said, smiling.

Date. Grady Wilde was asking me on a date. Maybe I needed to pinch myself again because there was no way this was happening.

"Unless you don't want to?" he added nervously. "I'm sorry, I just assumed we were giving the same vibes—"

"I'd love to," I said in a rush before he took it back. "It's just that, um, I've never really been on one before."

"You've never been on a date before?" Grady asked. "Really?"

I shook my head, looking down at my hands. I shouldn't have mentioned it. Now I felt dumb. He probably was looking for a girl who had more experience, one who wasn't going to be so awkward. "It's okay if you don't want to go now. It's totally cool."

Grady reached out, taking my hand lightly. I looked up, meeting his gaze. "I dunno what's wrong with the guys around here, but I'd be honored to take you on your first date."

I laughed, but there was little humor to be found. "You don't have to do that, you know. You don't have to follow through because you feel obligated."

"What's your favorite flower?"

"What?"

He squeezed my hand. "Your favorite flower. What is it?"

I chewed on the bottom of my lip. "Um, I don't know. I like daisies, I guess."

"And your favorite color?"

"Blue," I said without hesitation. "I love blue."

"Mine too," he said, smiling. "Okay, so how about this… I'm going to head out with Mr. Riley so I can go home and shower, then I'll come back and get you in like an hour and a half? Does that work?"

"Sure," I said, ducking to hide my blush. "That'd be great."

His smile was blinding, nearly knocking the wind from my lungs as the farrier called his name. He walked backward, pointing at me. "I'll see you soon."

cleo

. . .

"TODAY'S THE DAY," I murmured to myself, holding my clipboard tightly. "You got this."

A car was making its way up the drive toward our house. My nerves were frayed, and my anxiety soared, but I managed to keep it together as it came to a stop. I didn't have time to break down. Not today.

The door opened, and a little boy jumped out, excitedly pointing at the animals we'd brought up to the holding pen near the barn. Most kids who'd grown up in Ashwood were familiar with horses and cattle, but it didn't mean they saw them every day. There was something magical about the look on their faces about being near creatures we were somewhat desensitized to because we worked with them daily.

Lennox walked up beside me, bumping my hip with her own. "You ready for this?"

"Of course," I said, nodding nervously. My hands were already drenched in sweat, and the day hadn't even begun. "I mean, it's no big deal, right? It's just a weeklong day camp we've been working on for the past seven months. It's okay if nothing goes to plan and everyone hates it. We can say we gave it our best shot."

"Oh boy," Lennox said, blowing out a breath. "Have you talked to Laura lately?"

No, I hadn't, but I wasn't going to tell her that. "Of course."

She crossed her arms, giving me a look that said she knew I was lying. I waited for her to push the subject, to challenge me, but she didn't. She knew I'd only shut down more. "You know this is going to be amazing, right? People all over Ashwood are talking about it. We've already gotten inquiries about sign-ups for next year. Everyone knows Black Springs is the place to learn about horsemanship."

For adults, absolutely, but kids were a new market for us. After stepping away from professional team roping, my dad started training horses. It began as a hobby and grew into a side hustle. When he realized its potential, it became a way to use what he loved to diversify the ranch's earning potential. He traveled the country to teach, but he was renowned for the clinic we held here every June.

Last summer, Dad hired Lincoln to help him manage the load. Even before his health scare, we knew he wasn't going to be able to do this forever. We'd taken every precaution to mitigate his retirement. Lincoln was talented on his own, but under Dad's watchful eye and instruction, he'd truly flourished.

Despite that, this was the first year we hadn't hosted the annual training clinic. It'd been a hard call to make, especially since it helped financially carry the ranch through the winter. With Dad unable to work and the birth of Baby Hayes, we all agreed it would be best to let everyone settle in and return the following year with a bang.

It did, however, mean we had the opportunity to test out something different. When I started teaching at the local elementary school again, several parents complained about the lack of educational programs during the summer. Our school district would hold one or two camps during the two-month summer break, but they were mostly tailored toward math or science.

During one of my parent-teacher conferences, I was asked if the ranch had anything tailored toward kids. The nearest outdoor camp was over forty minutes away, which wasn't feasible for those who worked. When I'd said no, I found myself wishing I could say yes. We didn't need anything else on our plate, but once the idea was planted, it had sprouted roots I couldn't help but water.

Lennox's eyes had sparkled when I brought the idea to her. She immediately said yes and jumped headfirst into planning. I almost felt bad dumping something else on her plate, but honestly, no one would be able to pull it off like she would.

For all my skills, I hadn't even known where to start with this one. I may have grown up on the ranch, but it'd been a long time since I'd included myself in any of the day-to-day operations. I didn't know about licenses, insurance, or funding. I didn't know how to go about gathering staff or which horses would be best with tiny humans.

But my sister did.

Organization and paperwork were my areas of strength. I could take a bunch of random information and compile it into nice, neat stacks. My eyes dropped to my trusty clipboard, where I had at least two pages of kids who'd be showing up today, all alphabetized and color-coded by age group. If someone asked, I could probably recite their names by heart at this point because I'd studied them for so long. It helped that I knew most of them. Our town was small enough that I'd either had them in my class or gone to school with their parents. Some, though, were a mystery.

Lennox snatched my clipboard out of my hands, jerking me back to reality. "What?"

"You didn't listen to a single thing I just said, did you?" she asked.

"I don't know why you're in the business of asking questions you already know the answer to," I snapped, reaching for my stuff. She danced out of reach, holding it high above her head as though it would stop me. "Will you give me that back, please? People are here, and I need to check them in."

"Are you going to stop overanalyzing?"

No. "Yes, I'm done. I'm laser-focused." I held out my hand. "Now, give me my clipboard."

Lennox eyed me skeptically before dropping it in my palm. "Fine. But if I so much as see a single frown line or pout, I'm texting Rachel."

"You know, it's concerning that you have my best friend's number," I called out as she began walking backward.

She shrugged. "She was just reaching out to check on you, Cleo. You better be thankful I don't ask for Laura's number, too."

Note to self: Keep Lennox away from Laura

"Miss Hayes! Miss Hayes! Miss Hayes!"

I looked up to find a little boy running my way. He and his brother were both in my class last year. "Well, hello, Liam! How are you this morning?"

He skidded to a stop with a big, goofy grin on his face. His mother, Teresa, trailed behind, shaking her head. "So good. Mom made me have oatmeal instead of cereal this morning. She said it was because I was gonna be so busy today that I needed extra energy," he said, holding his hands behind his back.

"Oh, did she?" I asked when she came to a stop beside him. Teresa and I went to high school together. We'd never been close, but she was always nice to me. Her dad ran the livestock barn, so we had seen each other more outside of school than we did within the halls.

"Which ended up not mattering because someone put four

spoonsful of sugar in while I wasn't looking." She grimaced, putting her hand on top of Liam's head to stop him from bouncing.

"Oh yeah, I did do that," he said, nodding. "It tastes so much better that way."

Teresa and I shared a look. "I'm sure it does, buddy. Here, I'm going to give you this name tag," I said, taking out my pen and writing his name on the blank label. "I need you to wear it all day, okay?"

Liam's bottom lip stuck out. "Do I have to?"

"I'm afraid so."

"But you already know my name."

I crouched down to his level. "I do, but other people don't. You don't want people calling you Timothy, right?"

He scrunched his nose. "No way."

"Alright then. You'll need to wear this so that doesn't happen. It's just for today, okay? Look, I'm even wearing one." I pointed to the silver one pinned to my chest, which bore the BSR logo.

"Ooh, I want one of those!" he shouted, jumping up and down again.

I pushed to my feet, ruffling his hair slightly. "Unfortunately, these are just for adults, but maybe one day you'll work here and get one."

Every member of our staff had a nametag. They didn't get much use, but they made things easier during our events. It was an easy way for patrons to distinguish between employees and non-employees. Now that we were throwing kids into the mix, they needed to know who they could turn to if they needed help.

"Really? That is so cool." Liam turned to Teresa. "Momma, I wanna be a cowboy when I grow up!"

She smiled down at her son. "Well, your grandpa's gonna love hearing that. Now, gimme a hug so I can head to work. I'll be back later to pick you up, okay?" Liam made quick work of his hug before running off to say hi to some of his friends. "I'm so sorry about the sugar high," she said, grimacing. "I'd set the sugar out to put some in my coffee, but got distracted. By the time I turned around, there was already a mountain on top of his oatmeal. I didn't have time to make another bowl—"

I waved her off. This wasn't my first time dealing with sugar rushes, and it wouldn't be my last. "You're fine. I know today's a late start, but the rest of the week, we'll be providing breakfast, so you won't have to worry about it."

"Y'all are amazing for doing this. My dad's been wanting to teach him to ride for ages now, but you know how it is. Things slip through the cracks when you're busy."

I was trying so hard to focus on what Teresa was saying, how her dad had been struggling with health issues of his own. Still, I couldn't help but overhear snippets of two women somewhere behind us.

"Oh my gosh, is that—"

"No, it can't be. There's no way..."

"I'm so sorry to interrupt, ladies, but could you tell me where I need to check my daughter in?"

I froze, my blood running cold. Goosebumps cropped up along my skin. I knew that voice. God, I hated knowing that voice. This wasn't happening. There was no way it was happening. Not here, not now.

Nope. No, no, no. Not again.

"Of course! It's right up there," one of the women said. She sounded way too chipper if you asked me. It only got worse as she dropped her voice into this weird sultry tone and added, "Can I just say I'm a huge fan of yours? Your music helped me through some *really* dark times. I recently went through a divorce, and I've never heard lyrics that spoke to me like yours did."

Are you freaking kidding me right now? Did she think that would work? As if his fucking ego wasn't inflated enough…

"Excuse me, Miss?" There was humor in his voice, which pissed me off more than anything. How dare he come back after everything? "Rumor has it you're the one to see about checking my daughter in?"

Teresa glanced behind me, eyes going wide before she gave an awkward wave and headed back to her car. I returned the gesture, if only to buy time as I sucked in a deep breath and whirled around, coming face-to-face with Grady Wilde and his daughter on my goddamn ranch.

grady

· · ·

DID I expect to be met with a warm welcome when Cleo found out I was not only back in town, but had also enrolled my daughter in her summer camp? Absolutely not. Did I, however, expect it to be slightly warmer than the Arctic tundra look she was sending my way now? Maybe.

A fool can dream.

Cleo's deep blue eyes narrowed into tiny slits as I came to a stop in front of her. "Fancy running into you here," I drawled, giving her my best smile and slipping my hand into my pocket. It would probably be in my best interest not to piss her off even more, but in my defense, it didn't take much. Anyway, her anger was better than indifference. It meant I still got under her skin.

Déjà vu hit me hard and fast as Cleo glanced down at the clipboard in her hand. For a moment, we were sixteen again, standing in the barn with her cheeks flushed. I didn't give a shit if it'd been twenty years since it'd happened; it was the start of our journey. It was the moment I knew I wanted Cleo Hayes to be mine, and mine alone.

Hindsight might have been twenty-twenty, but sometimes I wished it wasn't. Sometimes I wished the details of our past were unfocused and blurry, or that I could remember the smiles rather than the tears.

I'd never forgive myself for all the tears. Not for one single second.

When the page flipped, her eyes dipped down the page and headed straight for the W's, likely trying to find my daughter's name. Joke's on her, though, because I hadn't used Wilde for that very reason.

If she'd seen my last name on the list, she would've immediately issued a refund and followed up with an email that said, "Absolutely the fuck not." There would be no questions. No time to explain or plead my case. It'd be one more door shut in my face, and I couldn't let that happen. Not when this was my chance to settle our past once and for all.

"I think you might be mistaken. I don't have anyone with the last name Wilde on my list," Cleo said, straightening her shoulders. *Called it.* "Unfortunately, we can't make exceptions. Our slots are all filled. I'm sorry you made the trip for nothing." Her words were professional but with a razor's edge. She was already slipping on the cold mask I'd seen her don in October.

It'd been strange seeing a side of her I never had before. The Cleo I knew was far too afraid of upsetting those around her to stand her ground. On the one hand, I was damn proud of her for not taking any shit. On the other, I hated it being used on me.

"Try Hart," I said, gesturing toward her clipboard.

With a small sigh, she turned back to the first page. Her lips drew into a tight line when she found what she was looking for. "Charlie Hart?"

"That's my girl." I placed my hand on my daughter's shoulder, giving it a slight squeeze. "And she is so excited to be here. Aren't you, sunshine?"

Cleo's eyes glanced over the edge of the clipboard, staring down at Charlie, whose little body was damn near vibrating with excitement. I was worried if I lifted my hand, she'd bolt out of here before I had a chance to stop her. "Daddy said I can ride a pony here!" she said, looking up at Cleo.

When we left the ranch last October, Charlie cried all the way home. She talked nonstop about coming back to the ranch so she could pet all the animals. Olivia and I both tried to do what we could to console our daughter, but words didn't seem to work. Nope, Charlie wanted to see results and follow-through.

Honestly, there were many times when my daughter reminded me of Cleo. It was as maddening as it was endearing to be surrounded by little reminders of her. Sometimes I found myself staring at Charlie with an aching heart, but I didn't let it show.

Cleo lowered the clipboard. Just like the last time she was faced with Charlie, her eyes grew distant. Glassy, almost. It took every ounce of self-restraint I had not to ask what was going through her head. To know if it was our memories and my broken promises that stared back at her from my daughter's eyes, or if it was something else entirely.

"You absolutely can," Cleo said, clearing her throat. "Do you, uh, have a pony at your house?"

Charlie shook her head, looking down at her feet. "No. I asked Mommy and Daddy if I could have one, and they told me no. They said I had to know how to ride one first. I keep asking, though."

"Maybe they'll get you one after this," she offered, softening her tone a touch.

"Daddy already said I'd need more lessons before I could get one." Her little face lit up, cheeks pink as she took a step forward. God, she really was too cute for words. "He said you were a really good rider. Can you teach me while we're here?"

Cleo looked up, mouth dropping open and snapping shut like a fish out of water. I couldn't help myself. I just smiled wider. She probably thought I was using Charlie against her, which wasn't exactly true. If my daughter wanted to learn how to ride a damn horse, then I was going to make sure she had the best teachers around.

Did I, however, know there was no way Cleo could say no if Charlie asked? Sure. Kids had always been her weakness. My dimples were her second. It was safe to say the odds were in mine and Charlie's favor here.

"We'll see. I don't think you'll be here long enough for me to do that." Cleo kept her eyes on mine as she said it, so I knew her barbed words were aimed at me. I was okay with that because it meant she was at least listening.

Charlie looked up at me, confused. "You said we were staying here for a long time?"

"I didn't say a long time…" I said slowly, scratching the scruff along my chin. I didn't have time to shave this morning. Between Charlie running down the halls screaming and my overthinking, we were almost late. "I said we'd be here for however long it takes."

My daughter furrowed her brows. "What's that mean, Daddy?"

"That's a great question, Charlie," Cleo said, adjusting her stance so I had the full weight of her attention. "I'd love to know, too."

It seemed presumptuous to say, "Until you're mine again," because I honestly didn't know if that would ever happen. What I did know was that until Cleo told me she didn't want anything to do with me, I was going to stay.

Because if there was even the slightest chance of redemption, I was going to fucking take it.

"It means I have some things I need to take care of in Ashwood, and my daughter wants to learn how to ride a horse. Seems like we can kill two birds with one stone, ya know?" I held my breath, waiting for her to call someone over and kick us out, but it didn't come. Cleo glanced back down at my daughter, shoulders slumping ever so slightly.

"Where are you staying?"

"My dad's. We're keeping an eye on the place while he's out of town on some once-in-a-lifetime fishing trip." Technically, it wasn't a lie. Dad was on a fishing trip, but I'd been the one to plan the whole damn thing for him and a few of his friends, so we had a verifiable excuse for coming back to Ashwood other than Charlie's newfound interest in farm animals.

Cleo's forced smile faltered at the mention of my parents. Did she know how hard it was to not only be back here, but also stay in the house I grew up in? Did she know how badly those ghosts haunted me?

But before I could give voice to any of that, she straightened her spine and stuck out her hand. "Well, Charlie... Let's take it day by day, okay? We have a long way to go before you can call yourself a cowgirl." Cleo sucked in a breath as Charlie's palm landed in hers. It was short and quick, but I'd seen it all the same. She thrust a packet of papers into my chest. "Here is her information packet. It has all our numbers in it if you have any questions about camp curriculum or safety."

"And this includes *everyone's* number? I really want to make sure I have more than one point of contact," I said, trying to hide my absolute glee as I found her phone number. It was the same one I'd left a message for last October. Even after we left, I tried to call and text her, to explain to her why I had to go back and that it was temporary, but every one of them went straight to voicemail.

Cleo's cheeks flushed a bright pink. "Yes," she mumbled. "But it's for camp purposes only. Any other topics of conversation will go unanswered."

We'll see about that. "Of course. It'd be unprofessional otherwise."

"It would," she agreed, finally meeting my gaze.

"Maybe I should call you right now so we can make sure you have my number," I said, reaching into my pocket for my phone.

"No, it's fine," Cleo squeaked, scrambling for her own. "I have your information on the sign-up—"

Too late. I scrolled through my contacts, pressing the little call icon beside her name. It rang once before going straight to voicemail—just like it always had. "Straight to voicemail."

"So strange," she said, tapping furiously at her screen. "Must be bad service or something. I'll have to look into that."

"You should. Especially since this appears to be an ongoing issue."

Cleo glanced away, jaw set in a hard line. Was it a dick move to call her out like that? Maybe, but she needed to know I hadn't walked away last year without trying to make amends. The ball had been in her court for too damn long, and I was done waiting to play by her rules.

Charlie stepped in front of us with her hands on her hips. "Can we see the ponies now?"

Cleo's gaze dropped. "I need to stay behind and check everyone in so they can see them, too."

"Oh," Charlie said, shuffling her feet. "Can my daddy take me?"

"I'm sure your dad is busy—"

"Sure, baby girl. I can do that. You don't mind, right? I mean, I know my way around here pretty well if you recall," I interrupted before she got the chance to shoo me away. I bent down, hoisting Charlie in my arms, and began the short trek to the round pens.

"Grady…" Her voice was a low growl. A warning. I fucking loved it. Maybe if I pushed her buttons enough, she'd finally stop hiding behind this aloof version of the girl I used to know.

"Bye, Cleo! Have fun checking off your to-do list! Don't forget to check into that issue with your phone, though. I'd hate for you to miss an important call, or something." I'd only taken two steps before her hand snagged around my bicep, halting me.

We both stopped, looking down to the point of contact where we were skin on skin. The moment she touched me was like an electric current. Based on how fast she withdrew her hand, I was willing to bet she felt it too.

"Charlie needs a nametag," she said with a huff, popping the cap off her marker. With careful strokes, she spelled out my daughter's name and peeled off the sticker. "Here you go."

I took it from her, carefully sticking it onto Charlie's shirt. She looked down at it, beaming. "Look, Daddy! It's my name."

I hugged her a little tighter. "It sure is, sunshine. Can you tell Miss Cleo thank you?"

"Thank you, Miss Cleo!" Charlie sang.

Cleo hesitated before I heard her say, "You're very welcome, Charlie."

She turned on her heel, heading back to the growing line at registration. To everyone else, I bet her smile seemed genuine, but I knew it was anything but. Every move she made was rigid, like it was taking everything she had not to run for the hills.

God, I wished she would let me in. I wished she would let me show her how desperate I was for her. How, after all the years and bullshit and distance, I still found myself yearning for her like I did when I was sixteen. I wished she would let me make up for all that lost time and show her what it would've been like if I hadn't had my head stuck so far up my ass I lost sight of what was truly important.

Her.

Charlie tapped my shoulder, bringing my attention back to her. "Daddy, can we go see the ponies now?"

I gave her a squeeze. "Yeah, baby girl. We can do that."

We walked over to the pen, where a couple of horses and cows lazed around, munching on hay to keep them content. Kids and parents alike giggled when one of them came up and nuzzled their palms. I glanced at my daughter, noticing the way her eyes grew wide with the same excitement reflected in her face.

Charlie and I'd had a tough couple of months, so seeing her joy made me feel like I was doing something right for the first time in years. Especially when Cleo looked at me with such contempt, like rocking up here with my daughter ruined her life.

I could admit it was strange being back here. Even more so with Cleo not at my side. I didn't have the opportunity to enjoy coming to the ranch when the band performed for Doug's birthday celebration, especially not when the night was over before it had begun.

I don't know how long Charlie and I stood together watching all the animals come and go. It seemed like just the blink of an eye, but before I knew it, Cleo clapped her hands and thanked everyone for signing up and coming by before launching into a spiel about the camp, the ranch's history, and what the kids would be learning over the course of the week.

She'd always been lauded for her public speaking ability throughout high school and into college. So much so that our debate teacher once asked her to lead the team because he knew she was the only one capable of taking them to state. He never understood why she said no, but I did.

Anytime she was stressed or nervous, she clenched her fist in a white-knuckle grip. Like holding onto something would stop her from losing it altogether. Right now, it looked like the poor clipboard was about two seconds away from shattering in her hold.

As Cleo finished up, she called for all the kids to follow her and Lennox into the barn for their first lesson of the day. Just before she turned, her gaze met mine, and I felt it. That pull to go to her, that incessant need to tell her how sorry I was. It was taking everything I had not to fall to my knees in front of this whole goddamn town and beg her to listen to me.

I'd grovel if she wanted me to. Hell, I'd kiss her fucking boots if that's what it took.

Charlie tugged on my shirt. Reluctantly, I dragged my eyes from Cleo's to my daughters. "See you later, Daddy."

I bent down, wrapping her in a big hug. It was the only thing stopping me from following Cleo immediately. "See you later, sunshine. Have fun and be sure to listen to Miss Cleo, okay?"

She nodded. "I will. I promise."

"Alright." I kissed the top of her head before standing. "Go have fun."

Without another word, she ran from my side. Instead of falling in line with the other kids, though, she bounded straight toward Cleo. She looked down as Charlie asked her a question, hesitating only a moment before holding out her hand for my daughter to take. I waited for her to look back, but neither of them did.

Instead, I watched them disappear into the barn hand-in-hand, finding myself slightly jealous of my daughter for being so close to the woman I loved.

grady

. . .

16 Years Old

SPEEDING down the street in my old truck, I skidded to a stop in my driveway and rushed out into the balmy summer air. Old man Riley had gone about five miles under the speed limit and talked my damn ear off the entire drive back to town from Black Springs Ranch. It'd taken every bit of manners my momma taught me not to tell the old bastard to shut up so I could get home.

I smelled like shit, sweat, and horses, which wasn't really the first-date impression I wanted to make, even if Cleo was used to being surrounded by it.

When I got to the ranch that day, I hadn't expected to ask her on a date. I knew who she was, knew my chances of seeing her were high, too. Maybe that was why I jumped on the chance to help Mr. Riley when he asked if I felt comfortable enough to go out on my first call with him. "Don't fuck this up, boy." That's what he'd told me. I just nodded and said, "Yes, sir," because I had no intentions of fucking anything up.

Especially not my first shot at talking to the girl I'd quietly been crushing on since we were kids.

Cleo was the kind of girl who was born to stand out—no

matter how hard she tried to blend in. She had no idea the effect she had on people. I'd have to have been blind not to notice her.

My plan was simple. Honestly, I was just hoping she'd notice me. If I were lucky, maybe we'd share a conversation that lasted longer than a greeting. Asking her on a date had been the furthest thing from my mind. I was content playing the long game. She was worth it. I didn't have to talk to her to know that.

But there was something today in the way her cheeks had flushed when we talked that cemented it for me. God, she'd been so pretty. I'd never felt such pride before because I swore, at least for a moment or two, she felt the same way I did.

I wanted—no, *needed*—to know more about her. Asking her a few of her favorites wasn't enough for me. If anything, it only made me more curious. Now it was more like a craving.

It felt cliché to say I'd never felt anything like it before, but it was true. I'd been on a few dates before, shared a few kisses here and there, but nothing that ever really stuck on my end. Things fizzled out fast before turning into a relationship, much to others' dismay. I just hoped I wasn't about to learn what it felt like to be on the other side of things.

I darted up the porch, hearing my mom call out for me the moment our screen door swung open. She was standing in the kitchen with a towel over her shoulder, brows furrowed as she watched me dart past her. "Hey, baby! How was your first big day?"

"Can't talk, Mom! No time," I called, bounding down the hallway toward my room.

"Whoa, there. Where's the fire?" my mom asked, rounding the corner. My shirt was already halfway off before she stepped in front of my bathroom door, hands on her hips. "No time to talk to your mom?" she asked, eyebrows raised.

"Mom..."

"What a shame. I'd love to know what's got you in such a

rush." She plastered on her best smile, staring up at me like she had all the time in the world.

I tipped my head back in a groan. "Maybe I just smell bad and want to shower."

She leaned in, nose scrunched as she sniffed the air. "No more than usual."

"Hey!"

Mom rolled her eyes. "You're a teenage boy, Grady. Stink follows you wherever you go. Your father, bless his heart, stunk to high heaven until he was eighteen." She leaned forward, loudly whispering, "He wasn't a big fan of deodorant until college."

"I heard that, woman!" he boomed from somewhere in the house. Knowing him, he was likely tinkering with something in the kitchen. Dad was the type of man who couldn't sit still to save his life. Since we lived in an older house, it worked out, because he saw it as an endless supply of projects to keep him busy.

"You still got the girl in the end, stink and all!" She turned to wink and smile at me before adding, "Which is just a lesson for you before you go off on this big date of yours."

"What?"

"If she's the one—"

"Whoa, Mom. Slow down—"

She threw her hands in the air. "I'm just saying."

I cocked my head to the side. "How'd you even—"

"Know that there was likely a girl involved?" she asked, finishing my sentence. Mom looked at me like I'd suddenly grown two heads. "Good lord, boy. I'm old, not stupid. You're never this quick to jump in the shower when you get home, and now you can't wait."

"Speaking of showering..." I said slowly, glancing behind her at the door she was blocking. I loved my mom, but there were other things on my mind. "I'm kind of in a rush."

But Mom didn't budge. If anything, she stood her ground hard. "Where are y'all going?"

I scratched the back of my neck, pausing slightly. I hadn't given much thought to that, hadn't had the time. The ride from Black Springs Ranch to home had been a blur. I'd just been riding the high of her saying yes. "I dunno. Figured that was a problem for future Grady."

She scoffed. "Well, your future and present selves are about to collide, boy. You want to make a good impression, right?" I nodded. Of course, I did. This was Cleo's first date ever, so it needed to be special. "What about Hardy's? They have a bit of everything, but it's a lot nicer than the Burger Shack."

"I don't really have Hardy's money," I confessed. Hardy's was a local joint, kind of like a fancy Chilis. It'd been run by the same family since it opened over thirty years ago. It was damn good, but it was more expensive than I'd bargained for.

I'd been working for the farrier for the past week but hadn't gotten my first check yet. All I had to spend was the little bit I had left from doing odd jobs around the neighborhood or for my dad. Half of that had to go to filling my gas tank, though. Which meant I had even less than I thought. "Maybe I should just cancel. Wait until I can do it right."

Cleo came from money, even if she never flaunted it. I knew she wouldn't really care where I took her, but there was this subconscious need to show her I was able to give her what she deserved. A half-cocked date wasn't gonna cut it.

I sighed, shoulders slumping as I tried to give my mom a smile. "I'm gonna call her really quick and explain. Maybe I'll say I got stuck talking to Mr. Riley and he wouldn't shut up in time for me to make it."

No sooner had I turned to trudge towards my bedroom than Mom called out my name. I faced her, even though I didn't want to waste any more time. She waited for a beat, her eyes searching my face. "You really like this girl."

There was no point in lying. Not to my mom. She knew me too well. "Well, yeah—"

"That wasn't a question," she said, cutting me off and stepping forward. "Don't worry about the money, Grady. It'd be rude to cancel, especially since I'm sure the poor girl is already stressing about what she's gonna wear."

There was a reason I was working this summer instead of hanging out with my friends or playing summer sports. We didn't come from wealth like some of the other families around town, Cleo's included. Mom and Dad worked their asses off for everything. While we had what we needed, we didn't always have extra cash to spend on things we wanted.

I still remember the crushing look on their faces when my friends and their parents invited us to join them for lunch at that expensive steak house after Saturday football practices, and they had to politely decline because we couldn't afford to go. It was burned into my memory, sometimes keeping me awake at night, as I wondered what more I could do to help. I vowed from an early age never to ask for more than what I needed, to do whatever it took to put them in a better position.

"Mom, no," I said, shaking my head. "I don't want you to do that."

She held her hand up. "Grady Elliott Wilde, don't you dare back-talk me. If I wanna do this for you, and also for that girl, then let me do it." She placed her hand on my cheek, eyes softening. "You've never asked your father and I for anything. You work harder than any sixteen-year-old I know. Let us do this for you, baby."

I was at war with myself, knowing how badly I wanted to impress Cleo, yet not wanting to use money I was sure Mom and Dad had saved for a night for themselves. "What about you and Dad?"

Her eyebrows rose, wiggling slightly. "Why do you think I want you out of the house so badly?"

I groaned, slapping a hand over my face. "Mom…"

I heard Dad's chuckle in the background as she looked me up and down. "Now that that's settled… What are *you* going to wear?"

I SHIFTED on my feet nervously as I stood in front of the Hayes' front door. There was a bouquet of wildflowers in hand. Mom helped me put it together while I got ready. The floral stuff was kind of her thing. She worked at a local flower shop on weekends and had a large flower garden in our backyard. When I'd told her Cleo liked blue and her favorite flower was daisies, she said she had just the arrangement in mind. It wasn't fancy, but she'd found a pretty blue ribbon to tie around the stems to keep everything intact.

For the briefest moment, I worried Cleo would look down on a homemade bouquet. She didn't seem like the type, especially not when she was out there sweating her ass off with the rest of the hands. Still, she came from a life of comfort, while I'd never experienced that kind of luxury in my life.

I rapped my knuckles against the wood, taking off my hat when I heard someone yell, "Coming!"

The door swung open, revealing an older woman who must've been Cleo's mom. They looked a lot alike, except for the eyes. Cleo's eyes were dark and shimmered like sapphires beneath the Texas sky. It'd been nearly impossible to ignore, especially not when they'd grown so wide during our conversations.

I smiled, dipping my chin in greeting. "Evening, ma'am. I'm here to pick Cleo up for our date."

Her mom fought a smile as she ushered me inside. "Come

on in outta the heat! It's stifling," she said, stepping out of the way. "I think she's almost ready—"

"I'm here!"

I glanced up as Cleo rounded the corner and stopped sharply in front of us. If I thought she was pretty in nearly one-hundred-degree heat and covered in sweat, nothing could've prepared me for how beautiful she was all done up.

She was wearing a pale blue dress with little wildflowers all over it. It stopped just below her knees, and there were thin straps over her shoulders holding it in place. I couldn't help but slowly drop my gaze, noticing her toned, tanned skin and freshly painted toenails that matched her dress. The front of her hair was pulled out of her face, but it flowed down her back in soft waves.

Holy shit. She was beautiful.

A sweet pink hue filled her cheeks as she broke eye contact and looked at the floor. "Sorry to keep you waiting—"

"I just got here," I said, cutting her off. There was an awkward beat of silence before I remembered the bouquet clutched in my hand. "These are for you. I know you said you loved daisies, so my mom made sure there were a couple in there for you. I'm not sure what the others are, but I could find out for you?"

Cleo's face broke out in a big smile as she took the flowers from my hand and brought the petals near her nose and inhaled their sweet scent. "They're lovely," she whispered. "You made this?"

I scratched the back of my neck, not wanting to lie. "My mom, actually. She works at one of the flower shops in town and has her own garden, so she helped me throw something together." When she didn't say anything more, I panicked and started to ramble. "It's okay if you don't really like them. It's just all we had, and the flower shop was already closed—"

"I think they're beautiful, Grady. This is so thoughtful," she said, turning to her mom. "Do we have a vase to put them in?"

"We should have one or two lying around somewhere," her mom said, giving me a wink before taking the flowers from Cleo. "I'll take care of this. You kids go have fun, now."

"Thanks, Mom," Cleo said, readjusting her purse strap over her shoulder. She walked to my side, still smelling like the flowers from the bouquet. There was the softest hint of something sweet beneath it all. Vanilla, maybe?

"Don't forget curfew," her mom called over her shoulder.

Cleo winced slightly. "Yes, Mom. I know," she said through gritted teeth. I couldn't help but wonder how many times they'd had the conversation. My parents didn't care much when I came home so long as I didn't wake them up coming through the door, and I was in bed before the sun rose the next morning.

"Alrighty then." Her mom smiled, waving at me over the top of her daughter's head. "Don't get into too much trouble!"

The look Cleo gave me said she was itching to get out of here. So was I, but probably not for the same reasons. Mine were purely selfish. I couldn't wait to be alone with her, even though I'd likely need to loosen her up to get her talking. Every bit of her was rigid and stiff, like she didn't know how to act or what to do.

She was nervous, which was so damn cute. Honestly, there wasn't a single part of her that wasn't.

I moved, gesturing for her to step into the balmy summer night. My hand found her back on instinct as we walked, guiding her to the passenger side of my truck. She faltered slightly, looking at me beneath furrowed brows as I reached across and opened it for her.

"I can get it, you know," she said, climbing inside. She wrapped her fingers around the handle and tried to pull it closed, but I held it in place until she looked up at me. "What're you doing?"

I kept my eyes locked on hers as I slowly let the door close. The window was open, so I braced my elbows in the empty space. That damn sweet floral scent wrapped around her must've been getting to my head because I couldn't stop myself from leaning forward.

"I know this is your first date and all," I said, smirking as her lips pursed tightly. "But let me tell you how this is gonna go. If there's a door that needs opening, I'm gonna do it for you. When it comes time for dinner, I'm gonna pay the bill. And maybe, just maybe, I'll be lucky enough to give you a kiss if you want one at the end of the night."

Cleo stared at me for a minute, her lips slightly parting at my honesty. "You want to kiss me?" Her words were slow, like she didn't really believe what I'd said. I hated that more than her thinking she should get her own door. Why was that so hard to get through her head?

"Sure do," I said. "But I'm trying to play my cards right, so you'll wanna kiss me, too."

Before she could say anything else, I pushed off the door and rounded the truck. The moment my ass hit the seat, I reached over and grabbed the aux cord and plugged it into my phone. Hands Down by Dashboard Confessional filled the speakers, and I turned to Cleo. Her face lit up with recognition.

"I love this song," she said. "I put it on all my summer playlists."

I laughed, making my way down the long driveway. "Oh yeah? And how many summer playlists do you have?"

"Three, I think. No, wait! Maybe four," she said.

A woman after my own heart. I loved the idea of creating a playlist for every mood, but not everyone else felt the same way. "Why so many? Can't you just throw them all together and have one big playlist?"

Cleo looked over at me in horror. "Uh, no way. Like, I have a playlist for work, which has a completely different vibe than one

I made for driving around the backroads with my windows down or sitting by the lake in the evening."

"Okay, so that's three. What's the fourth then?"

She chewed on her bottom lip. "I guess I was wrong. There were just three."

I didn't believe her. Not for a second. Not when she had that damn blush creeping along her cheeks and wouldn't meet my eye. "Alright, fine. Don't tell me. I'll figure it out eventually." I glanced down at her purse clutched tightly in her lap. "Even if I have to pry it outta of you."

Cleo laughed, but the sound was somewhat hollow. She stared out the window at the blurred landscape as we flew toward the highway. "I feel like I'm going to disappoint you."

I tried to keep my voice even as alarm bells began sounding in my head. "Why's that?"

She shrugged. "I'm really not that interesting, Grady. There's not much more to me than what you've already seen."

"I guess it's a good thing I like what I see, huh?" I joked, but her smile didn't return. "Besides, we're always our toughest critic. I'm willing to bet there's more to you than you think." I tapped my fingers along the steering wheel as I drove, trying to melt the tension between us. So far, I felt like I was fumbling this date harder than our football team during the playoffs. We hadn't even made it to the restaurant. At this point, I wasn't sure if we would.

"You barely know me," she said, her voice a little stronger than before. "I could actually be a horrible person. Maybe I'm just putting on a front since it's our first date and all—" I burst out laughing, unable to contain myself. Cleo whipped her head in my direction, narrowing her eyes. "What's so funny?"

I glanced over at her, noting the scowl that seemed to be etched onto her face at this point. Up ahead, there was a little clearing off the county road. I pulled over hard, skidding to a stop. Cleo grabbed onto the handle as dust kicked up behind my tires.

"What the heck was that for? What're you doing?" she asked, eyes wide. Her fingers had turned white from how hard she was clutching onto the flimsy plastic.

I didn't answer as I got out and marched around to her side. She called my name, but I ignored her until I reached her door. I yanked it open, reached over, and unclipped her seatbelt, forcing her to turn my way.

"Grady, what—"

I put my finger over her lips, trying to ignore how soft they were or the fact that I now wanted to feel them against my own. "I'm gonna talk, and you're gonna listen, okay?" She didn't say anything as I pulled away, but she slowly nodded her head. "Alright, first of all," I said, holding up that same damn finger. "I know you, Cleo. You may think I don't, but I promise you I do. We've known each other since we were kids. We may not have talked, but we literally started school together. Our graduating class will have—what? Fifty kids in it?"

"Sixty-seven, actually," she said, sitting taller.

"Alright then, sixty-seven kids. And correct me if I'm wrong, but most of us started in kindergarten together?" She nodded again. "Could you, in theory, name every single person and tell me something about them?"

Cleo watched me closely, clearly waiting for me to get to the point, but I was going to drag this out until she understood where I was coming from. "I'm on the student council—"

"Nope. Not what I asked. It's a simple yes or no question."

"Why don't you do it then?" she snapped back. Her dark blue eyes sparked with subtle defiance, and there was something about it that got my blood boiling.

I shrugged, smirking as I began going through a list of names. "Sara Baker. Her birthday is in June, along with her best friend, Allie Wills. Tanner Holstein just got a new truck after he ran his old one into a ditch at the beginning of summer. Jessie Chavez wants to get into bull riding so badly he lies to the event organizers and tells them he's eighteen. And then there's—"

"Okay, point made! You know people, but that doesn't mean you know me."

"You're on the fast track to becoming valedictorian and student body president."

I widened my stance and folded my arms over my chest. The way her eyes dipped to my biceps had me showing off just a bit. I flexed, enjoying the way her breathing changed ever so slightly.

"Everyone knows that," she mumbled. "People have to be voted into the student council, and my grades aren't a secret."

"Alright, you want me to go past the superficial shit?" I blew out a breath, not waiting for her to answer. Mom always said it was rude to cuss in front of a lady, but I think even she would make an exception right now. "You bring your lunch every day, except for Pizza Fridays—which I've always found weird because it isn't even good pizza. Whenever you have to make a speech in front of our class, you always make it look easy, but I think it terrifies you because you always have at least one fist clenched at your side or on the podium." She stared at me, completely stunned by my admissions, so I continued. "This is new, but I've noticed you do this little shoulder shimmy thing when you're trying to pull yourself together—which would be so freaking cute if it didn't mean you were hiding something from me. And you blush every time you see me. Did you know that?"

Cleo looked away, biting her lip to hide a smile. "No, I don't."

I stepped forward, taking her chin between my thumb and forefinger and forcing her to look at me. "Then why're your cheeks strawberry red right now?"

"I don't know," she muttered. "Because you said all that stuff. I'm not used to it."

"Not used to what?" I asked, chuckling.

Cleo's face sobered. "Being seen."

Without thinking, I let my hand slide along her jaw and ran my thumb across her cheekbone. My eyes dipped to her lips as she sucked in a breath. It was taking everything I had not to kiss her, to let her know just how much I saw her.

"What're you doing?" she whispered.

"Trying not to kiss you," I answered honestly. There was no point in lying. Not when there was so much tension lingering between us.

Her tongue darted out to moisten her plush lower lip, and I bit back a groan. "I've never been kissed before."

"And I wanna change that," I said hoarsely. "But I wanna wait until I take you home because if I kiss you now, I know that's all I'll want to do."

Cleo swallowed, nodding slowly. "Yeah, I think that'd probably be best."

She tried to pull away, but I didn't let her. "You shine bright, Cleo. Brighter than anyone else I know. Remember that." I let my hand fall away from her face, intentionally brushing my fingers along the exposed skin of her arm.

cleo

. . .

I COLLAPSED ONTO THE COUCH, letting out a low groan as my body sank into the leather and stared up at the ceiling. Every part of my body ached. I may have been used to running after kids all day, but not with the additional concern of wide-open spaces and teaching animal safety. By the end of the day, I'd nearly had twenty heart attacks from every time one of the kids launched themselves toward a horse they thought was cute.

I struggled to make it through dinner. Thankfully, we had leftovers from the weekend I was able to scarf down without having to worry about cooking a full meal. The only reason I hadn't made a beeline for my bed was the fact that I always tried to spend time with Mom and Dad before they went to sleep. Not that it seemed to matter tonight. Some old TV show they loved played in the background, but neither of them was paying attention to it. Instead, their attention was focused on me.

"How'd the first day go?" Dad asked. The leather groaned as he shifted into a comfortable position. "Saw a lot of cars out front."

"Oh, it looked like it was so much fun," Mom cooed from his side. She walked in from the kitchen and perched on the ottoman. "I kept watching all the parents drop off this morning, and those kids—they were just precious!"

I squeezed my eyes closed, trying to forget about one father and daughter duo in particular. I still don't think it'd hit me that Grady was back in town, or that his daughter had clung to my side at every chance she got.

Lennox and I agreed to split the kids in half by last name to make pick-up go a bit smoother. When the time came, I'd all but begged my sister to take the first half of the alphabet so I didn't have to see Grady again.

She may not have fully known my reason for the switch, but if there was one thing I cherished about my sister, it was her unyielding loyalty. That girl understood if I was asking for a favor, there was likely a damn good reason. Especially if I begged.

I never begged.

Someday Lennox would ask me about it, but not yet. She would give me the time I needed to figure things out myself before asking questions I didn't have answers to.

"I think it went really well," I said, pushing thoughts of Grady from my mind. Or at least, I tried to. It didn't really work as planned. In fact, the more I thought about the day, the less I could recall about the actual camp.

He'd been at the forefront of my mind, even when I tried my hardest to get him out. There was only one blissful moment of the day that'd been Grady-free, however, it quickly came to a screeching halt when Charlie came running up to me after lunch and asked to see my pony.

Her affection should have made me uncomfortable, but it didn't. The truth was I loved being someone she could rely on. Loved the way she seemed carefree and full of life. There was never a moment she censored herself, nor was she afraid to ask for the things she wanted.

If anything, I was jealous in a way. I wished I could've been more like that when I was her age. Maybe if I were, I wouldn't have spent my life waiting around for something—anything—to happen. Maybe I would've gone out into the world and demanded what I deserved, instead of settling for something I'd known in my bones hadn't been right.

Maybe I would've fought a little bit harder, too.

After we walked into the barn this morning, she divulged her entire life story—including the fact that her real name was Charlotte and she'd never been around so many kids before. When I asked her about school, she just shrugged and said her parents worked a lot, so she had a private tutor.

Seeing her again was like a fever dream. Whether I wanted to admit it or not, I'd spent a portion of my life wondering what Grady and I's kids would look like. He used to tease me relentlessly, saying he hoped our little girl would be my mini-me. I'd secretly hoped for the opposite. I wanted a little blonde-haired beauty running around that had eyes as crystal clear as his were.

That was Charlie to a T.

As hard as it was to be around her, I also couldn't deny my curiosity. Her willingness to share literally everything was somehow distinct from the other kids. She was special in a way that made me sad and happy at the same time. There were so many things about her that reminded me of the boy I used to know, the one who has always held my heart.

"That's great, sugar," Dad said, giving me a sleepy smile. "You and your sister have worked so hard on this project. It must feel good to see it come together so nicely."

"Huh?" I asked, lifting my head to stare at him. "Oh yeah, it feels great."

Mom and Dad shared a look. "You feeling okay?"

"I think I'm just tired."

He nodded, but I didn't miss the flash of concern in his eyes. "You don't have to babysit us old folks, ya know. Why don't you head on to bed?"

I nodded, faking a yawn for their own benefit. I was tired, but there was no way I was getting to sleep now that I'd let myself go down the rabbit hole that was Grady Wilde. "Good idea." I stood up, walking over and kissing the top of their heads before saying goodnight. "And for the record, I'm not babysitting."

Dad snorted, and Mom rolled her eyes as she settled into the crook of the chair next to him. "Sure you aren't."

The house was quiet as I walked down the hall. It felt empty. Devoid of everything other than my parents' fading conversation in the living room. I remember the days when our home was overflowing with life. It was such a strange contrast to the silence.

It used to be nothing to hear my sisters giggling and scheming from the other side of their doors. They would be up for hours, chatting until the early morning about boys and Cosmopolitan magazine. When I was younger, it used to annoy me, especially when our parents were working from sun up to sun down to grow this ranch into the enterprise it was today.

But now with Josie, baby Stella, and Lincoln living in their newly built home on the property and Lennox in love and shacked up with Bishop, I found myself missing my sisters more than I ever realized. It wasn't that I didn't see them daily, because I did. Lennox and I still worked together during the summer, and I frequently meal-prepped for Josie so she wouldn't have to worry about it.

This was different, though. It was sad. Desolate. Empty.

Stepping into my bedroom, I quickly closed the door behind me and ran for my phone. I needed to talk to someone. Someone who knew everything, who wouldn't judge my warring mind.

With trembling fingers, I texted Rachel.

CLEO

I need my friend and not a therapist.

I waited, my anxiety ratcheting up as the three dots popped up at the bottom of our messages.

RACHEL

1. I'm not your therapist

2. Hit me with anything and everything.

I chewed on my lip, wondering what I should say. Might as well cut straight to the chase.

CLEO

Grady's back.

The bubbles popped up, then quickly disappeared. Time seemed to drag as I waited impatiently for her reply. There was likely going to be a worn path on my rug from pacing back and forth.

RACHEL

What do you mean, he's back? Back where?

CLEO

I mean, he showed up on the ranch with his daughter in tow, talking about how he enrolled her in my camp. Then he told me, yet again, how he doesn't plan on leaving. I swear to God the universe is gaslighting me.

RACHEL

How did you not know he'd signed up? You've been monitoring that list like a hawk.

CLEO

Apparently, he used her mom's last name.

RACHEL

Ah

Well

CLEO

Very insightful. Thank you for your wise words. *eyeroll emoji

My phone vibrated in my hand, and I quickly swiped to answer it.

"Okay, you can't just drop that on me in a text message," she said, huffing slightly. Her voice was breathy and low, like she'd just gotten done running a mile. "I don't know what you expected."

"Are you okay?" I asked, looking at the time. It was well past ten, which wasn't late per se, but Rachel was almost always in bed by this time. She'd always been an early riser. "You sound a little—"

"I'm good," she rushed out, cutting me off. "Now give me a rundown on everything that happened today."

So, I did. I told her every single detail from the moment I looked up and saw Grady standing there with Charlie in tow, to the moment I watched him pick her up, scanning the front lawn and leaving with a smile that didn't quite reach his eyes when he didn't find what he was looking for.

When he didn't find me.

The thought alone nearly made me laugh, because all of this was beyond insanity. Why couldn't I just suck it up and put the past behind me? Why did he still have this freaking pull on my heart, the capability of turning me into a bumbling idiot who couldn't stop sweating at the mention of his name?

Honestly, I was overreacting. He wasn't looking for me. He wasn't sad. No, it was just my mind giving me the slightest hint of hope so I'd be disappointed yet again when he packed up and left in his stupid, shiny new truck.

It was hard for me to unblock his number. I didn't know why I'd felt so embarrassed when his call went straight to voicemail. We both knew it wasn't going to go through, but that knowledge sat unspoken between us like a bomb waiting to go off.

Now that nothing was keeping him away, I was all too aware of the silence on his end. There'd been no texts or calls to make sure they'd go through. No bullshit questions about the camp to get me to respond like I thought there would be.

It was silent, just like this stupid house.

"Wow," Rachel said. "That's... a lot."

"Tell me about it," I muttered, reaching for the worn daisy on my desk. I squeezed it, feeling the dried edges crack beneath the pressure.

The silence lingered for a moment before she hesitantly spoke again. "Maybe this is a good thing."

My laugh was hollow. "Yeah, okay. In what world is Grady freaking Wilde showing back up in my life a good thing?" Surely, she was joking, right?

"I dunno, Cleo. Maybe the universe is giving you a chance—"

"A chance at what?" I asked, instantly wincing at my tone. It was harsher than I intended, but I didn't apologize.

She sighed. "Aren't you tired of spending your life hating him?"

I shook my head. "There's no way—"

"Nope. Stop," she said sharply. "Think about it, Cleo. You've been hung up on this man for over twenty years. He was your first love. Your first everything. Don't you think it might warrant a conversation?"

"He's never given me the chance before, so why should I? Every opportunity saw him running for the hills."

Back to work.

Back to Tennessee.

Back to her.

"Why're you letting him be the moral compass you judge your actions against? It seems to me the best thing would've been to put this to rest ages ago, but you're both too goddamn stubborn to do it." Rachel blew out a breath. "Just talk to him, Cleo. I think you'll regret it if you don't."

"I'm not stubborn."

Rachel barked a laugh. "Yeah, okay, and I don't have a great ass."

"Whatever." I gnawed on my lip, mulling over her words. "What would we even talk about? The weather? You know small talk isn't my thing."

She sighed. "Well, he's obviously back for a reason. Put all the shit in the past aside and find out why."

"He's watching his dad's house while he's on vacation. That's it. That's the reason."

Even though I couldn't see her, I still knew Rachel was rolling her eyes. "Oh my god, you don't seriously believe that, do you?"

"Well, yeah—"

"You're telling me his dad conveniently chose to go on vacation at the same time you're holding a children's summer camp his daughter is attending? Come on, Cleo." I opened my mouth to respond, but she cut me off. "Listen, I've got company, but—"

Company? I heard a man's voice on the other end, which she promptly hushed.

Oh. *Company.*

"Oh my god! Why'd you let me ramble, then?" I cringed, knowing exactly why she was out of breath at the beginning of our phone call now.

"Because you needed me. Now, I'm gonna go get fuc—"

"Goodbye, Rach," I said, hanging up and tossing the phone onto my bed.

With a sigh, I stepped into my small ensuite bathroom.

There weren't many perks to being the oldest kid, but I was grateful for it. Especially when my sisters became obsessed with going through my things.

I looked into the mirror, running my fingers along my face. After years of having to wear full-coverage foundation, I found quiet joy in simply applying a tinted moisturizer before walking out the door. The problem now was it didn't hide just how exhausted I was.

It didn't take long for me to mentally catalogue everything I saw that I didn't like. My lips were too thin. The bags beneath my eyes stood out more than the wrinkles between my brows. Gray hairs were showing along my temples because it'd been way too long since I'd gotten my hair done.

I hadn't cared about any of that twenty-four hours ago, so why did it suddenly feel like there were neon signs and flashing arrows above my head pointing them out?

"Pull yourself together, girl," I muttered beneath my breath, and turned toward the tub.

All I needed was a hot shower. That would make me feel better. Maybe even some of those stupid undereye patches Rachel was always raving about. It couldn't hurt, right? Maybe it was one of those things where if I believed they'd cure every issue then they would.

I closed my eyes as I stepped beneath the water, letting it run along my skin like a comforting embrace—which felt a lot more depressing when I realized how long it'd been since anyone touched me. Sure, I was around my family who gave out hugs like candy on Halloween, but from a partner? I couldn't even remember the last time I'd felt that kind of tenderness.

Thomas had been overly affectionate at the beginning of our relationship, to the point I probably should've caught on to some red flags. The sad truth was I was so desperate to be loved and desired after Grady and I broke up that I didn't see them until it was too late.

That affection dimmed over the years until it became a chore —something I felt like I had to do so he wouldn't get angry. It worked for a while, until it didn't. I could still remember the first time I felt his violence. How he'd come home after a bad day at work and started yelling at me the moment he stepped through the door about dinner not being ready yet. With heated words and burning anger, I felt the sting of his palm long after he left me crying on the floor clutching my cheek.

It only went downhill from there. By the time we separated, it'd been over a year since we'd had sex. He would ask occasionally, telling me he was so sorry for the way things had been, but I'd been hearing that for years.

I was mentally checked out and wanted nothing to do with him or the pain he caused me.

But now, standing here in the same bathroom I grew up in, I found myself missing that kind of affection. Not with Thomas, obviously. But it'd be nice to experience an orgasm without turning over and reaching for the vibrator tucked away in my nightstand.

Rachel had gotten the thing for me as a joke. She called it my *"Congrats on getting divorced!"* gift. It was bright pink and had way too many settings—most of which I'd never used.

The orgasms were better than anything I'd had with my ex-husband, though.

I'd never been the most adventurous partner in bed. I never really gave myself the chance. Grady and I were each other's first. In the time between our end and the beginning of me and Thomas, there'd only been a handful of drunken make-outs that never turned into anything more. I'd been too nervous to take it any further. Sometimes I wished I hadn't been. Sometimes I wished I'd let loose and run a little wild instead of staying home and crying.

Maybe if I had, getting over him wouldn't have been as hard. Maybe I wouldn't have married some asshole just to fill a void or found myself carrying around an irrational anger for almost twenty years.

I didn't realize how long I'd been standing beneath the water contemplating my life until the shower began to run cold. Quickly, I shut it off and stepped into the small, steam-filled space. The fabric of my towel felt rough against my skin as I quickly dried off. Now that I'd acknowledged how long it'd been, my body was inherently aware of what it'd been deprived of.

Even though I knew I could handle the problem myself, my body was rejecting the idea. She knew it wouldn't be as good as it could be with someone who knew what they were doing. Someone who would draw out the pleasure and let it build until it met a cataclysmic crescendo...

Someone like Grady.

I squeezed my eyes shut, trying to force out the thoughts of what it would be like to kiss him again. To touch him in ways that were neither appropriate nor possible. I had no idea what was going on with him personally, not that I had a right to. Not anymore.

Charlie spoke highly of both her parents. It was obvious she was well-loved and cherished, but there was no mention of them living separately or her bouncing around between two houses. Something had to have happened, though. Otherwise, why would Grady be here when he'd built his life in Tennessee?

I was stuck somewhere between desperately wanting answers and hoping they never came. Looking over at the clock, I cursed as I noticed the time staring back at me.

11:11 p.m.

It may have been a lifetime since our last kiss, but I still remember it.

I was cursed to remember everything.

cleo

. . .

16 Years Old

"DO you think we'll be home before my curfew?" I asked, glancing down at my phone. It wasn't even eleven yet, which meant we had over thirty minutes to make it back to the ranch.

Grady glanced over. "You realize we're only like five minutes away, right? I told you I'd get you home with plenty of time to spare, and I'm gonna deliver on that."

He was right, and he had said that plenty of times. I wasn't sure why I was so keen to be back at the ranch. It was probably because I didn't want to give my parents a reason not to let me see Grady after a handful of dates, which would be devastating.

I wanted to see him again so badly it hurt.

Not that I'd said it out loud or anything. That would be way too embarrassing, especially if he decided this was all we'd have. Just some sweet summer fling that kept the two of us busy until school started back in the fall and we went our separate ways.

He hadn't kissed me after our first date, or our second. It'd been a struggle not to ask him why, especially after he kept talking about how much he was looking forward to it. Maybe it was for the best. Maybe I needed to protect myself a little longer because I wasn't sure I could get over that kind of heartbreak.

Though I'd never experienced it, I'd seen girls from school go through break-ups. Some of them cried for days. One of them even dumped a soda on their ex's head after she found out he was already seeing someone new. While I don't think Grady was the kind of guy to do something so careless, he'd already wrapped me around his finger after three dates. Seeing him with someone else, especially in our small town, would probably send me into hiding forever.

I tucked my hair behind my ear, returning his smile. "I know. I'm sorry. Guess I'm just nervous."

"For what?" Grady asked. His fingers drummed against the steering wheel in perfect timing with the melody. I realized he did that a lot, and to nearly every song.

Somehow, music came up every time we spoke. Grady knew way more about it than most kids our age. He appreciated the craft—like he felt each lyric and melodic note on some soul-deep level. And when he sang along to the grainy radio, it'd nearly taken my breath away. I'd never heard someone sing like their very life depended on it, like he would simply die if he didn't match that melody.

His voice wasn't where his knowledge ended, though. Apparently, Grady's mom had taught him how to play the piano as a kid. When he told her he'd wanted to learn the guitar, too, his dad had reached out to a family friend who didn't mind giving him lessons. When he would call me late at night after both our parents went to bed, sometimes I'd hear the faint strum of his guitar as he spoke. It was so dang cute that he couldn't help himself.

"What am I sorry for or why am I nervous?" Both were about him, but each was vastly different.

"Both."

Normally, I wouldn't feel comfortable being this vulnerable with someone, especially someone I wasn't close with, but there was something familiar about Grady that made me want to try. Maybe it was the fact that we had technically known each other since kindergarten, or maybe it was just *him*. "Well, I guess I'm sorry for this not being the best date—"

"Whoa," he interrupted, slamming on his brakes as we turned into the ranch. "Who said this wasn't the best date?"

I'd been nervous and fidgety all evening. Every time he leaned forward to dip his fry into ranch or snag a napkin from the dispenser, all I could think about was whether he was finally going to kiss me. It'd been so bad at one point I'd missed the big dollop of mustard that'd splattered against my shirt until he pointed it out.

I shrugged. "No one, I guess, but—"

"'Cause it certainly wasn't me," he continued, pointing a finger in his direction. "And if this is your way of telling me you had a horrible time—"

"No! Oh my gosh," I mumbled, covering my face with my hands. "That wasn't what I meant at all."

He tugged gently on my wrists, and I let them fall to my lap. The heat in my cheeks told me all I needed to know about what I must look like right now. "I was just teasing, I'm sorry. I didn't mean to make you go all red like a lobster," he said.

"I'm not good at this," I admitted. "I don't know what I'm doing."

"Neither do I. I think that's the point of this," he chuckled. "Don't worry, though. We'll learn together. You'll be a pro in no time. I bet it won't take long for all your friends to hit you up for relationship advice."

It didn't make much sense, but something about his words scared the hell out of me in the best way possible. He seemed so sure about us after only a handful of weeks, which was crazy, right? We were sixteen. This should be our time to fall in and out of love in the blink of an eye, but the way Grady was staring at me made it seem like he had no intention of running for the hills.

"You sound so sure."

This time, he shrugged. "Because I am. Look, I'm not trying to scare you or anything, and there definitely won't be a marriage proposal anytime soon—" I laughed as he continued "—but I really like you, Cleo. I don't know how long this will last, but I wanna find out if you're down."

"I really like you, too," I mumbled. I couldn't look at him right now, too nervous about embarrassing myself again.

I should've known he wouldn't let me get away with it. His fingers found my chin, guiding me to look at him. There was no judgment or hesitation, only patience. "Can you look at me when you say that?"

I nodded as his hand fell away. "I really like you, too."

Grady's gaze darted down to my mouth before glancing at the clock on his dashboard. His tongue darted out, leaving a wet trail across his bottom lip. I looked in time to see it change. "It's 11:11."

"I should probably get you back," he said, but he didn't move. His eyes dipped to my lips.

"Or you could make a wish," I said on a shaky exhale. "It's supposed to be lucky."

Grady's brows furrowed. "Did you make one?"

Yeah, I wish you'd kiss me. "I just did."

I didn't realize how close we'd drifted until I could smell the spicy mint of his gum. "Can I—"

Without letting him finish, I launched myself at him. It was awkward at first. I was too nervous to do the wrong thing, so we sat there for a moment with our lips just kind of smushed together, but then he took charge. I let him guide me, matching his movements the best I could, but it was so hard to focus.

Grady freaking Wilde was kissing me. He took me on my

first date, gave me my first kiss, and wanted more. He wanted more with *me*.

I didn't really know what more meant, but I wanted it, too.

I fell forward as he pulled away with a groan. Oh god, was I horrible? Did he not feel the fireworks I just felt? How was I going to ever show my face—

He turned back, threading his hands in my hair and pulling my face toward him. This time, his kiss wasn't tentative. It was entirely intentional. It reminded me of those kisses you see in movies, the ones you only dream about experiencing because they've made it seem too good to be true.

This time, Grady pulled away gently before giving me a single peck. I reached up, brushing my fingers across my lips. They felt strange. Swollen, almost. Was that normal?

"I don't wanna stop," he said slowly. Something about his voice was different. It made me feel warm all over. "But I wanna get you home a few minutes early so your parents don't get the wrong idea."

"Yeah, that's probably a good idea," I breathed. My heart was racing so fast, it felt like it was going to beat right out of my chest. How did people kiss and not be swept away in the rising tide? "I'm sure one of them is up waiting."

"Probably." Grady's eyes dipped again, but he didn't act on it. Instead, he pulled his gaze forward and put the truck in drive. Neither of us spoke until he pulled up in front of our house. The porch light was still on, which meant I was right—someone was still awake.

Grady hopped out of the truck and came around to open my door. He stuck out his hand for me to take as I stepped out. I expected him to let go, but he didn't. If anything, he held it tighter.

"Thank you for tonight," I said, fighting an inevitable blush. "It was everything and more."

His smile was so bright, it nearly outshone the full moon overhead. "I didn't scare you off, yet?"

I shook my head. "Not yet."

"That's good. It means I still have a chance."

"A chance?"

"Yeah," he said, leaning forward to press a kiss to my cheek. "A chance to make you mine."

grady

. . .

"CHARLIE, baby, it's time to eat!" I called, then put my phone away and set our dinners down on the table. I'd spent most of the afternoon staring at the one-sided text thread under Cleo's name, wondering if I should stop being a chicken shit and text her. Even though I hadn't checked to see if I was unblocked, I knew Cleo had done it anyway.

My calling her out like that yesterday was a dick move, but it was effective. There was no way she would've risked missing an important message for Charlie's sake. She cared too much about those around her. It was something I admired.

"Is it cheesy mac, daddy?" Charlie asked. She flew into the kitchen like a bat out of hell, nearly knocking the chair over as she jumped into the seat. There was still dirt on her face from camp. She'd been too busy yapping about what happened today to clean up for dinner like I'd asked, but I couldn't be too mad. Not when she was this happy.

I ruffled her hair as I walked by. "Yeah, but you gotta eat your veggies, too. Thems the rules. You know that."

I wasn't the best cook, but I had a few tried-and-true staples up my sleeve. Thankfully, they were all things my daughter would eat without much fuss, so I didn't have to worry about messing up anything new.

Charlie's bottom lip stuck out in the cutest pout. That was one of the hardest parts about being a dad, especially when she learned from an early age how to play me like a goddamn fiddle. "Fine," she huffed, stabbing at the roasted broccoli like it offended her. "If I finish, can I have more cheesy mac?"

"What'd broccoli do to you?" I asked, unable to stop myself from laughing as she stuffed it into her mouth. There was no way she'd still want seconds after finishing her plate—if she finished it at all. Her eyes were usually ten times bigger than her stomach.

"Keep me from more cheese," she said with a mouth now stuffed full of chicken.

Guess I couldn't argue with that logic. "Alright, fine. But let's see how you feel first. You may be too full."

She furiously shook her head. "No, Daddy. I'm *so* hungry. I'll have room."

The two of us sat in silence for a moment as we tucked into our meals. To Charlie's credit, she did seem like she was starving. I didn't think I'd ever seen her devour food so quickly. "They're feeding you at camp, right?" I asked, raising a brow.

I didn't mean that literally, of course, but Charlie's appetite had increased significantly since Monday. Maybe I should pack some extra snacks or something. Was that allowed?

Barbeque sauce and cheese joined the smeared dirt on her cheeks. "Oh yeah. They give us the best sandwiches ever! And Miss Cleo always has cookies for us." She slumped back in her chair with a dramatic sigh. "I'd do anything for one of them right now."

Even though I knew it wasn't just for Charlie's benefit, somehow the knowledge of Cleo baking cookies for the kids every day made my chest hurt. When that woman put her mind to something, she really gave her all.

"You'd rather have a cookie than my cheesy mac?" I asked, quirking a brow.

I could see the gears turning in my daughter's mind as she thought about it. "Yeah, I think so."

My hand landed over my heart. "Ouch. Way to hurt your old man's feelings."

Charlie just shrugged. "If you'd had one of these cookies, you'd get it, Daddy. They're the best in the whole world."

"But you haven't tasted every cookie out there," I countered.

"Don't have to. I just know," she said, stuffing her mouth full of the last bit of broccoli. She looked down at her cleared plate. "I think I'm full now. Can I video mommy?"

"Sure, baby." I fished my phone out of my pocket and held it out for her. The moment I remembered her sticky fingers, though, I held back. "How about you go wash up first? She might not recognize you with all that stuff on your face."

Charlie blew out a breath. "Fineee," she said, trudging out of the kitchen to the hallway bathroom.

"I'll be in there in a minute to help! Pick out your jammies while you're waiting," I called, picking up our plates and taking them to the sink. Cleaning up was easy since it was just Charlie and me.

When I'd sent my dad out on that trip, I thought it was for the best. It gave me a reason to give to Cleo when she inevitably asked why I was in town, but there were moments I regretted it. I hadn't been home since Mom's funeral. That last visit, the weight of the loss we all experienced, was so much heavier sitting here in this tiny house.

Even after all these years, the silence in these halls was suffocating now that Mom's lively presence wasn't here to fill it.

She'd been the reason these four walls had felt like a home. The reason there were always fresh flowers on the countertops and laughter echoing off the worn hard wood floors. Music filled the space, whether from the radio or the old upright piano that had once stood in the living room. Everything felt brighter. Better.

Now, it was cold and gray. Gloomy. No more flowers or sunshine or music. When Dad had tried to sell the piano, I'd nearly lost it on him. He was so determined to keep the place as a shrine to their life together, and yet it felt like he was doing it a disservice. Eventually, he relented and moved the instrument into my old bedroom so it was out of sight, out of mind.

One less reminder she was gone.

Looking back now, I understood why he'd ever considered it. Dad loved listening to Mom play. He'd sit beside her and belt the lyrics of whatever song she was playing. It was horrible in the best way. The man couldn't carry a tune to save his life, but each song ended in a fit of giggles, so I guessed he was doing something right. Sometimes, he'd watch from his recliner as she taught me a new song, occasionally chiming in with some notes of his own, like he had any business critiquing an instrument he couldn't play.

My phone vibrated on the counter, and I looked down, heart sinking when I realized it was just an email. What did I expect? For Cleo to sense I was in my feelings about my mom and just text me out of the blue? No, that'd be stupid. I could dream, though, and I did so often.

In those dreams, she reached out because she missed me like I missed her. She reached out because talking to me was better than silence, no matter how much it hurt us to be apart. After all, who could understand her heartbreak better than I could?

That could be the key. That may be what I needed to make her understand. Even if she didn't realize it, her pain, my pain, it didn't matter. It was one and the same.

Before I could overthink what I was about to do, my fingers flew across the screen.

GRADY

Did you fix your phone?

Minutes ticked by as I meticulously dried each dish before putting it away. I didn't remember the last time I'd been this nervous to send a fucking text before. Honestly, it was probably back when Cleo and I had first started dating. I was so careful about everything I said, desperate to make a good impression.

I was about to give up when I saw bubbles appear at the bottom of the screen.

CLEO

I'd never been so goddamn happy to see an emoji in my life.

GRADY

Oh, good. I was worried it was a permanent issue, seeing as I've been trying to contact you for months.

More bubbles, more waiting. Charlie impatiently called out for me while I stared at my screen like it held the answer to all my prayers.

CLEO

We didn't have anything to talk about then. Outside of Charlie, we have nothing to talk about now.

GRADY

Is it still considered talking about Charlie if I tell you she prefers your cookies to my mac-and-cheese? What're you teaching her at that camp? How to wound my pride?

"Daddy, are you coming?" I turned to see Charlie hovering in the doorway. She held her pajamas close to her chest as her foot tapped against the floor.

I put my phone down on the table. "Yeah, sunshine. I'm coming."

OLIVIA HAD a late-night event and couldn't talk as much as she and Charlie wanted. She'd propped the phone up on the dresser as she got ready, listening keenly as our daughter crammed as much information as she could into a fifteen-minute call. They'd both been gutted when Liv's assistant interrupted, letting her know the car was waiting outside. Even though she tried to hide it, I saw tears glinting in her eyes as she said goodbye and blew our daughter a kiss.

It hadn't taken Charlie long to fall asleep. She'd been exhausted the past two days after camp, but I'd lain in bed holding her a little longer and tighter than usual. No matter how excited she was to be here, I knew it was hard for her to be away from her mom for so long.

Over the past year, the number of business trips Liv had to take skyrocketed. She was now entirely in charge of her family's record label. Every meeting required her input, and every decision needed her signature. While the Hartstrings' headquarters was based in Nashville, most of the other executives and board members lived on the West Coast, which meant she had to go to them.

That was why I had to go back last year. Liv had barely gained control of the company at the time, and neither of us knew what our new normal would look like. I'd planned to stay in Ashwood longer than I did. I wanted to explain everything to Cleo so she understood how I felt, how I'd always felt, but everything changed when Doug collapsed. Sifting through our past was the last thing she needed, and so I'd left without warning, without question.

Looking back, I would've done that differently. I would've at least told her that my running away was for a good reason and I'd be able to explain it all when I got back. But I didn't. I'd been too much of a coward, so scared of her inevitable rejection that I ran.

What I hadn't expected was to be gone so long. Liv's workload was grueling, and if I wasn't flying out to California with Charlie, then I was in the studio, recording and writing music that would never see the light of day.

Then there was the matter of our marriage and subsequent divorce.

Liv and I had never planned on being married for the rest of our lives. At the beginning, it'd been purely a business arrangement. She needed to prove to the board she could run a multi-million-dollar company, and one of the many stipulations was marriage. So, I married her. The whole thing seemed antiquated and unreliable. I mean, could a piece of paper truly determine whether a person was capable of taking on something of that magnitude?

But then, in one drunken night of loneliness and despair, Liv and I crossed lines we never had before, and she got pregnant. There was never a question of whether we would keep the baby or not. We'd both always wanted kids, had talked about it in the past with a dark cloud hanging over our heads, knowing our chances of having that were diminishing with each year we stayed in our sham of a marriage.

Suddenly, we had a reason to stay together. Even if it wasn't romantic, Liv and I shared so much love. She was my best friend, and who better to raise a child with than your best friend?

It wasn't lost on either of us that we were settling, but we were okay with it. We had a good life, after all. One full of laughter and good times. I was at the height of my career, she was training beneath her uncle, and had the company she desired at the tip of her fingertips.

It'd been that damn night at the Lonestar that'd changed everything. Seeing Cleo for the first time in twelve years was, to say the least, shocking. It was like she'd plunged her hand into my chest cavity and fisted my heart, squeezing it until it was ready to pop. As quickly as it happened, though, it dissipated. Suddenly, I was cold and empty.

Just like this goddamn house.

When Liv had to fly to Ashwood to pull me out of a drunken stupor, I didn't even have to voice the words. She knew I couldn't go on like we were. It'd been written all over my face the moment she opened the hotel door and found me slumped on the ground.

By the time we landed, she'd called her grandfather, who then called the attorneys about filing for divorce. They were the only people who knew the truth about our marriage because they'd played a part in carefully crafting our prenup, which was overly generous if you asked me. I didn't want anything other than what I earned.

All they'd asked for in return was time. Liv's grandfather needed to announce his retirement and appoint her as the company's CEO. Once the dust settled, the paperwork would be filed, and we would make an announcement before it became a part of the public record.

Essentially, I was in one big, tangled web of fuckery, constantly waiting on things that were contingent on something or someone else.

I made my way to the living area after slipping out of Charlie's room and plopped down on the couch. I wanted a beer, or ten, before drifting off to sleep, but that didn't seem productive. Instead, I pulled up my phone and started scrolling mindlessly through social media. I was about twenty videos deep when a notification caught my attention.

> **CLEO**
>
> Don't ask questions you don't want the answers to.

I was about to reply when another message popped up.

> **CLEO**
>
> Tell Charlie I made her a bag of cookies to take home tomorrow.

I couldn't help my smile. The thought of her baking cookies just for my daughter did something to me.

> **GRADY**
>
> Is the sugar rush you're about to send her on intentional?

> **CLEO**
>
> You said she liked them, so I made them. I'm not forcing her to eat them.

Each text was short and to the point, which wasn't surprising. Cleo wasn't going to make this easy on me, I knew that, but she was responding. That was good enough for me.

> **GRADY**
>
> You're a teacher, right? I'm sure you know what happens when you give a six-year-old a bag full of cookies to take home.

> **CLEO**
>
> Right. It's one of the perks. By the time the high hits, I'll be sending her back to you for the crash.

I let out a laugh.

GRADY

So, it IS punishment! I knew it.

CLEO

Take it however you want. Now, will you stop
texting me? It's late, and I need sleep.

GRADY

Why? You're beautiful already.

Was it stupid and corny? Absolutely. But I didn't give a shit. As I watched, bubbles popped up and disappeared repeatedly. There was a high chance Cleo was fighting with herself about responding, which was something I reveled in.

I waited five minutes before sending something reckless. Something that would either save me or damn me.

GRADY

Sweet dreams, bluebird.

The bubbles never popped back up.

grady

. . .

17 Years Old

"WHY'RE you still down there? I told you it was safe." Cleo stared down at me from her treehouse, trying and failing not to laugh at my hesitancy. She may have thought she was slick, but I saw the twinkle in her eye. She was getting way too much pleasure from this.

I eyed the rickety ladder skeptically. "For you maybe, but we're not exactly the same size." Each rung on that deathtrap had groaned when she'd climbed up. I had an easy fifty pounds on her, and that was being modest. There was no way my ass wouldn't break it.

There was also the issue of being deathly afraid of heights, but telling her I had concerns about my safety seemed like a better reason to keep both feet planted on the ground.

She laughed. "Oh, come on. Stop being such a scaredy cat. Dad has climbed up here a million times. You'll be fine."

Well, that made me feel a little bit better, but I still wasn't convinced. She'd been trying to get me up this damn tree for about six months now. I'd always been able to navigate around it before, but I had a feeling my luck was running out.

"Okay. Say I got up there. What happens if it breaks on the

way down? Then I'm supposed to—what? Live in a tree for the rest of my life?" I asked, putting my hands on my hips.

Her giggle was infectious. It was almost enough for me to throw caution to the wind and climb up, the prospect of a horrible death be damned. "Only for a year or two. Nothing long-term."

"Uh-huh. Makes sense. Is there food up there, or will I be forced to eat leaves and twigs?"

"No. I'll throw bags of Doritos up here so you don't starve. Maybe a Dr. Pepper or two if you're lucky." She rolled her eyes. "Honestly, Grady. Just get up here or else I'll call Bishop and tell him to bring the tractor with a lift."

"Yup! Coming." That wasn't a threat I wanted to mess with. I didn't know Bishop well, but I'd never seen someone so young with such a permanent scowl. The dude always looked like he was ready to fight someone.

"Thought so!" she called, scooting back. "Now, hurry up!"

"The things I do for you," I mumbled, blowing out a breath. I climbed slowly, testing out each rung. Every time something made a noise, I cringed. It didn't even matter if it was from this stupid ladder or not. I didn't want anything to send me crashing back down.

"Just keep your eyes on me, baby," Cleo cooed, blowing me a kiss. "And how I'll reward you once you make it."

I paused, raising a brow in question. "A reward, huh?"

Her nod was the only answer I needed. Only a few feet separated, so I hurried up the final rungs and hopped inside. She squealed as I grabbed her waist, hauling her into my arms. She wrapped her legs around my waist as I peppered kisses along her cheek and neck. "Well, shit. Why didn't you say so earlier?" I asked, setting her on her feet. "I'd have jumped right up here."

Cleo swatted at my chest. "You're the worst. I don't understand why you threw a fit to begin with."

"Uh, because I value my life. I'm far too young and handsome to die at the hands—or rather, trunk—of your childhood treehouse," I said, taking a seat against the wall.

The space was exactly as I had always expected it. Dark wood and dusty floors with the occasional spider web in the corner. But there were also so many little pieces of her scattered around. Old pictures lined the faded blue walls, and handmade vases with fake flowers sat on the shelves.

Cleo sat down in front of me, bracing her hands on my thighs. "You're definitely too handsome to die. Not to mention how hard it'd be for me."

"Oh yeah?" I tucked a piece of her hair behind her ear. "Would you miss me?"

She looked down and bit her lip. "So much. And then I'd have to go through the trouble of finding another super-hot boyfriend who plays guitar and knows how to ride horses. It'd be a *whole* thing."

"Damn, that'd suck. Maybe you shouldn't make the one you have risk his life to climb a freaking tree."

Cleo laughed as I kissed her again. I meant for it to be quick —nothing more than a peck I'd steal from her when we were around our parents or between classes at school—but goddammit, I couldn't tear myself away.

Kissing Cleo was like finally nailing the hardest part of a song after months of practice. It was a rush, a high like no other. Except I think I loved it more than music or the thought of getting out of this small town for good. I loved it so much I often dreamed about it every night. Which, admittedly, made for an awkward morning sometimes when my mom came in to wake me up.

I didn't know what it was about her that made it so different. I'd dated other girls before her, but they didn't compare. Not by a long shot. I think part of me had known that since our first date.

The two of us had fallen hard and fast for one another, and there was no sign of slowing down.

Without realizing, we'd planned our lives together. It wasn't intentional; it just kind of happened. From conversations about which colleges we were looking at and what jobs we wanted to do afterward as we drove to school, to asking the big questions about marriage and babies when we were curled up in the bed of my truck. All of a sudden, I had a future I was looking forward to.

Even if none of it happened, even if all our plans went up in flames tomorrow, I knew I wanted her by my side.

But there was one line we hadn't crossed. One that was getting harder to ignore with each press of her lips against mine and stolen moment alone.

Cleo and I agreed to hold off on the whole sex thing until college. Some of it was out of respect for our parents, considering we spent most of our time together at her house or mine. It felt weird thinking our first time could be on a twin-sized bed that used to have Power Ranger sheets.

It wasn't as if we didn't know what could happen. Both of our parents had given us the rundown when they realized Cleo and I were serious about one another. They said they'd rather us be informed and intelligent than ignorant and stupid, which was more than I could say for some of my friends. When I asked my best friend Cooper about it, he said his mom had turned bright red, and his dad had pulled him off to the side and given him a condom.

All things considered, we got pretty lucky.

Some part of me was still nervous, though. What if we did it and then things changed? What if we finally took that step and she realized she didn't like me the way she thought and ended it?

Cleo climbed forward, setting herself on my lap as she threaded her fingers into my hair. Each kiss was greedier than the last, and I was trying like hell not to add to it. The last thing I needed was to embarrass myself.

"Cleo," I said, pulling back with a groan. "You're not playing fair."

She giggled. "I told you there'd be a reward."

This girl was trying to kill me. "Time with you is reward enough," I said through gritted teeth.

I tried to think of everything I could that would prevent my body from reacting. Sports teams. Grandpa Gary's dentures. An ice bath in the middle of winter.

Cleo leaned back. "Am I doing something wrong?"

"God, no," I breathed. "Uh, it's... Well, it's the opposite."

Her brows knitted together as she studied my face. It wasn't until I shifted beneath her that she understood, lips parting as she looked down. "Oh."

My chuckle turned into a groan. "Yeah. *Oh.*" I brought my hand up, running it through my hair. "I promise it's not you. It's just..."

"No, I get it," she said, biting down on her lip. "I guess I just wasn't thinking about that."

"Lucky you," I mumbled jokingly. "Sometimes I feel like it's all I think about."

"Really?" I nodded. "Like... in general?"

I shrugged. "Yes and no. I think about you, too."

Her cheeks flushed, hot and pink and oh so sweet. It wasn't hard to bring color to her face. I leaned in to kiss her again, unable to help myself when I heard something that caught my attention. "What's that noise?" I asked.

"What noise?" she asked, pressing her lips to the corner of my mouth.

"I dunno. Chirping?"

"Well, we are in a tree," she deadpanned, pulling back. "Birds do live in those."

"Thank you, smartass," I said, tickling her until she

squirmed. Honestly, it wasn't the best idea with her still on top of me. "Doesn't it sound close to you?"

Cleo sighed, dropping her head against mine before standing and making her way toward the window. "There's noth—" she paused, narrowing her eyes. "Oh my gosh, come look!"

I pushed to my feet and followed suit, standing behind her and caging her in against the window. "Where?"

"There!" she said, pointing to the small planter box just below where we stood.

Peering over her shoulder, I noticed the small, empty nest tucked away in the corner. "Doesn't look like anyone's home."

Her elbow connected with my stomach. "Now who's the smartass?" she muttered. "Do you think it's being used? Maybe we scared them away."

I didn't know a damn thing about birds, but the thing looked old. "I dunno, honestly. Maybe?"

Cleo's bottom lip stuck out in a pout. "That'd be cool. I hope they come back. That way, when you get stuck up here, you'll have a friend or two to keep you company."

I moved my hands to her hips, slipping beneath the fabric of her shirt and tickling her softly. "Oh, you got jokes, huh?"

"I didn't want you to be worried about being alone," she squealed, dancing out of my hold. "You seemed so worried earlier. I thought it might make you feel better."

"The only thing that's gonna make me feel better is getting my ass outta this tree."

Cleo put her hands on her hips. "You hate heights that much, huh?"

"What gave it away? Was it the months of excuses or the thirty-minute pep talk you just had to give?" I teased.

She tilted her head from one side to the other. "Maybe a bit of both."

"Well, now you know my fatal flaw. My biggest secret."

"Oh yeah," she deadpanned. "I'm sure it would make the

front page of the Ashwood Gazette if I sent in an anonymous tip." Her hands came up dramatically, framing the fake headline in the air. "Treehouses: Grady Wilde's Mortal Enemy."

I couldn't help but laugh, especially as I saw her own lips twitch in amusement. "Listen, it's a real fear. Just because you were a bird in your past life—"

"*A bird?*"

"—Doesn't mean tree life is for me."

"I don't know about this past life stuff, but..." Cleo shook her head and stepped closer, intertwining our fingers before bringing them to her mouth for a kiss. "I could be your bird right now."

My brows furrowed. "Is this supposed to be where I say something about being a bird if you're a bird? Because I need to be honest, I don't think I want to be."

She groaned, dropping my hand to cover her face with her own. God, she was so damn adorable. "No, you idiot. Nevermind. I was trying to be cute, but it was stupid."

"Oh, no, you don't," I grabbed her wrist and tugged her closer. She came without effort, wrapping her arms around my waist. Her nose was pressed into my chest as she sucked in a breath. "Lemme try that again..." I cleared my throat and felt her lips twitch through the thin cotton fabric of my T-shirt. "If you really wanna be a bird, then I'll—ow!"

I looked down at the spot Cleo still had pinched between her fingers. "Don't be a jackass."

"I was gonna say I could be your tree, but whatever, but fine. I'll keep the declaration to myself."

She quirked a brow. "You know, for someone who is supposed to write music, you seem to be lacking some originality."

I gasped in fake shock, looking down at her bemused expression. "You take that back right now, bluebird."

I didn't know where the name had come from, but it just

rolled right off my tongue and into the open like it was the most natural thing in the world.

"Bluebird?" she asked, pulling back.

I shrugged. "You like birds and the color blue, it seemed fitting."

Her smile was soft. "I think I like that."

"Yeah?"

"Yeah, but there aren't any cute tree names I could use for you, so I guess I'll just have to call you baby."

I pressed a kiss to her temple. "I think I can live with that."

cleo

. . .

"ALRIGHT, EVERYONE! LET'S TAKE A SEAT." I called out, even though it didn't seem to make a bit of difference. Only a few of the kids turned their heads my way. There was way too much noise for such a small space, it was hard to even hear myself think.

Today was proving to be a real bitch. Everyone seemed to be on edge, from the kids to the ranch hands to me. The heat was making being outside unbearable, messing up most of our planned activities for the day. Lennox had told the guys working in the arena to clear out for the day. Being in the shade brought the temperature down slightly, but not enough to make a noticeable difference.

And while the temperature seemed to be the only thing affecting everyone else, other things were distracting me. A lack of sleep, for one, that was caused by the stupidest conversation I should have never indulged in.

When Grady's first message came through, I almost ignored it. I should have ignored it. But I didn't want to give him a reason to believe I hadn't unblocked him. I'd stared at it for a minute before I made the decision. After all, his daughter was in my care, and her safety came first above any of the bullshit and years between us. If the roles were reversed, I'd want to know I could get in touch with him in case of emergencies.

I was trying to be responsible, not reckless. Even if it turned out to be a little reckless after all.

My stomach had done these stupid little flips at seeing his name flash across my screen after so many years. Then came the shortness of breath, the sheen of sweat along my palms and at the back of my neck. No matter how many breathing exercises I did, or how I tried to tell myself I didn't need to engage in conversation while silently padding down the hall to the kitchen to make an additional batch of cookies for Charlie, my body reacted all the same. It was like it remembered, even after all this time, how he used to make me feel.

But then he went and ruined it with one simple word. A word I'd tried my hardest to reclaim, to make it mine and mine alone.

Because at the end of the day, it didn't matter if he'd brought back a tidal wave of memories; he was married. He was married and had a kid, and I was divorced. There was no way to act on the feelings, no way forward that didn't end up with me eating a pint of Bluebell ice cream over a man who'd broken my heart.

I tossed and turned all night. Even when sleep finally came to claim me, I was haunted by charming smiles and pretty words. By tender kisses and crystal-clear blue eyes. There wasn't enough coffee in the world to mitigate the pounding in my head or near-constant yawning. I'd even forced down one of Josie's horrible energy drinks to see if it would give me what I needed to make it through the day. Instead, it left me feeling even crankier than I had been and with a bad taste in my mouth.

I clapped my hands together, finally catching a few more sets of eyes. "Hey! Let's focus, guys."

One of the kids, Jeremy, came up. He'd just lost a few baby teeth and had a broad, gap-filled smile. "Miss Cleo! When is lunch going to be here? I'm starving." A chorus of agreement followed his declaration, but I finally had their attention.

Thank god.

"Miss Lennox is bringing it in right now," I said, looking over my shoulder to the door. "Should be just a few more minutes."

My dear sister only had about five more minutes before I had a total mutiny on my hands. No one did hangry quite like a group of kids who'd been running around in the heat all day. And if that didn't scare her enough, she'd have to deal with me afterward. Trying to contain this rowdy group on two hours of sleep was starting to fray my patience.

"Who's hungry?" Lennox sang from the alley. She rounded the corner with Cook, who was pushing a giant cart stacked with brown paper sacks loaded with sandwiches, chips, and my homemade cookies.

The room erupted into chaos as all the kids raised their hands and started shouting. I took the opportunity to catch a quick breath as Lennox and Cook began handing out meals to everyone.

Since they were here, I could sneak away for a few minutes and grab another coffee. And Tylenol. I'd definitely need some Tylenol before this turned into a full-blown migraine.

"Hey, Lenn—" My words faltered as I noticed her expression. She was glancing between the cart of food and the tables, mumbling something under her breath. "What's wrong?"

"There's an extra bag," she whispered, confused.

"That'd be mine," I sighed, rubbing my temple. "I'll grab it in a second when I—"

Lennox shook her head. "I'm not talking about yours."

"What do you mean?" I asked, stepping closer. "Did Cook make too many?"

"You know how he is about wasting food. He made sure

there was enough for everyone, and we counted the bags together while I helped him put them together."

No, no, no. I glanced back over the room, mentally taking a roll call and ticking off familiar faces, even though some part of me already knew who was missing.

By the time I met my sister's gaze, I was ready to throw up all over the linoleum floor. "Charlie," we said at the same time.

I thought back, mind racing to remember the last place I saw her. She was there when we lined up for lunch, but my mind couldn't place her in this room. Had she gotten lost trying to go to the bathroom? Had she managed to stay behind in the arena somehow? There were no animals out there, so I didn't see why it would be of any interest to her, but what if she'd wandered through the fence to find some?

"Hey guys! Listen up!" I clapped my hands forcefully this time, which seemed to work as twenty-seven little heads swirled my way. "Has anyone seen Charlie? I'd hate for her to miss lunch." I tried to smile, but it didn't reach my eyes. "I know how hungry she was!"

Most of the kids shook their heads before quickly turning back to their meals, but Jeremy quietly got up out of his seat and made his way over. "I did, Miss Cleo. We saw a treehouse earlier, and she said she wanted to see it." He ducked his head. "I told her it wasn't a good idea to go alone, that we'd get in trouble, but she said she'd be right back."

I bent down and grabbed his little hands. He looked scared and sad. "It's okay, Jeremy. You're doing the right thing. How long ago? Was it before we came in here, or did she slip out?"

Jeremy chewed on his bottom lip. "Um, it was before we came in here. She slipped out of line after you and Miss Lennox took roll."

I closed my eyes, giving a gentle, reassuring squeeze before standing. "Thank you for telling us. Now, go finish your lunch, okay?"

He nodded before heading back to his seat. Lennox came over, running a hand along the back of her neck. "What can I do?"

"Stay here with them," I said, nodding behind her. "Maybe text Bishop and ask him and the hands to be on the lookout for her. I'll check the arena and then head to the treehouse."

She nodded and gave a small salute. "Yes, ma'am."

I turned around and quickly scanned the stalls and the bathrooms to make sure she hadn't gotten lost wandering back. All were empty. And when I finally stepped into the arena, the breath I'd been holding threatened to choke me.

"God-fucking-dammit," I cursed, rubbing my temple. I looked up and stared through the thick steel fence to the treeline up ahead for a moment before I slipped through the bars and into the field.

I wished I'd let Dad demolish the stupid thing years ago when he talked about having it rebuilt, but I didn't. I couldn't. Even though I'd been remarried, even though I cursed his name every chance I got, that damned treehouse was one of the last things I had of Grady. A remembrance of summer love, heated kisses, and sweet moments that never failed to make my heart ache and keep me up at night.

I might as well have kept it as a shrine to my youth, a hidden memorial that never let me forget the memories it held. It wasn't like it got much use anymore. Though I supposed that would change in a few years, since my parents finally had their first grandchild to spoil. I hoped, for my own sake, that Josie's daughter could make it her own. Maybe then I wouldn't be filled with dread at the thought of seeing it again.

Last October had been the exception. It'd been the one time in years I'd let myself settle into grief that was so bone deep, I knew there was nowhere else I could go. That sanctuary in the trees understood my pain. It knew what I'd lost, and it mourned right along with me.

I stood beneath the thick oak branches, staring up at the open hatch. "Charlie? Are you up there, honey?" Silence greeted me, which did nothing but increase my anxiety. "It's okay if you are. You're not in trouble, I'm just worried."

This time, the wood groaned like someone was moving. I could make out the briefest hint of blonde hair through the hatch. "That's what Mommy and Daddy say before telling me they're disappointed." She paused, sniffling. "I don't want you to be like that, Miss Cleo."

"Oh, honey…" I said, softening my voice. "I'm not disappointed, okay? I promise. I was worried, though, and I will be until we get you down from there. Do you think you can do that for me?"

"I—I'm scared," she whimpered. "I don't think I like heights very much."

Just like her father.

I was stuck somewhere between pride that she did something that terrified her and sorrow knowing she'd been up here all alone for the past twenty minutes. "That's okay! I'm right here," I assured her. "Do you think you could try, or do you want me to come up to get you?"

"C—Can you help me?"

Charlie didn't need to ask twice. I was already testing the ladder's strength. It'd been fine when I used it in October, so it should be fine now. "I'm on my way. Just sit tight."

cleo

· · ·

I TOOK my time climbing up, making sure I wasn't going to end up falling and landing on my back. When I finally reached the top, I popped my head and saw Charlie sitting in the corner. Her knees were pulled up to her chest, her arms wrapped tightly around them. My heart broke as I noticed the dried tear tracks on her cheeks.

"I'm so sorry, Miss Cleo. I'm so sorry," she cried. "I didn't mean to scare you. I just wanted to see the treehouse."

I was over to her in an instant, pulling her into my arms. "It's okay, Charlie." My hand rubbed small circles across her back as she clutched my shirt, soaking the fabric with her tears. "It's okay."

"I've never seen one before, but my daddy used to tell me stories of one when I was little. He said the treehouse was magical." I closed my eyes, trying to keep my own tears at bay as she spoke. "He said there was a princess up there who made wishes come true, and I wanted a wish to come true, Miss Cleo, so I climbed up here, but it was empty. There was no princess. There was no magic."

Oh god, how could I do this? How could I pretend like her

words didn't tear me the fuck up inside? Why oh why did he ever tell her about this place? A place so inherently special it tied me up in knots that he'd share its magic with his daughter. Because that's precisely what it was.

But she was right. There hadn't been any magic here in a long time, and the princess had lost her crown to another.

"I could've saved you a lot of trouble if you'd asked, you know," I said. "It's been a long time since this place had any magic in it."

Charlie pulled back. "But it was here?"

There was no point in lying, so I nodded. "A really long time ago."

Her eyes widened. "And the princess?"

"I don't know that she thought of herself as a princess, but yes."

"What happened to her?"

I gave her a sad smile. "I don't know. I think she got lost. Maybe you could take her place."

Charlie shook her head. "No way. I don't think I like being up here that much. I'd much rather stay on the ground."

I could help but laugh, remembering similar spoken words that seemed like a lifetime ago. "You're just like your father, you know? He's afraid of heights, too."

It wasn't until I looked down at Charlie that I realized my mistake. I wasn't sure how much Grady had told her about our past, or if he'd told her anything at all. "You must know my daddy pretty well," she said.

"Why do you say that?"

"He doesn't tell anyone about the things he's scared about except for me and Mommy." She shrugged. "And I guess you."

And I guess you.

There was so much I could add to that statement. Some deep, twisted, jealous part of me wanted to scream it was me, that *I* was the princess in the story, and her dad was right—it was magical and wonderful and all those things. I wanted to tell her that he loved me before anyone else, and maybe, just maybe, he still loved me now. After all, he was here, wasn't he?

But what good would it do? It wouldn't change the situation. It didn't matter if he loved me now because he was still married. This perfect girl in front of me was a reminder of that. If I could do nothing else, I would protect her from the ugly depths of my soul.

"Well, it was a long time ago," I said, waving it off. "Your dad and I went to school together. That's all."

"I think my daddy likes it here," Charlie said, toying with the hem of her shirt. "He's always excited to bring me here in the mornings. When he picks me up, sometimes he seems sad. Like, he doesn't wanna leave. And I feel like that, too." She looked up at me. "Do you like it here?"

Lie, Cleo. Tell her you love it. Tell her this is your dream, that you're happier than ever.

But I couldn't.

"Sometimes I do," I answered honestly. Shakily. "Sometimes I don't. Sometimes I worry I don't fit in here."

And that was my truth. The one I'd never even voiced to Rachel or Laura, because how could I explain how I felt like I needed to love every aspect of this ranch like my family did to deserve the love they gave me in return? That I'd always felt like I needed to compensate for not entrenching myself in the life they held so near and dear to their heart?

It wasn't their fault. Realistically, I knew if Mom and Dad lost everything tomorrow, their love for me would go on like it always had. I knew if I told Josie and Lennox that, other than an occasional hard ride on the back of my horse across the pastures, I hated everything about working this land, they wouldn't look at me any differently.

The issue was me. It was my mind, and the way it twisted

the most inconsequential thoughts into these vicious lies I found so easy to believe.

Charlie's little hand covered mine. I looked up, hating the frown I saw tugging on her lips. "I think you should find somewhere you like, Miss Cleo."

"Yeah," I choked out. "I think so, too."

"Everything okay up there?" Lennox called out, shifting my thoughts back to the real world awaiting us outside of these four walls.

I wiped away the tear, hoping Charlie hadn't seen it fall, and poked my head out of the hatch. "All good. We're coming down now."

But as we moved toward the hatch, I heard the softest sound. A sweet chirp.

Bird song.

"Do you hear that?" I asked, turning my head toward the window.

Charlie stayed silent for a moment, eyes widening in surprise as she nodded her head. "I do!" She tried to whisper, but her little voice was loud in the quiet of the treehouse.

I pressed my finger to my lips as I beckoned her forward. She tiptoed in front of me, carefully conscious of her movements as we both peered through the window.

There, in the worn planter box just below, was a large bird nest with three tiny baby birds inside. They squawked angrily, tilting their heads to the sky and demanding food. In the blink of an eye, one of the parents swooped in, ready to feed their young. Its chest puffed out, displaying a bright, vibrant blue that had emotion clawing at my throat.

"Look, Miss Cleo!" Charlie said excitedly. "It isn't empty at all!"

This time, I couldn't fight the tears. I couldn't fight the memories, the longing, the adoration. Instead of snuffing them out like I did every other time they came around, I let myself feel each and every one. The sunshine warmed my face, and I prayed its warmth would sink into my skin and touch my soul.

"You're crying," Charlie said. I looked down and noticed she was staring at me instead of the tender family moment taking place beneath the window.

"Happy tears." I dabbed at the moisture with my palm. "It's beautiful, isn't it?"

Charlie chewed on her lip. "Maybe there's some magic here after all."

"Maybe so," I whispered.

"Do I need to go get the tractor?" Lennox called out once more. "Are y'all stuck?"

I moved over to the hatch, sticking my head out. "Patience is a virtue, you know."

"Not one of mine," she snapped back. "I'm much more about instant gratification."

I narrowed my eyes as she smirked, knowing all too well what was on the tip of her tongue to say. "There is a child present, Lennox."

She shrugged. "Better hurry and get down then."

I could feel Lennox's stare on my back as I started to climb, carefully ignoring it as I coached Charlie on how to get down. The time for answering questions was coming quickly, but I wasn't any closer to figuring out what to say. The truth felt too heavy, but I didn't want to lie. Not to her. Not when I knew Lennox was one of the few people who'd never dare judge me.

It still didn't make it any easier to show the rawest parts of me, the parts I'd kept hidden even from the people who loved me wholly and completely.

"You've got this, Charlie," I called up as she made the descent. "Nice and slow. Keep your eyes forward, don't look down unless you have to."

Charlie clung to the rungs like her little life depended on it, but she gave a nod and moved slowly. Every so often, I'd call up, telling her to breathe when I saw her muscles stiffen from fear, her hand tremble as she tried to find the proper footing before letting go.

Her smile was wide by the time she finally made it to the bottom, turning triumphantly to Lennox and me and shouting, "I did it!" at the top of her lungs. We both laughed as she barreled toward us. I didn't think when she launched herself at me, only opened my arms wide and let her leap into them before giving her a little twirl.

"I'm so proud of you! It wasn't that bad, was it?" She shook her head. "See, I told you. I bet you're a natural now."

I set her down, watching as she scrunched up her face. "No, I think I'll be like my daddy and stay on the ground." And then, like a million-dollar idea just popped into her head, she started jumping up and down. "Ooh! Do you think we could have a treehouse on the ground? Do you think he'd build me one, Miss Cleo?"

"I think that's a wonderful idea, Charlie," I said, sticking my hand out for her to take.

She did so eagerly and tugged me back toward the barn. "If he did, would you come visit me and see it? Maybe that can be your place!"

"Your place?" Lennox asked, stepping up beside me.

"Yeah, Miss Cleo said she gets sad sometimes, so I told her she needs to find somewhere that makes her happy. Maybe we can share my treehouse." Charlie said it like it was the simplest thing in the world, like she hadn't just outed my unhappiness to my sister.

Lennox's steps faltered only for a moment before she fell back in line beside me. I expected her to question Charlie, to question me, but she didn't. She remained silent as we got back to the room full of kids and watched Charlie tear into her lunch. When I called for everyone's attention, we marched back to the arena, double checking all children were present. We were going to spend the afternoon watching my sister and a few ranch hands show off what their horses could do.

It wasn't until we were done, standing outside watching the line of cars pulling up the drive, that she finally turned to me. Her blue eyes scanned my face, but nothing gave away her thoughts. She was stone-faced and quiet, which was even more terrifying since Lennox was never one to censor herself or her emotions. I envied that about her.

"What is it?" I laughed, trying to dispel the awkwardness hanging between us. "You've been acting strange all afternoon."

Lennox trained her gaze ahead. I couldn't be sure, but it felt like it was on one very specific shiny truck at the back of the line. "I've been thinking—"

"Uh oh, that feels dangerous," I mumbled.

I expected her to laugh, but she didn't. If anything, her jaw grew tight. "You know I love you, right?"

I blinked. "Uh, yeah? You're my sister. It's obligatory."

"No, it's not," she said. "Everyone thinks families are required to love each other, but they aren't. I love you because I chose to. Because it makes me happy, *you* make me happy. And it's because I love you that I say this..." She put her hand on my shoulder, giving it a single squeeze. "I want you to find your happiness, too, Cleo." And then she walked away, waving at a parent who'd just wrapped their kid in a big hug.

Charlie tugged on my hand, pointing excitedly to where Grady had just pulled to a stop. He hopped out of the truck, smiling when he saw the two of us standing together. "Daddy!" she squealed, jumping up and down. "Can I go see him, Miss Cleo?"

"Go ahead," I said, nodding his way.

Before I'd even finished, she took off like a bolt of lightning. Her tiny body collided with his, the force of her nearly toppling him as he bent down to give her a hug.

Normally, I would've turned away by now. I would've focused my attention on anything, or anyone, else, but I couldn't bring myself to. There was too much joy between them. Their smiles were wide, their eyes were bright, and the love they shared was nearly overwhelming. It wasn't until Charlie turned my way and pointed that I remembered I was gawking awkwardly at a tender moment between my ex and his daughter.

He stood up confidently, maybe even a little smug, and clasped Charlie's hand as they strode over to me. The cotton of his faded t-shirt bunched along his muscled forearms and broad shoulders. It was strange seeing the whole ass man in front of me when I'd only known the boy he used to be. He'd come a long way from gangly limbs and wild blond hair tucked beneath a cap.

"Daddy! Guess what Miss Cleo and I found today?" Charlie said as she skidded to a stop in front of me.

"What do you and Miss Cleo find today?" he asked, blue eyes flitting between me and his daughter. I think he was waiting for me to shut it down, to walk away, but I didn't. Some part of me wanted to, but I selfishly wanted to see his reaction.

"When we were in class, I saw this treehouse and wanted to explore it." His gaze jumped to mine, and I nearly burned with the intensity I saw in his eyes. "So, I did, and at first I was sad because this treehouse didn't have any magic like the one from the story, but then Miss Cleo and I saw baby birds outside the window!"

I didn't have to feel my cheeks to know they were flushed from thinking about what Grady had told Charlie, and how our past was now intertwined with the present. Grady's voice was hoarse as he said, "Birds, huh?"

"And they were blue, Daddy! I've never seen bluebirds before, but they were so pretty. Can I have one as a pet? Can we take them home?"

Grady and I shared a laugh. "I think they already have a home, sunshine."

Charlie's shoulders slumped for only a moment before she swung around and grabbed my hands. "Will you keep an eye on them while I'm gone tonight? And can we check on them tomorrow?"

"I thought you said treehouses weren't for you?" I asked, raising a brow.

"I changed my mind."

"If you're sure," I said slowly. "But let's wait until I can get someone to replace the ladder, okay?"

"And what about Daddy? Can he come too?"

I looked over her head to where Grady stood. The emotion on his face was hard to read. Pained but filled with relief. Happy and yet there was sorrow, too. Honestly, it didn't make sense, but when had it ever? We'd once gone from mere acquaintances to everything to nothing in a matter of years. And now he was here, and I would've been a liar to say there wasn't something still between us. What that was, I had no idea.

But I wanted to find out.

Maybe Rachel was right. It was time to stop running and just ask the questions that needed to be asked. To hear him out once and for all.

"If he wants—"

"I do," he said eagerly. His fists clenched tightly at his side. "I mean, I think I'd like that very much."

"Have you gotten over your fear of heights?"

He chuckled. "Nope, but I think I can take a page out of Charlie's book and change my mind. Maybe it won't be as bad as I remember."

Charlie's jaw dropped, her little eyes growing about ten sizes bigger than usual. "You're not tearing any pages out of any of my books, Daddy. I love them."

Grady held up his hands. "It's an expression, sunshine. Just means you're being courageous, so I think I can be, too."

Maybe, I could be, too.

cleo

. . .

18 Years Old

BUTTERFLIES DANCED in my stomach as I heard a knock on the front door. Looking out the window, I saw a familiar, faded orange truck in the driveway. "I'll get it," I muttered as my mom put down her spatula. It was hard not to miss the knowing look she shared with my dad, but I didn't care. I rounded the corner to the entryway, glancing down and smoothing the wrinkles from my dress before sucking in a breath and opening the door.

Grady stood on the threshold holding a massive bouquet of flowers in his arms. They were all different shades of blue and cream, with an occasional pop of golden yellow. His smile widened when he took in my dress, even more so as his gaze dipped to the short hem and my long legs on display. "Bluebird," he said, leaning in to give me a chaste kiss. "I missed you."

"I missed you, too," I whispered, stepping aside to let him in.

It was dramatic, I knew that, but I really had missed him. It felt like we'd hardly had a moment alone the past two weeks. We were both getting ready to leave for college on Sunday, so our parents were holding onto their time with us a little more than usual. Plus, Grady had spent nearly every day working as much as he could since he hadn't had a chance to find a part-time job in Austin yet.

Mom and Dad decided to turn our weekly dinner into a celebration for Grady and me. Usually, Friday nights were strictly family. Every now and then, one of them would ask me to invite Grady over, but it didn't happen often. When they made the suggestion, I jumped at the chance. It felt right having everyone together.

"Oh, sweetie, you look beautiful!" his mom, Marsha, called, coming up behind him with her arms laden with sweets.

"Here, let me help!" I said, stepping forward to grab the pie pan in one hand and a plate of cookies in the other.

She smiled, tossing her head back toward her son and husband behind her. "I don't trust either of them with all these goods. I already had to smack Robert because I found him sneaking a cookie before we left."

Robert frowned and rubbed the back of his neck. "It's not my fault they're so good. You said you were going to make a batch for the house, too."

Marsha turned around, mouth agape. "I did, and you ate them all before we left the house!"

"Did I hear someone say cookies?" my dad asked, coming around and rubbing his belly. "I do love cookies."

"And it shows!" Mom called from the kitchen. "Now, y'all help that poor woman in this house so she can have a drink."

My mom was a fan of all things sweet and was a great baker, but she didn't have the patience Grady's mom had. Marsha Wilde and I had first bonded over our love of sweets. The first time I met her, she was busy in the kitchen making a batch of dark chocolate croissants entirely from scratch. When I asked her for the recipe, she told me to wash my hands and grab an apron off the hook so she could show me how.

Ever since, she would invite me over when she found a recipe she wanted to try. I was always much more nervous than she was, never wanting to make a mistake, but she waved me off and told me that was half the fun of baking.

I still wasn't sure if I felt the same way, but failing didn't seem so bad when we did it together. Sometimes, Grady would even help, although he was incredibly hopeless in the kitchen.

Grady took my hand as our moms giggled and our dads disappeared into the garage for a couple of beers. He tilted his head toward the living room, tugging me around the corner and out of sight from our parents.

The moment we were alone, Grady's lips were on mine. He pressed my body into the wall, hands roaming until they settled on my hips. It took every bit of effort I had not to moan at the urgency in his touch.

True to our word, Grady and I had remained abstinent. I mean, we weren't chaste by any means—we definitely did other things, but we hadn't gone *there* yet. It was extremely dramatic, but sometimes I felt like I might die waiting for it to happen. No matter how many times we kissed until our lips were swollen or lay in each other's arms, drunk on lust, nothing had filled the ache left behind.

"You're killing me, bluebird. It should be illegal to wear a dress like that in front of our parents when I can't do a damn thing about it." His voice was heady as he pressed his groin into mine. The pressure was almost too much. "I'm gonna have to recite baseball teams or something so I don't get a hard-on in front of everyone."

I could relate, although my need wasn't as obvious to those around us as his was. Grady would know, though. He would notice every time I squeezed my thighs together or shifted in my seat. For some reason, that only made it hotter. Like it was a secret only the two of us shared.

His lips trailed down my neck, and I smiled. "I wore it for you. I knew how much you liked it," I confessed.

"I can't wait until we can finally be alone," he whispered, pulling back and pressing a gentle kiss to my lips. "I can't wait for—"

"Cleo and Grady, sittin' in a tree! K-I-S-S-I-N-G—" Josie and Lennox peered around the corner, giggling and smiling as Grady and I jumped apart. Their smiles fell as I narrowed my eyes in their direction, and they took off back toward our parents.

I followed them, cheeks flamed from being caught and center aching from being interrupted. "You little sh—"

But it was too late. They were already cowering behind our mom when I stepped into the kitchen. "Language, Cleo!" Mom shrieked. She put her hands on her hips as my sisters peeked out from behind her. "You're an adult, now. You can't be chasing your sisters around like this."

Josie looked slightly embarrassed at what she witnessed, but Lennox stuck her tongue out at me as a taunt. When Mom turned around, I narrowed my eyes again and mouthed, "I will end you." All the color drained from her face, which was enough for me. It wasn't like I would be here to follow through on any threats, although I'd keep this in mind when she got a bit older and brought her first boyfriend home.

Being so much older than them hadn't gotten easier over the years. It was so painfully obvious now that I kept to myself most of the time. Sometimes Josie would come to me for advice. I'd been the one she called when she started her period for the first time, which I was grateful for. Thankfully, it'd been over the summer, so she hadn't needed to worry about explaining a change of clothes in her locker or why her bathroom breaks made her late to class like I had.

I crossed my arms as Grady walked past me toward his mom. "Well, if I'm an adult now, I'd like to be able to have a private moment alone from time to time. They shouldn't be sneaking up and embarrassing me—"

"Oh, hell no," my dad groaned. He joined the fray, plugging his ears as he took a seat at the table. "I don't need to hear about private moments—"

"It's only natural," Marsha interrupted, ready to play devil's advocate. "You remember what it was like to be young and in love, I'm sure."

I smiled at her words, looking down at my feet. It was no secret I loved Grady or that he loved me, but hearing her say it made it feel real. We weren't dismissed as two crazy kids who had no business feeling the way we did. It was legitimized.

"Just keep it away from me," he muttered before taking a sip of his beer. "I got two more daughters to worry about after this. My heart can't take the stress."

"Douglas, your heart is just fine," Mom called over her shoulder. "Just count your blessings we still have a few years before worrying about this stuff with Josie."

Josie's head snapped up. "Wait, worrying about what?"

"I think they're talking about boys," Lennox said with a roll of her eyes.

"Ew, gross." Josie scrunched up her nose, but not in time to hide the hint of curiosity I saw there.

"That's what I'm saying," our youngest sister mumbled.

Dad looked between the two and shook his head. "God, help me."

Robert clapped him on the shoulder. "Ain't enough prayers in the world to save you from three daughters."

"No shit," Dad snorted, pushing to his feet. "Let's get these steaks going so I don't have to sit here and listen to this."

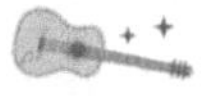

GRADY'S FINGERS lightly traced the exposed skin along my shoulder as the cicadas sang loudly in the summer night. Kenny Rogers was playing on the radio, and Dad belted out the words while Robert played the air drums in the background. We all laughed until our sides hurt, calling for an encore as the music faded away.

They both groaned, wiping the sweat from their brows. "I'm too old for a fuckin' encore," Dad panted.

"Yeah, drumming takes a lot out of a person," Robert said. He sat down and reached for his beer, pausing before it reached his lips. "But I bet if y'all asked nicely, Grady here would love to sing everyone a song."

Grady immediately shook his head. "Oh no, I'm good being an audience member. Y'all do your thing."

"Come on, son. We were just your openers," his dad teased. "You'll have to get over that stage fright sometime. Might as well be now."

"I didn't even bring my guitar—"

"Isn't it in the truck?" Marsha asked. "I could've sworn I saw it..."

"But I haven't warmed up—"

She snapped her fingers. "It's a good thing you've been singing along with these two buffoons all night, isn't it?"

"Mom—"

"I'm afraid you can't out bullshit a bullshitter, son. I will win every time."

Robert laughed. "Might as well get used to it. I'm sure you don't win many arguments as it is."

I chuckled. "No, he definitely doesn't."

Grady pinched my side and leaned in to whisper, "You're not helping."

"And I'm not gonna," I said back, kissing his cheek. "It's just family, baby. If you can't do it here, how are you going to in front of strangers?"

He bit down on his lip, eyes darting around the backyard before landing on me. "Alright, but only because you asked. Let me go grab my guitar."

"Already got it," Dad said, walking outside with the instrument clutched in his hand. I hadn't even seen him leave, but he must have snuck out while everyone was bickering. He walked over and knelt in front of Grady, the case outstretched for him to take. "Show us how it's done, son."

I didn't miss the slight tremble in his hand as he took the guitar from its case, or the way he sucked down the rest of his sweet tea before nervously strumming the strings. "What do y'all wanna hear?"

Our parents bickered back and forth on song titles until his mom finally shouted out Wonderful Tonight by Eric Clapton. Grady smiled, and I knew it was one of their favorites to play together. I'd listened to them come together on quiet nights spent at their house. She would start it off, staying up until the first chorus had ended, and then he'd take over while she asked Robert to dance. Sometimes I felt like an intruder, but it was love in its purest form—stripped back until the noise of the world had faded into silence and there was nothing between two lovers but the connection they shared.

The moment Grady opened his mouth and began to sing, it was like the world stopped. Would I ever get used to this? No matter how many times I'd heard his voice or watched him play, my skin always broke out in goosebumps, and I felt like I couldn't breathe. This talent was the kind people prayed for, and he didn't even realize how gifted he truly was. He shrugged it off like anyone could do, like he wasn't any better than any other musician with a dream in their heart and a story to tell.

I glanced around the yard, soaking in the expressions of awe and adoration on our parents' faces. They, maybe more than I, understood how extraordinary he was. My father clapped his on the back, while his mother let her tears fall as mine held her hand. Even Josie and Lennox sat still, listening intently with something like wonder on their young faces.

And just like in his parents' house, Robert asked Marsha to dance. My parents followed suit, joining the fray as they all slowly danced beneath the moonlight.

It was at that perfect moment in time I knew unequivocally what I wanted, and what I wanted was Grady to be the one to take my virginity. For so long, I was scared to lose this last piece of me I'd held near and dear to my heart. Like it was one last thing that belonged to me and me alone. Mine to keep or use as I saw fit, and I didn't want to wait any longer.

When Grady finished, he was met with thunderous applause. He kept his head ducked low, trying his best to downplay all the compliments and praise ringing in the air. The faint creep of a blush stained his cheeks, which was ridiculously adorable.

"I think we're gonna have to give them another song, don't you, Doug?" Robert asked, downing the rest of his beer. "Show him some old dogs can learn new tricks."

Dad laughed, wandering over to the stack of CDs next to the stereo. "What'll it be?"

As Grady slipped the guitar into its case, he turned over his shoulder to give me a smile. God, he looked so beautiful, haloed by the soft yellow glow of the strung-up Christmas lights over our heads. I wasn't sure what he saw on my face, but he slid his hand onto my knee and squeezed. "You okay?" he asked.

I nodded once, clearing my throat. "Y—Yeah, I'm good." I glanced around, noticing our parents lost to themselves. "Wanna get out of here?"

There was a moment when I wondered if he would say no, to remind me we had agreed to wait until we were away at college and that this was reckless. My heart was beating out of my chest, and I felt like I couldn't breathe.

But then his face softened, eyes darting to the door behind us. "I'll go anywhere with you, bluebird."

grady

. . .

"MOMMY!"

"Hi, sweet girl! How are you?" I smiled as Olivia's voice came through the speakers. Charlie always turned the volume up way too loud, but I never minded. The time away from each other was hard. It always was. No matter if I was on tour and Olivia stayed home, or if she was across the country in meetings for the label.

This was my favorite part of the day, listening to the two of them talk about nothing and everything. Charlie insisted on calling her mom every night. Some chats were longer than others. Last night, Olivia and I listened intently as our daughter gave us a complete account of her day at camp. Then she asked her mom to read her not one, but two, bedtime stories before she finally passed out.

I grabbed a beer and made my way out to the front porch, taking a seat in one of the large rocking chairs. It was humid as hell. The scent of rain hung heavy in the air as thunder rolled in the distance.

Dad's neighborhood was quiet, but lively. There were always couples walking along the sidewalk, or kids playing in the small park just down the street. That was what I missed most about living in a small town. Nashville was too busy. Too loud. We'd lived in the middle of the city for so long, I'd almost forgotten what this kind of peace was like.

Olivia's family lived in a small town a few hours from the city, so we didn't get out there as much as we liked. It reminded me a lot of Ashwood and had become one of my favorite places. I could easily see myself settling there. Liv and I briefly talked about building a place out on their land, even if it wasn't going to be our full-time home. With our careers, though, it never made much sense.

Now that I was out? That I was free? Yeah, I wanted to live that quiet life again. I wanted to sit out on the porch and watch the storms roll in over my own stretch of land. I wanted Charlie to be able to run wild and free, just like I had when I was growing up.

And I wanted Cleo at my side for all of it.

It was strange to think about what our lives would've been like had we not broken apart. Would we have kids? Cleo had grown up with a large family, and I'd always wanted one. We used to talk about them as if a big family was a done deal. What they looked like. If they'd be quiet and stubborn like her, or loud and a little wild like me. Or maybe they'd be a mishmash of both.

Besides a weak moment here or there when curiosity got the best of me, I hadn't kept up with Cleo's life after she got married. It hurt too damn much. I was better off pretending she was happy and thriving. It was a mantra I'd repeated over and over again to try to get it through my head. *She's happier without me.*

I'd admit to being surprised she never had kids, though. Not that there was anything wrong with that. I expected to see a whole gaggle of them when I finally caved last summer and looked her up. Maybe her dreams had changed over the years. Maybe I didn't know her as well as I thought.

Her social media gave nothing away. A picture here or there with her family or of the ranch, some with her ex-husband. I hated those the most. Not that I had a right to. I couldn't fault her for moving on with her life when I'd done the same. Especially when my relationship with Liv was all over the place.

Even though what we had was different, even if Liv hadn't signed me to her company's label, I would've married her anyway if she'd asked. I was pissed off at the world and on a road to nowhere good. Mom had just been diagnosed with cancer, I was in debt up to my fucking eyeballs, and Cleo had moved on with another man.

"Daddy!" I turned around as Charlie burst into the summer evening with my phone in her hand. "Mommy wants to talk to you before you tuck me in."

I gave her a smile. "Alright, sunshine. Go brush your teeth for me? I'll be there in just a second."

"Okay!" she said, running full speed back into the house. The screen door slammed, sending the nearby birds scattering from their perch.

"You know that girl is gonna spend the next five minutes making funny faces in the mirror, right?" Olivia laughed. "I doubt she'll even remember to wet the brush."

"Don't worry. I'll make her do it again when we go inside." I closed my eyes and rubbed my temples. "What's up?"

"Just wanted to check in with you. How's everything going?"

I chuckled and took a sip of beer. "That's a loaded question."

"Is it?"

"Yup."

Olivia propped her elbows on the table at her hotel. She was in L.A. for the entire month, attending meetings during the day and galas in the evening. Out of all the things I would miss about our relationship, the constant publicity was not one of them. I had to deal with it on my own, but dealing with it together was something entirely different. Liv was a media darling, and having to be "on" all the time was exhausting. There was never a moment in time when we weren't under public scrutiny. "Why's that?"

"Well, Charlie is doing great, obviously. She's settling in nicely here and is loving camp. The other evening, she told me she preferred their cooking over mine, so that was fun."

The past two days, I'd picked Charlie up, and she had a bag of cookies clutched in her hand. Most of them were crumbled by the time we got home, but she was right. They'd tasted way better than anything Liv or I had ever made.

Today, I noticed a few more cookies than I had yesterday, which made me smile like a goddamn idiot. It was foolish to think she'd done that for me. We still hadn't spoken, but I swore I noticed her gaze lingering longer than before. Noticed the way she didn't run and hide when I came up to sign Charlie out for the day.

Liv tried to hide her smile behind her hand. "Oh yeah, I've heard all about it. Sounds like you've got some real competition."

"Apparently so."

"And what about the other thing?"

I took another swig of my beer and shrugged before meeting my soon-to-be ex-wife's gaze. "As to be expected. I think I'd have better luck fist-fighting a bear than getting her to look my way, let alone have a conversation."

"Should I send you the address for the nearest zoo? Maybe that'd win her over?"

"Ha, ha. Very funny," I deadpanned. "I don't know what I'd do without you."

She leaned back in her chair. "Honestly? I don't know either. Probably be off fighting bears or some shit."

"Weren't you the one ready to push me into the exhibit

thirty seconds ago? Did you want to try and settle the whole man versus bear debate once and for all?"

Liv waved me off. "Sounds like a threat from your other ex-wife."

I grinned. "You're the one and only."

"And don't you forget it."

"Daddy, I'm done!" Charlie skipped out, smiling widely and pointing at her mouth. "See? All clean!"

Liv and I shared a knowing look. "Breath check?" I asked, quirking a brow. When Charlie clamped her lips shut instead of answering, I had my answer. "Nice try. Get your butt back in there. Let's go."

I stood up, tossing the empty beer bottle in the trash as we made our way back into the house. This time, we both watched Charlie begrudgingly brush her teeth before hopping into bed and demanding a story. I set Liv up on the charging stand next to her bed, and we took turns reading her favorites. It wasn't long before Charlie was fighting sleep.

"Alright, sleepyhead," Liv said softly, closing the book in front of her. "It's time to get some shut-eye."

Charlie sighed as she burrowed deeper into the pillows. "I don't want to."

"Why's that? Aren't you excited for camp tomorrow?" I leaned forward and gently tucked a strand of hair behind her ear. "And for those cookies you apparently love more than my cheesy mac?"

She gave me a sleepy smile. "Yeah, but tomorrow means it's almost over."

"You still have two full days, sunshine," Liv said. "That's so much!"

"I still don't know how to ride a pony, though. And if I don't know how to ride a pony, then I can't get a pony." Charlie's bottom lip wobbled, and a tear slipped free, a clear sign we were dangerously close to an exhaustion crash out.

My stomach dropped as Liv tossed a nervous glance my way. I knew what she was going to suggest before the words ever left her mouth. "What if we asked for private lessons? Surely, they have someone at the ranch who could do it, right?"

Charlie's impending tantrum cleared almost immediately. "Really?" She looked my way. "You think we can ask Miss Cleo tomorrow? You think she'll say yes?"

Goddammit, Liv. How the hell was I supposed to get out of this now? Sure, I could tell Charlie no and stand my ground, but I didn't want to. Not when she'd been so happy the past three days. Liv knew that. She knew I'd do anything to see my daughter smile.

Fucking hell.

"I don't know, sunshine. They may not be able to. I don't know what their schedule is—"

"Surely it can't hurt to ask," Liv interrupted. "Worst thing they can say is no."

That wasn't true. Not at all. The worst thing that could happen was Cleo thinking I was using my daughter to spend more time with her and telling me to fuck off. The temporary truce was just that—temporary. Despite my overwhelming desire to go all in, I was worried doing so would scare her off faster than I could blink.

"Yeah, Daddy! You tell me that all the time," Charlie reminded me. "That's why I ask so many questions."

Well, shit. I did say that, but I never expected her to throw my words back in my face. It was inspirational at the time. Were all the women in my life determined to test my patience? How was this fair?

"Why don't I teach you?" I asked, rubbing the back of my neck. "I did my fair share of riding when I was a kid."

Charlie and Liv both shared a look. "When's the last time you were on the back of a horse?" Liv asked, hiding a laugh.

"It's been a while," I admitted.

"Because I don't think I've ever seen it," she continued. "Like ever."

Charlie giggled. "Daddy, you can't teach me if you don't know how. I want Miss Cleo."

"I can ask—"

"Yay! Thank you, thank you, thank you!" Charlie shot up and wrapped her little arms around my neck. I glared at Liv over her shoulder, making sure she knew we would absolutely be having a conversation about this later. She just shrugged, completely unbothered.

"Just don't get your hopes up, okay?"

"I promise," she said, hopping back beneath the covers and closing her eyes. "Love you so, so, so much." Based on the smile on her face, I knew the chances of her keeping calm about it were slim to none. She was probably already riding off into the sunset on her imaginary horse.

"Alright. Goodnight, sunshine." I pressed a kiss on her forehead.

"Sweet dreams," Liv cooed.

Charlie mumbled something that sounded like "goodnight," but it came out as an incoherent jumble of sounds. I grabbed my phone and snuck out of her room, leaving the door cracked as I made my way to my own.

Since Dad had been determined to stay here, Liv and I helped renovate the house a bit. It was getting hard for him to keep up with everything by himself. Before the updates, Mom had left my childhood bedroom untouched. It looked completely different now, but somehow still felt like mine.

"What the hell—"

"Well, would you look at the time?" Liv interrupted, staring at the smartwatch on her wrist. "It's so late—"

"Nice try," I deadpanned. "You're two hours behind us. It just turned seven."

"Yeah, but you know how work is. I have an early meeting I

need to prep for." She blew out a breath. "Damn. Really wish I could stay and chat."

I pinched the bridge of my nose. "Why are you meddling, Liv? All this is gonna do is piss off Cleo and disappoint Charlie. You're putting me in the shittiest position possible."

"She doesn't have to be the teacher. Maybe she knows someone else who could do it. Besides, it's not like you're making any headway in that department."

"I don't want her to think I'm using our daughter to manipulate her. She has a soft spot for kids." I shook my head. "This isn't gonna end well."

This time, Liv hesitated before she spoke. "Look, Grady... I understand you're trying to take this slowly, but your time in Ashwood does have an expiration date. You can't stay there forever." She bit down on her lip. "Sooner or later, you'll just have to lay all your cards out on the table and respect her decision. Whatever that may be."

She was right. I hated that she was right. I had been trying to avoid thinking about the end as much as possible, but there would come a time when I couldn't anymore. "I know," I said, running a hand through my hair. "I just don't want to fuck this up."

"I get that. I really do. Putting yourself in a position to potentially have your heart broken is terrifying."

"I never said I was going to be heartbroken," I mumbled.

I would be—we both knew that—but admitting it felt a lot heavier than denying it. Just for a little bit longer, I wanted to live in denial. To believe I actually had a shot at winning her back and taking control of my life for the first time in over a decade.

"My point," Liv said with an eyeroll, "is you need to shit or get off the pot."

I scrunched up my face. "You have such a way with words."

"I can't hold off filing the divorce papers for long," she said, rubbing her temple. "It's been a month, and the lawyers have asked me about it at least twice a week. God knows I don't want the media attention any more than you do, but I don't know if I can defer it much more."

They'd been calling me, too, but I ignored them every time. "I know, it's just…" I blew out a breath. "Am I making a mistake in all this, Liv? With us? With Cleo?"

Liv tilted her head. "How would this be a mistake? It's what you want, isn't it?"

"Wanting something doesn't make it right," I said, letting my head fall back against the headboard.

"It doesn't, but I'm a firm believer in fate, and that's what I think the two of you are."

I snorted. "You've never been around her. You can't possibly—"

"I know you better than you know yourself, Grady. I've seen every high and every low, and I'll tell you one thing… I've never seen your eyes light up the way they do when you talk about Cleo. Not even for music. That tells me all I need to know." Liv sat back in her seat, staring down at her hands in her lap. The ring we picked out together shone bright on her left hand. "And maybe I need to believe in that kind of magic. Maybe I need to hold onto the hope that I can find even a sliver of it for myself."

"Oh, Liv…" My heart broke for her. She'd given up so much to have the one thing she said she wanted most, but sometimes I wondered if it wasn't out of some twisted sense of duty to carry on the family business. Her brother chose a different path, and her uncle never had kids. Everything fell to her.

She waved me off. "I don't need your pity, Grady. I need you to cowboy the fuck up—"

"I wasn't ever really a cowboy—"

"And get the girl. For your sake and mine. Otherwise, what the fuck was the point of the past thirteen years? It's not like we were together for the sex—"

"Oh, but what a great night it was," I joked.

Liv laughed. "Shut up. You know what I mean."

And I did. Just like I knew with every fiber of my being she was right. If I didn't go after what I wanted, then all the heartbreak and pain and tears and misery were for nothing. Liv and I lived a good life together. If we wanted to, we could do it forever.

But we didn't want to. Not anymore.

For the first time, we wanted to choose ourselves. We wanted to feel fulfilled in every aspect of life, not just the career highs the public celebrated.

My voice was hoarse when I finally answered. "I promise, Liv. I'll make it count."

"Don't do it for me. Do it for you. Do it for her, Grady." I nodded, unable to find the words to say anything more. "Same time tomorrow?"

"Same time tomorrow," I said, ending the call and tossing it on the bed.

grady

. . .

18 Years Old

CLEO'S HAND was warm in mine as she led me through the house and back out into the humid summer night. It hadn't been hard to slip away from the party, not as our parents laughed and drank and ate, reminiscing about the good old days and bickering about the best bands of the eighties.

"Where are you taking me?" I asked. Cleo didn't answer, but she giggled as I pulled her back into my arms as we stopped near my truck. "It would be awfully rude of you to break things off now that I've made your family fall in love with me."

Cleo rolled her eyes. "They already loved you."

"I don't know. I think your dad still had reservations, but after that performance? I don't know, I think I sealed the deal."

"Oh, you do, do you?"

"Mmhm," I nodded, placing my hand along her stomach and pushing her up against the side of my truck. Her eyes darted between us as I stepped closer, leaning in until our lips were only an inch apart. "You'll never be able to get rid of me now."

"What if that was part of my plan, anyway?" Her voice was so small, so casually cruel to herself that it almost broke my heart. She tried to laugh, to make it seem like she was joking, but I knew better. "What if I did it so you won't leave me?"

Cleo had come a long way from the unsure, shy, bumbling sixteen-year-old girl she was when we first started dating, but that didn't mean she wasn't still dancing with demons I never understood. I could see them sometimes. I didn't even think she realized she was mentally detaching sometimes until it happened. It was hard to watch her become a shell of her former self, but I did my best to show up and reassure her I wasn't going anywhere.

"Oh, bluebird… I could never leave you. You're stuck with me. Don't you see that?" I set the guitar down at her feet and cupped her face. Her eyes matched the night sky, sparkling with hope and barely contained nerves. "I'd give you anything you asked for—anything you needed—to get that through your head."

"Anything?"

I nodded. "I mean, I may not be able to hand over a million dollars right now—" she smacked my chest lightly "—but if you give me a few years, I could probably get it."

I'd save up every penny I ever made if she asked me to.

She bit down on her lip. "What if I didn't want to wait anymore?" I blinked, staring down at her perfect face in the pale moonlight. She looked like an angel. She looked like mine. "What if I wanted to give you the last piece of myself that I—"

I kissed her, tentatively at first, but it didn't take long for her hesitancy to bleed away to urgency like always. It seemed to be one of the few times Cleo didn't get lost in her head. She let her body act on what her mind would never let her. The anxiety was gone, and in its place was a quiet sort of confidence that only got me hotter.

"Is that a yes?" she asked a little breathlessly.

"That's a hell yes," I told her, maybe a little too eagerly.

Cleo chuckled, intertwining our fingers as she brought her

hand up to kiss each knuckle gently. "Then you better put that guitar up and follow me."

I didn't need to be told twice. Hell, I wouldn't have even needed to be told once if we'd already crossed that line before. "Oh, yes, ma'am."

I did as she told me, quickly setting my case on the backseat of my truck. And then, just because I could, I shut the door and scooped her into my arms. She shrieked as I hoisted her over my shoulder and smacked her ass. "Where are we going, bluebird? Tell me right now."

"Someone's eager," she murmured.

I was an eighteen-year-old kid. Of course, I was fucking eager. I'd spent more nights than I could count taking care of myself because her kisses and soft touches left me wanting more after I left. And sure, we'd done other stuff, but it never satiated that need for her. If anything, it only spurred me on.

"Cleo," I warned, letting my hands travel up the length of her thigh. Somewhere along the way, I'd forgotten just how short her little dress was. It wasn't long until I was grazing the soft cotton of her underwear. "Two can play the teasing game."

I ran my finger along the seam, enjoying the way her body reacted. She sucked in a sharp breath, clutching at my shirt as I made my way toward the back of the truck. I didn't think anyone would come out to look for us, but it was better to be safe than sorry.

"The treehouse," she gasped as my hand slid between her thighs. "Right now."

I turned my head, pressing a kiss on her hip. "Someone's eager."

"Now I know how it feels," she murmured.

We made it to the treehouse in record time. Honestly, I was shocked I hadn't tripped and taken us both down to the dirt. Even if we had, I didn't know if that would've stopped us. I'd kept my hand where it had been before, fingers splayed against the smooth expanse of skin. Something Cleo was all too aware of as she tried squeezing her legs together and squirming for just a hint of friction to relieve her ache.

"Now, unfortunately, I can't be romantic and carry you up this damn death trap," I said, setting her down and staring up into the trees. "So, you'll have to settle for me meeting you up there."

"It's not a death trap," she laughed, beginning to climb. "You're being dramatic."

Her hips swayed lightly with each step she took, and I couldn't look away. Soft blue panties peeked out from under her dress. I wasn't sure if it was intentional, but the little smirk she gave me as she climbed up and stared down at me from the top was enough to make me think it was.

Oh god, I was so painfully hard. Watching her, combined with the anticipation of what we were about to do, was more than enough. I needed to cool it down or else she was going to look back on our first time in disappointment.

I made quick work of the climb and closed the hatch behind me. I sat back on my heels, suddenly feeling nervous. I wasn't sure what to do or how to start, but then I found Cleo's big blue eyes. With the moonlight spilling through the window, she looked beautiful. Like a queen.

Our positions were nearly identical, with her hands in her lap and a soft smile on her lips. She fidgeted slightly, shifting her weight from one leg to the other.

"Um, before we do this," she began, tucking a piece of loose hair behind her ear, "Do you have a condom?"

I didn't want her to think I was presumptuous, but I'd been carrying one with me for a few months now. It wasn't that I thought something was actually going to happen, but I wanted to be prepared when it did. The last thing I wanted was for the two of us to do something that would force us into conversations and decisions neither of us were ready for yet.

"I do," I said, reaching into my pocket and pulling it from my wallet.

"You came prepared," she said, reaching into the small chest on the shelf. I didn't realize what she was holding until it hit the light. "But so did I."

Something about it made me smile, that she was just as eager as I was. I tried to be very intentional with my words and actions, especially when it came to sex. The last thing I wanted was for her to feel pressured. I'd seen it happen a few times with friends from school and hated the thought of anyone pushing someone past their comfort zone.

"How long have you been planning this, bluebird?"

Even though it was dark, I could see the pretty pink blush across her cheeks. "I just wanted to be ready. I was planning on taking them out before we left, but…"

"But," I said softly, reaching forward for her hand. My palm was sweaty, and so was hers when I gave her a reassuring squeeze. "We'll take this however fast or slow you wanna go, okay?"

"I trust you." Her whispered words in the darkness were the only confirmation I needed.

I leaned forward and kissed her. My hands slowly ran up her arms until her hair was threaded between my fingers. Cleo melted in my hold, letting me tilt her face however I wanted, which only made me greedy.

She let out a little gasp as I bit down on her lip—a sweet little sound that had blood rushing to… somewhere. It was freeing to do what we wanted, to not worry about having to stop. I knew it was selfish, but as she ran her fingers across my denim-clad thighs, I realized she was being just as greedy as I was.

There were times I wondered what this moment would look like. Most movies and TV shows painted one of two pictures when it came to characters losing their virginity. Either it was this overly romantic serenade with rose petals and candles in some ridiculous hotel room with soft jazz playing in the background, or it happened in the back seat of a truck and lasted only a matter of minutes.

Location aside, when I imagined Cleo and me in that position, I'd assumed I would take a more dominant role, that I'd have to guide her and force myself to go at a pace she was comfortable with. It seemed, however, I might've been wrong about that.

It was like a dam broke. After two years of heated moments and sexual frustration, neither of us was able to hold back any longer. Cleo broke our kiss to straddle my hips. The angle was awkward until she wrapped her arms around my neck and began grinding down on me. We were a tangle of limbs, frantically clawing at each other through our clothes as we explored the other's body.

Having her in my arms felt so damn good. To be able to take and take and take, to hear the sounds of pleasure I took as encouragement. All of it went right below the belt, something I was increasingly aware of with each sweet drag of her hips.

"Jesus Christ, baby," I breathed, tipping my head back on a groan as she moved. Her tongue danced along my earlobe, dragging it into her mouth with her teeth. "You gotta stop doing that. I'm gonna come in my pants."

Cleo leaned back, giving me a Cheshire smile before rolling her hips yet again. "I heard the first time is usually quick for guys, but you recover pretty easily. I thought we'd get the first one outta the way."

I wasn't the religious type, but this fucking woman had me praying more in the past five minutes than I ever had in my life. "Okay, uh, well, do you think we could not do it like this?" I panted. "Like literally any other way? I'll do it myself if you want, but please, for the love of god, don't tease me like this."

Her lips parted in surprise, and then she snapped them shut. "You'd do that?"

I nodded eagerly. "Yeah, I don't wanna be a one pump kinda guy. I'd like this to last, too."

"Can I watch?" she asked, looking at me through long, fluttering lashes. There was something in her voice that sounded coy and unsure, a hint of the shyness I expected from her, but that twinkle in her eye gave her away.

"Is my girl a little kinky?" I asked, raising my brows.

She shrugged. "I don't know. It's just… I don't know, Grady, I like the idea of watching you. Of knowing what you like, what turns you on."

"That's a short list," I laughed. "It's you, you, and—oh yeah, that's right—you."

"Be serious," she said, pushing at my chest.

I caught her wrist, smiling as I brought it to my lips. "I'd never joke about what got my dick hard."

"You're so full of yourself."

"Mm, I'd rather be full of you," I said, pausing before we both burst out laughing. "Uh, not like that."

Cleo bit her lip. "Maybe later then."

I wasn't sure that was going to be up my alley in any sense of the word, but maybe a bit down the road? Sure. I'd give it a try. I wasn't too proud. "Maybe later," I agreed. "But for now, lift your hips a bit so I can reach between us."

She did as I asked, and it was the sweetest relief and also the greatest torture. Part of me wanted to pull her back down and let her have her way. It must have felt good for her, too. But we needed to be smart about this. Eventually, we'd need to return to our parents, and I didn't really know how to explain jizz stains to my mom right before I went off to college.

I reached for the button of my jeans, but Cleo beat me to it, tugging gently to loosen it. Before I knew what was happening, she guided the zipper down and reached inside to palm my length through my boxers.

"Bluebird," I breathed as she gave me one long tug. She flicked her gaze between my face and my dick, licking her lips and letting out a shaky exhale as she did it again. "You're not gonna get to watch if you keep this up."

"Right," she said, shaking her head.

My hand took the place of hers as she ran her fingers along her thighs. She stopped at the hem of her dress, hesitating only a moment before pulling the fabric up and revealing her perfect body inch by torturous inch.

This was the first time I was seeing my girlfriend naked, and she was fucking beautiful.

The other times we'd messed around, it'd been through frantic touches beneath clothes so it would be easy to right if we were caught. We'd never had the luxury of nakedness, and honestly, I might not have made the move if she hadn't done it first.

Her dress fell to the ground, making a soft sound that might as well have been a loud, resounding bang that stole all the breath from my lungs. I didn't say anything for a moment. How could I when she was kneeling above me in nothing but her underwear?

"Is this okay?" she asked nervously. Her body curved in slightly, as if she were about to grab the fabric and hide for being so bold.

It was taking everything in me not to come right here and now after one stroke. If she wanted to watch, I wanted to try to make it good for her. "It's perfect," I breathed. "You're perfect. Jesus, Cleo."

She lit up under my praise, scooting back just a bit so she could see me better. "I like my view, too."

Her gaze flicked down my hand, lips parted as I gave myself one long drag. I did it again and watched her breasts swell on a ragged breath. She said she wanted to watch me to find out what I liked, and I realized I felt the same way.

Cleo couldn't hide a damn bit of her excitement each time I worked myself. From the goosebumps that cropped up as she ran her hands along her body to the way she moaned with each gentle pluck of her nipples, I realized how reactive she was to the things I did. The way it excited her beyond anything else we'd done.

It was too much. All too damn much. With a muffled groan, I came all over my hand like I was back in my bedroom with a hard-on that wouldn't go the hell away. "Shit," I sighed. "I'm sorry. That probably wasn't as hot as you were thinking it would be. I swear I can last longer."

At least, I fucking hoped I could. It'd be embarrassing if that was going to be my legacy.

But any doubts bled away as I looked at Cleo's lust-drunk face. "Are you kidding me?" she asked, reaching over and tossing me a blanket so I could clean myself off. "That was the hottest fucking thing I've ever seen. Way better than the porn I found."

"You watched porn?" I asked, laughing.

She ducked away but nodded. "Yeah. One of the girls at school was passing it around."

I smiled. "You really are a little bit kinky, bluebird."

"Shut up and kiss me," she said before moving toward me.

I was all too aware of the fact the only thing separating us was the thin fabric of her underwear. Especially as she dragged herself against me, showing me exactly how much she liked watching. "You're soaked," I rasped between kisses.

"It feels strange," Cleo said, pulling back slightly. "Obviously, I've been turned on before when we've done other things, but," she paused, "This feels different."

Yeah, it did. Probably not in the way it did for her, but even my body could sense something was happening. I wasn't getting myself off to scratch an itch like normal, or to make sure I wasn't going to pitch a tent in my shorts when I walked out to breakfast with my parents.

I was acutely aware that this was about more than me and my needs. This was about making Cleo feel as good as I possibly could. "Can I see you?" I asked hesitantly, gazing down her body to her center. "All of you?"

Cleo nodded, ready to swing her leg over but I was faster. I wrapped my arms around her waist and flipped us so her back was flat on the ground and I was hovering over her. She let out a sweet, but nervous, giggle as my fingers played along the waistband of her underwear.

"I think I like you beneath me," I said, working the fabric slowly down her hips until she was bared to me.

Holy fucking shit. This was real. This was happening.

I dropped the cotton scraps beside her dress, hesitating to get my first honest look at her beneath the moonlight. Soft blonde curls were nestled between her thighs, just a few shades darker than her hair. My nostrils flared as she squeezed her legs together.

"Don't do that," I said, dragging my gaze up to meet hers. "Don't hide."

"You're staring at me weirdly," she murmured.

"I'm staring at you like I want you, like it's taking everything in me not to rush things and make sure this is just as enjoyable for you as it already has been for me." Her lips parted, and I could see the way she relaxed a fraction, so I continued. "You're the most beautiful thing I've ever seen."

"Clearly you need to get out more."

"What would make you more comfortable?" I asked, sitting back on my heels. Something had changed from moments ago, and I didn't like the way she seemed to revert to shyness.

Cleo blinked. "What do you mean?"

"Five seconds ago, you were confidently calling shots, practically drooling as I jacked off to the sight of you watching me do it."

"I was not drooling," she muttered.

"And now that the positions are reversed, I feel you clamping up. Is it the position? Do you not want to go any further? And to be clear, it won't hurt my feelings if the answer is yes, but I won't know unless you talk to me."

Cleo took a breath and sat up. "I think I like it when I feel like I have some semblance of control. It's like I know I can stop at any time, and it makes me feel... sexy, I guess. Right now, with you staring the way you are, I'm too in my head. I keep wondering if you're noticing how bloated I am, or the bruises and scrapes I got last week when Houdini dragged me six feet across the pasture."

"Okay then," I said, holding out my hand.

"I don't want to stop," she said, panic flaring in her eyes.

My lips tilted in a smile. "Oh, bluebird... We're not stopping. Just trust me." I reached behind me, grabbing hold of the neck of my shirt and tugging it over my head. It felt unfair she was completely naked while I still had everything on. She stayed still as I quickly removed my jeans, boxers, and boots.

The moment I was done, I held my hand out once again. That was all it took for her to place her palm against mine. I pulled her close to me, earning a soft laugh that probably shouldn't have made my dick harder than it already was, and then I flipped us once again. She was on top, straddling my hips and staring down at me with such awe.

"This better?" I asked, and she nodded. "Good. Don't worry about telling me what you need, baby."

"You said you liked seeing me beneath you," she said, looking away.

I gripped her chin and brought her face back to mine, kissing her. "I love you anyway I can get you. That doesn't mean you have to like all the same things as me, and it can be something we can try later if you want. Whatever does or doesn't happen tonight won't define the rest of our lives."

Cleo kissed me again, but this time she guided my hand where she wanted it—which, lucky for me, was right between her pretty thighs. I groaned against her lips as I felt how eager she was. She began grinding against my hand, rocking back and forth so I brushed her clit with each keen movement.

"Take what you need, bluebird. Make yourself feel good," I panted, pulling back to watch her do exactly as I said. Her hands landed on my shoulders for support, digging deeper into my skin with each rock of her hips. It wasn't long before I realized how close she was, and then she detonated.

I held her through each wave of pleasure and stutter of movement, murmuring my praise in her ear as sweat clung to her skin. I didn't even feel the bite of her nails until her grip lessened, leaving me with indentations I knew would bruise.

Good. I'd proudly wear whatever marks she gave me.

"I want you so much," Cleo panted, leaning back to grab one of the many condoms she brought out. Her fingers shook as she tried to open the foil packet. I chuckled, plucking it from her hold and tearing it open.

We both paused as we stared at it between us, the reality of what we were about to do evident by the rubber between my fingers. Cleo took the condom from me, slowly making her way down and rolling it onto my length. I hissed at the contact, suddenly thankful she had come prepared with plenty of protection. Honestly, I was grateful for the thing. There was no way I wouldn't come the moment I entered her without it.

She sat back to stare at her handiwork, eyes widening as she came to some sort of realization. "How is this thing gonna fit?" I couldn't help myself. I burst out laughing. "It's not funny! What if this thing destroys me?"

"You're great for my confidence, bluebird, but I'm pretty

average." I mean, I might have been on the bigger side of that spectrum, but I definitely wasn't what she was describing.

Her eyes widened. "*Average?*"

"How are you just now realizing this?" I laughed, leaning back on my hands. "It's not like you haven't seen it before."

Cleo waved her hand dramatically. "Yes, but now this is going to be inside of me."

"Hey, hey," I said, pushing up. "We'll go slow, okay? And whatever position you want."

She bit her lip. "Can I still be on top?"

"If that makes you more comfortable, absolutely." I didn't care how it happened, as long as she was okay. "If there's any pain, though, you'll have to either push through it or stop. I won't be able to do that for you."

"Yeah, okay," she mumbled, nodding and moving closer. I could feel the way her body trembled in my arms, or maybe it was my own. I wasn't sure.

"I love *you*," I whispered, making sure she understood the emphasis on the word.

My love wasn't conditional. It wasn't there because we were about to have sex. It wasn't there because I was riding a high from everything we'd done so far. I loved her because she was the single most important thing in my life.

Her gaze met mine, and she smiled. "I love you, too."

cleo

. . .

"YOU'RE HERE LATE."

I looked up to find Lennox standing in the doorway of Josie's office. Even though she was champing at the bit to come back, our sister was still out on her semi-forced maternity leave. Every time she wandered up to the barn or the main house, she had deep circles beneath her eyes and clothes littered in spit-up stains, so we'd tell her to march her happy ass back home.

Stella, as cute as she was, was a bit clingy to both her parents. When Lincoln walked out of the room, she cried. Every time Josie sat her down for two seconds, she screamed. The only exception was when our dad was present. I already knew that girl was going to be spoiled rotten by the time her first birthday came around.

But Josie being out meant no one was handling the admin work full-time. Mom and I split it when we could, and Lennox hopped in when Bishop didn't need her help on the back of a horse. With the camp taking so much of my time and attention, though, I hadn't had a chance to dig into the emails and invoices like I should've been.

I nodded toward the computer. "It's only 6:30. Besides, no rest for the wicked, or however the saying goes."

"Oh yeah, I get that," Lennox said. She sauntered forward, sitting down in one of the jade green chairs Josie had bought, and propped her feet on the desk. "That's what Bishop mutters every night before bed when I'm still curled up with one of my books."

"He's not wrong," I snickered.

She stuck her tongue out. "Are you almost ready to go?"

"To bed? Uh, no," I told her, confused. "Ready to go where—oh shit." Josie was coming over to the main house for a girls' night, while Bishop helped Lincoln drink a few beers and Dad got cuddle time with his new favorite girl.

I'd been looking forward to it since we made the plans a few weeks ago, but that'd been before Grady came barreling back into my life and sent me spiraling. It turned out actively trying not to think about someone only made you think of them more. Who knew?

The issue was I was supposed to be on snack duty, and I had completely forgotten.

"Lucky for you, I loaded up on all the chips and dips anyone could ever want. I'm talking salsa, guac, and queso—the holy trinity—hummus, French onion, spinach and artichoke, ranch—"

"What the hell, Len?"

"—and ranch dip," she finished, ticking them all off her fingers.

"Did you buy the whole freaking store? What about the stuff you were supposed to get?" I asked.

She shrugged. "Look, y'all put me on drinks for a reason, and as always, I delivered. I tried volunteering for the main course, and Mom shot me down. Then I tried to take desserts, and Josie stole that—even though this whole evening was supposed to be a way for her to relax—and you had snacks."

"So, you stole the snacks?"

"Is it stealing if you forgot?"

I mean, I guess she had a point, but it didn't make me feel any less shitty. Usually, I was the one picking up after my sisters, anticipating anything that might go wrong and what I'd need to do to make sure things ran smoothly.

I sighed. "I'm sorry, Len. I've been really spacey this week. I'll get better once the camp's over, and I can get back to some semblance of normality."

"I suppose I can hand the snacks back to you next time," she said, steepling her fingers.

"I don't know, you may be stuck with it now. Especially since you picked up Mom's favorite. I'll probably be demoted to drinks."

Lennox jumped out of her seat and pointed in my direction. "Aha! I knew it. Drinks *do* go to the least reliable."

I smiled, saving the spreadsheet I was working on and shutting the computer down before pushing to my feet. "I never said that."

"You didn't *not* say it either, though." She narrowed her eyes. "I'm gonna ask Mom."

She probably wouldn't like the answer she got. It wasn't that Lennox was unreliable—she wasn't in the slightest—it was just that my dear sister had little to no patience for cooking. Given the choice between a home-cooked meal and grazing on random things for dinner, she'd choose the grazing.

"I think it's more the fact that Mom doesn't consider 'girl dinner' a real thing," I said, locking up the office as we walked into the barn.

As I turned, Lennox looped her arm with mine and led me outside. "Well, that sounds like Mom's problem. Who doesn't love a good charcuterie board? Those little salami roses? I mean, come on. They're so cute."

"Do you even know how to make those?" I asked.

"No, but that isn't the point. It's the fact that it's a real thing." She tipped her head back in a groan. "Ugh, that's what I should've done for tonight! It would've been a chance to show her I was right."

"Alright, well, let's make a deal," I chuckled. "We'll switch next time. That'll give you plenty of time to practice meat art."

Lennox turned to me as we reached the front door of our parents' house and gave me a wink. "Meat art is a pastime I can get behind."

I shoved her forward as she stepped inside. "Gross, Len. I don't want to hear about what you do with Bishop's dick—"

A spluttering cough caught our attention, and we both looked up to see Lincoln, Bishop, and our dad standing in the living room staring at us in a mixture of horror and humor.

"God fucking dammit, Lennox," Bishop cursed. Lincoln burst out laughing, earning a jab from the grumpy bastard beside him. "It's not funny, you asshole."

"I mean, it's a little funny," he said, glancing down at his feet to hide his smile.

Bishop jerked his head toward the kitchen. "You want Josie to walk in talking about that shit in front of everyone?"

Lincoln shrugged. "I don't believe in gatekeeping, buddy, and I've got nothing to hide. Josie asks to try things all the time."

Dad shifted on his feet, shaking his head as he headed back toward the kitchen. "Y'all are gonna send me to an early fuckin' grave."

"I don't either, but—" Bishop gestured around, his cheeks flushed "—there's a time and a place." Then he smacked the back of Lincoln's head. "And don't call me buddy, asshole."

Lennox walked up to her fiancé and gripped his chin, forcing him to look at her. "If you take that stick outta your ass, I'll do that thing you like so much," she dropped her voice, "*daddy*."

I groaned and waved my hands in the air. "Too far, Len. Too far!"

Lincoln, on the other hand, looked like a kid in a damn candy shop. "I always knew you were a kinky fucker."

Bishop's face was bright red at this point. He pointed his finger at Lincoln. "You're gonna pay for that shit," and then he looked down at Lennox with fire burning in his eyes. "And I'll deal with you tonight."

"Promises, promises," she smirked, reaching up on her tiptoes to give him a chaste kiss.

Dad appeared in the doorway, cradling Stella to his chest. "Y'all better behave in front of my granddaughter, or I'm gonna have to kick your asses. Let's get this sleepy girl home."

I walked over, running my fingers along her cotton onesie. She still had that sweet newborn smell. It called to something deeply biological inside of me, and I ached for it. "Oh, don't take her away just yet. I haven't had my turn yet."

I held out my hands, gently taking her from Dad and laying her against my chest. She wiggled in my hold and let out a soft coo that had everyone in the room melting. "Hi, sweet girl," I whispered. "You're getting so big."

"Isn't she?" I hadn't heard Josie come up beside me. She peered over my shoulder at her daughter. "I can't believe she's already closing in on one month. It seems like just yesterday—"

Lincoln stepped up, covering Josie's eyes. "Nope, none of that, or else you're gonna start crying again. We've already had three tantrums before leaving the house, and only one of those was Stella's."

Josie turned in his hold, pushing at his chest. "I only cried once, you ass." Lincoln stared at her, and she rolled her eyes. "Okay, twice, but calling them tantrums is a bit much."

"Are you talking about my grandbaby?" Mom said. She had a glass of wine in one hand and a baby blanket in the other, which she shook at Lincoln. "Don't you go forgetting this now."

Lincoln grabbed it from her hold. "Oh, thank god. We wouldn't have made it far without this."

Lennox stepped up to my other side, resting her chin on my shoulder. She stared down at Stella like she was in love, and I couldn't blame her. "My ovaries are literally aching right now," she said, turning toward Bishop. "I want one."

The frustration from her earlier antics was gone as he said, "Let's get through the wedding first, killer."

"You're not getting any younger, old man. Gotta strike while the iron is hot and all that," she teased, motioning down to his crotch.

"Lord, what did I do to deserve this cruel punishment?" Dad mumbled, sending everyone into a fit of giggles.

I could help but smile at how much love was in the room, and how lucky Stella was to be surrounded by it. Watching my sister become a mother was surreal. Because I was the oldest, I assumed I would be the first to have babies. The first to explore motherhood in all its spit-up-covered glory, so if Josie and Lennox decided to walk the path, they wouldn't have to do it alone.

But being here amidst all the happiness and jokes and future promises also reminded me I was painfully alone. I had no one to plan for the future with. Even if I did, it wouldn't change the fact that motherhood was never going to be in the cards for me, no matter how much I wanted it to be.

Stella yawned and began kicking her little feet as I held her. Small, frustrated grunts had her parents immediately tensing. Before my sister could swoop in, Lincoln beat her to it. He pulled the crying baby gently into his arms before giving Josie a stern look. "I've got her," he said, stepping forward to press a kiss to her head. "You have fun tonight, okay?"

Josie bit her lip, looking like she wanted to argue but didn't. She nodded her head and sucked in a deep breath. "Alright," she mumbled. "But will you let me know if she needs me?"

Lincoln's eyes softened. "Of course, darlin'."

I excused myself as everyone said their goodbyes, walking

swiftly to the kitchen where there was an unopened bottle of tequila ready for margaritas. Tapping my fingers against the counter, I eyed it warily. I wasn't much of a drinker, but certain occasions called for it. Surely it was warranted on a girl's night, right?

Without thinking, I popped off the cap and poured a shot into one of the plastic cups on the counter. They were bright pink, which made sense since they screamed Lennox. I downed the liquor, letting the warm burn settle all the way into my stomach.

"Starting without me?" Lennox pouted, strutting into the kitchen with confidence and grace. "How rude. Everyone knows it's not a party until I've given a toast."

"Is that really necessary?" Mom asked, following her in.

Lennox gasped in faux shock. "Of course, it is! How could you say that?"

"I don't know where you got your flair for the dramatic. It must be your father."

Lennox and I shared a look before busting out laughing. "Mom, you are the most extra person I've ever met," she said.

"Present company excluded," I added, nodding toward my youngest sister, who stuck her tongue out at me. "I rest my case."

"I am not!" Mom cried. "I'm just—"

"Passionate?" Josie finished for her, joining the fray. Her eyes were red-rimmed, and it looked like she'd been crying. This was her first time truly being away from Stella, which I imagined was hard after having every moment of her life dedicated to her daughter.

Mom crossed her arms over her chest. "What on Earth have I ever done to be considered dramatic?"

"Well, you make us coordinate and match for every holiday," I said.

"And you get done up like you're going to the PBR or some-thing every time you go into town," Josie added.

"I do not—"

"Oh yes, you do," we all said at once.

"Need we remind you about the time you threw yourself your own birthday party because you thought we had all forgot-ten? When in reality, we'd spent weeks planning a surprise party and you ended up ruining the surprise because all your friends were confused about when and where to show up," Lennox deadpanned.

Mom glowered at each of us and snatched the bottle of tequila from my hand. "Give your damn speech then," she grumbled, pouring each of us a shot of the clear liquid.

"Oh, I've already had one," I said, waving her off and holding my cup to my chest.

Josie walked by, snatching it from my hand and passing it to Mom. "Too bad, so sad. Looks like you're going to have another."

"You know," I said, narrowing my eyes, "I forgot how pushy you can be."

She snorted. "If anything, it's gotten worse. Get used to it."

Mom passed out the shots as Lennox cleared her throat. "Here's to men and horses, and the women who ride them!"

"That's a new one," I murmured, smirking into my cup before letting this shot join the one I'd just taken. "At least you got good tequila."

"Don't offend me. Of course, I got the good tequila," Lennox scoffed. "What do you take me for? An amateur?"

"My daughter, the tequila connoisseur. Lord help me," Mom whispered, downing her shot with a grimace. "No more shots. Could someone please make me a margarita on the rocks with extra salt? Two limes, please."

Josie elbowed Lennox in her side. "And she says she isn't extra."

"I heard that!" Mom called as she turned and began fussing with covered dishes. "Now, someone make me that drink while I get dinner ready."

THREE MARGARITAS and two shots later, I was sitting on the couch and staring at the ceiling while Josie and Lennox chatted next to me. What was I doing? I was going to hate myself tomorrow. It was nearly midnight, and tomorrow was the last day of camp. Showing up hungover wasn't quite the plan, but it looked like it was inevitable.

"How's the wedding planning coming along?" Josie asked, pulling me back to the present. "Get him to budge at all?"

Lennox sighed into her cup, downing whatever was left. "Nope," she said, popping the P. "I still want to elope, but he isn't having it. He wants the big white wedding and all the stuff that comes with it. I told him with all the things he's done to me, a white wedding was the last thing we were going to have," she joked.

I couldn't help but laugh. The thought of Bishop being the one who wanted to make a big fuss out of declaring his love for my sister was honestly the cutest thing I'd ever heard, but strangely, it kind of fit him.

Bishop had a difficult start to life, and I knew there were a lot of insecurities and demons he was battling on his own. The fact he'd opened up enough to want to do this, to believe he and Lennox deserved a big celebration in front of their friends and family, was a testament to how far he'd come. Before they'd gotten together, I was sure he was going to be a bachelor forever. It wasn't that he had any shortage of options, but they never stayed long—whether that was his doing or theirs, I wasn't sure. I never pried.

"Okay, but that's kind of cute," I said, turning to face them.

"I know, but I'd much rather have something small in the middle of a field and then go on one hell of a honeymoon, ya know? Or grab y'all as witnesses and run away to a beach."

Josie noisily slurped at her drink. "Why don't you want a wedding? It seems like that'd be right up your alley."

"The wedding industry is a total sham. They charge out the ass because they can, because they know people will pay it." Lennox scrunched up her face like she'd tasted something awful. "Plus, I am not conventional, so why would I want to do one of the most conventional things?"

"You'll do it for him, though," I said.

Lennox's eyes softened, a smile tipping the corner of her lips. "Yeah, I will. The things I do for that man, I swear." Then she nudged Josie. "What about you? When are you and your baby daddy getting hitched?"

Josie rolled her eyes, but there wasn't a hint of annoyance. "We want to wait until Stella gets a bit older before we do anything, but," she bit her lip and looked down at her hand, "we're going to look at rings next month."

"Mr. Romantic isn't going to plan some elaborate surprise?" Lennox asked, placing her hand on her chest. "How disappointing."

"Well, since the ring is going to be on *my* hand, he wants to make sure it's something I really love," Josie said, straightening her shoulders. "I mean, I don't think it's any secret we'll get married eventually. We're kind of obsessed with one another."

"Really?" Lennox and I said sarcastically, busting out laughing when it came out at the same time.

"Yeah, yeah," Josie muttered, waving us off. "Judge me all you want, but you and Bishop are always sneaking away for lunchtime sex breaks. Don't think I don't know!"

Lennox shrugged. "Can't help myself, honestly. Have you seen the man?"

As I listened to my sisters taunt and tease one another, I couldn't help but feel a little left out. It was stupid, and I was absolutely going to blame the alcohol for bringing out my insecurities, but hearing them talk about their futures with such surety had me feeling nauseous.

Or maybe that was the alcohol. Who knew? Certainly not me. Certainly not now.

Faking a yawn, I stretched my arms over my head. "I think I'm gonna crash, girls. I'm struggling to keep my eyes open." I pushed to my feet, leaning forward to grab ahold of the empty cups when a hand shot out and grasped my wrist.

"Oh, no, you don't," Lennox said, narrowing her gaze. She pointed to the worn leather spot I'd just vacated. "Don't think you're going to get off the hook from everything you have going on."

Josie turned to me in surprise. "What's going on with you? What have I missed?"

Over Josie's shoulder, Lennox looked entirely too pleased with herself. I knew this talk was inevitable, especially with how I'd been acting lately, but this wasn't really what I had in mind for a sisterly heart-to-heart. "Nothing," I said, just as Lennox said, "Her ex is back in town."

"Thomas?" Josie asked, sitting up. She was the picture of concern. "Do we need to call someone? File another restraining order? Are those universal?"

"Of course it isn't Thomas. Do you really think he'd still be breathing if it was? Give me some credit," Lennox said, crossing one leg over the other. "This is the other one. The high school sweetheart who disappeared under a stage name and popped back up one day with a freaking kid."

Josie's lips curled into an O. "That makes much more sense." She turned back to me. "When's your first date?"

"Oh, we aren't going on a date," I said, coughing. "That ship has sailed. Been there, done that." I tapped my chest. "Got the broken heart to prove it."

"You can't be serious," Josie whined. "You can't just let him go. What about fate? Destiny? It can't be a coincidence he showed up here—twice."

"Thrice now," Lennox interrupted.

I rolled my eyes. "I'm pretty sure that's the first time you've ever used that word."

"What a time to do it, huh?" she said, giving me a smile. "Don't change the subject. Have you asked him why he's coming back around?"

I sighed, sinking back into the couch. "No."

Josie and Lennox waited, unmoving, for me to say more, but I kept my lips shut. There was nothing to tell. No great second-chance love story for the ages that'd warm hearts and have my sisters turning to a puddle right here where they sat. It was just two people who, yes, may have shared history together, but that was it.

Wasn't it?

I kept telling myself that was what I wanted, but after the other day, I wasn't so sure. I'd felt such a kinship with Charlie in the treehouse, and when Grady and I had talked, it hadn't been awkward. If anything, it'd been... nice. Which seemed like such a cop-out answer, even to my own ears, but it didn't make it any less true.

If someone had told me I'd be talking to Grady Wilde again in any capacity, I would've called them crazy. I would've told them there was no way in hell the two of us would ever be in the same spot, let alone chatting about going back to that goddamned treehouse like we were two old friends and not brokenhearted fools.

"Well, why not?" Josie pouted.

"I—"

"Because she's scared," Lennox finished for me. She waited,

begging for me to correct her, to argue with her, but there wasn't any point. Nothing changed the fact that she hit the nail on the freaking head with that observation.

"I know what that's like," Josie said quietly. "I felt the same after Lincoln came back, and you know how hard it was for me to even look in his direction. It was like walking barefoot on pins and needles, knowing you'd eventually get poked but still wanting to get to whatever's on the other side. But then—"

"Oh, don't say it," I grumbled. "All you needed was a little push, and that's what I gave you. I don't need a pep talk, Josie. I need a lobotomy, a time machine, or a memory eraser. Maybe all three."

"You were the reason I put all the fear behind me, though. You told me you regretted it." Her voice was stronger this time. "That'd you do anything to have it back, and now you have your chance."

It seemed like so long ago Josie had cried on my shoulder, not knowing what she should do about Lincoln. She'd been too damn scared and stubborn to go after what she truly wanted. In the end, I just had to make her see that—which I should've known would come back to bite me in the ass sooner or later.

"It's different with us, Josie. There are a lot of wounds I don't think we could heal. It's too much," I stammered. Hopelessness, my familiar friend, settled back into my chest and down into my stomach as I searched my mind for all the reasons talking to Grady was a bad idea. "For one, he's married." When neither of them responded, I added, "And they have a kid!"

"Do you know if he's married? Has he said that?" Lennox pressed, leaning forward.

I thought back on our conversations, carefully sifting through each interaction. Grady had mentioned the woman in passing, mostly just when referring to something about Charlie, but I couldn't remember him laying any claim to her while I was around. And he didn't strike me as the cheating type.

Then again, people changed as life went on. I was no exception. It would be stupid to think the Grady standing in front of me was the same Grady I knew from high school.

"I don't know," I said, shoulders slumping in defeat. "I suppose not."

"Then what're you waiting for? An invitation? A red carpet rollout? Believe me when I say that man would do literally anything you asked for."

"He would not," I snapped back. "He's just—*I don't know*—being nice."

Lennox raised a brow. "Being nice for what exactly? He has no stake in this game with you, not anymore. It's been years, and yet he's standing in our yard every day, damn near panting after you for everyone to see." I tried to speak, to argue, to tell her she was wrong, but she beat me to it. "Girl, don't even try to tell me you haven't noticed."

"So, what, Lennox? What if he does? It doesn't mean anything."

"It means everything, actually."

I snorted. "What would you have me do? Walk over to him tomorrow morning and kiss him? Or what if I sent him a dirty text right now, would that—"

Lennox's eyes flashed with trouble. I instantly regretted my choice of words as she said, "That's exactly what you should do! Oh, Cleo. You're brilliant! Where's your phone?" she asked, scanning the immediate area. "We can sort through your lingerie, too, if you're feeling a little bold. I know all the best poses."

Lingerie? Did she not know me at all? I hadn't worn anything outside of cotton staples for years now. They were comfortable, and it wasn't like anyone was going to see them anyway, so it didn't matter.

"It was a joke," I deadpanned. "I'm not actually going to do that."

She stared at me expectantly. "Yes, you are. Now give me your phone."

I felt the strange sense of something tugging out from under me and surged forward as I realized Josie had my phone in her pocket. "Give that back right now."

Josie had the decency to look a little sorry as she gave the device to our youngest sister, who instantly began typing. "It's for your own good. I mean, I had some of the best sex of my life after talking to you about Lincoln—"

Lennox plugged her ears and shook her head, and my phone dropped into her lap. "Nope, don't want to remember that."

"Just because you don't want to talk about it doesn't mean it isn't true," she snapped, taking the phone back. I sagged in relief when Josie handed it back, mouthing a quick, "Sorry."

"Hey! What'd you do that for?" Lennox whined. "I was really getting into it."

I looked down at the screen, feeling both relief and horror at the words on it. Thankfully, Josie had snatched it before she could hit send because I would've died if it'd actually gone out.

CLEO

What're you doing right now? I can't stop thinking about you.

Just thinking about Grady in that context had my cheeks flushing hot and thighs squeezing together. The text was suggestive, slightly flirty, but it had thoughts so vulgar, so filthy, so utterly decadent in every wrong way flitting through my mind. I'd always struggled to embrace sex the way my sisters did, and honestly, I was grateful they didn't shy away from it like I did.

Most of the time, I was too deep in my head to actually enjoy it. The only time I'd been able to let myself be free was with Grady because he let me take control if it was what I needed. Even though my experience was limited, I knew Grady was the best I would ever have, which only made me want him more.

I knew I should delete the words, should tell my sisters they'd overstepped, before heading off to bed and waking up tomorrow with my hangover as my only regret. But as I stared down at the words, something stopped me.

Why shouldn't I be bold? Why shouldn't I go after something I wanted for once in my life? Tomorrow was the last day of camp. If all of this backfired completely, I'd only have to see Grady one last time before he packed it up and went back to Tennessee. And even if the thought of dirty texting him sent shivers down my spine, it didn't have to go that way. Maybe I could just be bold and say what was on my mind. It wasn't a lie to say I was thinking about him, that I'd been thinking about him longer than was appropriate.

I could feel Lennox and Josie's eyes on me as my finger hovered over the send button. Neither of them said anything, for which I was grateful. If I were to do this, it would need to be my decision. No one else could make it for me.

So, with a deep breath, I ignored every single warning bell going off in my mind, closed my eyes, and pressed send.

grady

. . .

BRINGING the bottle of beer to my lips, I scanned the email from my attorney. Barring any complications and Liv's approval, they would be filing our divorce papers first thing on Monday morning. After getting off the phone with my soon-to-be-ex-wife, I listened to the myriad of voicemails I'd been avoiding from our legal and PR teams. It was time to stop ignoring my problems and tackle them head-on, regardless of the shit storm that would follow.

There were already rumors circulating about Liv's and my separation, despite our teams trying their hardest to squash them before they garnered media attention. They ranged from cheating scandals to addiction troubles, none of which were true. However, truth never seemed to matter to the vultures circling for a single juicy morsel of gossip. Some part of me wanted to say fuck it and let them fly, but I wasn't the only one who'd be affected. It was vital for us to control the narrative so Charlie remained unscathed, and Liv's company didn't take any heat.

The moment we filed those papers, it would be mayhem. It was all on public record, and I was willing to bet that people were watching. It wouldn't take long for our phones to start ringing off the hook and paparazzi to station themselves outside our Nashville home. Though it probably wouldn't take long for someone to come sniffing around here, it would at least buy us more time for Charlie's sake.

And Cleo's.

When Liv and I first talked about separating, I'd wanted a clean cut. It wasn't fair to come down here and pursue Cleo when I was technically married to someone else, but Liv asked to wait for both her sake and Charlie's. I couldn't say no to her, not when she'd given me such a wonderful life. Besides, nothing was happening with Cleo anyway. It wasn't like I'd popped down here, professed my love, and was ready to run hand-in-hand for the hills. There was plenty of muddy water we would need to wade through before that ever became an option.

I thought back on my conversation with Liv, unable to stop myself from wondering if I was doing the right thing. I stood by what I said. Just because I wanted something didn't make it right. Despite Cleo not immediately shying away from me when I picked Charlie up earlier, there had been no signs she was receptive to anything other than cordiality.

It was strange to see her now, compared to when we were kids. Even though she was guarded back then, it paled in comparison to how she was now. I couldn't help but wonder if it had to do with her ex-husband. It wasn't my place to pry. By all accounts, I should let it lie until she told me—if that day ever came—but my curiosity was too strong. I needed to know if there was anything to worry about, for her safety and my daughter's.

Grabbing my phone, I typed in Cleo's name in the search bar. The only thing I knew for sure was she'd never changed her last name. I scrolled through the results, finding nothing beyond brief mentions in articles about the ranch or a story about local teachers in Ashwood Independent School District. I scanned for anything that might give me some sort of clue about her life before.

Nothing. Zip. Zilch.

"Dammit," I muttered, taking another sip. Where had she lived before? Montana, wasn't it?

Adjusting the search, multiple hits with her name popped up. Most were similar to what I'd just seen, discussing the connection between Black Springs and a dude ranch in Montana. Apparently, Cleo's ex-husband and his brother were trying to revitalize their parents' legacy by leeching onto the Hayes name.

There was a picture of the three of them standing in front of a large wooden fence. At first glance, they looked content. Happy, even. If I hadn't known her the way I did, I probably would've assumed the same and minded my business, but there was something off. I just couldn't quite place it.

I zoomed in, immediately noticing Cleo's stiff posture and rigid smile despite the grainy black and white picture. Without thinking, I popped his name into the field and waited. It was likely going to be a dead end, but I was desperate enough to try anything at this point.

The moment the search loaded, my blood ran cold. Assault, battery, and harassment were the first few things I saw. I clicked on the first link, seeing his haggard face staring back at me from his mug shot. I'd only met the guy once in passing, right after my mother's diagnosis and my agreeing to marry Liv, but I didn't see a single hint of familiarity in his features. His eyes were soulless, beady little things that were damn near black. I couldn't make out a lick of color in his irises, despite them being listed as blue. He looked high out of his goddamn mind.

"What a low-life piece of shit," I muttered in horror. Was this the type of shit she was dealing with? I was going to be fucking sick.

A notification from the last person I ever expected appeared at the top of my screen, drawing my attention away from the jail log.

CLEO

What're you doing right now? I can't stop thinking about you.

I stared at the message, wondering if I was reading it right.

GRADY

Are you drunk?

That was the only explanation I could think of, because there was no way in hell Cleo was texting me at nearly midnight, telling me how much she missed me. No way at all.

CLEO

Maybe a little

GRADY

Ah, that explains it

CLEO

You didn't answer the question. What're you doing right now?

I fought a smile, knowing damn well I should shut it down. But I could picture her sitting there, frustrated at my avoidance, brows pinched together. Bringing the bottle to my lips, I typed out my reply.

GRADY

Talking to you. I thought that was obvious?

CLEO

One of us is very bad at sexting...

I choked on my beer, spilling what was left of it down my shirt. "Shit, shit, shit," I cursed, pulling it over my head and using it to wipe at my skin. What the hell was happening right now?

GRADY

Sexting? Is that what this is?

CLEO

omg *texting

But sexting was Lennox's idea

God help me.

GRADY

You're gonna regret telling me that in the morning, bluebird.

CLEO

Maybe, but you know what?

I can do what I want

My dick shouldn't be getting hard right now, but I couldn't help it. Especially not as I wondered what she was doing on the other side of the phone. Was she naked? Was she touching herself? God, what I would give to hear her quiet little whimpers of pleasure.

GRADY

Is that what it takes to get you to talk to me? A little liquid courage?

I watched the text bubbles pop up and disappear multiple times before her response finally came through.

CLEO

Unfortunately, I always want to talk to you. I try to stay away, though.

Well, that was the best goddamned news I'd heard all day.

GRADY

Out of curiosity… What's your poison tonight?

CLEO

Why?

GRADY

So, I can slide some your way tomorrow when you come to your senses

CLEO

Not gonna happen. This is a one-night-only deal. Text tonight and forget tomorrow.

GRADY

What about sexting? Is that on the table?

CLEO

This was a horrible idea.

GRADY

I kid, I kid! Don't block me again.

Why can't we talk sober?

I waited for the text bubbles that never came. I was about to give up when my phone rang. Cleo's name flashed on the screen, and I nearly dropped the phone to answer with a hurried, "Hello?"

She laughed, actually laughed, and it was the sweetest sound I'd ever heard. "Someone's eager."

"When it comes to you? Absolutely." I wasn't afraid to admit it, and maybe that was what she needed to hear. Maybe she needed to know I was done playing it cool, not that it'd ever been my forte, and that she held all my cards.

Cleo sighed. "That's why we can't talk sober. It'd be too easy to fall into your trap."

"There's no trap here, bluebird. Just a foolish man waiting with open arms."

I could hear her shifting on the other line and held my breath, wondering if I'd gone too far. To be fair, we could both blame our brazenness on the alcohol, but I didn't want to. If she would let me, I'd have admitted all this sober, too.

"I think I missed that, you know," she breathed.

"Missed what?"

"The nickname."

"I missed you," I replied honestly.

She sucked in a breath. "You can't say things like that." I was about to ask her why, to tell her it was just my way of being honest, when she said, "I'm sorry, this was a mistake. I've got to go."

"Wait, Cleo... Don't—" but it was too late. The line clicked, and I pulled my phone away to stare at the blank screen, mentally berating myself for being such a fucking idiot.

cleo

. . .

19 Years Old

I TAPPED my fingers against the pristine white tablecloth, trying and failing to ignore the pitying looks of guests at their tables. Instead, I stared at the half-burnt candle in the middle of the table near a small vase with a single rose that looked like I felt.

Rain pelted the window as a storm raged outside. The weather had taken a dark turn the moment I stepped inside, something I'd initially been grateful for since I'd spent way too long on my hair and makeup before leaving the dorm. I didn't want all that hard work to go to waste before the night had even begun. Though each minute I stared at the empty seat across from me, I wondered if that was a long shot to start with.

My phone buzzed in my pocket, and I scrambled to get it.

RACHEL

Happy birthday, bitch! Grady better get you something good or I'll kick his ass *winking emoji

My shoulders slumped as I clicked out of her message and into the last one from Grady I'd gotten this morning.

209

GRADY

Can't wait to see you tonight, bluebird <3 I'll be waiting for you!

I stared at the words, trying my hardest not to cry. I'd called him multiple times when I realized he wasn't at the restaurant like he said he'd be, worry bleeding into humiliation as I heard staff whispering about the sad-looking girl who got stood up on her birthday and how pathetic it was I was still here waiting.

As much as I didn't want to believe the hateful thoughts, I couldn't. It wasn't just that he was late; it was the fact I'd gone all evening without a single text or call letting me know he was on his way. I was sick and tired of feeling like a forethought. Silly me for thinking tonight of all nights would be different. I should've known better.

I thought college was supposed to be this grand start to the rest of my life. Everyone told me how much I'd love it, that it was going to be nothing like high school, and I'd finally have some semblance of freedom I'd never had at home. But so far, I was highly unimpressed. Classes took up most of my time, which was my own fault for signing up for the maximum hours allotted, but it was still draining. My roommate was horrible. She spent most of her time screwing the entire athletic department rather than studying, which wasn't even something I cared about. What I didn't appreciate, though, was coming back to the dorms after late nights in the library and seeing her scarf on the handle. I was forced to sit outside in the hallway listening to her fake screams of pleasure through the thin walls. There was no escape from it. At this point, it seemed like I spent more time outside of my room than I ever did inside.

The one saving grace had been Rachel, whose roommate had the same proclivity for extra-curricular activities as my own. She lived just across the hall. We met one night when I came home after class and saw her sitting on the floor. It didn't take long for us to hit it off, often spending our evenings sprawled out in the study room since our dorms were occupied. She was one of the only friends I had, and I was okay with that. Friendships had never come easy to me, not even as a kid. Since I was much older than my sisters, I rarely relied on them for that kind of comfort.

And then there was Grady.

When we made it to Austin, everything had been great. We signed up for most of the same classes so we could spend extra time together, and our dorm buildings were nearby, so it wasn't a long trek across campus to meet up. He snagged a job at a nearby restaurant that doubled as a bar in the evenings. After a month, they allowed him to fill in when someone in the house band called in sick. Seeing him pursue something he loved made me think about my future and what I wanted. He seemed so happy, so carefree, and I wanted that for my life too.

But then he started skipping classes. What started as an occasional thing became a habit, and the random fill-in for the band became permanent. After the end of our first semester, he decided to drop out and pursue music full-time, without considering the consequences of losing his housing and all financial aid. For the past four months, he'd been crashing on his bandmate's couch because he couldn't afford a place on his own. His parents had been so upset when he came home and told them, but what could they do? There was no way to force him to re-enroll. At the end of the day, they wanted him to be happy, and he told them it was what he wanted.

With his focus on music, our relationship suddenly felt like more of a chore than a treat. I spent most of my time trying to fit my schedule into his, which proved nearly impossible. Whenever we did get together, we were usually at some dive bar on Sixth Street, where I often felt like an outlier, or having hurried sex in the front seat of his truck before I walked back to my dorm. Anytime Rachel invited us to hang out, it seemed like Grady always had an excuse as to why he couldn't go. Or when he agreed to go, he would show up hours after he said he would. I heard the same excuse every time. "Sorry, babe. I got held up with the band."

I tried to be understanding. Really, I did. After all, if the situation were reversed, I would want him to support me the same way I tried to support him. But after nearly a year of fighting for his attention, I couldn't help but wonder when I was going to be a priority again. The thought alone made me feel selfish, but I hated having to ask for his time and attention when he used to give it so freely.

"Miss?" I glanced up, meeting the annoyed stare of the waiter who'd come by to check on me no less than fifteen times. "I'm sorry, but—"

"He's going to be here," I insisted, fisting my hands on top of the table. "He's just running late."

"It's an hour past your reservation," he said, loud enough to pique the interest of the couples around me. "We simply can't hold the table any longer. I've already gone against our policy to let you wait this long."

"Please… Just five more minutes," I mumbled, turning pleading eyes his way. "He said he was going to be here."

The man sighed. "I'm sorry, but I have to ask you to leave." The way he held his hand out toward the door told me there was no reasoning with him. Honestly, it was foolish to even try. Even though he never said it, I could tell what he was thinking, and he was right.

Grady wasn't coming.

"Alright." Reaching down, I gathered my purse and looped it over my shoulder. I kept my head down and held onto the strap as though it would save me from the awkward glances around the room, even though I felt every single one bore into me as though they could see the fragile state of my readily breaking heart.

Tears blurred my vision, making it nearly impossible to make out the waiter carrying a tray until it was too late. It felt like it happened in slow motion. Our bodies collided, and marinara sauce splashed down the front of my bright blue dress as the plate landed at my feet. It shattered, sending shards of white porcelain in every direction. The sound echoed off the high ceilings and marble floors, drawing everyone's attention to the spot where I stood.

" I-I'm so sorry," I muttered, bending down to help pick up the broken pieces. "It was an accident—"

The waiter looked up, and I recognized him from one of my classes, though I had no idea what his name was. He glanced at the sauce now staining my dress and began profusely apologizing. "Oh, no. That was my bad. I'm so sorry. I wasn't paying attention—"

"Miss? Let me help you out," the hostess said, coming over with my coat slung over her arm. She ushered me to step over the broken dish, wrapping her arm around me until we reached the entrance. As if this night couldn't get any more embarrassing, now I was being physically escorted out of one of the nicest restaurants I'd ever been in.

I looked around for a place to sit and wait, but each seat was full of waiting patrons who turned up their noses at my distress. The girl glanced over my shoulder to a bench that was half covered by an awning just outside the building.

Point taken.

I pushed open the door, stepping out into the torrential downpour, and took a seat. The wooden slats were still wet, but I guessed it didn't really matter, seeing as I was covered in spaghetti sauce anyway. The brand-new dress I'd bought just last weekend was ruined. Even if I could save it, I wasn't sure I wanted to. There wasn't much about today I wanted to remember.

I didn't know how long I sat there, staring out into the busy Austin streets. Headlights illuminated the sidewalk as cars drove by, and people scurried from building to building to get out of the rain. Music from nearby bars floated out, accompanied by laughter from couples, making me feel even more alone than I had when I left the restaurant.

"Hey! I'm so sorry I'm late." I shifted my gaze to see Grady running up with a big smile on his face. He was completely soaked; his dark band tee and blond hair plastered against his skin. "The band and I—"

"Let me guess..." I mumbled, staring down at my hands. "You lost track of time."

He laughed and ran a hand through his hair. "Yeah, we're working on a new song and hit a groove. You ready to eat? I'm starving." He gestured toward the restaurant and held out his hand for me to take.

I glanced between it and his face. "The reservation was for six, Grady."

He winced, checking his watch to see how late he was. "I know. I'm so sorry, Cleo. Let me make it up to you."

"I waited alone at our table for over an hour," I said, pushing to my feet. "People gawked at me when I told the waiters you were coming and begged them not to kick me out. Do you understand how humiliating that was?"

He glanced at my dress, seeing the large stain down the front. "What happened?"

I wasn't sure why the question made me snap, but it did. All the sad, pitiful feelings I'd experienced moments ago gave way to anger, and all I saw was red. I felt so stupid, waiting in the goddamn rain like some love-sick fool.

I stood up and pushed past him, heading out into the rain. He called my name as I stomped down the sidewalk, but I ignored it. I needed to get out of here. I felt like I couldn't breathe. Why did I wait? Why did I let him see me like this?

His fingers found my arm, and he tugged me back. "Cleo, hey! Where are you going?"

"Let me go, Grady," I said quietly, looking down at our point of contact.

He shook his head. For the first time tonight, I saw real fear in his eyes. Like he knew he'd made a cataclysmic mistake that was about to change the trajectory of his life. I wondered if he saw that same fear in mine. "Bluebird, please—"

"Don't call me that," I choked. I couldn't take it. If he called me that, then I'd fold. "You don't get to call me that anymore."

Grady dropped his hand but stepped forward. I could smell the stale scent of cheap beer and cigarettes clinging to his clothes. Not even the expensive cologne I bought him for Christmas last year could cover it up. "Please, listen—"

I pushed at his chest, hating how wrong it felt. I didn't want the space between us, but I needed it. "Listen to what? Another excuse? Another apology?" I scoffed, feeling the tears begin to fall. "What is that going to do, Grady? Huh? It doesn't erase the memory of yet another one of your disappointments."

"I'll do better," he said, voice breaking. "I promise, I'll do better. Just don't walk away."

"I want to believe you," I whispered. "God, I want to so badly, but I just can't anymore. I'm so sick of feeling like I'm not a priority. Like I don't matter."

Grady's brows furrowed. "Of course you matter! How could you say you don't?"

I stared at him in shock. Was he serious? "It's my fucking birthday, and you were an hour and a half late!" I shouted, balling my hands into fists at my side. People around us stopped and stared, but for the first time tonight, I didn't care. Let them look. Let them see how desperate and pathetic I was. Nothing could hurt as badly as this. "You didn't answer any of my calls or texts. You didn't even send one when you were on your way. The fact remains that not even this was important enough for you to show up on time. I just…" I sucked in a breath, barely able to choke out the next words. "I can't do this anymore, Grady. I can't sit around waiting for you to give a shit about me."

"No, don't do this," he begged. This time, when he stepped closer, I let him. "I love you, bluebird. Please don't leave me."

He framed my face with his hands, bringing his forehead to rest against mine. For a moment, we stood there, breathing each other in. It would be easy to forgive him. To tell him it was okay like I did every other time before, but there was something about tonight that felt different.

I wanted him to succeed so badly, but I wasn't sure he could do it with me at his side. It was always going to be like this. The late nights, the missed calls and texts… None of it was going to change. Even if he did land a record deal, then what? He'd be leaving Austin for Nashville or Los Angeles, and I would still be here—insecure and alone. My broken heart wasn't all his doing. It was also knowing that I wasn't strong enough to weather this storm like I thought I was.

"It's not fair," he said. "It's not fucking fair. I don't want to lose you, and I don't want to choose."

"You don't have to. I'm the one making a choice. I can't do this, Grady. I wish I were the woman you thought I was. I wish I were strong enough, but I'm not." I could barely hear myself over the pounding of the rain around us.

His tightening grip was the only thing holding me together. I wasn't sure how I was supposed to stumble my way home like this, but I knew I had to. "Cleo, please…"

"I hope you make all your dreams come true," I said, stepping back. "I really do. You deserve it."

"Don't fucking say that," he snapped. "Fuck the dreams. Fuck the music. It doesn't mean shit if I don't have you."

I shook my head. "You don't mean that. Not really. You just feel that way right now because this hurts like hell, but there will come a day when you understand all this pain will make sense. Maybe the song you write about this will be the one that does it." I tried to smile, but it broke into a sob.

Grady pulled me into his arms, both our bodies shaking from the realization that this was over. We were done.

"Please don't go, bluebird. Please don't leave me."

I sniffed into his shirt. "I think you left me without knowing it the moment we set foot into Austin," I confessed, and his hold tightened around me. "And I'm not secure enough to handle coming in second place right now. I don't know if I ever will."

"You're first, Cleo. You're the most important thing—"

I gently pulled myself out of his grip and stared at him. "No matter how much you want that to be true, we both know it isn't. Not anymore."

"But I love you. This can't be the end of us. What about the plans we made, huh? Do those not matter?"

"Love isn't always enough, and plans change. The things we wanted… I don't know, Grady. People change."

He scoffed, and the dismissive sound hit me right in the chest. I knew what he was doing, knew he was trying his hardest to protect himself in the same way I was, but it still hurt. All of this did. There wasn't a good way around it.

"Tell me how to come back from this. Tell me we might not have a present, but that we have a future," he pleaded.

I wanted to say that more than anything, but in my heart of hearts… I didn't know what the future had in store for us. Because while I knew I'd never love another person the way I loved Grady, I couldn't say the same for him. Despite his faults, he was the best person I had ever known. Someone else, someone better than me, would come along, and it was only a matter of time before I was forgotten.

"I love you," I said, backing away. My arms wrapped themselves around my waist as if I could hold myself together. "I will always love you."

Grady's fallen face was the last thing I saw as I turned around and headed back to my dorm alone, knowing I'd just made the biggest mistake of my life.

grady

. . .

I DIDN'T SLEEP at all last night, spending the remaining hours before dawn tossing in my bed. I replayed the phone call on repeat, wondering what exactly I'd said that'd crossed the line. Cleo seemed fine with the nickname, but somehow it was me telling her I missed her that triggered her sudden need to flee.

I was already up when Charlie came bouncing into my room thirty minutes before her alarm was supposed to go off. She climbed into my bed, her stuffed unicorn at her side, and curled up next to me. These moments were few and far between. She wasn't overly affectionate unless something was wrong.

"What's wrong, baby?" I asked, pressing a kiss to the top of her head.

She pouted, a trait she'd perfected in her short six years, and turned to me with big, watery eyes. "Daddy, I don't want the camp to be over."

I hated that it was ending, too, even if it was for different reasons. "I know, but we're gonna ask Miss Cleo if someone on the ranch can give you private lessons."

She nodded, snuggling deeper into my side. "What if Miss Cleo says no?"

It was a possibility. While I didn't want to lie to my daughter, I also didn't want to ruin her day before it started. "We'll just talk to her and see what she says, okay? I told you last night I can't make any promises."

Charlie was silent for a long moment. "I'll be sad if she says no, Daddy."

"Me too, kid. I know how much it means to you." It meant a lot to me, too, but I couldn't say that. She was too damn inquisitive, and I didn't have half the answers she was looking for. Instead, I squeezed her tightly. "How about we do something fun tonight, huh? Just you and me?"

This kid rolled her eyes. "We do that every night."

I pulled back and gasped. "Are you saying you don't like hanging out with your dear old dad?"

"I wanna hang out with Miss Cleo, Daddy. Do you think we can ask her to come over for dinner?"

Jesus, kid. Just put me on the spot, why don't you? "Uh, probably not. I'm sure Miss Cleo already has plans."

Charlie gave me a wild grin full of mischief. "But we can ask, can't we, Daddy? And we can ask her to make some cookies?"

"You're gonna make yourself sick with all the cookies," I warned.

She just shrugged and said, "Worth it. They're *so* good."

"Alright, you little cookie monster. Anything else to add to your list of demands?" I asked, brow raised.

Charlie tapped her finger against her little chin, looking ten years older than she was. "Will you play music for me? On the guitar?"

Her eyes darted to the corner of my room where my old case sat. It was littered with stickers from small towns across the country and bands we'd opened for over the years. Inside was the same old instrument I'd played for Cleo a thousand times. I wasn't sure if it was sentimentality that led me to keep it, but it was one of my most prized possessions.

"Alright, baby girl. I think I can do that."

She clapped before turning and throwing her arms around my neck. Her squeeze was tight enough I wondered if I was going to tap out, but she relented and sat back on her heels. "Can we leave early, Daddy? I wanna check on the birdies in the treehouse."

My stomach clenched at the thought of facing that particular memory, but I ignored it. Now wasn't the time to get cold feet about pursuing Cleo. Not when I could feel her walls crumbling bit by bit. Maybe I could talk to her this morning, try to figure out what had her running for the hills when we'd been so close to something. "Anything for you."

THE RANCH WAS ALREADY PACKED when we arrived. It seemed like everyone had the same idea to show up early, which was pretty damn annoying considering the conversation I wanted to have with Cleo.

It didn't take long to spot her. She was in the middle of an eager group of bouncing kids, laughing as they danced around her. She pointed toward the chuckwagon, where a familiar big, surly man with a thick beard was cooking breakfast. It smelled like fucking heaven. Bacon, eggs, and something sweet wafted through the air, covering the scent of horse shit that always hung around.

Casualties of living on a ranch, I suppose.

As though she could feel my stare, Cleo looked up. Her smile faltered as she saw me. I'm sure I looked like an idiot. When her eyes dropped to Charlie, who took off at a dead run in her direction, it returned. My daughter slammed into Cleo, knocking her slightly off balance with the force of her attention.

I couldn't help but laugh, especially as Charlie seemed to mutter an apology before wrapping her arms around Cleo's waist in a hug. She closed her eyes, basking in my daughter's embrace before they stepped apart.

I took my time walking up, stuffing my hands in my pockets so as not to reach for her hand when I stepped up beside them. Cleo glanced at me from the corner of her eye and tucked her hair behind an ear, giving me a view of pink-tinged cheeks. "Morning," she mumbled.

"Morning," I said back, keeping my voice low. "How're you feeling?"

Cleo winced. "Better than I deserve, probably. It was a... long night."

"I know the feeling. I didn't get much sleep last night, either. Too much on my mind, ya know?"

Charlie looked between us. "Were you thinking about what we talked about, Daddy?"

"What were you talking about?" Cleo asked, shifting on her feet. Was that worry or anticipation in her voice? I couldn't tell.

I cleared my throat, placing my hand on top of Charlie's head. Here goes nothing. "Well, someone—and I'm not naming names here—wanted to know if you gave private riding lessons. They're very sad camp is almost over."

"It's me!" Charlie shouted, throwing her arms in the air. "I wanna be able to ride like you and I wanna watch the baby birds grow! Have you checked on them this morning? I asked Daddy if we could get here early so we could check on them. Do you think they're there?"

Cleo laughed—an honest to god laugh that had goosebumps skittering along my skin. It'd been so long since I'd heard it. Especially since I usually got the forced, polite version that I often had to pry out of her. "Well, I have checked on the birds. They were sleeping, so we'll need to let them rest."

"Oh." Charlie's shoulders dropped. "What about the lessons?"

This time, Cleo hesitated. Her gaze flicked between Charlie and me with question. "I'm not really the best one to teach—"

"Please, Miss Cleo?" Charlie begged, clasping her hands in front of her. "It's gotta be you. I don't trust anyone else to teach me."

She crouched in front of my daughter, taking Charlie's hands in her own. "Riding a horse is a lot of work. It's not like riding a bike, so you'd have to practice regularly to make sure you don't lose the skill."

Charlie giggled. "Yeah, Daddy said he could teach me, but Momma and I just laughed at him. She said she'd never seen him on the back of a horse before."

I smiled down at Charlie. "Yeah, apparently the thought of me on a horse was hilarious," I said, glancing toward Cleo. When I did, I noticed the way her demeanor changed. How every muscle in her body seemed rigid with tension.

"Well, I've seen your dad on a horse, and he used to ride very well, but your mom's right. He probably shouldn't be teaching anyone if he hasn't ridden in a while." Cleo stood up. Her fingers danced against her thighs in anxious contemplation. "Alright, Charlie. I have a few weeks before classes start in the fall. I'll do it."

"You will?" Charlie and I asked at the same time.

Cleo nodded and plastered on the fake smile she seemed to have mastered. "Of course. We'll make a horse girl out of you yet."

"Did you hear that, Daddy?" Charlie turned toward me with a grin. "Miss Cleo said I'll be a horse girl!"

"I did, baby girl."

"I can't wait to tell Momma. Can we call her tonight after dinner?"

"Of course. She'll want to hear all about your day." A muscle in Cleo's jaw ticked as I spoke, and I hated it.

"Oh, Miss Cleo! Will you come to dinner tonight? Daddy said you probably had plans, but I told him I was gonna ask anyway."

"Your dad was right. I have plans tonight."

Charlie pouted. "You can't change them to hang out with us?"

"It's a Friday night tradition," Cleo said gently.

"What about tomorrow?" I asked, stepping in. There was so much I wanted to say, that I *needed* to say. My best bet was going to be getting her somewhat alone to do it. And I didn't want her to put space between us because of what happened last night, or what she thought she knew about Liv and I's marriage.

I could only imagine what she was thinking, the way she was likely beating herself up for flirting with who she thought was a happily married man. I wanted to set her straight once and for all, but there was a time and a place for that, and this wasn't it.

"I couldn't possibly—" she began when her youngest sister, Lennox, stepped up beside her.

"Hey, Charlie, girl!" she said, holding her hand out for a high-five. My daughter gave her one, beaming under all the attention. "What's up?"

"Miss Cleo said she's going to give me riding lessons! And we asked her to come to dinner tonight, but she said no."

Lennox slid her gaze to her sister, whose cheeks were flushed entirely. "She did, huh? Why'd she say that?"

"Because we have plans, Lennox," Cleo hissed. "Just like every other Friday night."

Lennox's smile grew into something fierce and wild. "Yeah, but aren't they invited to the potluck too?"

"A potluck??" Charlie asked, turning to Cleo. "Can we come, Miss Cleo?"

"Charlie, we can't go inviting ourselves to someone's house for dinner," I said, cutting in.

Lennox shrugged. "It's an end-of-camp potluck, you should have gotten an email."

Cleo sighed heavily.

"Hmm, must have gotten lost in the mail," Lennox said, throwing a thumb over her shoulder. "I bet Charlie would love some of Mom's homemade banana pudding, huh?" My daughter nodded furiously. "Yeah, I thought so. She's a little sugar fiend."

"Don't I know it," I chuckled. "She's been begging for more of Cleo's cookies."

Lennox nodded, lips twitching as she said, "I'm sure she's the only one, huh?"

"Lennox!" Cleo said, smacking her sister's arm.

"No, Daddy likes them, too!" Charlie said, completely unaware of the shit storm she was creating.

"Oh my god," Cleo muttered, looking utterly mortified, as I uttered a quiet, "Jesus Christ," beneath my breath.

"Kids," I said, clearing my throat. "They say the damndest things."

"I've heard they're super truthful, too," Lennox said, hiding her smile. "Their little ears hear everything while their mouths tell it all."

"Alright, well, I guess that settles it, guess you missed the invite," Cleo said, putting an end to the conversation. When she looked at me, I couldn't help but take a step forward. There were so many emotions in those blue depths. "Dinner's at seven."

"You can hang out after camp is over, though!" Lennox said, holding out her hand for Charlie to take. "Maybe we could see those riding skills."

grady

· · ·

19 Years Old

MY CLOTHES SQUELCHED as I shifted on the shitty wooden barstool in this shitty run-down bar listening to a shitty cover of Hank Williams. I'd ducked inside when the rain turned into a torrential downpour, the neon sign shining like a beacon of hope in a dark tunnel.

I was hoping to drown my sorrows and earn a five-star hangover to distract my mind from the all-consuming agony that settled into my bones. So far, all I'd accomplished was a pounding head from the wailing happening on stage. Apparently, my luck was destined to be shit.

Seriously, I wasn't usually a dick to performers, but I'd make an exception for the man on the stage. It was an open mic night, but he was treating it more like a karaoke bar. His friends sat in the front row, laughing and clapping as he wailed the final note and took a bow.

Fucking idiot.

"God, he was terrible, right?"

I turned to my right, noticing a woman standing beside me who definitely hadn't been there before. She was facing the stage with her elbows braced behind her on the bar. Her blonde hair was piled into a messy bun on top of her head, with thick pieces pulled free to frame her face. She turned toward me, the cheap neon lights above us casting a colorful glow across her features.

"Yeah, he was pretty bad," I agreed, reaching for whiskey and shooting it down. The bartender came back around, and I signaled him for another. Thank god he didn't question the fake ID when I'd slammed it down an hour ago.

"I thought men from the South were supposed to be gentlemen. Shouldn't you have asked if I wanted a drink, too?" she asked. Her tone was flirtatious, but I could tell her heart wasn't in it. And I wasn't in the mood to keep it going for the sake of polite conversation.

Not when I'd just lost the best thing that'd ever happened to me.

"Pretty presumptuous to assume the character of someone you just met," I muttered. "And stereotypes are just that. Not real."

"Ah, but there's usually a nugget of truth in there somewhere." The woman turned my way, giving me a blinding smile. She looked so out of place here. "For instance, I'm from Tennessee and know a thing or two about southern hospitality. Men tend to be chivalrous. They buy your drinks, hold the door for you, get you flowers on a first date—"

I huffed a laugh. "I hate to break it to you, but most men don't do it out of the goodness of their hearts."

"And how would you know? Is that why you won't buy me a drink?" She leaned in, and I got a whiff of her perfume. "Because you don't want anything?"

The bartender came by, pushing a fresh shot in my direction. I stared down at it, trying to avoid her question. I didn't want to lead her on, but I also didn't want to completely shut myself off. I'd blame that decision on the liquor tomorrow. If I thought too hard on it tonight, I was sure I'd lose the last bit of my sanity.

Her laugh captured my attention. "I'm totally messing with you." She stuck out her hand. "I'm Olivia."

I returned the gesture hesitantly. "Grady."

"Oh man, that sounds like a good boy name," she said, scrunching up her nose. "It doesn't match you at all."

"What matches me, then?" I asked, raising a brow.

Olivia plopped her elbow down on the bar. A manicured finger tapped her chin as she studied me. "I don't know. You have this bad boy country vibe going on. Like, you're in boots and jeans—which is common as hell in Texas, don't get me wrong—but the tight black t-shirt and leather jacket give more of a rocker feel."

"Bad boy country vibe," I echoed, shaking my head and taking a sip. The liquor burned going down, and I liked it. Enjoyed it even. I wanted the pain. "I guess that fits."

"Exactly! But the name doesn't match. We should find you a new one."

"I'm not gonna change my name."

She rolled her eyes. "I'm talking about a stage name. You know, one you only use for your public persona."

"I don't need one of those," I replied, slightly annoyed. I mean, I'd toyed with the idea before as a way to separate the two aspects of my life. It'd come in handy when I become somebody.

Well, *if* I became somebody.

Maybe that was why I'd never done it before. It felt like I was pretending to be someone I wasn't. For some reason, it felt like counting my chickens before they hatched. Sure, it could be great in the long run, but what if nothing happened? How silly would I feel? Would it even matter?

A hand waved in front of my face, snapping me out of my spiral. "What'd you say?" I asked, clearing my head.

"I asked what your last name was. We need to see if it's got enough grit," Olivia said, sliding into the seat next to mine.

"Wilde."

"Wait, really?" I nodded. "Okay, well, for starters… There are so many things we could do with that. Can you imagine the merch possibilities?" She splayed her hands in front of her, squinting slightly. "Lawson Wilde—the ride of your life."

I coughed, the beer I'd just taken a sip of going down the wrong way. "That's so corny."

Olivia smiled widely. "That's kind of the point. People love that kind of thing. It can become a key component of what makes you marketable. We've already established you have the bad boy thing going for you," she said, gently smacking my arm. "Capitalize on that. Build your brand from the ground up and make yourself stand out."

I narrowed my gaze, pointing her way with the beer bottle. "How do you know all this shit?"

She shrugged. "My family runs a little business up in Nashville, and I'm a business major with a minor in marketing. This is kind of what I do."

"Then what're you doing here?"

"What do you mean?"

I gestured around the hole-in-the-wall bar. "A girl like you doesn't fit in here." She opened her mouth for a rebuttal, but I held up a hand. "Not like that. I mean, I don't think this is your normal kind of joint, but you live in Tennessee." I held up one finger. "I'm assuming you go to school there, too?" She nodded, and I added another tally. "And your family business is there." Another finger.

"I'm glad to see you can count to three," she said, nodding toward my hand. "But what's your point, Mr. Wilde?"

"I'm just trying to figure you out."

She hummed, reaching out to push each finger down. "I'm actually here on my first business trip. My uncle wanted to check out a few places in Austin, but he had a few last-minute meetings he couldn't reschedule, so he sent me."

"Ah, so it's a test."

She nodded. "Something like that. As for why I'm here,"— she tapped the bar—" I just happened to wander into this little gem when I saw the open mic night. So far, it hasn't been great."

We spun around, looking toward the stage where someone else was trying their hand at George Strait. It was better than the last guy, but it still wasn't great. The kid was pitchy and seemed uncomfortable with the guitar sitting in his lap. Unlike the other, though, you could hear the conviction in his voice.

At least he got more applause than the last guy.

"Yeah, it's not great," I agreed.

She glanced back, nudging me with her elbow. "Why don't you give it a shot?"

"Me?" I asked. "No way. I don't even have my guitar."

"The last time I checked, a guitar wasn't a requirement for using your voice," Olivia deadpanned, reaching over to snag my bottle and take a sip. She made a face that told me she wasn't much of a beer drinker. "God, that's so gross."

I laughed. "Then why'd you drink it?"

"Because I knew you'd give me some bullshit about doing things you didn't want to do. I've done something I didn't want to do, so now it's your turn," she said, gesturing toward the stage.

"That doesn't seem fair since I didn't have a say in it. And I'm sure it's already full. You have to sign up for these kinds of things."

"It's called open mic for a reason," the bartender interjected. "And anything would be better than this shit." He jerked his chin toward the woman who looked like she was trying to deep-throat the microphone.

Well, that was disturbing.

"Got a different mic by chance?" I asked, trying and failing to get the image out of my head.

The bartender reached beneath the bar and pulled one free. I watched, pulling my brows together. "You just keep them handy like that?"

He snorted. "You'd be surprised how often people get rowdy as shit and break 'em."

"Now you have to do it!" Olivia shouted, grabbing my arm. For someone so tiny, she was surprisingly strong. Or maybe it was the alcohol that caused me to stumble ever so slightly. I turned over my shoulder, noting how she covered up her laugh behind her hand.

"You owe me more than a sip of beer," I said.

She straightened her back, jutting out her chin in a challenge. "If you get up there and sing, I'll let you name your terms."

"Is that so?"

"Within reason!" she said quickly. "You have to be reasonable."

"Just like you're being right now?"

"We're at an open mic night, dude. This is kind of what people are here to do," she deadpanned.

And that was when an idea struck. One she'd probably shoot down immediately, but I'd give it my best shot anyway. "Alright," I said, heading toward the stage. I was going to check their list of instrumental songs when I noticed a guitar perched by the stage.

Picking it up, I strummed a few chords to check if it was in tune. It was slightly off, but nothing I couldn't work with. I'd played on worse before, and it wasn't like there were record executives in the crowd to be nervous about.

I grabbed a stool off to the side and brought it to the center. A spotlight shone down as the half-drunk crowd threw out their song requests. I wasn't going to listen to any of them, though.

Olivia had been a great and welcome distraction, but there was nothing that could take away my hurt. Not anything in my control, anyway. Music was my solace, though. My therapy. If anything was going to dull the ache, this was it.

"Well, I didn't plan on doing this tonight, but thanks to a new friend, I'm gonna sing for y'all," I said, turning on the new mic and switching it out with the other. Olivia hooted and hollered as I took a seat and played the first few notes. It was a slower, acoustic version of Slide by The Goo Goo Dolls.

"Holy shit, the kid can sing!" someone from the crowd drunkenly whispered to one of his friends. The rowdiness settled a bit as they listened. I could feel their eyes on me as I stepped back into a moment in time I could never forget.

For a while, it was our song. Instantly, I was taken back to the summer when we'd turned sixteen. Wild. Carefree. We'd been driving down a back road with the windows down, our hair whipping around us and smiles on our faces. She was mine, and I was hers. The rest was supposed to be history. I guess, in a way, it still was.

I wasn't ready to accept defeat, but maybe the only way to prove I was the man for her was by focusing on myself. Maybe I needed time to be a bit selfish without worrying about what it would do to the person I loved.

Before I'd even finished, the patrons erupted into a thunderous, albeit offbeat, applause. I looked to the back of the bar where I'd been sitting. Olivia's fingers flew across the screen of her phone, her tongue peeking out like she was concentrating too hard. When she looked up, there was this sense of wonder on her face that suddenly made me nervous.

Thanking the crowd, I headed back to my seat. I was fully prepared to tell Olivia it was time to pay up on her end of the bargain, but before I could, she stood and extended her hand for me to take.

"I'm getting a weird sense of déjà vu," I joked, looking down at her hand. "Haven't we already done this?"

Her smile was big and bright as she tilted her head side to

side. "Yes and no. I left out a few important details. My name's Olivia Hart."

Hart? Hart. Why did the name sound so familiar? And she was from Nashville...

Oh fuck.

I swallowed. "As in...?"

She nodded. "As in Hartstrings Records. And I'm about to change your life."

cleo

. . .

I STARED at myself in the small bathroom mirror, taking just a single moment to compose myself. With a pounding head and sweat on my brow, I was grateful for how busy the day had been. It meant I didn't have time to sit and dwell on the humiliating conversations of last night and this morning.

Honestly, once Lennox stepped up, I knew there was no way I was going to get out unscathed. I already felt like I was flayed open, all my wounds on display for the world to see, once Charlie had dropped the innocent reminder of her mom. You know, Grady's wife.

God, Cleo, you're so goddamn stupid.

It wasn't like I didn't know he was married. In fact, I often tried to remind myself of that so I wouldn't lose myself in Grady's gravitational pull. But the longer I spent in his presence, the more that little tidbit of information went to the back of my mind as though it was insignificant.

Well, it wasn't. It was actually very significant. There was no way I could keep flirting with a married man, let alone one who broke my heart on multiple occasions over the past seventeen years. And he had a kid for crying out loud. What the hell was I doing? This wasn't like me. It wasn't like me at all.

And why, oh why, did I agree to give her private riding lessons when Grady was on the way out of my life? I should've told them no. I should've referred them to literally anyone else. It wasn't like Ashwood had a shortage of people who could teach her. I knew several people who could use the extra cash and were way better riders than I was. But there was something in Charlie's eyes that made me give in. When it came to that girl, I found it super difficult to say no.

Her father had the same effect.

When I called him last night, I was feeling bold. I thought if I could keep things light I could get this restless feeling out from under my skin, but it backfired. He'd been so intentional with his words. All it did was mess with my head more than ever.

I'd lived with the nickname my entire adult life. Even when he wasn't in my life, it haunted me. I tried to reclaim it. To make it mine and mine alone. So, while it'd been a shock to hear it on his lips after so many years, I knew I'd be able to move past it.

But there was something about the earnest way he'd said he missed me that had done me in. It was too much. It was too far. How could he say he missed me when another woman was wearing his ring? That wasn't fair to me. It wasn't fair to her.

God, did she even know about me? And what did it mean if she did? I was just a blip on the radar, a moment of his past. I didn't mean anything. Not really. At least, that's what I used to think.

"I know what you're doing in there," Lennox sang, rapping her knuckles against the door. "Stop spiraling and get your ass out here. Parents are starting to show up. Even ones you conveniently left off the email list."

I sucked in a deep breath and turned to open the door. Lennox was standing with her arms over her chest, looking far too pleased with herself. I loved my sister dearly, but I was more than a little annoyed with her at the moment. "What? You can't handle some parents?" I asked, brushing past her. "Seemed like you were doing one hell of a job earlier."

She laughed. "Oh, come on, sissy. Don't be mad. You looked like you needed a push, so I gave you one. It's just that simple."

"I needed a push?" I asked, turning to face her.

"Just like last night—"

I waved my hand to cut her off. "Len, he's married. He's got a kid. Last night was an epic mistake, and inviting him into our home for dinner would be another one. I need to put as much space between us as possible before—"

Lennox raised her brows, waiting for me to finish, but I snapped my mouth shut. There were some things I wasn't comfortable admitting out loud, and the fact that I was opening myself to the possibility of getting hurt was one of them. It sounded ridiculous when I thought about it. It'd been less than six months since Thomas and I's divorce was final, and I'd sworn off all relationships until I figured out what I was doing with my life. Not that I'd expected to jump headfirst into anything this soon anyway.

Not that there was anything to jump into in the first place.

"I just mean it's inappropriate. That's all," I said, shifting on my feet.

Lennox studied me, her gaze all-knowing. I wasn't sure how she did it. I was nine years her senior, and yet it somehow felt like she knew so much more than I did. She was fierce and had the drive I wished I could have. When it came to what she wanted, she didn't ask for permission to take it. She just did. That was why she and Bishop worked so well together. He needed someone to coax him out of his shell, and she needed someone to keep her grounded. I loved seeing her so in love, but this side of her made me feel small. It was my own insecurities, I knew that much. But I should've been the one urging her to follow her dreams. Not the other way around.

"Inviting someone to a camp potluck isn't inappropriate, Cleo. It's a fucking camp for kids, not a sleazy nightclub. No one said anything had to happen. Plus," she gestured behind me to the crowd of people milling about, "It's casual. A chance to hang out without the pressure of all the bullshit."

"Nothing *can* happen," I stressed. I was choosing to ignore the rest because even though we may have been hosting a little party for the parents and the kids, there wasn't a chance in hell I would get out of this night unscathed. It's why I'd tried to avoid it altogether.

Lennox looked down and bit her lip. "But do you want it to?"

"Of course not," I said, shaking my head. No, that would be insane. It would be crazy. Grady was a thing of my past, not a moment in my future. We'd had our chance, and it hadn't worked out. Plus, he was married.

Married, married, married.

I hated the word. Hated everything it represented. But I especially hated it when thinking about Grady.

Lennox hummed but didn't say anything else. Instead, she wrapped her arm around my shoulders and led me from the barn into the afternoon heat. Cook was at the chuckwagon dishing out grilled hamburgers and hot dogs to everyone in line as music filtered through the speakers of Bishop's truck. Kids ran back and forth from table to table as parents chatted about their weeks. Everyone seemed to be having a great time.

Up ahead, I could see my parents by the wagon talking to Cook. Dad's hand was tucked into the back pocket of Mom's jeans, and she was leaning into him like he was the only thing keeping her up. Even as a kid, before I truly knew the meaning of love, I always admired their relationship. They loved each other like they were in some epic romance novel. It wasn't always perfect. In fact, they were often messy, but their love never wavered. Not even when they fought like cats and dogs.

Sometimes I wondered what their secret was, how it was possible for two people who seemed so different to fit together so perfectly. Everyone always said opposites attract, but I didn't believe that much. Grady and I had been opposites, so had Thomas and I. Neither of those relationships worked.

The reason Thomas and I broke apart had more to do with the abuse than our differences. If things hadn't turned dark, I knew we would've still been married. We'd been content with one another, or at least, I had been. It was easy, convenient. Love had never been a factor in our marriage. After Grady and I broke up, I'd vowed not to seek it out again. I couldn't let myself be hurt like that. Not by him. Not by anyone.

I needed to remember that vow.

"They look happy, don't they?" Lennox said, pulling me tighter.

I smiled, though it felt weak. "They do," I agreed. "It's good to see them smile like this. The past year has been hard. I think it killed Dad not to do the clinic in June."

"This was a good call, though." She gestured around at the people around us. "Not just for what it added to the community, but for all of us. I think we've been so preoccupied with Dad's heart and Josie's pregnancy we forgot what it's all about."

There was a subtle upturn on Lennox's lips as she scanned the scene in front of us. She was made for this life. Both of my sisters were. Of that, I had no doubt. It felt good knowing my parents could pass down their legacy to people who were worthy of it. I certainly wouldn't know what to do with it, nor did I want it.

I bumped her shoulder. "You're gonna run the shit out of this place someday."

"Someday?" she asked. "I run the shit out of it now."

We both laughed. "Bishop may disagree," I said, nodding in the broody man's direction. He was leaning up against the fence line, talking to Lincoln, posture relaxed, even though I knew he'd been working his ass off in the heat all day.

Lennox smirked as Bishop glanced over at us, eyes narrowing at his fiancé's expression. "Oh, he knows it, too. Although I let him take control in the bedroom. It's so much more fun that way."

"I swear to god, Lennox," I muttered, shoving her out of her little daydream. "I don't want to think about that!"

Lennox shrugged. "Might do you some good to submit a little sis. If only there was a very willing and eager participant." She turned, tapping her lips with her pointer finger until she made a triumphant little sound. "Ooh, like that one!"

I turned in the direction she pointed and nearly stopped breathing at the sight.

Grady was stepping out of his old truck; the same one he'd had when we were kids. The paint was slightly more faded and chipped than it had been before. I could still remember the feel of the scratchy cloth interior against my bare skin after we made love, or the smell of the leather air freshener always hanging from the rearview mirror.

He was wearing a green, short-sleeved Henley that show-cased the rippling muscles in his forearms, paired with jeans and boots. The fabric was tight around his shoulders in a way that l sent heat rushing to places I'd rather not think about. My body was not on the same page as my heart. If it were, I wouldn't be in the unfortunate predicament I currently found myself.

Grady had always been in shape, but had leaned more on the tall and lanky side of the spectrum when we were kids. Now, his six-foot, three-inch frame had filled out with muscle, and I wasn't mad about it. This version of him was all man, but I could still make out the features of the carefree boy I fell in love with nearly twenty years ago.

"Goddamn," Lennox said, shaking her head. "He's ten times hotter than your other ex."

I jabbed her in the stomach. "Will you stop it? I can't go down that road."

She groaned beside. "My god, Cleo. Will *you* stop it? Get out of your head and live a little."

"He's married—"

"Have you asked him?"

I paused, ready to tell her it didn't—or rather, shouldn't—matter. He was off limits regardless, wasn't he? "No," I grumbled.

She clapped her hands together. "Wonderful! So, you'll ask him if he's still married, and if he is, that'll put an end to it. If not..." she trailed off, waggling her brows like a teenager who just found out something scandalous.

"If not nothing," I snapped. "There's no universe in which Grady Wilde—"

"Oh, this outta be good," came a smooth, deep voice that made me want to melt. We both looked over, noticing the man in question standing right in front of us. He had an amused smile tilting up his lips, and I hated how much I loved it. "What am I, or am I not, doing in this universe?"

"Noth—"

Lennox pulled me tighter. "She thought you'd show up empty-handed, and it looks like she was right! Didn't your mom ever tell you good guests bring dishes to dinner?"

At the mention of his mom, Grady's smile faltered a touch. We hadn't spoken about Marsha's passing at all since he'd been back; it'd never come up. Now, I was kicking myself for staying silent as years of grief and pain flashed in his eyes.

"Marsha was actually the best host," I said, meeting his gaze. "I'm sure Grady has something in his truck."

"Y—yeah," he said, clearing his throat. "Made some mac-n-cheese. It's kind of my specialty. Although" he paused, looking around, "I don't think I've made enough for everyone."

Lennox, who didn't appear to catch the ripple of unease, continued as though nothing had happened. "We'll hide it in the house so we can keep it to ourselves. Cleo can show you where to drop it off." Lennox waved at someone behind Grady. "Now, if you'll excuse me…" She flitted off before I had a chance to beg her to stay.

"I'm sorry about her," I rambled, glancing at my feet. The words kept tumbling out before I could stop them. "She's never had a filter, and she said the first excuse that popped into her head, which isn't always the best one. Lennox didn't know about your mom, and she wouldn't have brought her up if she had—"

Two large, warm hands fell on my shoulders, moving up to brace my face. Grady tilted my head up, forcing me to look at him. "It's okay, I'm not worried about it. Breathe for me." I did as he said, letting my eyes drift close as I sucked in a deep breath and held it for four long seconds. "Let it out," he said smoothly. I did, opening my eyes to find his trained on me. His thumb grazed my cheekbone, and I was lost to his touch, thoroughly grounded in the moment by him. "Better?"

"I'm sorry. I just—"

"Why're you apologizing?"

"Daddy! Are you and Miss Cleo going to kiss?"

We both jumped apart at the sound of Charlie's voice. She was staring up at us with a popsicle in one hand and a smile on her face.

"What? No!" I said quickly, smoothing out the wrinkles in my t-shirt. "Of course not."

Charlie's brow furrowed. "You don't wanna kiss him?"

"Oh my god, what is happening?" I muttered under my breath as Grady howled with laughter.

"Yeah, Cleo? Don't you want to kiss me?" he asked, turning to me with the smuggest grin I'd ever seen.

I was going to kill him. Lennox would be my accomplice. She always said how many good spots there were to dispose of a body. Maybe it was time to give her a chance to find out just how good.

"That would be inappropriate," I said back, ignoring how wrong it felt to say out loud. And then, just for the sake of putting everything out there, I said, "I bet your mom wouldn't like that too much."

"Mommy?" Charlie asked, scrunching up her little nose. "She wouldn't care. She always says she hopes Daddy finds someone to give him kisses the way he deserves."

"Charlie," Grady warned, but it was too late. The truth was out, spilled straight from the lips of a child, whether I wanted it or not.

I turned to Grady, suddenly connecting dots I'd been too stupid to put together before. I mean, he'd literally driven across state lines to bring his daughter to a one week horse camp, made sure his father was out of town so he could have the house to himself, and was constantly making flirty digs about wanting me back. Would a married man do that? He could, theoretically. Married men did stupid shit all of the time. But I knew Grady better than that, didn't I? Despite the years between us, despite the fact we'd grown from clumsy sixteen-year-old kids to adults who didn't have their shit together, I still knew him.

"What, Daddy?" Charlie asked, tilting her head to the side. Her lips were tinged blue from the sweet concoction currently melting all over her hands. "It's true." One of the kids called her name, and she took off running in their direction, leaving us alone with the weight of her confession.

He looked away, giving me a full view of the muscle feathering along his jaw. Was it from irritation or embarrassment?

Maybe both? If the roles were reversed, I'd probably feel some type of way, too. Grady didn't know it, but Charlie's revelation had given me the motivation I needed to ask the one question that had been consuming me since he showed back up on my ranch a week ago.

"So, you and your wife—"

"Ex," he said, shifting his gaze back to me with a careful assessment. "We're separated. The papers are being filed next week."

Oh. For some reason, that wasn't what I was expecting. I would've assumed they were already divorced, or in the middle of some heated custody battle, not on the eve of filing. Was that why he got out of town so quickly?

He turned toward me, rubbing his hand along the back of his neck. "There's so much I want to tell you, so much I need to say, but not here. Not like this." He gestured around us, and I couldn't help but chuckle.

"Yeah, this probably isn't a conversation you want to have out in the open," I agreed.

"But I want to have it, bluebird. Please don't think I don't."

I nodded. If his words hadn't convinced me, there was something in his voice that would've done the trick. It was teetering on the edge of desperation—a feeling I had more experience with than I cared to admit.

"I believe you," I said, ducking my head. And then, before I lost my nerve, I asked, "Is the option for dinner tomorrow still on the table? Literally and metaphorically, I mean."

Grady bit down on his lip. The move was so damn distracting it should've been illegal. "The table, the floor, the fucking bed. Anywhere you want."

"Let's start with the table," I said slowly. Oh god, what was I doing? Was this *flirting*? When was the last time I'd done that? It was strange and foreign, but I couldn't help myself on some level. It was like he drew out the side of me that wanted to be cute and playful.

"Table it is," he agreed. "Mind if Charlie and I stay for dinner, though? Those burgers smell heavenly, and I have a feeling you'll fall in love with me again once you try my mac-n-cheese. I've come a long way from spicy ramen and microwaved nachos."

I waved toward the chuckwagon. "I'd hate to deprive you of sustenance, and will admit to being the slightest bit curious to see how your cooking skills have evolved."

"You won't be disappointed. I promise. Wanna get us two burgers while I go grab the casserole dish?"

"Sure. You still like everything on it?"

He nodded, grinning. "Heavy on the—"

"Mustard," I finished for him. "I remember."

"I guess you do," he said, staring at me for a beat longer before he turned and headed toward the truck.

As I ambled over to Cook to put my order in, I couldn't stop thinking about what he said. "I have a feeling you'll fall in love with me again once you try my mac-n-cheese." Sure, it was corny and silly, but it left me feeling all twisted up inside because all I'd wanted to say in the moment was, "Maybe I never stopped."

grady

· · ·

23 Years Old

GROWING UP, I always heard people talking about how fast life could change. How, in the blink of an eye, you could go from living on top of the world to feeling like the dirt beneath someone's boot. I never believed them until I was standing out in the pouring rain, watching the woman I loved walk away from me.

I thought I had learned my lesson, but life had other plans.

"You would think they'd have more comfortable seating arrangements in there since, ya know, they're telling people they have cancer," I muttered, settling into the driver's seat of Mom's tiny car. "For fuck's sake, it's the least they could do."

Mom giggled but smacked my arm with the stack of pamphlets the doctor had given her when we walked out. "Young man, you may be an adult now, but that does not mean I want you saying the word fuck so freely," she scolded half-heartedly.

"You swear like a sailor," I said, pulling out of the parking lot and hitting the road back to Ashwood.

"Yeah, but I have fucking cancer now. What's your excuse?" she joked, although it fell flat. The car was filled with uncomfortable silence as I came to a stop at a red light. We hadn't put on music, but my fingers tapped along the steering wheel to a tense beat only I could hear.

When Dad called a few weeks ago to tell me Mom was having health problems, I thought it was some kind of joke. I hadn't taken it seriously, thinking it was just their way of telling me she was having a root canal or some shit, but then he hadn't laughed.

There wasn't a trace of humor in his voice as he told me about the lump they'd found in her right breast, or the way the biopsy had come back with detection of cancerous cells. She now had a meeting with oncologists and surgeons to develop a plan for her future.

He told me I needed to come home, and so I did.

I didn't stay in Austin long after Cleo and I broke up. It was too hard, and without her, I had no reason to stay. I'd only come to the city because it was supposed to be the best of both worlds for us. While the music scene in Austin was growing rapidly, the one in Nashville was even more impressive.

Meeting Liv that night had changed my life in more ways than one. When my life felt like it was coming to an end without Cleo, Liv had given me a purpose. Hope. She wasted no time setting up a meeting between her uncle, John, and I in the weeks after our run-in. Before I knew it, I was flying up to Nashville, standing in a flashy skyscraper, and shaking hands with one of the men who helped shape the music industry as we knew it.

Now, I had a band, and we were travelling around the country, opening for artists I'd only dreamed of. John signed me with one of their sister labels and told me I needed to give him a reason to sign me to Hartstrings within five years. The guys and I were well on the way to doing that. Our recent album was selling significant numbers, and we had a meeting next month, hopefully to bring us up to the big leagues.

But now, I wasn't so sure what my future would look like.

Mom was going to need help with all the doctor's appointments and radiation treatments. She was going to get worse before she got better. It wasn't fair for Dad to handle on his own.

Luckily, the band and I didn't have any appearances scheduled until our tour kicked off next month, so I was relatively free to figure my shit out from the discomfort of my childhood bedroom.

"Grady, I—"

"My mom has fucking cancer. That's my excuse," I said, forcing a smile for her benefit. The one she returned was small enough, but I'd take it. There was enough on her plate. She didn't need me to break down or show every single fear I had. I needed to be strong for her like she'd always been strong for me.

Mom settled back into her seat. "I guess that makes sense then. I'll allow it."

BY THE TIME we made it back to Ashwood, Mom was asleep. I quietly put the car into park and looked over at her peaceful features. At a glance, it was easy to forget she was sick. There was no pain, no worry, no stressful talk of radiation or surgery or cancer.

But then my gaze drifted to the papers clutched in her fist, which had the six ugly letters printed across the top of almost everyone, and the realization kicked back in.

My mother had fucking cancer.

Up ahead, I saw Dad standing on the front porch. He was leaning against the railing, staring at the car. He looked exhausted. The past few weeks had drained a lot out of him, and now it was catching up. His work had been lenient, letting him take as much time off as he needed, but he wasn't sleeping. I'd only been here a week and almost every night he'd taken to sitting in the recliner in their bedroom or staring out the kitchen window into the dark, empty night.

I got out of the car, nodding his way as he came down the steps. "Thanks for taking her today," he said, clapping my back. "Couldn't miss this meeting at work."

"It's no problem, Dad. I was happy to do it."

"She asleep?"

"Yeah, she passed out pretty early on."

He shifted on his feet. "That's good. She doesn't seem to get much these days."

"You don't either," I said, nudging him with my elbow. "Don't think I don't notice."

"I'm not worried about myself," he grumbled. "Just wanna make sure she doesn't wake up and need me."

I sighed. "You need to take care of yourself just as much as she does," I said, following him around the car to Mom's side. He gently pried open the door and undid her seatbelt before hoisting her into his arms. She stirred slightly, but he quietly murmured reassurances before walking her into the house.

I walked into the kitchen as Dad helped Mom settle into bed. Might as well get a drink because I didn't have anything else to do. Opening the fridge, I saw two choices. Sweet tea that looked like it was ready to be thrown out, or an array of Coors bottles. Opting for the harder of the two, I grabbed a beer and twisted the cap off.

Being back in Ashwood made me restless. I was haunted by the past, assaulted by memories. Even in my own home, I couldn't escape Cleo's suffocating presence. The kitchen? We had a brownie batter fight with my mom the night after our last high school football game. The living room? It was the first time she'd ever heard me play. My bedroom? God, that one almost hurt the worst. I still remember the sounds she made when we messed around for the first time when Mom and Dad had gone out to pick us up lunch.

I was halfway through my beer when Dad came in. He looked down at the bottle with raised brows before letting out a breath and grabbing his own. "You hungry?" I asked. There wasn't much in the fridge, so I'd definitely have to pick up some groceries tomorrow to avoid starving, but I'm pretty sure there were some Hot Pockets in the freezer or something.

"Naw," Dad said. "Don't have much of an appetite right now. I'll make your mom some soup later. It's about all she'll eat right now. I think the nerves are keeping her stomach tangled in knots."

I knew the feeling well. "Let me know if you change your mind. I can pick us something up."

Dad stared at me as I finished off the bottle, immediately tossing it in the trash before I reached for another. "Why don't you go out tonight?" he asked, snatching it from my grasp.

"What? Go out where?"

He shrugged. "I don't know. The Lonestar? Heard there's some live music. Might be fun."

I chuckled. "Spending the night alone at my hometown bar, listening to music doesn't really sound like a great time, Dad."

"There's a rodeo tonight. Could be fun, ya know?"

I stared at him. "A rodeo? How in the world would that be fun?"

"I don't know, Grady. Just thought you might wanna get out of the house for a bit."

"I'd rather go sit alone at the bar," I muttered.

"What if I want to go?" Mom asked from the doorway. She padded over and snatched the unopened beer from Dad's grip. We both watched as she twisted the cap and took a sip. Mom had never been much of a drinker, so to say it was more than a little out of character was putting it mildly.

"Marsha! You can't have that," Dad chided.

She rolled her eyes. "I can do what I want. I don't start treatment until next week, and I don't want to spend this last weekend moping around the house with you two. So either we'll go to this thing together, or I'll go by myself."

"Like hell you will," Dad mumbled.

Mom looked at me, brows raised in question as she brought the bottle to her lips. "Well? There's one in. Care to make it two?"

"Mom, you slept all the way home from your appointment."

"Exactly! I've had plenty of rest. I'm ready to go. Come on, Grady." She set the bottle down next to me and took my hands in her own, tugging on them slightly. "Let's have some fun tonight. Who knows how many nights like this we'll have?"

"Jesus, Marsha," Dad cursed.

Mom waved him off. "I don't care if it gets him to say yes."

She looked up at me with big, wide eyes. I was crumbling and fast. It didn't matter how much I definitely didn't want to go to an Ashwood rodeo; I'd have walked through flames for her if she asked me to in that moment.

Maybe it wouldn't be too bad. I could stay put in the stands, I didn't have to venture out and mingle with people. It'd be fine. Everything would be fine.

"Fine, but just because you pulled the cancer card," I said, lips twitching into a smile.

Mom flung her arms around my neck, squeezing tightly. "This is why you're my favorite kid," she said before grabbing the beer and heading back to their bedroom.

"I'm your only kid!" I called back, listening to the sound of her laughter as a response.

Dad finished his drink and chucked the bottle in the trash. "That woman's gonna be the death of me," he muttered.

"At least you won't be bored."

He paused, tilting his head to the side. "Ya damn right about that."

grady

. . .

23 Years Old

JUST LIKE I thought it'd be, the parking lot of the Ashwood fairgrounds was jam-packed with trucks as far as the eye could see. If people weren't at the bar getting drunk, they were at some roping or bull riding event, watching other people fall on their asses. It looked like everyone and their damn mother had shown up. Looking over at my company for the evening, I guess I was no better. "Oh, this is going to be so much fun," Mom said, squeezing my hand. She hadn't let go since I helped her out of Dad's truck. "We haven't gone to the rodeo in years."

It hadn't been an accident. At least on my part. I'd stayed far away from Ashwood since Cleo and I had broken up. Cleo's family was at damn near every rodeo event, so this was the last place I wanted to be. I wasn't dumb, I knew someone from the Hayes crew would be here tonight, and there would be no avoiding them. My only hope for the night was to make Mom happy while hoping none of them saw me and went back to Cleo to tell her I was in town.

I'd heard she'd moved back to Ashwood after she graduated. Mom kept in contact with her and said she was now teaching at the local elementary school. I was happy for her. It seemed like she was following her dreams and doing all the things she'd said she wanted to. I knew it couldn't have been easy, but she did it anyway.

All without me.

Though the thought fucking killed me, sometimes I wondered if she'd been right all along. That neither of us was ready for the level of commitment we pledged to one another, and our goals weren't attainable if we couldn't give them one hundred percent. I still held on to the notion of *someday*, because the one thing I refused to believe was we weren't meant for one another. Even after all this time, I still felt her beneath my skin.

Some days it was comforting. Others it was consuming. I just didn't know which one it would be when I woke up each morning.

I paid for our admission, and reluctantly let Mom drag us across the grounds to the bleachers nearest the chutes. If I had my choice, I would've picked the opposite end. My chances of running into someone were less likely that way, but Mom had always liked being close to the action. She always said she couldn't see very well, and while, yes, she did have terrible eyesight, I couldn't help but wonder if that was the case in this instance as I stared at the Black Springs Ranch logo pasted on the front of the gates.

The events had already begun by the time we took our seats. We watched the last few contestants in the steer wrestling round finish up as the announcer started talking about team roping. I didn't listen to most of it. I'd heard the speeches before. It was damn near the same no matter where you were, but as I heard a familiar name, I perked up. "This sport owes a lot to Ashwood's own Douglas Hayes and the crew out at Black Springs Ranch. You know his daughter is competing tonight in the barrel race? Truly, such an amazing and gifted family."

My chest constricted as the first mention of the Hayes family settled around us. Mom tried to talk to me about Cleo for years.

At first, I opened up. I didn't want to admit to my mistakes at first. Acknowledging I'd lost myself in the excitement of the Austin music scene felt like such a cop-out. It was easier to blame her for not being more understanding. But after the restless nights turned into restless months, I began to wonder how much of that was true.

Could she have approached things differently? Sure. But so could I. My list of faults was a mile long, and if I could go back, I would've done so many things differently. I wouldn't have dropped out of school and prioritized music over everything, especially not over her. I hadn't realized it in the moment, too focused on all the shit I was trying to do for me.

I think, even before she spoke the words, I knew I was going to lose her. Maybe it was why I subconsciously tried to preemptively fill the void with something I knew I wanted. If I'd known that was going to be the nail in our coffin, I would've given it all up. Even if only to avoid seeing the look of complete and utter devastation on her face, the way every bit of light remaining in her eyes had died as she walked away from me for good.

Mom squeezed my arm, and I gave her a tentative smile. I was sure my thoughts were written all over my face. Being back home was hard. Too complicated for my liking. At least in Nashville, I didn't have to watch my back around every turn. Maybe that was why I liked it so much, why I never came home anymore. It was too hard. I wasn't even sure I could do this, but I knew I was damn well going to try for Mom's sake.

"I'm thirsty, baby," Mom said, turning my way. "Will you go and get me a beer?"

"You trying to get drunk?" I asked.

She looked away, hiding a smile. "I don't know. Maybe. I just want to live a little tonight. I want to have a perfect night with my perfect family."

"You sure you're not already drunk?"

"Oh my god, you're being a buzzkill. I knew you were like your father, but I didn't realize you got that from him, too."

"Hey!" Dad and I protested at the same time. "I'm not a buzzkill," he murmured.

"Honey, you've kept one hand on that damn cell phone for the last month, just in case I go down. I wouldn't be surprised if you had 9-1-1 on speed dial."

Dad looked down, noticing the way his hand was, in fact, resting beside his pocket. "I don't know what you're talking about. Doesn't sound like me."

I leaned over and pecked Mom on the cheek. "Alright, fine. But just because you asked so nicely," I deadpanned.

"There's the sweet boy I raised," she said, lightly patting my cheek with her hand. "Thank you, baby."

I squeezed past the folks sitting next to us and jogged down the stairs, keeping my head down in hopes I didn't run into anyone from high school. I didn't consider myself well-known in any capacity, but there were a handful of times people slid into my DMs after years of silence, asking for autographs or concert tickets.

Yeah, absolutely the fuck not.

After standing in line for far longer than it should've taken, I had three beers in hand and was walking back to my seat when someone bumped into me from behind, spilling all three drinks at the feet of two women. I turned around, ready to tear into whoever it was, but I only saw the backs of three kids' heads as they sprinted to the far end of the arena.

"God-fucking-dammit," I cursed, reaching down to pick up the cups as a pair of boots turned to face me. "I'm so sorry, ma'am. Let me help you clean—"

"Grady?"

I jerked my head up, staring into the deepest blue eyes I'd ever seen. The ones that continued to haunt me to this day, every time I closed my eyes. "Cleo?"

Her mouth gaped open, quickly snapping it shut as she scanned the area. "What're you doing here?"

I stood up, clocking the way her eyes tracked the movement, how the pulse point in her neck kicked up several notches as she sucked in a breath. God-fucking-dammit had been right. What had I been thinking earlier, telling myself she'd been right to let us go? Looking at her now, all I could think about was how wrong it was her hand wasn't in mine.

"Uh, I'm in town to see Mom. You know, just helping with stuff," I stammered out. "She asked to come tonight, so..." I gestured to the fairgrounds around us. "Here I am."

Her fake smile faltered. "She told me. I'm so sorry, Grady."

"It's fine. She'll be fine. She's too tough to be taken out by something like this." I knew she talked to my mom on a somewhat regular basis, but for some reason, the fact she knew about the cancer kind of pissed me off. It wasn't about me, I knew that at the end of the day, but why didn't she reach out? Why didn't she ask how I was doing? Losing my mom would destroy me. Didn't that warrant a text message?

Then again, what was she supposed to do? Text me out of the blue and tell me she was sorry about the diagnosis? It would've pissed me off more. None of this was fair.

"She is," Cleo agreed. "How long are you in town for?"

"Dunno," I said, rocking back on my heels. "I don't have anything going on until next month. Figured I'd probably hang around until then."

Cleo nodded. "Good. That's good. I know she misses you. She talks about you all the time."

I couldn't help but laugh. The sound must've taken her by surprise because those big eyes widened like she'd done something wrong. "I'm sorry. It's just... This is fucking weird, right? The small talk bullshit? I mean, it isn't like we're strangers." I shook my head when she continued to stare at me like a deer caught in the headlights. "Maybe it's just me, but—"

"No," Cleo said hurriedly, stepping forward. Her hand landed on my arm in what I'm sure was supposed to be some kind of polite gesture, but it burned like fire the moment our skin touched. She jerked her hand back, clinging to the beer can in her hands instead. "It's definitely not just you. I was just thinking about that, honestly. It's like I'm second-guessing what I want to do or say right now because I could say the wrong thing."

"Well, what's going on in your head right now?" I asked.

"Right now?"

"This very instant."

Cleo bit down on her lip, gaze trailing from my eyes to my boots and back up. My style hadn't changed much, but I did learn how to dress it up a bit. Gone were the days of throwing on a wrinkled T-shirt and jeans and walking out the door. Now, they were hung up and starched. I wore rings and a watch. Even put on a spritz of cologne before walking out the door.

Okay, maybe I put on two because I knew I'd likely run into someone I knew here, but still.

"You want honesty?" she asked, raising her brows.

"Don't I always?" *Even if it fucking kills me.*

"On some level, you look the same. I can recognize the same boy I used to know, but I can see how much has changed. Like, you're turning into an actual adult? It's weird," she laughed.

I could tell she was still holding back, but for her to admit what she had was huge. Cleo usually kept her thoughts and emotions close to her chest. The fact she was willingly giving them away like that was reassuring.

"I could say the same about you, you know. You look amazing, Cleo." She blushed under my praise. Some part of me got a twisted sense of satisfaction about still being able to elicit that kind of reaction. "Beautiful," I added, because fuck it. Why not?

"You too," she said, before smacking her forehead. "I mean, handsome. You look handsome."

"You can say I look beautiful," I chuckled. "Handsome is overrated these days, anyway."

"Is it? I wouldn't know." She tucked a strand of hair behind her ear. "Are you still doing the music thing?" Her words faltered ever so slightly over the last two words. Not because she wasn't interested, but I think because it was obviously a sore spot—the big ass elephant between us. It was what drove us apart.

And it hurt me, too. I never asked my mom about what Cleo was doing, she just told me. I had no choice in the matter. Did she not do that with Cleo, or was this just a polite conversation?

I nodded. "Yeah, I am. In Nashville, actually. I didn't stay in Austin for long…" I trailed off, sucking in a deep breath. "Mom tells me you're teaching now. Elementary, right?"

Cleo's eyes flashed in surprise. "Yup. This is my second year full-time. I had some substitute teaching experience before I accepted the position. I wanted to get my master's at UT, but I think it was hard for Mom and Dad when I was gone, so I'm doing it online. You know how it is. Being the eldest daughter isn't easy."

"Yeah, no. I often tell myself the same thing," I said, and she laughed.

"Okay, smartass."

I placed my hand over my chest. "Cleo Hayes, was that a curse word dropping from your pretty lips?"

She pushed on my shoulder, letting her fingers softly trail down my arm before dropping altogether. That was twice now she'd touched me, but the first time she hadn't immediately pulled away. Goosebumps erupted along my skin, and my dick, who had been lying low like a good boy, suddenly decided now was the time to wake up.

Clearly, I was doing great.

"I've grown up a little bit," she said, shimmying her shoulders and straightening up. "I'm not the same little girl you used to know."

God, wasn't that the truth? It didn't take the word ass slipping out to tell me that much. She was standing before me in a knee-length dress and boots, her skin sun-kissed and freckled from summers outdoors. Her hair was lighter than I remembered, probably for the same reason. But she didn't look timid like she had when I took her out on our first date. There were nerves, obviously, but she stood her ground.

"I can see that," I murmured. My shirt rose up as I lifted my hand to run through my hair, and her eyes drifted to the ink peeking out from under the fabric.

"What's that?" she asked, pointing toward the exposed skin.

Quickly, I dropped my arm and pulled down the shirt. "Oh, it's nothing. Just something I got a few years ago."

"Can I see?" she asked, stepping forward. Her eyes stayed glued to the secret on my skin.

"Sure, let me just take my shirt off in public," I joked, trying to distract her with humor.

It didn't work.

Cleo, persistent as always, lifted her gaze and batted those blue eyes like she used to. "Come on, just lift it up a little. It's not that big." When I just stared at her, she rolled her eyes. "You show me yours and I'll show you mine. Sound fair?"

"Wait, what?" I asked, blinking in surprise. "You have a tattoo?"

The smile she gave me was coy. Slightly shy. "I do. You'll have to settle for a picture, though, because mine isn't as... accessible as yours."

What. The. Fuck.

"Are we talking about a foot and ankle situation, or..." I couldn't help but drag my eyes along her skin, looking for any hint of ink and cataloguing all the parts of her that were covered.

Again, Cleo blushed. "Definitely *or*."

And there went my dick, rising from half-mast to fully stiff. Honestly, how was I supposed to make it back to my mom and dad like this? Talk about freaking awkward. This was horrible. All I could do was wonder where it was, what it looked like, and how she would shiver if I ran my tongue along the inked lines.

Christ. Get it together, Grady. You can't be out here lusting after your ex-girlfriend like this. Especially when you haven't seen or talked to her in over four years.

No matter what I told myself, it didn't work. It'd been too damn long since I had a woman in my bed. After the breakup, I'd drowned myself in anything that could numb the pain, even if only for a moment or two. It wasn't until Liv told me that shit was going to get me a one-way ticket to a fatherhood that I straightened my shit out.

I still had company from time to time, but I was much more careful with my choices and made sure no matter what… I never had a one-night stand while on tour.

"Okay, fuck it," I said, taking a breath and lifting the hem of my shirt to reveal the artwork along my ribs. It was of two birds, one perched alone in a cage while the other took flight. Flowers bloomed along the vines coiled around the bars while the trapped bird sang its mournful lament.

It was the story of us. While most people would likely think of me as the one running away, I was, in fact, the one trapped because a life without her love was no life at all.

Cleo reached out the lines, and I held my breath, scared I would spook her if I moved at all. When she finished, she looked up at me through thick lashes. I expected her to pull away, but she didn't. "It's beautiful," she whispered.

"Thank you," I said, a little hoarse, letting my shirt fall. "So, a deal's a deal. Let's see yours now."

She straightened up, fidgeting with her the drink in her hands. "Can I see you again?"

"Is it a requirement of the deal? Don't you have a picture?" Not that I was opposed to the idea of seeing her again. In fact, I wanted to. And then I wanted to trace her own tattoo, just as she had mine. I wanted her to feel the torture of having me trace her skin and not be able to act on it.

Cleo smiled, but it was a nervous smile. "No, it's just I really think I want to see you again. It's been so long," she looked down, biting her lip, "and this has been really nice."

"Just nice?"

"More than nice," she murmured. "So, say yes. Say I can see you again, and—"

Just then, a tall man in jeans and a polo came up and draped his arm over her shoulder, pulling her to his side. He looked about our age, maybe a year or two older, with dark brown hair tucked beneath a Black Springs Ranch ball cap. "Thought I lost you."

"No, sorry. I got caught up talking to an old friend," she said, stumbling over the last word. "Thomas, this is Grady. Grady, meet Thomas." I could see how much he wanted her by the way he looked me up and down, like I was his competition, and he needed to squash me. "Thomas is visiting this weekend from Austin."

"Grady, huh?" he said, sticking out his other hand for a shake. "I've heard so much about you."

Was this her new boyfriend? Jesus, what a douche. What the hell did she see in him? "Thomas, was it?" I asked, squeezing his hand. "Funny. I can't say the same about you. How are you liking Ashwood?"

Thomas snapped his mouth shut, grinding his molars together before finally speaking. "It's been great. I love small towns like this. Reminds me of home back in Montana. And Cleo's parents have been so accommodating. Ruby and Doug have been great hosts."

Not only did he have his arm around her, but he was also staying at her place? At the ranch?

"That's great," I replied.

Silence stretched before Cleo pried herself from under his grip. "Is your phone number still the same?" she asked.

I nodded once, keeping my gaze locked on hers. Even though no words were spoken, no promises uttered, I still felt like the rug had been pulled out from under me. And it was my own fault. I had no one to blame but myself, because I was delusional enough to think maybe her wanting to meet up meant we would eventually get back together.

It had been a shit week on top of this, so I knew I was being irrational, but my mom had fucking cancer, and Cleo had a fucking boyfriend. I had what? A music career. Sure, it was great and all, but nothing was promised. Not even the big contract with Hartstrings. There were always better artists out there. Even if I met every parameter Liv's uncle wanted to see, there was always better talent out there. Someone could come in and blow them away, more than I ever could, and then where would I be?

"Well, I probably better get new drinks. I'm sure Mom is wondering where I've been." I pointed behind me to the concession stand. "It was good seeing you," I mumbled.

I'd only taken two steps before I felt Cleo's hand on my wrist, tugging me gently back. I turned as her body collided with my own. She wrapped her arms around my middle, hugging me so goddamn tightly it felt like she was trying to hold me together. Maybe she was, but I had to remember it wouldn't last. She would let go, and then I'd be left with all these emotions I didn't know what to do with.

"I'm here if you need anything," she said, pressing her face into my chest. "My number is the same, too. I'll text you tonight. We can grab dinner or something."

I held her to me for a moment longer, savoring her warmth,

her scent, before letting her go. "Yeah, sure. I'll text you," I said before quickly turning away. I didn't look back, and by the time I'd grabbed new drinks, she was gone.

THAT NIGHT, I stared down at the text message on my phone.

CLEO

> Hi, it's Cleo! Not sure if you have my number saved. Wanted to reach out and see when you were free for dinner?

This was my chance. I could ask her right now what was going on between her and Thomas. I could find out the truth without letting my mind spiral. The issue was I was too far gone. I'd let myself slip into the unknown, into the dark hole in my mind I often struggled to get out of.

When my phone rang, I almost didn't answer. I thought it might've been Cleo, and even though I wanted to hear her voice, it wouldn't have been the right call. Instead, it was Liv. I hit answer immediately, bringing it up to my ear only to hear her frustration clear as day.

"God, I fucking hate men," she grumbled. "I know arranged marriages aren't, like, super common, but come on! I'm hot, I'm super chill—"

"Oh yeah, totally chill," I laughed, cutting off her spiral. "I'm guessing your latest prospect called it off?"

I would never pretend to understand the lives of the elite. She was right; arranged marriages weren't common for us regular folk, but apparently it was nothing in the world she grew up in. And while Liv had concocted the plan herself to appease some bullshit contingency built into her inheritance, it was proving to be more difficult to carry out than she originally thought.

"Fuck off. You know what I mean. I'm just saying it's not like it's a chore. I'm not even requiring fidelity in the marriage agreement. Just, you know, keep your shit on the DL or else I'll take you to court."

"Is that a thing?"

Even though I couldn't see her, I somehow knew Liv shrugged. "I don't know, but it's what the family lawyers are for."

"Why don't you try dating for—and I know this is crazy—love," I suggested.

"Absolutely not! There's too much riding on my hypothetical marriage, Grady. You know that. I want to be CEO of Hartstrings more than I want the new Taylor Swift album, which is saying something. I can't risk it for something as fleeting as love." She sighed dramatically. "I really wish you could do it. I trust you, ya know? You wouldn't completely blow things up the week before our announcement was supposed to go live."

"Why can't I?" The words were out of my mouth before I could stop them.

The past week had been shit. My life felt like it'd been turned upside down and I was just scrambling to make sense of it all. Cleo had moved on, and I was done with love. I didn't want it if I couldn't have her. Besides, if I married Liv, maybe I could help Mom and Dad out with the cancer treatments. They were stressed enough about how they were going to make things work around here. She didn't have insurance and Dad's wasn't the best. Any money they'd saved over the years would be gone.

Liv laughed, but stopped when I didn't join in. "Wait, you're serious? Grady, we can't get married. You're still hung up on your ex, for god's sake!"

"I'm not hung up on her," I argued, even though we both

knew it was a lie. There would never be a day in my life I wouldn't think of her. I just hoped I could make it to a place where it would bring happiness over pain.

Liv snorted. "Says the man who got his love story tattooed on his skin."

"Do you want my help or not?" I asked.

"I don't know if it would be such a good idea, Grady. I mean, we're such good friends—"

"Best friends, actually."

"Right, okay. Best friends. I don't want to make it weird between us. I mean, we'd need to act all romantic in public and shit. And it would be for a long time, too. This isn't something that's only going to last a year or whatever. Like, this would be a commitment."

It was kind of terrifying, honestly, but what else was I doing? I was already living in Nashville. Liv and I spent nearly every day together as it was, and we were in the same business. Other than my previous proclivity for hooking up with strangers, everything would stay the same.

"I know, and I want to help. It would be so easy, Liv. People already think we're a couple half the time. Sure, physical intimacy might be weird, especially in public, but I think we can sell it, don't you? And then it can be normal at home. It's the perfect solution."

It was quiet on the other line which meant she was considering this. "And what do you want from it?"

"Other than to be labeled as your hot-as-fuck arm candy?" I asked, laughing. "Honestly, I just want to be able to help my mom with her cancer treatments. I think it's going to take a lot more than my parents anticipated. I can hear their conversations through the wall sometimes…"

"Oh, Grady… You don't have to marry me for that. I'd help them just because," Liv said. I knew she'd do it, but it didn't feel right.

"Yeah, but this way I can earn it."

"Well, I'm not going to let that be it. Of course we'll help your parents. That's non-negotiable, but what about you? Be selfish for a minute. What do you want?"

Music. It was what I always wanted but telling her felt like asking for too much. Still, I said it anyway. "A guarantee in this cutthroat business. A contract with Hartstrings."

I could hear her smile on the other end. "Now we're talking."

And then, before I could back out, I said, "And a new phone number."

cleo

. . .

"THIS PROBABLY ISN'T the best idea," I said warily as Lincoln led Sundance, his extra mare, into the arena.

"Sure it is," Grady said from beside me. He pulled his new Black Springs Ranch cap down on his head and flashed me a dizzying smile. "I remember how to ride, Cleo. I'll be fine. Lincoln said she's a good one."

Lincoln would know. While he was here last year, Sundance had been designated his horse until he could bring his from Tennessee. These days, he alternated between the two because the mare had become somewhat obsessed with him.

"If you're sure," I murmured, watching Grady wander over to Lincoln and take the reins.

Charlie came up and leaned into my side. "Is my daddy gonna ride that big horse?"

"Well, he's certainly going to try," I said. She scooted closer until my hand rested on her shoulder. It felt awkward at first, which was just because I still didn't understand what she saw in me to warrant such affection when she'd only known me for a week. But just like she was during the camp, Charlie was firmly glued to my side. Who was I to turn her away for seeking comfort?

Grady placed his foot in the stirrup and pulled himself up, sitting high in the saddle. As much as I didn't want to admit it, he looked way too damn good on the back of a horse. "What'd I tell you?" he called out as Lincoln stepped back. "I'm a natural."

"Don't get ahead of yourself now," Lincoln said, with a chuckle. "Let's see if you do a couple of laps without falling off."

"Yeah, maybe we can have a friendly competition!" Lennox called from the back of her horse, Strider.

After dinner, Charlie had asked my sister to bring out the barrels so she could watch her ride again. My sister, ever so keen to show off, immediately said yes. It led to bets about Grady's riding skills, which he immediately wanted to rectify. He'd seemed so cocky. While I didn't want him to get hurt, there was a small, petty version of myself that wanted him to fall on his ass at least once.

Grady clicked his tongue, urging Sundance into a trot around the edge of the arena. We watched and waited to see if her rough gait would be enough to throw him off, but he wasn't deterred.

"Well, would you look at that!" Lennox called out, leaning forward over the saddle horn. "Maybe the pretty boy has it in him after all."

"Oh, ye of little faith," he said back, turning over his shoulder to shoot us a blinding smile. "I told you it was like riding a bike."

"Except bikes don't spook when something runs out in front of them," Bishop said, stepping out of the barn with Titan. His horse was every bit the monster his name suggested. He was easily one of the largest horses I'd ever seen and would've been terrifying if he weren't such a sweetheart.

Charlie's eyes grew wide as she took in the gentle beast. "Oh my gosh," she whispered. "That's the biggest horse I've ever seen!"

Bishop, who'd overheard her excited gasps, walked over with Titan in tow. "Wanna pet him?"

She shied back into me a bit. "Uh, I don't know."

I chuckled, placing my hand on her back to guide her forward. "Want me to come with you?" Charlie nodded, and I took her hand. "Come on, he's a big softie—just like his owner," I joked, earning a scowl from the grumpy cowboy.

"My reputation has been tarnished," he mumbled as we stepped forward.

"That's what you get for falling in love."

He snorted. "I didn't fall. I was tripped. Shoved, even."

"Same thing," I said. "Alright, Charlie. Come say hi to this sweet boy." I held up my hand and gently ran it down the middle of Titan's face. "You just need to be gentle like we talked about in camp. You don't know him, and he doesn't know you."

"Okay." She glanced between the two of us before slowly stepping forward and lifting her hand. He met her halfway, and she laughed as he leaned into her touch. "He's so soft," she said with a giggle.

"He is, isn't he? Titan's one of my favorite horses on this ranch," I lowered my voice. "But don't tell any of the others I said so, okay?"

Charlie giggled again. "I promise I won't tell, Miss Cleo."

"Alright, good. You wanna feed him a little treat?"

She nodded enthusiastically. "What kinda treat? Does he like cookies?"

"I'm sure he would, but we're gonna go with a tried-and-true favorite." Digging into my pocket, I pulled out a peppermint and held it out to her.

She squinted, taking it from me. "Because he has bad breath?"

This time, Bishop let out a hearty laugh. "I mean, it certainly helps a bit. Peppermint is calming to them. Plus, they've got a bit of a sweet tooth, so it's the best of both worlds."

I squatted to her level and took her hand in mine. "Alright, palm up. Lay it flat, okay?" She did so, and I placed the candy in the middle of her hand. "Now just lift it up a little. There we go."

She giggled as Titan's nostrils flared and he bent down to nuzzle her palm, gently taking the mint between his teeth and chomping down. "It tickles," she said, wiping the slobber-covered hand on her jeans.

"I know, his whiskers are soft, huh?"

"They are," she said, staring up at the massive animal like she was in love. Titan leaned down again in search of treats. "Can he have another one?"

I glanced up at Bishop. He had a smile on his face and jerked his chin in confirmation. "Sure. Think you could do it by yourself now?"

"I think so."

Pulling another candy from my pocket, I dropped it in her waiting palm. "The most important thing is to keep your hand flat. We don't want him to accidentally bite you."

Charlie pulled back momentarily. "Would he really do that?"

"Not on purpose," I assured her. "But accidents happen, so let's make sure to keep your hand straight."

"Alright," she mumbled, holding it back out. Her face was pure magic, sweet giggles filling the air as Titan happily took another snack. He shook his head, letting out a soft neigh.

"Looks like you made a new friend," Bishop murmured, scratching the horse's nose. "You wanna ride him?"

Charlie jerked toward Bishop. "Can I?"

"We'd have to ask your dad," I said, pausing to find Grady, though it didn't take long.

I felt the weight of his stare before I found him. He was staring at Charlie and me from across the arena, a soft smile playing on his lips. I returned it, lifting my hand to wave him over. He urged Sundance forward, who was all too happy to come see Titan.

"Ah hell, we'll never get them apart now," Bishop said, greeting the excited mare as she approached. "These two are inseparable."

Grady laughed. "Yeah, she got a little feisty when she saw y'all walking in a few minutes ago. Had to rein her in a bit, but she's good now."

"I'm surprised she listened," Bishop muttered. "Lincoln's usually the only one who can keep her in line."

The man in question walked up with a smirk on his face. "Oh yeah, you reined her in real good. Tell me… Was that before or after she knocked your ass to the dirt and I had to stop her from bolting?"

Bishop busted out laughing as Grady's cheeks turned pink. Looking closer, I could see his pants covered in dirt he hadn't dusted off yet. "You couldn't keep that between us for like five more minutes, man?"

Lincoln shook his head. "Naw, we don't keep secrets around here. Especially not something like that."

I hid my laugh behind my hand. "Oh man, do you think the cameras caught it? I'm going to need to see this."

"What?" Grady asked, jerking his head up. "What do you mean by cameras?"

Bishop jerked his head toward the little domes hiding along the rafters. "Oh yeah, Lennox made sure they were recording before we headed in here."

"Just in case we get any hotshot country music stars who think they can still ride," Lincoln added with a wink.

"And here I thought we could be friends, man," Grady grumbled.

"Even friends need blackmail. You should hear some of the shit I have on Bishop—"

"That goes both ways, asshole," Bishop interjected. "You wanna get into that shit, I'll get into mine."

Lincoln didn't back down. "Whatever you say… Daddy."

"Hey! I'm the only one who can call him that!" Lennox called from the back of the arena where Josie was leaning against the fence with baby Stella in her carrier. "Don't forget I know the sounds you make when you—"

"Hi, hello! Children are present," I said, quickly covering Charlie's ears. "Is it too much to ask you to behave for once?"

She giggled, pulling my hands down to rest on her shoulder. "Daddy says bad words sometimes, Miss Cleo. He never behaves."

"Maybe he needs to stay late for detention to learn his lesson. That something you could help him with, Cleo?" Lincoln's words came through barely restrained laughter.

"I'm going to kill you," I mouthed over Charlie's head, which only sent him into a full fit.

"Alright, are we gonna ride or what?" Bishop asked, turning to Grady. "You mind if I take her around the arena a few times? You'll be beside me because I doubt she's gonna let Titan get far without her." He gestured toward Sundance.

Grady nodded. "Sure, man. I trust you."

Bishop walked around and pulled himself up into the saddle. Honestly, it was impressive every time I saw him do it. He was a big guy himself, but it still took some serious strength to get on the back of that horse. "Come on, Charlie," he said, motioning for her. "Lincoln, mind giving her a leg up?"

"No problem," Lincoln said, bending down and creating a cradle with his hands. "Charlie, you're gonna put one foot right here and grab hold of Bishop's hand so we can get you up there."

She glanced between Lincoln and Bishop warily. "Where am I gonna sit?"

Bishop patted the small space between his body and the

saddle horn. "Right in front of me so I can make sure you don't go falling off."

"Okay," she mumbled, stepping out of my hold. Just as they said, she grabbed onto Bishop's outstretched hand as Lincoln hoisted her up. She settled right in front of him, a giddy smile on her face as she looked down at all of us. "Oh my gosh, I'm so tall," she giggled. "Miss Cleo, why don't you ride with us?"

"I don't have a horse saddled up," I said, stepping back. "But I'll be right here watching you."

"You can ride with me," Grady said, smirking as he glanced down at his lap.

"Nice try." I couldn't help but smile when his lips dropped into an overexaggerated pout. "I'll catch the next one."

Stepping back, I let Bishop take the lead with Titan. Sundance didn't need any coaxing to follow suit, falling perfectly in step with her little boyfriend. I watched from the sidelines as Bishop let Charlie hold the reins, giving her gentle instructions on how to navigate the turns.

Then my eyes shifted to Lennox, who looked like she was ready to melt at her fiancé's coaching. It wouldn't surprise me if they announced a little surprise before long. They absolutely fawned over Stella and jumped at every opportunity to watch her, even if only for an hour or two while Lincoln and Josie ran errands in town.

In all my creeping, however, I forgot I wasn't alone. Lincoln walked over and let out a low whistle as he leaned against the railing. "Damn, you've got it bad."

"I don't know what you're talking about," I said, refusing to look at him. I'm sure he had a stupid, goofy smile on his face, which was the last thing I wanted to see right now.

"Sure you do. I see the same thing you did when you encouraged Josie to tell me how she felt. The same thing you see now with the way Lennox is staring at Bishop like that grumpy bastard is the most important person in the world." He bumped into my shoulder. "You're not as cool, calm, and collected as you think you are."

I rolled my eyes and turned to see I was right. He was trying to suppress his smile, but his lips were twitching. "He's not even officially divorced."

"That's more of a confirmation than deflection, you know," Lincoln said. "But so what? No one said you had to skip down the aisle, Cleo. Just don't shut it all down before you've given it a shot." He pushed off the gate and set his hand on my shoulder. "You should see the way he looks at you, by the way. Everyone sees it except for you. Just keep that in mind." Then he was gone, making his way across the arena to where Lennox was talking to Josie. He pressed a kiss to his daughter's head before doing the same to Josie. She leaned into his side, the picture of perfect happiness and contentment.

I deserved that, too, didn't I? I may have told myself I didn't, may have shut down the prospect of opening my heart because I was scared of getting hurt. But Grady was different. He wasn't some random stranger I'd never met. We had history. Even if it wasn't all perfect, the bad bits didn't seem quite so horrible these days.

The day I walked away, he asked if he had a chance in the future, if we had a someday. For so long I thought that door was closed, but I didn't think it ever really was. At the end of the day, there was always a sliver of space left open just for him.

It wouldn't be easy for either of us, but if he was open to it, I think I could be, too.

NIGHT HAD FALLEN by the time I followed Grady out of the barn. He was carrying a sleeping Charlie to his truck. She'd spent the last thirty minutes drooling on my t-shirt as Lennox and I watched the guys try to outdo one another on horseback. It started after she ran barrels, to which Lincoln and Grady both smarted off they could do better. Because Bishop was incapable of letting a challenge pass him by, he inevitably joined in.

To absolutely no one's surprise, none of them could beat Lennox's time. However, that led to betting about who could get the fastest time roping steers, which then led to the best shortstop.

Even though Grady came in last every time, he paid up and promised he'd be winning it back in no time. I didn't have the heart to tell him there was no way he would be able to win against either of those two con artists, so I just cheered him on with Charlie by my side.

"Oh man, this was great," Grady said as we stopped by his truck.

"It was," I agreed, stepping up to get the passenger door as he shifted Charlie in his arms. I laid my head against the door as he buckled her into her booster seat, watching as he carefully laid her braid over her shoulder so it didn't get caught behind her back.

"Mind turning on the truck for me?" he asked over his shoulder, nodding to the keys in the cup holder.

"Sure thing." I did so, walking around the vehicle to the driver's side and listening to the familiar hum of his engine as it came to life. There were nights I stayed up with my window open, hoping to hear the familiar rumble down at the gate so I could sneak away with him.

"You know, I'm surprised you still have this thing," I said, meeting his gaze over the center console. "Figured someone might have gotten rid of it."

His lips lifted in a smile. "You know, Dad tried at one point. He said if it was going to sit in the driveway, he was going to start charging me rent. Said it was going to waste. I almost agreed, too."

"But you didn't in the end."

He shook his head, closed the passenger door, and joined me on the driver's side. "How could I? Some of my best memories happened in this truck."

"Best memories, huh?" I asked with a laugh. "I don't know, that seems like a bit of a stretch. You've lived a whole life since then."

"I have, and don't get me wrong... I've done some amazing things. But I think the fact my mind keeps wandering back to you and I after so many years means something."

It made sense. I felt the same way about our time together. Those moments were deeply ingrained in my mind and heart. No matter how hard I tried to carve them out, they burrowed deeper.

"Who knew you were so deep?" I joked. He leaned against the closed door. Our bodies were separated by only a few inches of space. The way he looked at me felt too heavy, too personal. It made me feel things I hadn't felt in years, a longing I thought I'd never feel again.

"I don't think that's getting deep, bluebird. It's me being honest. I've carried those memories around my entire life, unable to get them out of my head." He turned his body, letting his head fall back against the truck, and looked up at the sky. "It was always you and me in the front seat of this truck. Our first date, our first kiss," he laughed. "Remember the day we played paintball on our Senior skip day and you got smoked? There's still a pink stain on the floorboard mats."

"Okay, in my defense, I didn't know Billy Stevens had such good aim. How was I supposed to know the kid who came in second place for class president was also a sharpshooter champion?" I said, laughing. "And you know you could just get new mats? I'll even buy some for you if it means so much."

"You're missing the point. The old ones mean so much *because* of the stain. For the longest time, it was one of the few pieces of you I had left." He let his head fall toward me. "I like having whatever pieces of you I can get."

I blew out a breath. Whatever was happening between us right now felt monumental. Walls were down, and honesty was flowing. It was taking everything I had not to run away. I looked at my feet, unable to meet his gaze as I admitted my truth. "I think you already have whatever's left of me, Grady. And that is terrifying."

I felt his fingers beneath my chin, gently lifting my head until I was staring into a pair of bright blue eyes. His thumb slowly brushed against my bottom lip, and I let them part on instinct. "So fucking beautiful," he whispered. "I wonder—"

But I didn't let myself find out what he wondered, because I wanted to see something for myself. "Fuck it," I muttered. My heart was racing as I raised onto my tiptoes and crushed my lips to his. He paused for only a moment before surging forward and taking my face between both of his hands, deepening the kiss. He rolled us so I was pinned between his hard body and the cool metal of his truck.

Oh god, what was I doing? I should've pulled back, I should've stopped it before it ever began, but it felt so good, so right, to have his lips on mine. When I thought about what it might've been like to kiss Grady again, I figured it would be awkward. Maybe it would've been easier if it had been. My memories, regardless of how vivid they were, couldn't compare to the real thing. He tasted like spearmint gum, and smelled like horses and sweat. It reminded me of the day he asked me out on our first date.

This felt like coming home.

Grady pulled back with a groan. I could feel the hard length of him, how desperately he was fighting to keep his hips from rolling into mine. Part of me was disappointed with his control. I knew it was for my benefit. I wasn't ready for that. Hell, I wasn't ready for *this*. I could already feel the panic settling in the longer we stared at one another.

Raising my finger to my lips, I felt how swollen and sensitive they felt after just one kiss. *Cleo, Cleo, Cleo… What are you doing? You're not thinking straight.*

"Please don't shut me out," he begged. "I can see it in your eyes, can feel your muscles tightening beneath my touch. Don't do this."

I cleared my throat and stepped out of his hold, trying to smile even though I knew it was falling flat. Of course, he could read every moment of panic coming to the forefront of my mind. He knew me too well. "It's getting late. You should probably get Charlie tucked into bed."

"Cleo—" he began, fists clenching at his side.

I shook my head. "I can't," I said, wrapping my arms around my waist. I just needed some time to figure out what the fuck was happening. Everything was moving too fast and yet not fast enough. It would've been nothing to let him drag me into the bed of his truck and make love to me all night beneath the stars, but he wasn't officially divorced, and he had Charlie. This was more complicated than either of us truly realized. If this thing, whatever it was, was going to be a possibility, there were things we needed to talk about first.

Even if I did let him back in, I wasn't the same girl he fell in love with twenty years ago. This new version of me had barely graduated from being held together by duct tape to superglue.

He hung his head, defeated. "Will you ever trust me again?"

"I want to," I admitted. It was the truth. And I'd come to accept it. But I still needed to protect myself, and I wasn't quite ready to give him the broken pieces of me yet. "It's just—"

Grady sighed, running his hand through his hair. "That bastard really fucked with your head, didn't he?"

I blinked in surprise. "What are you—"

"I'm not scared of whatever it is you're hiding, by the way.

I'm not scared of your scars, of your fears, of any other bullshit you think you're protecting me from. The only thing I'm scared of is losing you again." He opened the driver's side door, hesitating only for a moment. "I don't know what I have to do to show you I'm all in, but I'm going to try. I've lived far too long without you, bluebird. I don't want to do it any longer."

With that, he got in his truck, put it in reverse, and slowly drove away. I stood there until his taillights disappeared, and I knew I was actually alone.

I slowly trudged back into the house, barely making it to my bed before I reached for my phone and typed out a message.

CLEO

I need to see you next week.

cleo

. . .

23 Years Old

IT'D BEEN a week since I'd seen Grady at the rodeo. One week since I texted him and asked him out to dinner. One week of no responses.

Looking down, I saw the text was still unanswered. I debated texting him again. Maybe it hadn't gone through. It was late, he could've opened it and forgotten to respond. That was reasonable, right?

That was what I told myself to make me feel better, but it was losing its shine. Each day of no contact that passed, I felt the truth coming into focus.

Grady didn't want me.

I didn't know what I expected. Did I really think seeing each other once would be enough to have him knocking at my door? He had a whole life I didn't know about. When I visited his mom, she avoided talking about him unless I specifically asked. After we broke up, I did it a lot. It didn't take me long to realize I was only torturing myself. It wasn't as if his mom was going to tell me he was doing miserably. She only spoke of the good things, the success he was having without me.

While she never outright said it, that was how I felt. Without a nagging girlfriend, he was able to fully commit to the music scene, and it seemed like it was paying off.

I put those thoughts away as the familiar white house came into view. Marsha was sitting outside, holding a cup of tea between her hands. She smiled when she saw my car pull up, and I stepped outside. "Well, isn't this a surprise!" she called out. "I didn't know you were coming by."

I rounded the car with a covered casserole dish filled with fresh lasagna my mom and I had made. Ever since Marsha told me about the cancer, I had been taking them dinner three times a week. Mom helped me during the school year when I had late-night events I couldn't miss.

It wasn't much, but it was what I knew how to do. Food was my comfort, and something Marsha and I both loved. Half of the dinners I brought were from recipes she'd taught me how to make. It seemed only fair to share them back with her.

"School has been a little busy over the past week, but I finally had a free evening, so," I held up the dish, "feel like having some lasagna? The sauce is homemade, just like you showed me."

"You know, they keep telling me I'll lose my appetite with all these medications they have me on and the impending treatments, but I don't know how that's supposed to happen when you keep bringing me my favorite treats." I walked up the steps and let her pull me into a tight hug. "Missed you, girl. You can't be staying away like that. I don't care if that son of mine is home or not. He can get over it."

I couldn't help but laugh at the bluntness of her words. "Anyone ever tell you you're too damn observant?"

She smiled over the lip of her cup. "All the damn time. Can't help myself. Now, let's go see what you learned from my sauce lesson."

I followed her into the house, listening as she told me about what the last week had been like, how it'd seemed like an endless stream of doctor's appointments and pharmacy visits. The countertop by the fridge was littered with pill bottles, both prescription and over-the-counter medications.

She took a seat while I prepared plates for us and carried them to the table. I waited as she picked up her fork and took the first bite, closing her eyes and groaning. "My god, girl. You missed your calling. You should've been a chef."

I laughed, following suit and taking a bite. She wasn't wrong. It was damn good. Probably the best one I'd ever made. I couldn't imagine doing this as a job, though. Even though I was much better at baking, being in a kitchen in general was therapeutic. It was the only time I had to myself. It was the only reason I was halfway as sane as I was.

"Naw. Sometimes hobbies need to stay hobbies. I'll stick to my day job." It was silent for a few minutes before I cleared my throat and spoke again. "So, is it just you here today?"

I didn't look up from my plate, but knew Marsha was staring at me anyway. Her gaze was remarkably like her son's. I could always feel the weight of it when it landed on me. "Is that your way of asking if Grady is here?"

"Of course, not. It's not my business."

She sighed, leaning back in her chair. "Well, that's not entirely true, is it?"

"I don't see why it would be." I set my fork down on the plate. "I was just asking to know if I brought enough food for you guys."

Marsha stared at me a moment longer before she broke away. "No, he's not here anymore. Left the day after the rodeo, actually."

He's been gone all this time? Then why didn't he call and tell me? Why didn't he just tell me he didn't want to go to dinner?

"Oh," I said in surprise. "Did something happen? He seemed pretty set in staying here for a little while."

"He was at first, but he said he got a call that night from

some big recording label. Apparently, they want to sign him," she said, shrugging. "I don't know how it all works, but it seemed pretty important. He called me last night to tell me it was a done deal."

Of course, it had to do with music. Everything did when it came to Grady.

"Well, that's good," I said, injecting fake cheer into my tone. "He'll be great."

"He will," she confirmed. "I just hope he isn't making a mistake, selling his soul to the highest bidder just for a moment of fame. He's such a talented boy."

"I'm sure he knows what he's doing," I said, trying to offer some kind of platitude. "You raised a smart boy. Have faith in him."

"Well, he lost you. I don't know how smart he was for that," she grumbled, taking the last bite of her dinner.

I laughed. "You can't hold it against him forever. It's been years. Ya gotta move on."

"You haven't," she said, pointing a finger my direction. "Don't think I haven't noticed you haven't brought anyone home."

"You don't know that. I could be bringing home lots of men."

Marsha rolled her eyes so hard I thought they might get stuck that way. "Oh, please, don't give me that shit. If that was the case, you'd look a hell of a lot happier than you do now."

"Alright, fine," I muttered, standing from the table. I grabbed her plate and mine and took them to the sink to clean, so she wouldn't have to worry about it later. She kept telling me not to worry about it, that she had been sitting too long and needed to get up and move her weary bones, but I didn't let her.

"Wanna stay for dessert?" she asked, raising her brows. "I had Robert pick up stuff for chocolate chip cookies. Care to help?"

I pretended to think about it for a minute, even though it was a no-brainer. Marsha's cookies were a cure-all. I didn't know what it was about them that tasted so much better than when I did, but I wasn't going to pass up on the offer. "Do I get to take some home?"

"You know I am a firm believer in sharing the wealth," she said. "Now grab an apron and get my Pyrex mixing bowl from the top shelf. Let's get started."

I WAS STUFFED by the time I made it home. Not that it mattered. I still grabbed one of the cookies from the bag and brought it to bed with me. The bag was nearly sealed when I thought better of it and grabbed two. I would need it for what I was about to do.

Ever since Marsha told me about Grady's deal, I couldn't help but wonder if it was the reason he never texted back. There was no way in hell he would turn down that kind of deal. He would've been stupid to. This was all he ever wanted, and now it was coming to life.

Maybe his lack of contact stemmed from a place of growth. Maybe he hadn't wanted to hurt me by following through with a dinner plan, only to back out at the last minute because Nashville was calling. On some level, I could applaud that kind of growth. I certainly wasn't that mature.

I stared at my phone. There were a million questions I wanted the answers to, and most of them could be found if I just picked the damn thing up and did some digging. Even though I didn't follow Grady on social media anymore, there was sure to be something on there, right? I mean, this was a huge thing. It wouldn't go unnoticed.

Without thinking any further, I pulled up his profile and

began to scroll. The first image had a countdown attached to it, but it ended tonight. Most of his other posts were pictures of the band on tour. There were a few from the recording studio, but most of his pictures featured the same people. His timeline was uneventful for such an up-and-coming star. But amidst the handful of faces, there was one that stood out over all of them.

She was gorgeous with incredibly long blonde hair. Her wide smile were always bright, and she had this incredible way of looking poised in every photo. Surprisingly, it wasn't her beauty that caught my attention, although it was hard to miss. It was the way she was in the background of most shots, but all her attention was still fixed on him.

That was how I used to look at him. Full of love and adoration. My stomach twisted as I went further back, seeing how much things had changed. There were pictures of them going back for years. Sometimes they were casual, the two of them standing together for a posed photo. Others were silly and goofy —there was one with his arm around her shoulder, both of them smiling, their tongues sticking out. I recognized the background. It was an ice cream parlor we used to go to in Austin.

And then I looked at the date. It was taken only two weeks after we broke up.

I wasn't sure how I'd missed it before. This wasn't the first time I'd gotten curious and gone down a rabbit hole of shame, but I usually didn't make it back this far. Because if I continued down, I saw he still had pictures of us posted. Long forgotten, or somewhat suppressed, memories that killed me. It didn't matter how long ago they'd been taken. Seeing our young, innocent faces stole the breath right from my lungs. How did we get from there to here? From intense familiarity to complete strangers?

I scrolled back up, hesitating when I saw her profile tagged in one of the posts. This was likely the worst idea I'd ever had, but I clicked on it anyway.

I regretted it immediately.

Olivia Hart was a stunning woman. She was from Nashville and a year younger than Grady and me, and yet she seemed so much more accomplished. There were pictures of her at parties with celebrities, or sitting in what looked like an office in a skyscraper, surrounded by windows overlooking the city. Her feed was much more polished than Grady's was, the picture of professionalism at twenty-two years old. Mine suddenly seemed so immature—littered with photos of the ranch or brunch dates with my best friend, Rachel.

I didn't often feel inadequate, but I did then. I couldn't measure up to someone like that. She was perfect. Everything I wasn't.

As if she could sense the impending spiral, my phone rang. I answered and brought it up to my ear. "Hi, Rach," I mumbled.

"Oh god, you already know, don't you?" she rushed out. "Dammit, I really thought I would beat you to it."

"What are you talking about? Know what?"

"About Grady. I saw the announcement a few minutes ago and was hoping you hadn't seen it yet."

Oh, was she talking about the record deal? "Yeah, I went by and visited his mom this morning, and she told me. I'm happy for him. He deserves it."

Rachel was silent on the other end for a moment. "Wait, what? You're happy for him? He deserves it? Are you feeling okay?"

I laughed, though it felt forced. "He's worked so hard to get signed by a label, Rach. Of course, I'm happy for him. I know things didn't work out between us, but that doesn't mean I don't wish him the best."

"The record deal?"

"Yeah, isn't that what you're talking about? His mom said the label called him up and offered him a crazy deal, and he took it."

Rachel was silent for a minute. "Okay, so we are talking about two different things…"

I settled back into my pillows. "Well, I'm waiting on pins and needles. Why don't you enlighten me?"

She sighed. "So, I have a Google Alert on him, which can be a bit annoying because that thing is always going off. Seriously, I have to have a separate folder just for them because they keep coming in—"

"Please get to the point, Rach."

"Right. The point. So, yes. He did get signed, it was announced today," she hesitated, blowing out a breath. "But that wasn't all."

"What do you mean?" My fingers were wound tightly in the comforter as if I could hold onto my current reality before it crashed and burned around me.

Somehow, I already knew what she was going to say before she said it. It felt as though the world had shifted sometime in the last week, and this was me only now catching up. Though I hadn't thought I'd read the vibe between us wrong, apparently I had. Apparently, he was just trying to be placating and polite when he said he wanted to catch up.

"Babe… Grady got engaged tonight. It's all over the news. All over socials."

My heart was hammering in my chest as I put Rachel on speaker and refreshed his social media feed. Sure enough, there was a new post. It was filled with a bunch of random pictures. It was remarkable how, even in still images, I could sense the happiness radiating from them. He and his band smiled as they signed on a dotted line while someone popped a massive bottle of champagne in the background. There were toasts and spilled drinks, even more laughter. And then there was her.

She was poised at his side, smiling up at him as he rested his arm around her waist. Then she rested her hand on his chest, showing off the massive ring on her left finger. They sealed it with a smile-filled kiss, both with a demure blush across their cheeks.

It made sense he'd moved on. Why would he want me when he could have her? She was perfect. He would've gotten down on one knee for someone eventually. It was inevitable. I just thought it would've been later. I never thought about what it would feel like to see it, either. How it ripped open a wound I thought had long been healed.

"Babe? You okay?"

I hadn't realized I was crying until the first tear fell on my screen, distorting their faces into something as ugly as I felt. I couldn't help but let them fall. Feeling like this, missing him this much after so many years, couldn't have been healthy. It was time for me to stop holding on when he had clearly already let go.

I felt so stupid, so foolish, for the hope I felt a week ago. When I left the rodeo, I really thought this was the start of our someday. We'd both grown; that was clear enough to see. And being so close to him, I don't know, it felt right.

"Cleo, talk to me," Rachel begged.

"It's fine," I sniffed. "It's fine. I'm fine. Like I said, I'm happy for him."

"You don't have to be, you know? It's okay to be upset. I know it's been four years, but—"

"I said, I'm fine, Rachel. Please don't try to psychoanalyze me. He's happy. She's happy. Everyone's happy."

"Everyone except for you."

But that was a feeling I knew all too well. I was used to prioritizing everyone else's feelings over my own. Why would this be any different? I could compartmentalize, I could shove it down so it never saw the light of day again. Just like I did with everything else.

grady

· · ·

MY TEXT THREAD with Cleo was unnervingly silent, save for the few messages I'd sent with no response. It wasn't until I asked her what time I should bring Charlie by on Monday morning that she sent a single text.

CLEO

9:00 a.m.

For the past two days, our interactions had been limited. I'd drop Charlie off in the morning, sometimes lingering, much to her dismay, and then I'd pick her up later. Cleo didn't say much, and while she hadn't entirely shut me out, she wasn't exactly forthcoming either.

When I asked Lennox if Cleo was okay, she assured me she was. I didn't know if I really believed it or if it was just something I was being told, so I didn't barge through the door and beg her to talk to me.

As much as I wanted to push her for more, I didn't. I couldn't. She was struggling to come to terms with everything, with us. While I was determined to prove to her I was the man she needed, the one she deserved, I knew better than to push right now. If I did it too much, she would shut down entirely, and I refused to let that happen. Not when I was finally seeing her open up.

I played our kiss on repeat all weekend, lying alone in bed or in the shower as I fisted my cock. It didn't take long for me to come, not when I remembered the soft little moan that'd left her lips when our mouths touched, or the way she struggled to keep control of her body as I pressed against her.

I didn't know how long it'd been for her, but it'd just been me and my hand for far longer than I cared to admit. I hadn't touched another woman since Liv and I got together one drunken night. We both woke up after, feeling the mistake between us, but never admitting it out loud. Especially not when it ended up giving us the greatest gift neither of us expected.

While I didn't want to be too presumptuous, I knew well enough the first time I claimed Cleo's body again, I was going to make sure she was entirely satisfied before I ever tried to get my own. If not, it was going to be over far quicker than either of us wanted.

"Daddy, Daddy! Wake up! It's time to go to Miss Cleo's for lessons." Charlie came running through my door and pounced on my bed. "Come on! Get out of bed."

"Someone's eager," I said, laughing. "Haven't you ever heard of sleeping in?"

She sat back on her heels, looking at me like I had lost my mind. I mean, I had, but she didn't know that. "Sleeping in is for old people."

"Ouch. My god, kid. You're going to kill someone with that honesty one day."

"I'm not trying to kill you, Daddy," she whined, leaning forward. Her stuffed rabbit was squashed beneath her palm. "I just want you to get up so we can go see Miss Cleo."

I stared at my daughter, the way her little hands twitched in my sheets, and the pout on her face. Something about her words gave me pause. "Are you excited to see Miss Cleo or ride horses?"

Charlie blushed. "Can it be both?"

"It can," I said, opening my arms. She crawled over to me and settled against my chest. "Do you like Miss Cleo?"

My daughter turned and looked up at me. "Duh, Daddy. I love her."

"That's a big word, you know," I murmured. "Love isn't something you should throw around without meaning it."

Charlie was silent, but I could hear the gears turning in her mind. "But you love her, don't you, Daddy?"

I realized I was at a crossroads. I could either tell my daughter the truth or I could lie. But I'd always told her how important it was to speak honestly, and what would lying do other than eventually show her I didn't practice what I preached?

"I do," I said, hugging her tighter. "Is that okay with you?"

She nodded, but I could feel her holding back. "If you love her, does that mean I can love her, too?"

"Oh, sweetie, of course you can. You can love anyone you want, but especially Miss Cleo."

"D-Do you think she loves us, too? Like, both of us?"

My sweet girl was breaking my heart. I didn't know why. She was loved, so very loved, by Liv and me. Even if we hadn't fully explained to her what it would mean to be divorced, she was a smart kid. I knew she was picking up on the changes that were about to happen.

"How could she not? You're the best girl around." I pressed a kiss to the top of her head. "Miss Cleo... Well, she's been hurt by love before, so we've got to help show her it's okay."

Charlie nodded against my chest, burrowing in so deeply before bursting from my arms. "Can we bring her breakfast,

Daddy? I know she likes cinnamon rolls. Can we bring her cinnamon rolls?"

Just like that, the heavy moment was gone, with nothing but Charlie's bright, innocent smile filling my heart with happiness. "Yeah, sweet girl. We can do that."

BY THE TIME we made it out to the ranch, box of cinnamon rolls in tow, it was a bit later than we normally showed up. I didn't think it'd matter, especially since we had a box of her favorite treats in tow.

I pulled up and put my vehicle into park as Charlie clambered to unbuckle herself from her booster seat. I'd taken to driving the old truck as my daily now. There was something comforting about the familiarity of it. Plus, I wouldn't lie and say I didn't like how it'd felt when Cleo saw me rolling up in it last week.

"Hold on, baby girl. Give me a second to help you," I laughed, getting out and walking around to open the passenger door for my daughter. She hopped down with the white box in tow. Part of it was crushed beneath her fingers, and I wondered if there would be anything salvageable inside. I'd been smelling them for the past thirty minutes and would be a little heartbroken if they didn't survive.

"Lennox!" Charlie shouted, running toward the woman standing at the entrance of the barn.

Lennox met her with a smile, opening her arms wide for Charlie to throw herself into. "What's up, wild child? Whatcha got there?"

"Well, I asked Daddy if we could stop for cinnamon rolls, and he said yes, but we had to get enough for everyone." She held up the box, shaking it slightly. "So, here they are!"

Lennox laughed, taking the goodies from Charlie's hand. "That was so thoughtful, Charlie! I'll make sure Miss Cleo gets one before the rest of these rowdy boys dig in."

"Where is she?" Charlie asked, pulling back. "Is she okay?"

I walked up, catching the last bit of their conversation. "What's happening?" I looked at Lennox. "Everything alright?"

She nodded and smiled, but it didn't feel like the truth. "Yeah, she's fine. Cleo is out sick today, so I'm going to fill in for her. That sound okay with you?"

Charlie looked back at me before shrugging her shoulders. "Guess so. You'll make sure she gets the breakfast I brought her?"

Lennox held up her hand. "I swear. I'll take it to her right now."

"Can I come?" she asked.

Lennox winced. "We don't want you getting sick, sunshine. Why don't you stay out here with your dad while I take them to her?"

"Or I could do it," I said, crossing my arms over my chest. "I'm not really worried about getting sick."

"That's not necessary. I said I would do it," she said between clenched teeth. "I'll be right back."

With that, she jogged toward the house and slipped inside. I watched her, waiting for any sign Cleo was watching us, but found none. A few minutes passed before Lennox came out with a forced smile. "How's she feeling?" I asked, not taking my eyes off the house.

"Well, she's grateful for the cinnamon rolls, I can tell you that much!" Lennox said, ruffling Charlie's hair. "She wanted me to tell you thank you. Both of you," she added, looking my way.

I didn't like this at all. It felt like Lennox and Cleo were both hiding something from me, but I had no proof. Was it all over that stupid kiss? I knew I should've told her to stop, to make sure she was really ready to take that step, but it felt too good. I couldn't help but be swept up into such a perfect and simple moment with her.

Friday night had felt like being a teenager again. There we were, up against my old truck beneath the moonlight, stealing kisses and praying for more time. Except it had all come crashing down like someone had taken a wrecking ball and destroyed whatever facade we'd built.

"You'd tell me if something was wrong, right?" I asked, stepping closer to Lennox. "If I did something—"

"Chill out, Romeo. It's not that deep. Cleo's just," she sighed, scratching the back of her neck. "She's working through some shit right now and needs some space. She'll come around, I promise. Just not today. Probably not tomorrow either, if I'm honest."

"Am I fucking this up before it's even begun again?" I asked.

Lennox's eyes softened. "You're not. Keep doing what you're doing. Just don't push her too hard the next few days, okay? I'd tell you if you were overstepping." She reached out and squeezed my hand. "I promise."

"Alright," I said, defeated. "Just tell her I'll be here waiting for her." When Lennox looked concerned about possible stalkerish tendencies, I added, "Not here, here. Just in general."

"I was worried there for a second," she joked. "Thought I might actually have to make use of all my threats."

"Your threats?"

She smiled, but there was something slightly sinister about it. "Yeah, I keep telling everyone the ranch is an excellent place to dispose of a body, but so far I haven't been able to test the theory."

I raised my brows. "You sure my daughter's safe in your company?"

"Oh yeah, she's fine. You're the one on thin ice, so you better not fuck it up."

cleo

. . .

"DEEP BREATH IN. Okay, great. Hold it, Cleo. One, two, three, four. Now let it out. Four, three, two, one. Perfect." Squeezing my old stress ball, I did as instructed, closing my eyes and letting Laura walk me through a guided breathing exercise. We'd been doing this for the past three minutes, and I was beginning to get restless. This part of our sessions usually only got me so far, but I humored her nonetheless.

"How're you feeling?" she asked, settling back into her chair. "Any better from yesterday?"

When I texted her on Friday night asking for a session, I hadn't understood the depth of my despair. I'd made it through the majority of the week unscathed, but when I woke up on Wednesday, I couldn't get out of bed. My body refused to cooperate. At first, I thought I was getting sick, but when I checked the date, I realized what it was.

My wedding anniversary.

I wasn't sure how my body subconsciously knew what my mind hadn't caught onto yet. It was the first one since our divorce had been finalized. While I hadn't planned a celebration, I didn't think it was going to completely knock me on my ass either. I'd spent the majority of the day in bed, squeezing my stress ball, crying, and eating my weight in the cookies my mom had baked just for me. She and Dad both tried to get me to come out, but I refused.

That was when they sent in the cavalry, which came in the form of both my sisters and takeout from my favorite Chinese restaurant in town. We spent the night watching early 2000s rom-coms and taking turns falling off my full-size bed.

"I'm okay," I said. "Yesterday was hard. It was, well, it was tough."

"Do you think it has to do with the kiss you shared with Grady? Or is it mourning what you thought you had with Thomas?" Laura asked, tilting her head to the side. "Or perhaps both?"

I sucked in a breath. "I don't think I ever mourned anything with Thomas, except for the loss of myself and the years I wasted. I guess at one point I thought we had something special, or else I wouldn't have married him, but I don't even know if that's the truth."

"What do you think the truth is?"

"Aren't you supposed to tell me?" I muttered.

She smiled patiently. "No, my job is to help you work through this yourself. The fact of the matter is the truth is relative. It depends on who you ask. Even then, it can have variations depending on your feelings on the matter. So, tell me what you're thinking about it."

That was a loaded question. I wasn't even sure I knew what I thought. Most of that time in my life was such a blur, like I was looking out of a car window at the passing scenery that was my past. The only parts in focus were the ones with Grady.

"I think I was lonely. I saw my life passing me by so quickly, and none of it was turning out like I thought it would, so I felt the need to catch up. And when Thomas showed up, I don't know, he didn't leave. He stayed. He was persistent. And after

Grady let me walk away so easily, I guess I wanted the opposite? Not that I blame him, honestly. I told him to go, and he listened, but—" I paused, swallowing down what was left of my pride. "It still hurts. And even more so when I realized he was engaged. I think I wanted to hurt him back, but it ended up hurting me more. I've always been guarded, but I've struggled to let anyone in—even those I love the most."

Like Grady.

"I think that's an important realization, Cleo. And I think it must be complicated to mourn a failed marriage, even if it wasn't the one you always dreamed of. Especially if you're also mourning a failed relationship. And that kind of grief can make us do things that are out of our normal characterization, which for you, would be marrying Thomas," Laura said. Her fingers tapped against the notebook in her lap.

"So, then why am I sad if I can realize how horrible the relationship was? Thomas made me question everything, and I've been fighting to get back to the girl I used to be. I don't want to feel like this. I don't want to mourn, or whatever. I don't want to be scared of the future."

"You once told me you were scared of being so broken you couldn't be fixed. Is that still how you feel?"

Honestly, I was scared of a lot of things. I was afraid of becoming inconsequential, of my family not needing me anymore. I didn't have anything of my own to occupy my time without them. Maybe that was the saddest part of it all. My life existed to please others, never myself.

But there was one thing, one person, who scared me more than anything.

Grady had the power to hurt me more than anyone else ever could. If he walked through the door right now and told me whatever this was becoming was over, I would crumble. I didn't know if I could watch him walk away again. He'd already worked his way under my skin in less than two weeks, which seemed crazy. Absolutely wild.

Except it wasn't just him. Charlie was there right beside him, making me fall for her in all her wild, innocent glory. She loved so thoroughly without fear of falling, without fear of getting hurt, or rejected. I never thought a six-year-old would be able to teach me much about life, but she already had. She'd already made me question my current life choices and the ones I wanted to make for my future.

For what seemed like the first time during our session, I met Laura's gaze and she smiled. I wasn't sure what she saw in the woman staring at her, but I felt a strange kind of peace settling in my chest.

"What're you scared of, Cleo?"

"Myself," I whispered, meeting her gaze. "I'm scared of letting my fear rule my decisions. Of listening to all the awful things my mind tells me—that I'm not worthy of love, that everything is my fault, that I don't deserve good things. It's miserable living like this, but I feel trapped in my own mind. And while I used to be afraid of these things themselves— maybe part of me still is, if I'm honest—I think I'm more afraid of letting them rule me. I'm afraid of missing out on my chance for happiness."

Laura leaned forward. "Well, they don't call it 'growing pains' for nothing. Sometimes it hurts to grow, but it might hurt a lot more if you never give yourself the chance."

IT'D BEEN ages since I'd climbed out of my bedroom window. Still, here I was doing it anyway, so I could avoid the barrage of questions I'd face if I stepped into the hallway and ran into one of my parents. Mom had been hovering outside ever since I refused to come out for lunch. The sound of her pacing back and forth, likely debating whether to barge through the door or let me be, had driven me to the brink of insanity.

I knew she was just worried about me, but I hated it. If I knew what I could say to convince her I was weathering the storm on my own, I would have. But if I knew one thing about Ruby Hayes, it was that she was a certified hoverer.

After I ended my call with Laura, I felt like the walls were closing in on me. I wanted to get out, but wasn't sure where to go. If I took my car, I wouldn't put it past someone to follow me, which meant my refuge needed to be within walking distance. The barn would be crowded, and Lennox likely had the ranch hands on standby, ready to report my whereabouts if I stepped within three feet of the perimeter.

But then it dawned on me. There was one place I could go that was mine. One place where I could hide from the world and the people in it.

Which was how I found myself awkwardly climbing out of my bedroom window like a teenager sneaking out after curfew. It wasn't as easy as it used to be, but I didn't want to think about the reasons why. I was going to blame it on the fact that it had clearly shrunk in size since I was sixteen, and not the fact that I was nearly thirty-seven and wasn't as flexible as I used to be.

I peeked around the corner of the house to make sure there wasn't anyone wandering in the front yard who might see me. I knew how silly this would seem to anyone who might've seen me. After all, who feels the need to sneak around their own property? But anyone who'd met my family before might understand. After all, privacy and alone time weren't well-known concepts to the Hayes family.

The sun had nearly set by the time I made it to the tree-house. Thankfully, there was just enough light left that I didn't need to struggle with my phone in my mouth as I climbed the ladder.

When I made it to the top, I felt like I could breathe for the first time. I crawled across and let my head fall against the wall, feeling the weight slip from my shoulders. Birdsong filled the air, and I smiled. Just like I had promised Charlie, I occasionally climbed up here to keep an eye on our feathered friends. She'd been so excited it'd been hard to say no.

After lying dormant for so many years, I loved that she'd found joy here when it'd once been such an important part of my childhood. Aside from memories with her father, I had spent more time up here than I could remember. It was a haven from my sisters, a place I could go to when the noise in the house and my head became too much. Maybe that was why I could think of no better place to come tonight. I needed a semblance of the same peace I sought as a kid.

Not that it lasted long.

"Rapunzel, Rapunzel… Let down your hair!" I stilled at Lennox's voice coming from below the treehouse. Shit. How did she find me? Maybe if I stayed quiet, she'd go away. "I know you're up there," she called. I closed my eyes and drew my knees up close to my chest. She might have guessed it, but the only way for her to know for sure was to check for herself. There was no way she was going to do that, right? "You're really gonna make me climb my ass up there, aren't you? Alright, I guess…"

The sound of creaking wood had my molars grinding together. *I guess that answered my question.* "I'm not in the mood for company, Lennox. I'll be back at the house later."

"Tough titties. I'm coming up anyway."

Tough titties? Where the hell did she come up with this stuff?

A minute later, her blonde head popped through the floor latch. She scanned the space, narrowing her eyes when she saw me cowering in the corner. "Well, hello, Rapunzel," she said, batting her eyelashes my way. "It's so lovely to see you."

"Sometimes I wonder if Mom dropped you on your head as a kid," I grumbled. "Or maybe I did, and this is my penance."

"You're so dramatic," she said, rolling her eyes. She pulled herself up and scooted over next to me. "And that's saying something, coming from me."

"You did coin the term," I agreed, letting out a breath. Having this conversation was the last thing I wanted. I knew what she would say, but the thought of her over-the-top dose of positivity was nauseating. "I really wasn't lying, Len. I'm not in the mood for company. I don't say that to be rude, but—"

"You're sulking. I get it." She bumped her shoulder against mine. "But you don't have to sulk alone."

"That's kind of the whole idea."

"Well, not here. Not with me. I won't let you."

Some days I applauded her stubbornness, but today was not the day. Why couldn't my family just leave me be for two seconds? "And why not? Haven't I earned a little alone time?"

Lennox tilted her head, as if she was thinking about it. "Earned it? Sure. But I'm not known for my ability to give people space, and unfortunately for you, you're not an exception to the rule."

"God, you're annoying."

She laid her hand over her heart. "Oh, sis. I love you, too. Now... Tell me what has you hiding in your tower? Are you, per chance, waiting to be swept off your feet by a handsome prince with a killer singing voice?"

"I was just trying to get a little peace and quiet without someone, or multiple someones, coming by and knocking on my door, or trying to force feed me chicken-fried steak and brownies," I said, a little exasperated. "God forbid a girl take some time to herself."

"Wait, who made the brownies? Mom or Josie?" she asked. I mean, her question was valid; Josie could, and often did, burn toast if left unsupervised. While she'd gotten better over the past year, I was sure poor Lincoln had been forced to choke down her subpar cooking many times along the way. "Okay, you're right. We can circle back to that."

We settled into the silence, and I looked down, playing with the fringed hem of my shorts. Why was talking about my feelings so difficult? I could give the world's best pep talk to a random stranger if I needed to, but the moment the spotlight was on me, it was like everything I knew evaporated into thin air. All that good advice I gave other people? Yeah, I could use some for myself right now.

And there was something about talking about everything with Lennox that made me feel worse. It wasn't because I thought she would judge me. If anything, my little sister would be my ride or die, but I never wanted her to. I wanted to be the one she turned to, the one who was there to comfort her when she needed it. Not the other way around. I always strived to keep my struggles from my sisters, so letting my guard down and allowing her to see all the fucked up parts of me was jarring.

"I don't know, Len. Things have been confusing ever since Grady came back into the picture. I thought I was done with love. I thought my time had passed and that I needed to get used to being alone. Ever since the divorce became final, I've been trying to convince myself it was okay. That I'd be okay. And then *poof*," I mimed an explosion with my hands, "he fucked it all up."

Lennox chewed on her bottom lip. I could tell she was holding back, which wasn't like her. Her bluntness knew no bounds, typically. "Did he fuck it up?" she said, cautiously. "Or did he make you realize the things you were telling yourself were bullshit? I mean, in what world do you deserve to be alone? You're one of the best people I know, Cleo. You deserve all the good shit others deserve. Even more, probably."

I rolled my eyes. All of this was easy for her to say. She was barely twenty-eight. She still had her whole life ahead of her. "I'm old, Len—"

She held up her hand. "Jesus Christ, Cleo. You're thirty-six. That's not exactly Betty White. Even then, you think she'd let her age stop her from taking what she wanted? Fuck no. The idea that a woman's life dies with each year that passes is so ridiculous."

"I just mean—"

She barely took a breath before barreling through. "No, I know exactly what you mean. Cleo, look at Bishop. He's forty. He'll be forty-one in a few months. Do you think he doesn't deserve happiness because of his age?"

"Of course not," I said quickly. "But Bishop doesn't have two failed relationships behind him. There are zero expectations for him to marry or have kids, unlike there are for me. I don't know how many times I can be asked about my love life or have a pitying look shot my way when someone asks if I have children, and I say no."

Lennox let my words sink in before landing a killing blow. "It's easier to make yourself believe everything is over for you rather than dust yourself off and get your ass back in the saddle. What a miserable existence it must be to live in fear like that."

I barked out a cruel laugh. "Gee, thanks, Len. Appreciate your honesty."

She shrugged. "It's what I do."

"Yeah, well, I don't want to get hurt again. I don't know if I can survive it," I mumbled.

I felt her reach over, taking my hand in hers, the comforting embrace making my eyes sting with unshed tears. "You want the unfortunate, fucked up truth?"

"Not really, but I don't see how I have a choice now that you're here."

"Look… Even if you live your life in a bubble, never getting hurt again is out of the question. Pain is inevitable, whether you stub your toe or lose someone you love. There's no way to totally remove it from your life. What you have to do is make the pain worth it, which means you've got to put your cute ass out there occasionally. Now, tell me the truth… Do you love him?"

"Love?" I choked. She was giving me whiplash. "Are you crazy?"

Lennox stared at me, unmoving. "I am. Now answer the question. Do you love the man or not?"

Was the answer complicated? Sure. Absolutely. But I didn't even need to think about it. "Yes," I whispered. "I do, but it isn't that simple."

"Love never is, sis. But you know what? It's always worth it. If I had listened to all the bullshit going on in my head about Bishop and me… Well, I think I'd be pretty fucking miserable. But now I know what it means to feel true happiness, to know I'm loved for who I am and not just a fun time."

I stared at my sister, soaking in her features in the moonlight. She'd changed so much in the past year. I think, objectively, I always knew, but seeing and hearing it was different. Out of the three of us, Josie and Lennox had always been closer because of their age. And with nearly ten years between us, I struggled to gain even a fraction of the relationship they had. Maybe I was no better than all the other assholes who dismissed her because of her age, and yet, here she was, trying to pull me from my stupor. "Jeez, when did my baby sister get so wise?"

"I think it's because I'm getting dicked down by someone so experienced," she said, shooting me a wink. "Maybe some of his wisdom just transfers to me every time we have sex. Like wisdom osmosis. Does that make me an intellectual succubus?"

"God, no!" I laughed, and she joined in with me. We didn't stop until our cheeks were flushed and our sides hurt. "Please refrain from using 'dicked down' in your vocabulary, especially in front of me. That gives me a bad mental image."

Lennox sighed, rocking forward. "It's just the truth. If you only knew the way that man makes me scream—"

"Don't worry, I think the entire ranch has heard you two going at it one time or another," I said with a shake of my head. The same could be said about Josie, too. Their men were obsessed with them and seized every chance to show my sisters just how much.

"Cleo, some dick would do you good," she said, blowing out a breath. "Well… It's a good thing Grady's been standing right below us the entire time, huh?"

I froze, eyes darting to the hatch in the floor. "What do you mean?"

"Oh yeah," she said, smacking her forehead. "That's what I was coming to tell you. Loverboy showed up at the house looking for you. Mom went to check your room but it was empty. I was the kitchen, shooting the shit with Dad and Bishop, and she came back in on the border of hysterics. Because I'm so wonderful, I said I'd come find you. Grady, ever the gentleman, decided to tag along."

"Um, for the record, I was forced to tag along. I was all too happy to wait at the house," Grady called up.

Hearing his voice sent me reeling. What did he want? How much had he heard? Oh my god, I told Lennox I loved him. Surely, he hadn't heard me, though. No, there was no way. No way.

"Goddammit, Lennox! Why would you do that?" I hissed. "And you left the hatch open?" I pointed to the opening in the floor. This was so much worse than I thought. Honestly, if the earth could just swallow me up right now, it would be fucking fantastic.

"Duh," she said, rolling her eyes. "How else was he supposed to hear my awesome pep talk?"

"I'm going to kill you," I murmured. "I'm going to freaking murder you."

"Yeah, yeah, just talk to him. One way or the other, y'all need to figure this shit out," she said, crawling toward the hatch. "And listen, if you still wanna kill me after you talk to him," she trailed off, giving me a smirk as she lowered her body through the opening. "You're gonna have to catch me."

"Lennox!" I shouted, watching her disappear down the ladder.

"Love you, Rapunzel!" Lennox hit the ground and waved up at me. Then she pointed toward a figure in the shadows. "Don't fuck this up, Loverboy."

When Grady stepped up toward the ladder, the sight of him took my breath away. Fear had my heart rate spiking, making me want to run, but there was something else there, too. Something warm and comforting, like a warm blanket on a cold night. Seeing him here, in this place, *our* place, felt right.

He looked up, a tentative smile on his lips. "Hey, bluebird. Mind if I come up?"

grady

. . .

I WASN'T EXACTLY sure what made me drive out to Black Springs Ranch. One minute, I was sitting on the couch, listening to Charlie and her mom chat on the phone, and the next, I was telling Liv we had to go. Even though she had no idea what was going on either, my daughter was giddy as I buckled her in and told her where we were headed.

Lennox's words had played on repeat since we'd talked yesterday. I wanted to give Cleo all the space she needed, but how much space was too much? The last thing I wanted was to give her the idea I was giving up, and I worried if I didn't show up for her or push just a little, then that was precisely what she would think.

I knew my unexpected appearance at the ranch for the summer camp had come as a shock to her, but it was the only way I had of getting her attention. Electronic communication was clearly out of the picture, given her proclivity for blocking my number. I was sure if I'd sent her an email, it would've ended up the same way. And I had no doubt, if I'd sent a letter, it would've ended up in the trash without a second thought.

So, what was another random pop-up? I'd managed to break

through her walls long enough to steal an earth-shattering kiss —one I still hadn't been able to get off my mind—with the last one. Might as well try for number two.

Deja vu smacked me straight in the face as I walked up to her house and knocked, just like I had when I'd picked her up for our first date. And, just like before, it was Mrs. Ruby Hayes who'd answered the door. We just stared at one another for a moment before her gaze drifted to my daughter at my side. She was holding her stuffed bunny tightly to her chest, grinning widely at the dazed woman.

"Is Miss Cleo here?" she asked. "My daddy wants to talk to her."

I thought we were going to get turned away. Maybe we would've if Lennox hadn't popped her head around the corner and told her mom to let us in. Charlie ran past Ruby toward Lennox, who immediately opened her arms for a hug. Ruby excused herself to check on Cleo, which left me, Charlie, Lennox, her father, and her fiancé awkwardly staring at one another with nothing to say.

When Ruby came back in a panic and told us Cleo was missing, Lennox offered to look for her. I said I would stay behind with Charlie. Instead, I was dragged out the front door by a death grip on the collar of my T-shirt, and Lennox was telling her parents and fiancé to keep an eye on my daughter.

"You just don't listen, do you?" Lennox asked, finally letting me go.

I held up my hands. "I wanted to, I tried to, but I just kept wondering how much was too much. I don't want her to think I don't want her, Lennox. She needs to know—"

"I'm glad you didn't listen to me," she said with a sigh. "Sometimes I forget that while Cleo asks for space, sometimes it's the last thing she really wants or needs. It's like she wants time to think things through, but she also needs the reassurance of the chase. To know you're going to be here—"

"I am," I said, earnestly. "And this is me trying to prove it."

Lennox stopped near the fence line. I could make out the treehouse just ahead. "There just might be hope for you yet," she said with a smirk. "Now, I'm going to go chat her up, make sure she's alright, then the rest will be up to you."

Before I could say anything else, she skipped over to the tree and called out for Cleo. I couldn't hear much, but after a moment, Lennox climbed up the ladder and disappeared from sight.

Even though I knew I shouldn't, I was curious to know what they were talking about. What would Cleo tell Lennox she would be too afraid to say to me? Did she let her sister in, or did she meet just as many walls as I did?

Slowly and quietly, I walked over, careful to avoid tripping over a fallen limb that might snap and give me away. That was the last thing I needed right now. I looked up and realized the hatch was left open. I wondered if Lennox did that on purpose, or if she didn't care. Either way, I wasn't going to let the opportunity go to waste.

I could only make out little fragments that didn't make much sense on their own. Frustrated, I was close to giving up and slinking back to the shadows when I heard Lennox's voice, clear and strong. "Do you love him?"

I waited impatiently, straining to hear Cleo's answer, but nothing was clear. They were speaking in hushed tones and hurried whispers. Goddammit. I needed to know what she would reply to that question more than anything else.

If she loved me, it meant I had a shot.

If she loved me, we could make it work.

I never really stopped to think if love was in the cards so soon. I knew regardless of what had happened in the past, I never stopped loving her. If she asked me the same question right now, I would've said yes. No ifs, ands, or buts about it. I couldn't be sure about Cleo's answer, though. Her head was a minefield. At any moment, one misstep might see your whole world ending. I didn't fault her for it, knowing I damn well contributed to planting some bombs of my own. It was very well possible I sealed my own fate.

But only time would tell.

A loud shriek from above had my eyes drifting to see what the commotion was. Lennox climbed down the ladder as fast as she could, and I almost wanted to laugh at the look on Cleo's face as she stared after her sister, full of disbelief.

Lennox pointed at me. "Don't fuck this up, Loverboy." And then she ran back toward the house, her footsteps a rapidly fading rhythm.

Stepping out of the darkness, I placed my hand on the ladder and looked up. "Hey, bluebird. Mind if I come up?"

She narrowed her eyes. "Do I have a choice?"

"You always have a choice, Cleo." I took a deep breath. "I just hope you choose me."

For a moment, she didn't speak. I wondered if she was going to tell me to kick rocks, but something in her expression softened just a touch. "If you can make it up here without having a panic attack, I guess I'll let you stay."

"You've got yourself a deal," I said, beginning my ascent. Honestly, I was surprised this thing could hold my weight. I'd been worried about that as a kid, and I'd been nothing but a tall, lanky thing back then. I'd gained a significant amount of muscle over the years, and suddenly, every creak and moan felt more significant.

When I finally made it to the top, I let out a shaky breath. I wasn't sure I felt better about being off the ladder and in the treehouse, but at least if I was going to fall through the floor, Cleo would be the last thing I saw. That counted for something, right?

I sat next to her, waiting for the moment she'd tell me she'd changed her mind, to go away, but she never did. I stretched out my legs and looked around. So much was different, but it was familiar, too. It felt a little outdated and rundown, which is how I sometimes felt too. Time had that effect on everything, it seemed.

"What're you doing here?" Cleo asked, finally breaking the silence.

"I'm here to see you."

"I know," she said dryly. "But why? Why did you come out here tonight? What were you hoping for?"

"We kissed six days ago, and then you ran away. When you didn't show up to Charlie's riding lessons, I was worried about you, Cleo. I just wanted to make sure you were okay. Lennox told me to back off, but I clearly didn't listen."

"Surprising for that traitor," she muttered. "Especially bringing you over here to goad me into conversations I'm not ready to have."

"For what it's worth, I didn't really hear anything." She looked skeptical, and I chuckled. "I mean, it wasn't for a lack of trying."

This time, she smiled. It was small, but it was there. Suddenly, I felt sixteen again—watching her step into the room with that same cautious joy. I'd take it as a win. "That's good, at least."

I snapped my fingers. "There was one question, though, that I caught the end of. I was hoping maybe you could repeat your answer for clarity's sake. Something about love? I don't know. My hearing is shit these days. I blame it on the years of loud music."

Cleo stared at me for a moment before looking away, her mouth set in a hard line. "You want to know what I said when Lennox asked if I loved you." Her voice was deceptively calm, but her hands were shaking. She glanced down, squeezing them together to gain control.

"I do," I said. Any humor I had moments ago was gone. I

didn't want to hide behind it anymore. If there was ever a moment to lay all my cards on the table, it was now. It was here, in our spot. "I need to know."

She tipped her head back with a low groan. "Grady, you've been back in my life for less than two weeks after being out of it for seventeen years. How the hell am I supposed to answer that question when I don't even know how I feel about it fully?"

"Easy," I said, shrugging. "Ask me if I love you."

"What?"

"Ask me if I love you. It only seems fair for me to dish out what I'm asking you to. So do it. Ask me, bluebird."

Cleo's lip trembled as she turned her gaze toward me. "Do you love me—"

"Yes," I responded. I didn't even let her finish, because I didn't need to think about it.

"Grady—"

"The answer is yes, I love you. I love you now like I loved you then. Maybe more, if I'm honest. Back then, I was a coward who wasn't prepared to fight for you. I let the best thing I ever had walk away from me. But I'm not the same stupid kid I was then, bluebird. I'm a man who knows what he wants and is willing to do anything to get it."

It was terrifying laying my heart on the line like that. If Cleo wanted to, she could crush it beneath her pretty little foot without a second thought. I wouldn't blame her if she did. I probably deserved it. Still, it was a risk I had to take. She needed to know how much she meant to me, if she didn't already.

"You know, I've spent my life analyzing our relationship. I mean, we were only together for a few years. It was high school love. We should've been over it by now."

"Is this your way of telling me you're over it?"

"No. That's the problem." I tried to pretend I didn't notice the way she trembled, trying my hardest not to take her in my arms, rather than let her collect her thoughts. "Did you ever stop and think the issue wasn't that we didn't love one another, but maybe we were just too young for that kind of commitment?" Her voice was barely above a whisper as we sat side-by-side. The cicadas sang their summer song, keeping the silence from swallowing us whole.

"What do you mean?" I asked, rolling my head against the worn wood of the treehouse. I wasn't going to risk missing a moment of the vulnerability she was willing to show.

Her gaze dropped to her lap, where she fiddled with the hem of her shirt. "We fell for one another so hard and fast when we were kids. What we had... It felt like that forever kind of love, the type you never wanna lose, but what business did two teenagers have feeling things that deeply? It was terrifying."

"People feel that all the time, and they make it through, bluebird," I countered. "My parents—your parents—they have the kind of relationship others can only dream of. The kind books and movies only hope to convey," I paused, making sure she really heard what I said next. "The kind I wrote songs about because I could never get you out of my head or my heart."

Cleo's ragged exhale went straight to my aching chest. "We were just so young, Grady," she said, sniffing. "I thought love was supposed to be easy, but ours wasn't. Not once we left Ashwood."

"You didn't fight—"

I regretted the words as soon as they left my mouth, but it was too late. Her head snapped up, eyes narrowing into small slits as she turned to fully face me. "What'd you just say?"

"I didn't mean—"

"How dare you?" she whispered harshly, scooting away from me. Her hands fisted in the fabric of her shirt so tightly I thought it would rip. "From the moment we left for school up until that final fucking night, it's all I was doing. You prioritized everything over me—over *us*—and I let you. I made excuses for you when we had plans with friends, and you never showed.

God, there were so many times you let me down, and yet I kept telling myself it would be different someday. I kept telling myself it would get better, if I held on just a little longer, you'd show me an ounce of the attention you showed your music. Sometimes I didn't even recognize you. Especially not when you stumbled in drunk—"

"I was trying to make a name for myself," I gritted out. Her words, although spoken out of a place of anger and hurt, weren't untrue. That was the worst part. But it also wasn't fair. It wasn't fair she saw these things as failures when they led me to some of the most extraordinary highs in my career. I made something out of myself. Couldn't she see that? "I was trying to make sure we would be set for the rest of our lives. That I wouldn't be some big disappointment you'd look back on in twenty years, but I guess it didn't matter in the end, did it? I was always going to lose you."

"We stopped talking, Grady. There was no communication between us. Even when we did talk, it was always about your music, your gigs, the band you wanted to put together… It was never about us or the plans we made. We used to dream together, but I suddenly felt like I was alone even though you were right there in front of me," she cried. "You never asked me about school or my grades or even my family. Never asked about what I liked or wanted. It was all about you."

How could she think that? Despite what we'd been through, how could she not see everything I did was for her? For us? It was irrational, but it pissed me off. "Bullshit. Yes, I did."

"You missed so many parties with friends, you missed our anniversary, both of our birthdays, but I was there for every gig," she bit out, jabbing her finger into her chest emphatically. "Even if it meant giving up studying for finals or an extra-curric-ular, I was there because I knew how much it meant to you. And yet you dare to sit there and say I didn't fucking fight for us? You were the one who didn't fight, Grady. You never reached out. You just moved on like I was nothing. Like what we had was nothing."

"That's not true!" I said, voice rising. "I was ready to give you everything at that stupid fucking rodeo, and you were with *him*." My eyes darted to her hand, where another man's ring once sat. "You moved on—"

"What? I wasn't with anyone then—"

"He put his fucking hand on you so casually. Like he'd been doing it for years," I seethed. "He took my place and then you fucking married him."

If she hated me after my outburst, I wouldn't blame her. I hated myself in that moment. I hated that I brought him up when she was finally being honest. I hated that I was still filled with so much anger—at her, at me, especially at him.

Cleo blinked in surprised understanding. "That's why you left, wasn't it? You thought I was with someone else?"

I dropped my head. "I wasn't in a good place back then. Mom had just found out about her cancer. I thought we were going to lose her so much sooner than we did. When I saw you that night... I don't know. I thought it was fate. Some big fucking sign this would be our second chance. And then he showed up."

Her eyes turned to a blazing inferno. "Maybe if you hadn't let your bruised ego get in the way, you would've *asked*. Maybe if you weren't such a goddamn coward, you wouldn't have left without knowing for sure." She shook her head. "God, we are a fucking mess. Look at us, still harboring so much anger and resentment for things that don't matter in the long run."

"Help me understand, then, bluebird? Enlighten me."

She leveled me with a crushing glare. "Thomas was a drunken, abusive asshole who would rather lay a hand on me in anger than touch me like a husband should. He gambled away our savings and fell into debt with the wrong people. I had to get a restraining order after I filed for divorce because he called me incessantly, and I had to turn my phone off. I didn't agree to date Thomas until I found out about *your* engagement, you jackass. I texted him the night I found out about you."

The hate I felt for him and myself grew tenfold. "What?"

She scoffed, wiping beneath her eyes. "He'd been trying to date me for years, but every single time he asked me out, I turned him down. I made sure he knew I just wanted to be friends because my stupid heart still belonged to you."

Her words smothered the raging fire burning in my veins. I knew I'd been a selfish prick when we were younger, but having her lay it out so plainly was fucking agonizing. Cleo deserved someone far better than me.

"At some point, Grady, love isn't enough. It doesn't matter how much of it there is, or how long it lasted. I needed actions. I needed security. I fucking needed *you,* but you were never there. I had to make that call and break my own heart before you shattered it completely."

Tears ran down her face as she sucked in a ragged breath. This was worse than losing her all those years ago. Hearing her side of things, watching her break in front of me, was eye-opening in a way that left me feeling empty.

"Bluebird..." I whispered, voice cracking at the end of the word. I crawled toward her hesitantly. If I tried to take her in my arms, would she let me? I didn't deserve it.

To my surprise, she went willingly. Cleo lay her head on my chest, right above my heart. Her hot tears soaked through the fabric of my shirt, body heaving with heartbreaking sobs. I hugged her tightly to me; one arm banded around her waist as the other rubbed circles along her back. "I'm sorry. I'm so fucking sorry."

"I fucking needed you," she cried, echoing her previous statement. "You made everything better until you didn't. I might've been the one to walk away, but my life has been one disaster after another since that day. I've hated myself for not being stronger for us, for not riding it out, but goddamn it..." she hiccupped, and I squeezed her tighter. "I think I hated you, too. Now, I've made so many mistakes, and I don't know how to fix them."

I rested my chin atop her head, trying my best to stay strong for the both of us, but that control was slipping with each passing second. "Let me in. Let me help."

"You can't. You can't fix this. You can't fix *me*."

I couldn't take it anymore. I moved quickly, pulling her up to straddle my hips. My hands found her face, and I forced her to look at me. "You are not fucking broken, bluebird. The fact you think that? God, it breaks my fucking heart. You're perfect the way you are."

Cleo's eyes were closed as she pushed at my chest, trying to break free from my hold. "Stop, let me go."

"Not until you listen to me—"

Fresh tears fell as she tried to stand, but I needed her to understand this. To hear me. "Grady, please..."

"I will fucking kill anyone who made you feel like you aren't enough—"

"Goddammit, Grady. Fucking let me go!" Her nails dug into my shoulders, voice breaking as a ragged scream tore through her throat.

Cleo moved the moment I let go, clambering away from me. Her chest heaved as she fought to catch her breath. What the fuck was happening?

"Tell me what you need, Cleo. Talk to me, baby," I pleaded.

She closed her eyes, hands pressed tightly to her chest as tears fell. Every instinct told me to go to her, but what if I made it worse? She was barely holding on as it was. "I can't—"

Before I could think about it further, I slowly moved forward. Cleo was lost in her head. It was like I didn't exist at all.

Reaching up, I gently plucked her hands away. She resisted at first, but the moment I laid her palms flat on my chest so she could feel the steady beat of my heart, she paused. "Breathe with me," I whispered, sucking in a deep inhale. I waited for her to follow, but she didn't, keeping her eyes squeezed shut. "Come on, bluebird. Breathe with me."

On the next inhale, I felt Cleo's body shakily comply as the pain and anger she held onto melted away. She shuddered through each long breath, but took them in stride. I did my best to keep my tempo even, giving her something steady to focus on. "One more," I said, guiding her through another. As we let it go, she finally opened her eyes. They were still wary, but they weren't wild.

Neither of us spoke, too afraid to dispel whatever this was between us. Our gazes dropped to where her hands lay flat on my chest. I expected her to pull away, especially after she shied from my touch moments ago. Instead, her fingers curled into the fabric as if she was trying to claw through my skin for a better hold. Through our shared breaths, we'd drifted closer somehow. I didn't remember moving, but needing to be near her was an instinct I couldn't ignore.

She may not have said the words, but somehow, I knew she loved me. I knew she loved me despite my fuck-ups, despite my faults, despite the years and broken promises. I could feel it in my soul.

"Grady," she whispered. Her voice was raw, broken.

"Bluebird," I said back, shifting forward until our knees brushed. "Are you okay?"

She shook her head. "Not right now."

"How can I help?" I asked, resting my forehead against hers. "Tell me how to help. I'll do anything—"

"Kiss me."

The words hung between us, echoing through my head like the ringing of a bell. God, I wanted to. I wanted to kiss her, to hold her, to love her. I wanted to make up for lost time and erase every bit of pain I had ever caused her.

Her grip on my shirt grew tighter as she repeated herself in my silence. "Kiss me, Grady."

"I'm so scared to hurt you, Cleo." My hands ran up the smooth, exposed skin of her thighs until they rested on her hips. "I want to so badly, but—"

"I'm not going to run away again," she said earnestly. "Give me another chance."

"Oh, baby," I whispered, curling my fingers through her belt loop. "I don't deserve you."

We moved at the same time, closing the distance between our mouths in a clash of tongues and teeth. Unlike before, her arms wound their way around my neck, deepening the kiss until I no longer knew where I ended and she began. I couldn't get enough of her. Her taste, her scent, the subtle way she fought for dominance, it was all intoxicating.

"Would it be forward to ask you to come home with me?" I murmured against her lips. "I don't want to let you go now that I have you in my arms."

"What about Charlie?" she asked between impassioned kisses.

"She's at the house with your family."

Cleo pulled back, a single eyebrow cocked. "What do you mean?"

I sat back on my heels, trying to ignore the way my dick was straining against the zipper of my jeans. "Well, I couldn't leave her at home alone. It's just the two of us." I shrugged. "So, she's my wing-woman, I guess."

"That's kind of adorable," she said quietly, biting her lip.

"She is," I agreed. "So, what do you say? Come home with us?"

cleo

. . .

WHEN WE WALKED BACK to my parents' house, Lennox met us outside with a half-asleep Charlie and a packed weekend bag for me, which came with strict instructions not to come back until Monday for riding lessons. I wasn't sure how I felt about staying an entire weekend with them, but I owed it to myself and Grady to find out.

The ride was quiet. By the time we reached town, Charlie was out like a light. I had to stop myself from giggling when her soft little snores filled the silence in the cab. Sometimes I would catch Grady's eyes drifting our way, a smile on his lips. I wasn't sure if he was just shocked to find me in his truck, or if it was because he saw his daughter and me together. It wouldn't be the first time. I often felt him staring at us when we were together.

Up ahead, the familiar craftsman house came into view. I'd purposely avoided this area after Grady's mom died. The last time I was here was only two days before she passed. She'd called me, voice barely above a whisper, and I dropped every-thing to hurry over.

I held her hand the entire time we were together, laughing and crying as we dug into our past. Only for her would I walk down a Grady-filled memory lane. Before leaving, she had tugged me back into a hug and thanked me for being such a presence in her life. As I went to leave, Robert brought in a large blue box with a gold ribbon on the top. Marsha told me not to open it until I got home, but I was too curious. I ripped into it the moment I was in my car.

I wish I had waited.

Inside, there was an all-too-familiar set of vintage Pyrex mixing bowls. One of the first times Grady brought me home to meet his mom, we had gabbed about how much we loved baking. I'd admired the set, with its blue snowflake pattern. Marsha said it had been passed down to her from her mother, and she hoped to one day pass it to her daughter-in-law.

I think, somehow, she knew it was going to be the last time we saw one another.

And she was right.

Grady cut the engine in the driveway, but neither of us made an effort to move. So much had been said tonight. Every part of my body felt heavy. Slowly, he reached over and gave my hand a squeeze. My heart did a little flip as I turned toward him. He was already staring at me, lips quirking up ever so slightly as my gaze dropped to his mouth.

"Help me get her inside?" he whispered, motioning toward his sleeping daughter. I nodded and followed him outside. He dropped the keys into my palm before walking to the other side and helping her out of her seat. I couldn't stop my hands from shaking as I unlocked the door and held it open for them. I watched as he quietly padded down the hall and disappeared into her room.

The house had been remodeled at some point. The walls in the living room had once been a dreary off-white color Marsha used to complain about, but now they were a pastel blue that reminded me of her son's eyes. In the kitchen, a colorful back-splash was installed below new white cabinets. I wondered what his mom would think, since she was notoriously messy in the kitchen. She probably would've had a good time making Robert regret wanting something that was so easily stained.

I felt Grady's presence behind me before he tentatively slid an arm around my middle and stepped closer. I let myself lean into his touch, be grounded by it. How had I fought this for so long when being with him felt so right?

"What're you thinking about?" he whispered, tightening his hold on me.

I shivered, feeling his breath along my exposed neck. "That I'm an idiot." His body grew tense, and I moved to correct myself. "Not in the way you think."

"Care to enlighten me, then?"

"I keep wondering when this—being here with you—will feel awkward, but it doesn't. It feels right. I think that's what I've been fighting all this time." I spun in his arms, unable to read the expression on his face. He was just as guarded as I was now that both of our hearts were on the line.

With one hand firmly planted on my lower back, he brought his other up to cup my face. "I know what a big deal this is for you, bluebird. And I don't intend on fucking this up again. I hope you know that."

There were so many things we still needed to figure out and talk about. There was the matter of his wife, or soon-to-be-ex, I guess. How did she feel about this whole mess we'd gotten ourselves into? And then, of course, there was the living situation. His entire life was in Tennessee, and mine was here. With Charlie in the mix, that added a layer of complexity to the problem I don't think either of us knew how to navigate.

But I didn't want to think about all of that. Not tonight, at least. It was too exhausting, and my emotions were spent.

"I know," I said, sliding my hands up to rest on his chest. The feel of his heart beneath my palms was comforting. I hadn't realized just how much until he'd forced me to feel it in the treehouse. Laura would be pleased to hear about the breathing exercises, though. "I don't want to hurt you either."

"Is there a 'but' coming at the end of that sentence?"

"No," I shook my head. "Not yet anyway." A muscle ticked in his jaw, but he didn't argue or push it. He seemed just as spent as I was. "So, where am I sleeping?"

Grady pulled me closer until there was no space left between our bodies. "With me. I'm not letting you out of my space for even a minute, not now that I've finally got you back in my arms."

His words did something to me. I never understood what Grady saw in me when we were sixteen, and I was no closer to figuring it out now that I was thirty-six. I had changed a lot over the years, my body softer and battered. Thomas always made me feel insecure about not taking better care of myself, always telling me I needed to do more or I'd let myself go. But from the moment Grady saw me standing in the bar over a year ago, I'd never felt an ounce of anything but appreciation from him.

"You know you aren't going to get lucky tonight, right? There will be no funny business."

He chuckled. "Not even a little bit?"

"Nope."

"What about a kiss?" he asked, tilting my head so our mouths were nearly touching. "Surely that's acceptable."

I hummed as his lips swept over mine, but didn't claim me. "A kiss often leads to more," I said, barely managing to restrain myself.

"I can be good for you," he promised. "I can even beg if it will help my case."

Goddammit. Here I was setting the rules, and yet he already had me wanting to break them. I had to be strong, though. No matter how badly my body wanted him, I couldn't go there until we talked about all the things we'd left unsaid.

But a kiss? I refused to deny either of us that much.

"As much as I would love to hear you beg," I said, loving the way his chest vibrated in a deep growl at my words, "that's not necessary tonight."

Just like in the treehouse, we moved at the same time. We were like magnets, bound to collide no matter how hard we fought against the pull. The taste of him was intoxicating. He had me wanting to say fuck the rules and give in. I might be the one begging by the time we finally came back up for air.

Without breaking the kiss, he reached down and lifted me into his arms. I wrapped my legs around him as we began to move, not stopping to think about where we were going or if I was too heavy for him. My only focus was on him and the growing hardness between us. I was just glad my own arousal wasn't as obvious because I could feel how much of a mess I was.

"Don't scream," he said, breaking the kiss. I barely had time to register what he was doing before he winked and tossed me through the air. I landed on the bed with a soft thud, letting out a stream of giggles as he followed me down and settled between my legs.

I thought he would kiss me, but he didn't. Instead, he just stared down at me. The curtains were drawn, letting just enough moonlight in I could make out the stubble lining his jaw and the subtle curve of his swollen lips. Reaching up, I traced them with my fingertips, feeling the moisture left behind from our frenzied kisses and loving the way they parted at my touch.

"What am I going to do with you?" he asked, lowering to his elbows so he hovered just a few inches away from my mouth. Whether by his own doing or just his body seeking friction, his hips ground against my center. My back bowed and my mind short-circuited from the contact.

"You're making it hard—"

"No, actually, that would be you," he said, repeating the motion.

I laughed. "You know what I mean. We can't. Not yet anyway. You promised you'd be good."

Grady bent down, quickly kissing me before he rolled away with a groan. He settled beside me, both of us staring up at the dark ceiling. "I know, I know. I will."

I let the silence sit for only a minute before I said, "It isn't because I don't want to. You know that, right? I'm not doing this to torture you. I want it, want you, just as badly."

I kept my eyes up as the bed shifted and Grady faced me. He reached out, grabbed my hand, and brought it to his lips for a kiss. "I know, baby. You don't need to tell me." I felt him smile against my skin. "But if you want to tell me how wet I've made you, by all means… Go ahead."

"Grady!" I turned around to see the playful twinkle in his eyes. "You're only torturing yourself."

"Won't you put me out of my misery?"

My lips twitched as I suppressed my grin. "No. Only good boys get rewards."

He groaned, making me laugh. "You're killing me here."

"The wait will be worth it," I said, hoping I was right. It'd been so long since I'd been with anyone. Was it possible to forget how to have sex? What if I wasn't any good?

His thumb ran along the crease between my brows, smoothing it away. "When it comes to you, it always is."

grady

. . .

"DADDY?"

I heard Charlie's voice from down the hall, but there was a hot, sweaty body clinging to my own, and I couldn't move. Opening my eyes, I looked down to find Cleo curled into my side, sleeping peacefully. Our legs were tangled together, and her arm was banded around my middle, pulling me tighter. Though she would argue with me if I ever said anything about it, Cleo was so fucking adorable when she was sleeping. If this were how I woke up every morning for the rest of my life, I'd consider myself a lucky man.

But my daughter was about to burst through my bedroom door any minute, and while I didn't mind her knowing Cleo slept in here, I wasn't sure if Cleo would.

Gently, I reached over and ran circles across her back. Her body stirred, pulling me tighter and moving her leg up until it brushed my already hardening cock—which was going to be an issue if my daughter came in before it'd gone down.

"Morning bluebird," I whispered as she blinked open her eyes.

She let out a little groan as she burrowed into my chest and hid her face. "I don't want to get up. Not yet."

"I don't either, but Charlie—"

In an instant, she rolled away and clutched the covers to her chest. We'd fallen asleep in the clothes we wore yesterday, so it was comical she was trying to hide. "Oh my God. Charlie," she said, glancing at the door. We could both hear her padding down the hall.

"It's okay," I said. "She just normally likes to come lie in bed with me in the mornings, and I wanted to give you a warning."

"She can't see me in here," Cleo hissed, jumping out of bed.

"Where do you think she believes you are right now?" I chuckled. "I guarantee she checked the couch first and is coming in here to tell me you aren't there."

Cleo narrowed her eyes and dashed into the bathroom just before Charlie pushed open the door. She stood there, hair wild and drool stains on her cheek, with her bunny clutched in her arms.

"Good morning, sunshine," I said, holding my arms out for her.

She padded over and crawled into my bed, taking Cleo's spot at my side. "Daddy, Miss Cleo isn't on the couch."

"I know, sweetie."

Charlie's lip wobbled. "Did she leave without saying goodbye?"

I opened my mouth to answer when Cleo stepped out of my bathroom. "Nope, I'm right here. Just needed to use your daddy's bathroom really quickly."

My daughter smiled. "Yay! I'm so glad you're still here. I wasn't ready for you to leave. I wanted to show you my room and all my stuffies." She hopped out of my arms and held out her hand for Cleo to take. "Come on, let's go."

Without waiting for an answer, Charlie tugged Cleo toward the door. Cleo looked back at me, and I shrugged. "Duty calls," I mouthed to her before Charlie managed to get her all the way down the hall.

As I lay my head against the headboard, I listened to Charlie chatter a million words a minute. She began telling Cleo a complete history of each stuffed animal she had lined up on her bed, and the ones that were on the dresser. Occasionally, I'd hear Cleo ask a question or murmur her appreciation, but it wasn't enough. I wanted to see the two of them together. Curiosity finally won out, and I quietly got out of bed and tiptoed down to Charlie's old room.

"Did you know this used to be your dad's room?" Cleo asked. She was sitting on the blue and cream checkered rug on the floor, surrounded by every stuffed animal Charlie owned.

"Really?" Charlie asked, hopping down from the bed to sit in front of Cleo.

"Yup. But it looks so much better now that it's yours. It used to be filled with pictures of cars and sports, with dirty laundry all over the floor."

Charlie scrunched up her face in disgust. She looked around the room, and I wondered if she was imagining what the space used to look like before. "Yeah, I like this better for sure."

"In my defense, I really liked cars and sports." Charlie and Cleo both startled as I stood in the doorway. "And I hated doing laundry."

"I know for a fact your mom did your laundry," Cleo said, crossing her arms. "You were just a dirty teenage boy who couldn't be bothered to put his clothes in the hamper."

"You knew my grandma?" Charlie's voice was softer.

Mom had died well before my daughter was born, but I did what I could to make sure she knew how much they would've loved each other. When Dad was home, he always brought out the thick scrapbooks Mom made. Charlie loved looking at pictures of me from when I was a kid. Without knowing it, she'd seen Cleo, too.

Cleo cleared her throat. "I did. She was an amazing woman. Would've loved you to pieces, you know?"

"That's what Daddy says. He said she loved to make sweet treats, too. Just like you!"

"Your grandma actually taught me a lot about baking. She's the reason I'm so good now."

Charlie's eyes grew wide. "Really?"

"Absolutely."

"Can you teach me?" Charlie asked, hopping up and down on her bed.

"Of course, but," Cleo paused, looking between my daughter and me, "I need to run out to my house for something first."

Charlie instantly froze. "No, I don't want you to go," she said with a pout. "I want you to stay here with us."

"I'll be right back." Cleo pushed to her feet, placing her hands on her hips. "If I make a list of ingredients, do you think you can help your daddy get them at the store?"

I felt similar to Charlie. I didn't want Cleo to go either. What could she possibly need from the ranch that she couldn't wait for until she went home? This was supposed to be our time together. Selfishly, I didn't want to spend one more minute outside of her proximity.

"Is that okay, Grady?"

I blinked, focusing back on the two women in front of me. "Sure, yeah. I can get groceries."

Cleo studied me for a moment before nodding her head. "Great. Do you mind if I borrow your dad's truck to drive out there?"

"You can take mine," I said, jerking my head toward the table in the entryway where my keys sat.

"Do you need her booster seat?"

"No, he's got one in his. We'll be fine." I stepped out of the way as she walked past me, looking back at my daughter, who was sitting on her bed, clutching that damn rabbit to her chest.

I hoped to God this wasn't Cleo trying to run. Maybe she just needed some space, maybe I rushed into things, but I hoped she would tell me that rather than leave. Pushing off the door jam, I followed her.

My fingers latched onto her wrist, and I gently spun her back to me. "You're coming back, right? You're not leaving?"

I wasn't sure what I looked like or if she heard the worry in my voice I was trying to hide, but Cleo's eyes softened. "I'm coming back. There's just something I have tucked away I think Charlie will really love. I want to share it with her."

"You promise?"

Cleo stepped forward and cupped my cheek. "I promise. I'll text you the ingredients, okay? Maybe you can make some more of that mac-n-cheese you made for the cookout?"

I smirked. "You liked that, huh?"

"Maybe a little bit. I don't need you getting a big head, or anything."

Leaning in, I kissed her. It was so breathtakingly normal I almost forgot we hadn't been doing this domestic shit our entire lives. "Hurry back to us."

A soft blush crept across her cheeks. I loved the way it lit up her entire face. "I like the way that sounds."

The only thing I could think of was the truth. "So do I."

"CAN WE GET POPCORN, TOO, DADDY?" Charlie asked, leaning over to point at the box on the shelf.

"What do we need popcorn for?" I asked skeptically. "I thought you didn't like it because it gets stuck in your teeth?"

"Yeah, but you do. So does Cleo. And you can't have a movie night without popcorn and candy, Daddy. That's silly."

"So, the adults get popcorn while you get candy, huh?" I

asked, reading between the lines. My daughter was about as subtle as a freight train. She was already sneaking away toward the chocolate at the end of the aisle.

Charlie sighed. "I guess you can have some chocolate too, Daddy."

"What about Cleo? Does she not get any?"

She held up two boxes. "I was obviously going to get her some."

"Alright, alright," I said, snatching them from her hand and tossing them in the basket. "Anything else we need?"

Charlie shook her head, and I started moving toward the register. When Cleo asked me to go to the store, I was worried it'd be too crowded. Since I got back to town, I'd been having everything delivered using Dad's account. The last thing I needed was to be mobbed at the grocery store. People knew I was in town, sure, but I didn't want to take my daughter out there and run the risk of some dick from high school making things weird.

Still, I tugged my baseball cap down further as we stepped up to the register. Charlie was helping me place our groceries on the conveyor belt when I looked up and saw my face on the front of a tabloid magazine.

"Splittsville, USA. Country Icons Hart and Wilde Call It Quits!"

Fucking hell. I'd kept an eye on the media ever since our divorce was filed on Monday. Everything had been relatively quiet the first few days, but it didn't last long. Yesterday, Liv's PR team alerted us to rumors that were beginning to circulate. Talks of infidelity on both sides and bitter divorce proceedings were running rampant. It was all bullshit. A way for sleazy journalists to make a quick buck. We were working on getting them removed, but no matter how fast we worked, they worked faster.

If I had seen this when we walked in, I would've turned around and told Charlie we'd bake another day, but it was too late now. We were already here. The only thing I could do was hope the cashier didn't pay any attention to tabloids. Thankfully, she was a younger woman who seemed completely unfazed by anything happening around her.

Just to be safe, I grabbed the magazine and turned it around so I wasn't staring at a picture of myself.

When Charlie and I had everything unloaded, I helped her move the basket forward so we could put the bagged items into the cart. As the cashier rang up the final item, she looked up. All hope I had to go unrecognized vanished as her eyes grew wide with recognition.

"Oh my god," she squealed. "It's you!"

Shit.

"Hi," I said, quickly looking around to find curious eyes glancing my way. Charlie shrank back near me, knowing all too well how hectic public attention could become.

She played with the end of her braid, staring up at me through thick lashes. "I'm, like, your biggest fan. I know all the words to every single one of your songs, and I've been to, like, three of your concerts."

"Thank you. I appreciate your support." I gave her a closed-lip smile. She stared at me, and I wasn't sure what else to say, so I asked, "Would you like an autograph?"

"Yes! Oh my god, this is amazing. I can't believe you're here. My sister is totally going to think I'm lying when I tell her. Can we get a picture, too?"

"Of course, but would you mind not posting this on social media for a while? I'm just here to see family and want to make sure it stays that way for a bit." I squeezed Charlie's shoulder, grounding myself.

The cashier gave me an over-the-top pitying look. "Is it because of the divorce? I was so sorry to hear. I can't believe your wife would cheat on you. That's—"

"She didn't," I said sternly. There was no way in hell I was going to let that rumor fly in front of me or our daughter. "You should know not to believe everything you read on the internet."

Her smile fell. "Well, I read this in Star Finder, actually."

"Well, you should believe them even less," I said, pulling two one-hundred-dollar bills out of my wallet and handing them over. "I'm sorry. It's been wonderful meeting you, but I really need to go."

"What about my picture?" she asked, pouting.

I didn't answer her as I grabbed the cart and escorted my daughter out of the store. She'd gone quiet during the whole interaction, and I'm sure had a bunch of questions I didn't have answers to.

Liv and I had been talking to a therapist about how to break the news to Charlie. We wanted to make sure she never felt abandoned during our separation. For the most part, her life wouldn't experience a significant shift. Liv and I were apart more than we were together, so she was used to not having us at home all the time. However, the biggest differ-ence would come in media perception. The last thing we wanted was for her to get caught in the shit storm that was public divorce.

We were blessed to be best friends given the circumstances, but that didn't mean the act of separating wasn't difficult. And people's perception could change in an instant. We were already seeing that with the rumors flying around. I'd scrolled through the comments on one of my recent social media posts, horrified at what some people were saying. How could people get on the internet and be comfortable hurling insults at someone they didn't know? There was no information to back up their claims, and they didn't seem to care.

With the rumors, though, it was going to be hard to bring Cleo into this mess. We had to be careful. All it would take is one sighting, one anonymous tip and photo to a journalist, and she'd be splashed all over the front page of some bullshit tabloid by morning.

How could I have been so selfish to drag her into something like this? I'd wrongly assumed I could hide away in Ashwood without anyone finding out I was here. If I were a betting man, I would be putting money down that the cashier was going to be out for her five seconds of fame. Who knew what bullshit she'd spew, or if she would leak our location? I wouldn't be surprised if paparazzi showed up by the end of the day.

Pulling out my phone, I shot a quick text to my lawyer and PR team, letting them know about the interaction. At least if they knew about it, they could get ahead of any potential situation that may come up. I'd resort to bribery if I needed to, though it was never my first option. I'd leave that up to them, though.

Charlie and I wordlessly loaded the groceries into the truck. By the time she was buckled in and we were on the road back to the house, my anxiety was starting to spiral. How much had she heard? Did she understand any of it?

"You okay back there?" I asked, looking in the rear-view mirror. Charlie was staring out the window.

"Yeah, all good, Daddy," she said. It didn't feel all good, though. Not in the slightest.

"If there's anything you want to talk about, you know I'm here, right? So is Mommy," I hesitated before adding, "and Miss Cleo. You've got three adults who love and care for you very much."

At that, she smiled. The relief I felt was instantaneous. "I'm the luckiest girl."

"You are, sunshine. You're very lucky."

The spirits were lifted by the time we pulled up to the house. Charlie and I were singing along to the radio until I cut the engine. My truck was back and sitting along the curb, which meant Cleo had come back. I didn't know why, but part of me expected that something would spook her and she'd stay gone. I should've known better.

She came out of the front door, jogging down the porch steps until she slid to a stop. I could hear music coming through the screen door. "You're back."

"So are you," I said, glancing around. When I realized no one was looking, I pressed a quick kiss to her lips. "Did you get everything you needed?"

"I did. What about you?"

I nodded. "Cleared the list and then some. Charlie decided she wanted to have a movie night, so we got all the goods. Isn't that right, sunshine?"

Charlie came bounding around the truck with the bags in question. "Yup! We got popcorn and chocolates and pickles— which seems kind of gross, but Daddy really likes pickles, so I guess it's fine."

"Hey, don't knock it till you try it," Cleo said with a laugh. "I happen to love them, too. Want to take that bag inside and set it on the table?"

Charlie climbed the steps as Cleo and I grabbed the rest of the groceries. We were halfway up the stairs when my daughter came skipping out with a big smile on her face. "What's in the box, Miss Cleo? Is it a present? It looks like a present?"

"You'll have to wait until tomorrow to find out," Cleo said, laughing as Charlie began to pout. "Trust me, it'll be worth waiting. Grab the door for us?"

Charlie did as Cleo asked and held the screen door open so we could walk through. I didn't have to wonder what she was talking about for long because there was a big, blue box sitting on top of the kitchen table when we stepped inside.

"Now you've got me curious," I mumbled, setting the bags down nearby. "What is this?" I asked.

Cleo ducked her head. "It's nothing. Our conversation this morning made me think about something. So," she gestured toward the box, "It's something small, but I think she deserves it."

I wasn't sure how she did it, but Cleo had me falling more in love with her every day. I just hoped we weren't about to get pulled into a mess that'd fuck everything up before we even had a chance to rebuild.

cleo

. . .

"CAN WE WATCH ANOTHER ONE?" Charlie pleaded, glancing between her dad and me. "Please, please, please?"

Grady looked at me over the top of her head, and I shrugged. I didn't care how late she stayed up, but I wouldn't say no to some time alone together. All day, he'd driven me crazy with the most minuscule touches. When he laid his arm along the back of the couch, his fingertips would brush my shoulder, or if we were in the kitchen and he needed to get by, his hands would find my hips to subtly move me out of the way. It was such a silly thing to be turned on by, but I'd spent god only knew how long shying away from any kind of physical touch. Knowing it came from a place of nothing but affection and need had me craving more.

"While you bribe your dad, I'm going to make some more popcorn," I said, holding up the plastic tub with nothing but kernels at the bottom and giving it a little shake.

Since Charlie had mentioned a movie day when they'd gotten back from the grocery store, we decided to hold off on the baking until tomorrow. We'd already sifted through Marsha's recipe cards for a couple of treats that would be fun and easy for her to help with. She seemed genuinely excited. While I was nowhere near the baker Marsha was, I knew enough I could make the learning process fun.

Halfway through the second movie, storm clouds had begun to roll in. The sky looked ominously dark for most of the afternoon, but it seemed the weather was all talk and little bite. With the curtains open, we watched nightfall and lightning strikes in the distance. The smell of rain filled the air, and I knew it wouldn't be long before the downpour began.

Putting the bag in the microwave, I leaned against the table and gazed into the living room. Charlie and Grady were howling with laughter as he tickled her mercilessly. "Miss Cleo! Miss Cleo!" she screamed, holding out her hand for me to take. "Help me!"

I couldn't resist. "I'm coming!" I said, jogging up behind Grady. I ran my fingertips along his sides, and he shrieked.

"You're going to pay for that," he said, narrowing his eyes as he flew off the couch to the other side of the room. "Both of you."

"Run, Charlie!" I said, urging her toward the hallway as her dad started my way. "Save yourself."

I tried to follow, but he caught me around my waist and pulled me back toward the kitchen. He covered my mouth with his hand as I screamed. My shirt rode up as I fought back through giggles, giving him access to run his calloused fingertips across my abdomen. Did it tickle? Sure. But I was more attuned to the way his touch made goosebumps crop up along my skin. Charlie was just on the other side of the wall, likely hiding and waiting for someone to call a truce. The truth was, I didn't know if I wanted to. Not when his hand stopped just above the waistband of my pants.

"You're supposed to be fighting me, Cleo," he whispered. I could feel his smile against the shell of my ear. "You're supposed to stop me from having my way with you."

"What if I don't want to?"

Grady let go of my mouth, though it wasn't uncovered long. The next moment, he crashed his lips into mine, and I lost all sense of self-control.

"Did you get him, Miss Cleo?" Charlie called from the hallway.

We broke apart instantly, both of us aroused and panting. I glanced down at his crotch, raising my brows at the apparent bulge there. He hung his head, grimacing as he adjusted it.

"I sure did. Coast is clear," I called back breathlessly. "The tickle monster has been vanquished."

Charlie came running around the corner with a big, goofy grin. "Can we still watch one more movie? I'm not tired yet."

The alone time I wanted earlier only intensified after our heated exchange, but I couldn't stop myself. "Sure. Go pick one out."

She ran into the living room as Grady came up behind me, subtly squeezing my ass. "Bet she'll be out in twenty."

I didn't say anything as I got my popcorn out of the microwave and emptied it into the bowl. I just hoped he was right.

THIRTY MINUTES LATER, Charlie's snores grew loud enough that we knew she was out for good. It'd only taken fifteen minutes for her to close her eyes, and another five for her breathing to even out. We'd both held our breath, waiting until we knew we could move without her waking.

Grady leaned forward, hitting pause on the remote. "Gimme five," he mouthed, eyes darting toward his sleeping daughter between us. Her head was resting on my shoulder, so I just nodded as he pulled her into his arms and disappeared down the hall.

I got up and immediately started cleaning. Though I'd been looking forward to this moment all day, I was suddenly sick with nerves. I wasn't sure if I was going to be strong enough to resist him, and honestly, I didn't know if I wanted to. Were there things we needed to talk about? Absolutely. But who said that meant we had to abstain from sex in the meantime? There was a time and place for these conversations, but right now, with our excitement from being together, it didn't feel like the right moment.

I was in the kitchen washing up when I felt him come up behind me. Just like last night in the living room, he slowly banded his arm around my waist and tugged me closer. He crowded me against the counter, running his nose along the top of my ear and down toward my neck. I could feel him hardening already, and let my head fall back against his shoulder to give him access.

His lips moved along my skin, worshipful like a prayer. They were needy and desperate, each one more frenzied than the last. Neither of us spoke, but our bodies were communicating better than words ever could.

Before I could move, he spun me around, hoisted me onto the countertop and stepped between my thighs. The moment our mouths crashed together, I wound my fingers into his hair. Neither of us was coming up for air, but it was okay. I could die like this, right here and now, with his taste on my tongue.

"You're fucking killing me," he whispered. "I'm trying so hard to keep myself from doing something stupid and pushing you, but goddammit, you're too perfect. I want you too much."

I let my hands fall from his head to the hem of his shirt, running my fingers beneath. His muscles contracted at my touch, and he let out a groan as I explored his body. "Maybe we don't have to be good," I rasped as he bit down on my neck. I had no doubt we'd be covered in marks come morning with the way we both seemed to be losing our minds.

He pulled back, ripping my hands from beneath his shirt and pinning them above my head against one of the cabinets. "Don't say things like that, bluebird. Not unless you intend on letting me follow through."

I bit down on my lip. Normally, I wasn't the reckless or impulsive type. I'd stick to my decisions and wouldn't budge. Still, maybe if we got some of this sexual tension and frustration out of the way, it'd clear the path toward the conversations we needed to have.

Honestly, I'd justify just about any reason I could so I could feel his hands and mouth on me again.

"Take me to bed," I whispered.

Before I knew what was happening, I was in Grady's arms, and he was damn near running to his bedroom. I smiled into his neck before he kicked the door closed with his foot and tossed me onto the bed. I sat up on my elbows, watching the way he stood over me like a god. The room was darker than last night, and I could just barely make out his outline.

Reaching behind his head, he gripped the back of his shirt and pulled it off in one fluid motion before tossing it at me. I caught it with a laugh, though it abruptly stopped as I caught sight of the barest hint of ink along his abdomen.

His tattoo.

"Turn on a light," I whispered. "I want to see you."

Wordlessly, he walked over to the bathroom and flipped on the light so it spilled out into the bedroom. He stood in the doorway, hesitating slightly before he made his way back to the bed.

I sat up, staring up at him before reaching forward and tracing my fingers along the inked skin like I had at the rodeo when he first showed me. Regardless of how long it'd been, I never stopped thinking about it. The way I knew even at first glance it was about us. He didn't understand how eerie it was, and part of me wished he had. If he'd known the whole story, if he'd met me for a drink, and I could've spilled my secrets, maybe we would've had our second chance back then.

But I think, despite all the bullshit and hardships we'd gone through, our story was always supposed to end up this way. We were far too young to fall so fast. We crashed and burned before we had a chance to fly. Now, we knew what we wanted, and what we wanted was each other.

"I've thought about this more times than I can count," Grady murmured.

"Thought about what?"

"This. Us. Everything, honestly," he said. "Having you here, touching me, it's more than I ever dared to hope for."

Leaning forward, I pressed a kiss to the exposed skin above the button of his jeans. He bit his lip, letting his head fall back with a suppressed groan as I let my tongue explore.

Suddenly, his hands were winding in my hair. He tilted my face up and kissed me. "But there's one thing I've thought about even more," he said, stepping back.

I missed his touch already. "Oh yeah? And what's that?"

"*Your* tattoo," Grady said, eyes raking down my body.

"That's because you decided to run off and get married," I joked, though it fell a little flat. That was the reality of our situation, and it sucked. Avoiding it did us no good, though. We might as well face it head-on if we have any hope of a future.

"I did," he admitted. There were no excuses or platitudes. It was just his way of surviving at the time.

"Sit down," I said, pushing to my feet. He did so without question, trading places until I was the one standing in front of him. His hands came up to cup the back of my thighs, fingers tracing circles on my skin.

Reaching for the hem of my shirt, I pulled it up and over my head before discarding it on the floor next to his. Grady's eyes scanned my torso, searching for any hint of the ink he was desperate to see.

I let my touch trail down my stomach to the button of my shorts and popped it free. His eyes were on fire, lust-filled and crazed. His hands came up and began working the denim down my hips and thighs, and his lips parted when I was wearing nothing but my bra and panties.

The moment he spotted the markings, his lips parted on a gasp. It wasn't nearly as fancy as his, but there, hidden along my hip bone, was the word bluebird in cursive script.

"Oh, Cleo," he said, leaning forward to reverently place a solemn kiss along the ink. "Oh, baby. When did you do this?"

"The night I graduated from college. Rachel and I were drunk along Sixth Street and saw the sign. We decided to be a little wild and reckless. Tattoos had been on our bucket list for some time, so we figured what better way to close out our college days." I smiled as I thought of the memory. "I'd been missing you like crazy, you know. She took my phone so I wouldn't call you. Because of that, I decided to be rebellious in another way."

"So, you marked yourself with this," he said, finishing my thought.

"I've always been yours, even when I wasn't."

He stared up at me, and I felt myself crumbling. Tonight, it wasn't about conversations or logistics or getting rid of sexual tension. This was about Grady and me. It was about the love we shared, because even I couldn't ignore it anymore. I glanced at the clock, heart racing as I saw the time.

11:11 p.m.

And when he whispered, "I love you, bluebird," so tenderly, so reverently against my skin, I let whatever was left of my walls crash to the ground.

"I love you, too."

grady

. . .

"I LOVE YOU, TOO."

Four words had never sounded so fucking sweet. For a moment, I wondered if I was hallucinating. It was hard to believe Cleo Hayes was standing in my bedroom after all this time, wearing nothing but her underwear, telling me she loved me, but as I stared up at this maddeningly beautiful woman, I knew it was real.

She was real, she was here, and she fucking loved me.

She. Loved. Me.

I already knew it, and I never would've pressured her to say it before she was ready, or even at all, but hearing it fall from her lips so easily had soothed the anxious monster in my mind.

I reached forward, scooping her up. She fell forward with the sweetest little giggle as I peppered her neck with kisses. Her legs fell on either side of my thighs, and suddenly, she was straddling me.

My hands held her face, both of us letting the charged emotions speak in ways our words never could. Saying 'I love you' wasn't nearly enough to encompass what I felt for her. It was too limiting. Too finite.

"You are mine," I said, pressing my lips to hers.

"All yours," she replied, sweeping her tongue across my own, deepening the kiss. Her hands went behind her back, unclasping her bra and letting it slip down her shoulders. It took me a moment to realize what she'd done, until she was pulling away to discard the article of clothing. I stared at her, silhouetted by the light coming from my bathroom. The outline of her breasts, the way I watched her nipples harden under my gaze, it made me fucking ache with need. She was the most beautiful woman I'd ever seen, and she was all mine.

I bent my head forward, moving my lips down her neck to her shoulder before coming to a stop at her chest. She wound her fingers into my hair as I latched onto one of her nipples, sucking it into my mouth and letting my tongue lave over the tight bud. My hips rolled up as I switched to the other, trying like hell not to whip my dick out and tug her panties to the side so I could bury myself inside her tight, wet heat.

Why the fuck was I still wearing jeans? Why didn't I think ahead enough to take them off? Granted, I didn't know her secret tattoo would be hidden behind her goddamn underwear. That was a surprise I never saw coming, not even after she told me it wasn't anywhere the public would be able to see. I figured it was an ankle, or maybe even something along her back, but my girl was full of surprises.

Cleo ground down against me as I worshipped her breasts, both of us biting back moans of pleasure as we chased a high that would come too soon. I wasn't above embarrassing myself, especially not if she got her pleasure first. As much as I wanted to come, I wanted to make sure she was taken care of.

While I didn't want to think about her with someone else, I couldn't help but wonder how long it'd been since she was last touched. For me, it'd been a damn long time, which was why I was close to coming in my pants. Our current predicament reminded me of our first time, how she watched me masturbate to the sight of her just so I could make our first last more than a single minute.

Reaching between us, I found her clit through the fabric of her soaked panties, rubbing tight circles around the area. Cleo let out a moan, her fingers pulling tighter at my scalp as she rotated her hips. She pressed against my dick and my thumb, frantically searching for what combination felt good.

God, she was fucking beautiful. It wasn't like I was being entirely selfless. The way she was rubbing herself against me was enough to see stars. I wasn't even thinking about the way my poor dick would likely be chafed come tomorrow. What did it matter when she was using me how she saw fit? If this was what she wanted to lead us into a more physical aspect of our relationship, I'd gladly sit here and let her dry hump me to her heart's content.

The moment I felt her tense up in my arms and watched the peak of her pleasure crest and her orgasm take over, I was a fucking goner. She moaned my name, mouth open on a silent scream, and I couldn't hold back anymore. "Give it to me, baby," I rasped. "Let me see you come." I followed her, chasing that high just like she had, and spilling my own release in my pants like a goddamn teenager.

"Fuck, fuck, fuck," I chanted, muffling my own cries in the delicate curve of her neck. "Holy shit."

Cleo's head dropped to my shoulder as we sat there, both of us trying to catch our breath. "Oh my god, Grady," she panted. "Did you—"

"Come in my pants? Yup," I said, pressing a kiss to her shoulder. "But it was so worth it."

She pulled back, cheeks heated with exertion and pleasure as she laughed and looked down at the wet spot covering the fly of my jeans. "I'm not sure whose mess that is," she said, covering her face. "I'm so sorry."

"Why?" I said, gripping her wrists and pulling them away. "I'm not. I loved every second of what just happened."

"But you came in your pants…"

"So? Why does it matter where I come?" I smirked, lowering my voice. "Although I have some ideas for next time."

"You're already thinking about next time?"

"Baby, I'm thinking about the rest of our lives, but I figured it'd be best to start with baby steps."

Cleo blinked, eyes softening as she pressed her forehead against my own. "This is wild. It's crazy."

"Is it?" I asked, trailing my hands down her spine until they came to rest along her hips. I couldn't stop touching her now that she was in my arms. "The way I see it, this is a long time coming. We've wasted so much time, Cleo. I don't really want to waste anymore, you know? I want to spend every day showing you how much I love you and making up for all the years we lost."

Even though I couldn't see her tears, I knew they'd begun falling. I hated that they were there, that I wasn't sure if they were from happiness or if I'd done something to hurt her. "Don't cry, bluebird. I'm sorry. I'm sorry if I rushed you. We can take this at whatever pace you want, just don't shut me out. I'm begging you."

"I'm not crying because I'm sad," she said, with a little laugh. "Although that seems like something I would do." She sat up, letting me run my thumbs beneath her eyes to wipe away the moisture slipping down her cheeks. "I'm crying because, for the first time since I was a kid, I feel like I know what I want from my life. I've spent the last year feeling lost, but now I don't. Now I have you, a-and I hope it's not presumptuous to say Charlie—"

"It's not," I said without hesitation. When the time came to talk to Charlie about all of this, I knew she'd be ecstatic. "She adores you."

"I know there's a lot to sort through, and we will have to figure out a lot of logistics. Honestly, I'm so fucking scared of losing you again, Grady, but the thought of walking away to try and protect my heart would break it more than loving you ever could."

"You're never gonna lose me, bluebird. I'm yours. I've always been yours," I said, kissing her earnestly. "Now, if you'll let me, I'm gonna carry you into the bathroom, and we're going to squeeze into a tiny shower that's definitely too small for the both of us, and I'm going to clean you up."

Cleo bit down on her lip, nodding as she wrapped her arms around my neck. I stood with her in my grip and carried her through the door, depositing her on top of the counter. There was just enough space for her to sit comfortably. Try as I might, I was doing my best not to think about her being nearly naked because if I did, I doubted we'd make it far.

Reaching into the shower, I turned it on and adjusted the temperature to make sure it wasn't too warm. Cleo used to set it to the hottest possible setting. Secretly, I hoped her preferences had changed enough that I wouldn't get third-degree burns from a bath.

When I turned around, she was fidgeting. Her arms were covering her breasts, and her eyes cast down. I stepped up between her legs, gripping her chin. "You good?"

She nodded but avoided eye contact. "It's just that, um, I haven't been naked with anyone in a long time. And I don't look like I did when I was nineteen, so I'm kind of freaking out right now. Like, you look the same—better even—but I have cellulite and stretch marks, and don't even get me started on how my tits stare at the floor rather than straight ahead—"

"Hey," I said, cutting off the impending spiral with a kiss. "I don't give a shit about that."

Anxiously, she chewed on her lip. "I look a lot different than your ex, too," she said, voice breaking. "And I'm really nervous about this. I know it's silly, but I'm not going to live up to whatever fantasies you may have had."

Reaching past her, I flipped off the harsh, overhead lighting before pulling my phone out of my pocket and turning on the flashlight. Then I set it on top of the counter, so it filled the room with a soft glow.

"What're you doing?"

"Do you feel better?"

"You didn't have to do that," she murmured, but I could hear the relief in her voice. I'd do anything in the world to make sure she felt comfortable. If it meant living in the dark for a little bit until she was more secure, I'd happily do that.

"I know. I wanted to. You know what else I want to do?" I asked.

"Tell me," she whispered, reaching between us to deftly unbutton my jeans. I tried to speak but lost all train of thought as she reached inside my briefs and took hold of my quickly hardening cock. Holy hell. It didn't take much to get me going, especially not when I realized it was Cleo's hand and not my own. "Cat got your tongue?"

"Goddammit, woman." I let out a shaky breath. "I can't think when you're doing that."

"I've always preferred showing to telling." Her voice dropped low, sultry. I could just make out the flutter of lashes against her creamy skin.

"Is that right?"

"Mmhm. Absolutely."

"That," I said, grabbing her hips and pulling her forward against my hard cock, "I can do."

Cleo laughed as I walked us into the shower. There was barely enough room for the two of us to stand together, but it wasn't any hardship for me. I loved knowing she was within my grasp. The fact I couldn't move without touching her was a comfort I never realized I would ache for.

"Grady, our clothes," she said, looking down at my jeans, which were now sitting at my ankles. "You could've at least let me finish taking them off."

"They're just clothes," I said with a shrug. "And they're already stained with cum. I don't think a little water is gonna hurt them, bluebird."

"Oh my god," she mumbled, reaching behind me for the body wash. "Do me a favor and get those off so we have a little more room."

"Yes, ma'am," I said, earning an eyeroll when I gave her a salute. I loved this bossy side of her, how she'd become more assertive with age. Part of it was a front, I could tell. I think she assumed she needed to be bossy because she carried the weight of being the oldest, but sometimes I think she enjoyed it.

I opened the shower door as much as I could, tossing the sopping wet clothes in the sink before turning to her. I glanced down at the panties she still wore. They were so thin, completely soaked, and I could just see the outline of her pussy. "Your turn."

Crowding her against the wall, I let my hands trail down her arms until they rested at her waist. Cleo trembled as I slipped my fingers beneath the fabric and slowly tugged them down her legs. Part of the way, at least. The shower really was small, so she had to finish the job once they got past her knees.

Note to self: Make sure all future bathroom spaces are large enough to fit two people comfortably.

Suddenly, there was nothing between us. I could see all of her, and she could see all of me. There was something erotic about simply being able to look at her. I knew it made her uncomfortable, but her body was beautiful. Sure, it'd changed, but the only regret I had when staring at her was I missed it happening.

"You're stunning," I said, pressing a kiss to her forehead.

"Gorgeous." She opened her mouth, likely to protest, but I stopped her. "Can I wash you?"

"Wash me?" she echoed.

"If that's okay with you?"

Cleo furrowed her brows. "Why would you want to do that? I can wash myself."

My feelings about her ex were complicated. I hated the man, hated what he did to her—both mentally and physically—but I also wished he had treated her like the queen she was. The fact that I wanted to care for her on every level shouldn't have come as a surprise. It should've been the bare minimum, honestly.

Even though my relationship with Liv was complicated, I'd washed her hair more times than I could count, especially after Charlie was born. If she needed help taking a shower, I would've done it without hesitation. Things were only sexual if they were made to be. It was just a form of care, of adoration. Why would anyone shy away from that, especially if they loved someone?

"I know you can. The point is I *want* to wash you, baby. I want to shower you, literally, with affection. I want an excuse to touch you," I said, lowering my voice. I let my fingertip trail from her shoulder down her chest to her nipple. "To tease you." And then I went lower until I found the patch of trimmed hair between her thighs. Whether she meant to or if it was instinct, her legs parted for me. "To make up for lost time." She let out a soft moan as I brushed her clit. "But if you don't want that…"

"I do," Cleo said quickly. "I want it so badly."

"Then hand me the shampoo. We'll start there."

Cleo did as I asked, turning around and handing over the bottle. Her hair was already soaked through, so I poured some of the shampoo into my palm before gently running my hands through her strands. She closed her eyes as I began to massage her scalp, making noises that went straight to my cock.

"He never did this for you?" I asked, keeping my voice low. "Not even when you were sick?"

"Never," she said, giving her head a little shake. "But to be fair, I never asked him to."

That was the thing with Cleo. When it came to others, she never expected anyone to do something unless she asked. She carried the weight of everything on her shoulders, yet she would bend over backwards to help others without them so much as uttering a word. No matter how often I tried to get her to see that when we were kids, I'd hoped she would've changed her outlook.

"He should never have needed to be asked to do something nice for you, Cleo. He should've just done it because he wanted to, because he knew it would make you feel better or take something off your plate."

She didn't say anything as I grabbed the detachable showerhead and rinsed all the soap out before going in with conditioner. "Body wash, please." I held out my hand and she placed it in my palm. I looked around, realizing I had never grabbed a washcloth. It slipped my mind because I'd let my other head focus on the earth-shattering orgasms and Cleo's naked body instead.

My hand would have to do this time, but I sure as hell wasn't complaining. I kneaded her muscles as I let my soap-filled hands roam across her body. I paid attention to the spots that made her gasp or moan or shake. Her breasts were a favorite. When I delicately rolled her nipples between my fingers, she let her head fall back against my shoulder. By the time I made it to her back, I felt her relax fully into my touch. "How's that feel?" I whispered, noting the way she shivered as my breath caressed her ear.

Cleo let out a noise that sounded like "good," though I wasn't sure. That was how I was going to take it anyway, as I continued my way down her back to her ass. I wrapped my arm around her stomach and pressed her into the wall, taking my time to clean between her thighs until she was panting.

Without meaning to, I'd damn near brought her to the point of orgasm.

"Do you want to come, baby?" I asked. She nodded her head, muffling her cries with the back of her hand as I slowly traced a finger along her entrance, dipping in ever so slightly.

Holy fucking shit, my girl was tight. Her pussy was already greedily clamping down on my digit, and I'd barely begun to work it inside of her. I considered my cock slightly above average, but I couldn't stop myself from wondering if she would struggle to take me. She had, once upon a time, but that was years ago, when we were innocent and had barely explored our own bodies, let alone someone else. I suppose if it had truly been ages since she'd been with someone and had settled on a silicone replacement, it made sense.

It'd be so easy to make her come like this, but just like I had when she dry humped me to climax, I wanted to watch her every fucking second of her pleasure. I got off on the visuals of seeing my fingers, my cock, my tongue be what sent her careening off the edge.

I pulled back, laughing as she let out a frustrated groan. "What the fuck, Grady? You ask if I want to come and then you deny me?" She turned around, ready to hurl another insult my way, but her words died as I slipped the finger that'd just been inside her into my mouth.

"Well, if you'd stop throwing a fit and let me finish washing you off, we could get to the good stuff," I said, raising a brow.

With a squeal, Cleo quickly turned around and faced the wall again as I worked. The moment I turned off the water, she hopped out and reached for a towel. I stopped her, grabbing it first. "Let me," I murmured, sweeping the cotton across her skin to erase the beaded moisture. "I want to do this."

Cleo snapped her mouth shut as I worked, taking extra care between her legs just because I could. Only when I knew she was a panting, writhing mess did I pull back with a smirk. "That's not fair," she said, pouting. Her attempt at anger disappeared as her gaze dipped down my naked body appreciatively.

"If there's one thing we know, it's that life isn't fair, but," I said, stepping toward her until we were chest-to-chest. "It is always worth it."

Without saying another word, I tugged her out of the bathroom. The moment we fell back on the bed, Cleo pounced on me like I was little more than her prey. Her kiss was full of so much heat I thought it'd burn me alive. She tugged on my bottom lip, raking her nails down my chest until she gripped my cock.

As much as I wanted to get mine, I wanted her so much more. "Sit on my face," I panted, trying to pull her closer. "Let me fucking drown in you."

Immediately, she sat back on her heels and shook her head. I recognized the stubborn, resilient set of her jaw and knew she was going to fight me. "No. No way. Absolutely not."

"Do you want me to beg, baby?"

She didn't say anything, but I didn't miss the way she sucked her lip between her teeth. "I can't—"

"Please," I said. My fingers dug into her hips. I was barely holding myself back. I wanted to drag her over and force her to take a seat, but I didn't. I showed the restraint she deserved, but I wasn't above a little bit of begging. "Please let me taste you. Please, please, please…"

"But why do I need to sit on your face to do that? Why can't you do it the old-fashioned way?"

"Because I want you to work my cock while I eat your sweet cunt, bluebird."

Her lips parted at my crude words, and I didn't care. There were no thoughts of decorum when it came to my need for her. "Oh."

"Yes. Oh. Now, if you could just take a seat," I said, lying down on my back and patting my lips. "I could have my meal."

Cleo chuckled nervously but shuffled her way over. I didn't have to ask to know this was her first time doing this. I'd already had most of her firsts, so knowing I had this one too was so goddamn gratifying.

The moment she swung her leg over my face, I was greeted by the sight of her pussy for the first time in seventeen years. Oh god, I was a goner at the thought of having her taste on my tongue. The tease in the shower had been just that—a fucking tease. It did nothing to satisfy my hunger for her.

She yelped as I tugged her down on top of me, running my tongue along the seam of her pussy, delving past to suckle on her clit. Her hands landed on my stomach as she doubled over in pleasure. "Fuck," she whimpered. "Oh my god, Grady."

"Work my cock, bluebird," I whispered against her thigh. "Show me how much you love my tongue in your cunt."

Honestly, I was a little worried about coming the moment she grabbed hold of my dick. It was already painfully hard. Maybe if I did, she'd realize just how much she turned me on, how all it took was a few simple strokes, and I'd be spilling myself all over her hand and my stomach.

Would she clean it up? Would she let me watch?

The thought alone had me looping my arms around her thighs and forcing her down further until I could barely breathe. If this was the way I was going to go, so be it. I'd gladly die between her thighs if I made her come first.

"Grady," she panted. "Fuck, that feels so good."

I wanted to tell her how good she tasted, how much I loved her and this and us, how well she was stroking my cock, but I didn't want to stop what I was doing for a moment. Instead, I growled, letting her feel the rumble in my chest as I fucked her with my tongue.

Even though I knew whatever she was doing felt great—

amazing, even—I didn't realize how close I was until she squeezed the base of my shaft and slowly worked her way up to the tip. My hips moved of their own accord, fucking her hand as though I was fucking her.

"Bluebird, I—"

"Come for me, baby. Let me see it." My plan was for her to go first, but the breathy way her voice hitched as she spoke told me she wouldn't be far behind.

It didn't mean I couldn't try, though.

As I felt my own climax surge, I sucked down on her clit. Hard. Her hips jerked, body convulsing as I glided my tongue along the tight bud. She cried out, neither of us caring about how loud we were being. Not when our pleasure felt this good.

Cum pooled along my stomach as Cleo tried to continue stroking me through her own orgasm, but faltered. I couldn't breathe, couldn't think about anything other than how good it felt when she touched me, and how sweet her own release was as it landed on my tongue. Jesus Christ, it was fucking intoxicating. Her legs squeezed tighter around my head as she let out a low, carnal moan.

Slowly, I unhooked my arms from around her thighs. Cleo collapsed beside me, resting her hand on my abdomen and her head on my thigh. "Holy shit, Grady," she chuckled, turning to face me. "I think you had me seeing stars."

I looked down at my spent dick. "Yeah, I could say the same. Let me clean up really quick."

As I tried to sit up, Cleo placed a hand on my chest and pushed me back onto the bed. "Let me," she said, rolling away before I could stop her. She padded into the bathroom, grabbed a washcloth, and ran it under the water before coming back. Her eyes glanced between the mess on my stomach and my face, reaching out with gentle care as she cleaned me with reverence. It was a struggle not to get hard again as she worked.

When she was satisfied, she tossed the cloth on top of our

soaked clothes that still lay on the floor of the bathroom. We could get them tomorrow. Tonight, I was spent. So was she, judging by the way she crawled into bed and curled up at my side.

With her head on my chest, I pressed a kiss to her crown. "Goodnight, bluebird."

cleo

. . .

GRADY'S HEARTBEAT was steady beneath my ear as I pried my eyes open and peered around the room. It was bathed in a soft morning glow filtering through the window. I knew this was his dad's room, but there was still so much of his mom here, too. Pictures of them lined the top of the dresser, and the comforter was an olive green with a floral pattern stitched at the bottom. On what I assumed was her side of the bed, there was a vase of fresh flowers. Clearly, keeping that up was Grady's task, given he'd been here for nearly two weeks now. It was these tender touches that made my own heart ache for the woman who'd been so kind.

When Charlie started talking about not knowing her grandmother, I knew passing on the vintage Pyrex set she had given me was the right thing to do. Marsha would've loved Charlie. She would've spoiled her rotten, likely spending their time together tending the garden or baking cookies in the kitchen. While I definitely couldn't help in the floral department, I could try to bridge the gap with sweets.

At the sound of Grady's snoring, I turned my head and watched him. It was strange how peaceful he looked. We never had the luxury of many sleepovers when we were kids, so seeing him like this was a first for me. I was obsessed with the way his long lashes fanned out against his cheeks, and the way his pouty lips were parted just a touch.

If I were an artist, I would want to spend hours capturing his likeness to get it right. Since I wasn't, I'd settle for staring at him as though he was a work of art because to me, he was. Seeing him like this gave me an idea, though, one which would conveniently ruin whatever peace he'd found while profusely begging me for more.

Slowly, I extracted myself from his hold, waiting a moment as he readjusted his position. It'd be my luck if he woke up before I ever had a chance to have my fun. When I realized he was, indeed, back asleep, I slipped beneath the covers and settled myself between his thighs. Neither one of us had put on clothes after crashing last night, which meant I was staring at his semi-hard cock.

I'd always thought the concept of morning wood was a joke, a way for men to excuse themselves from being hornbags who demanded sex before even waking up, but being older taught me it wasn't always true.

Taking hold of his length, I let my tongue run from base to tip. His body shivered under my touch, head lolling to one side as I took him inside, moving slowly. The longer I worked him, the more restless his body became.

This was exciting. I'd never been the type of person to think about a spontaneous blow job, let alone actually giving one. By the time Grady and I were able to be a little more open and adventurous with our sex life, we were on the downhill slope of our relationship. And I never enjoyed giving Thomas head. It always felt like a chore versus something I actually wanted. I did it because he asked, not because I enjoyed it. Eventually, even that went away, though—not that I was complaining.

I wasn't sure if I was still drunk on orgasms or if my preferences had changed overnight, but I felt the shift. I woke up wanting the taste of him to start off my day, and I wanted to give him a surprise I knew he'd love.

I liked the idea of him being asleep, though. It took the pressure off having to ask him if I could suck his cock. Not that he would say no, but I wasn't exactly comfortable with being so open yet. A good morning blow job today could mean road head next week. Baby steps, and all that.

The feeling of him hardening in my mouth was strangely euphoric. Knowing I had that kind of control over his body? Yes, please. Sign me up. It was more than that, though. It was also knowing selfishly, he was getting hard for *me*. He was going to come down *my* throat, not anyone else's.

When one of his hands moved to my head, fingers tangling themselves in my hair, I smiled around his dick. The covers were thrown back a second later, and I looked up to find his ice blue eyes locked on me.

"Good morning," I said, releasing him with a pop. "Did you sleep well?"

"Oh, god, I love you," he said, as I let him guide me back on his length. I could feel the way he was fighting the urge to fuck my mouth, the way his hips rocked ever so slightly beneath me. His restraint was so goddamn sexy. It only made me want to see him lose control.

Doubling my efforts, I added my hand to stroke his base as I bobbed up and down. Saliva coated his dick, running along my skin, but I didn't care. I liked the messiness of it. His grip grew tight before he yanked me off with a sharp exhale. "Fucking shit, bluebird. Are you trying to kill me?"

"No," I said with a smile. "I'm trying to make you come. You definitely need to be alive for that."

Grady's head fell back on a groan. "You're making this whole abstaining thing really fucking difficult."

"So, fuck my mouth," I said, running my tongue along his

tip, earning another low rumble from his chest. "Show me how badly you want me, baby."

I wasn't big on the pet names like he was, but I liked calling him baby. It was endearing, and he folded every time.

"You want me to fuck your mouth?" I nodded. "It's going to be rough."

"I can take it," I rasped, feeling my arousal between my thighs as I shifted my legs together. There was no way I was going to be able to hold off on the whole sex thing for much longer. If I didn't fold right now, then I would by the end of the day. Conversations, be damned. There was only so much a woman could take, and I was at my limit.

Grady sat up quickly, taking my mouth in a bruising kiss. "I love you," he said, crawling off the bed.

"I love you, too," I assured him. "Now, do your worst."

Taking my hand, he helped me off the bed and dropped to my knees. I had to sit up straight, but it was the perfect height for him to have his way with me. With trembling hands, he gathered my hair and wrapped it around his fist, jerking my head back just a touch. "Tap my leg if it's too much, okay? I don't want to hurt you."

"You won't," I murmured, pressing a kiss to his tip. "I trust you."

Something about those words set him off. It was as though he needed additional reassurance, to know I wasn't doing this because I thought he wanted it or because it would please him. I was doing this because I truly wanted to. Because, after fighting him for so long, I finally trusted him not to hurt my body or my heart.

With a fistful of hair in one hand, he guided his cock to my lips with the other. I opened my mouth and laid my tongue flat, eagerly putting myself on display for him.

And then his restraint broke.

Gone was the timid man who'd been worried about hurting

me. In his place was someone ruled by the desire to give me exactly what he wanted, exactly what I asked for. His mouth fell open on a groan as he surged forward, letting his cock hit the back of my throat.

I wasn't a pro at giving head, and my gag reflex wasn't great, so I coughed and spluttered at first, but recovered quickly. Grady, to his credit, wasn't nearly as aggressive as I imagined he could be. He was still rough, though, forcing me to take every powerful thrust of his hips as though he wasn't choking me.

"Goddamn, bluebird," he hissed through clenched teeth. "Look at you being such a good fucking girl for me. You like it when I fuck your face?" I nodded as he pressed me down on his dick until my nose hit the flat expanse of his lower abdomen.

I gasped for air as he ripped me off his length, watching through tear-filled eyes as he started stroking himself to completion. Before he could come, I surged forward, capturing the end of his dick with my mouth. I hummed around him as the first spurt of his release hit my tongue. He let out a deep growl, looking in awe as I took every drop. The flavor wasn't great, and honestly, part of me wanted to gag a little bit, but the idea and act of what we were doing, the way he was claiming me, marking me, had me sitting still like the good girl he'd called me.

It appealed to some basic, biological part of me. The one that told me this man was marking me as his, and I reveled in it.

When he finished, he smiled, grabbing the trash can next to his nightstand. "You can spit it out, bluebird. I'm not gonna make you swallow."

Oh, thank god.

I leaned forward, barely having time to spit it out before he pulled me up and kissed me. I wanted to protest, to tell him I still had the taste of him on my tongue, but why did it matter? If I could kiss him after he'd tongue fucked me into oblivion, why couldn't the same be said of him?

"Good morning to you, too, by the way," he murmured, running his nose along my own.

IT TURNED out waking Grady up with a blow job came with more than just the satisfaction of a job well done. He was all too happy to return the favor, making me come with his fingers and his tongue until I could barely move. And then he let me watch as he pleasured himself and spilled his release in his hand. I'd tried to do it myself, but I was told I had to keep my hands to myself and stay far away so he didn't get hard again two seconds after he came.

Honestly, the way that man was obsessed with me should probably be studied, but I damn sure wasn't going to complain. When you spend your life running from the demons in your head, it's a relief to find the person who puts them to rest. They would come back, they always did, but I wasn't as worried with Grady at my side.

Thankfully, we were freshly showered and in the kitchen by the time Charlie wandered out of her bedroom. She walked to Grady, still half asleep, and he picked her up without question. He peppered her cheek with kisses, sending her into a fit of giggles that nearly had me melting into a puddle at their feet.

Grady's love for his daughter was one of the first things I'd noticed when he came back into my life. It was strange to see him as a father. It would take me a while to come to terms with it. Seeing how good he was with her, how much he doted on her, I couldn't help but wonder if he was content with only having one kid, or if he wanted more. What if he did? Would it change things between us?

"Miss Cleo, are we gonna make cookies today?" Charlie asked, pulling me from my thoughts.

I offered her a smile. "Of course. I told you we would, didn't I? I'm not backing out now."

Charlie cheered. "Yay! Cookies for breakfast!"

"Now hold on," Grady said, laughing. "You gotta eat some actual food before you go ruining your dinner with a belly full of cookies."

"But—"

Charlie began to pout, but Grady placed his finger over her lips. "No buts. Eggs and bacon first."

At the mention of bacon, she perked right up. "Oh, I could eat some bacon," she said, nodding.

"Yeah, I figured so," he said, setting her down on the ground. "But you have to eat your eggs, too."

"Daddy..."

"No eggs? No bacon. No cookies."

I watched, utterly enamored as they stared off with one another until Charlie sighed. "Fine," she huffed, before running off.

He turned toward me, widening his eyes. "Have kids, they said. It'll be fun, they said."

I wanted to smile, but I couldn't find it within myself. Instead, I turned to the fridge and grabbed the eggs. "Do you— uh—do you want more kids? Or is it a one-and-done situation?"

"Oh man, I'd love another one," he said. I could tell he was smiling from the way he talked, and it flipped my stomach upside down. "I used to be terrified of being a father. Mine was so great I was worried about fucking it up, but now that I have Charlie... I don't know. She makes the fear worth it."

My hands shook as I set the eggs down and braced myself on the counter. Grady came up behind me, caging me in. "Why? You're already thinking about trying? I'm game if you are."

"I can't have kids," I whispered, the words coming out so quickly I wasn't sure if he'd heard me at first. But when I felt his body tense, I knew he had.

"What do you mean?"

I sucked in a breath. "You know how much I wanted kids. I always thought my calling was to be a mother, but I knew there was a possibility I'd struggle to conceive. When Thomas and I got married, I was already older than I wanted to be when I started trying. I didn't want to wait any longer. We tried for about a year before I became pregnant. I was so excited. Ecstatic even."

I could feel the tension rolling off Grady before he spoke. "Did he—"

"No," I said, quickly. "Thomas didn't become physical until later. Just like me, he wanted a baby so badly. Because I'd been tracking, we had our first appointment early. Eight weeks. Everything looked great. We took the sonogram pictures home and hung them on the fridge. I looked at them every day, dreaming up all kinds of names for our little one." I didn't realize I was crying until I felt the first tear land on the back of my hand. "A few weeks later, I woke up cramping. I didn't think much of it at first and decided to go to work. I was halfway through my second class when it became so bad I ended up passing out. Apparently, I was only out for a moment, but I don't remember going to the hospital. I just know when I woke up, the doctor told me I'd had a miscarriage, and I cried alone in the Emergency Room until Rachel showed up and brought me home.

We tried a few more times, but the doctors said my uterus was too much of a hostile environment for a child to survive. They suggested IVF, but I was tired of having my heart broken. I went into a deep depression that Thomas didn't understand, going between mourning the lives I'd lost and hating myself for not being able to do the one thing I was supposed to."

"Jesus Christ, Cleo," he muttered, wrapping his arms around me. "I'm so sorry, baby. I didn't know—"

"How could you? It's not like we had a reason to talk about it before, and I don't offer it up."

Grady squeezed me tighter. "I know it wouldn't have made a difference, but I wish you'd been with me. You should've been with me. I just—god, bluebird—I'm so fucking sorry."

"It was a long time ago."

"Time doesn't just make the pain stop. It may lessen, but it never goes away entirely."

I wasn't sure how long we stayed like that, with him holding me so tightly it felt like he was trying to keep me from falling apart. I welcomed the comfort, letting myself fully feel the pain from the wound I'd just ripped open.

"If this is a dealbreaker for you—"

"What?" Grady asked, jerking back like I'd just slapped him. "Are you serious?"

I turned in his arms, purposely keeping my space. "You said you wanted more. I could understand how it may change things for you."

His crystal blue eyes flashed with anger. He moved so fast, cupping my face and forcing me to look at him. "You fucking listen to me, Cleo Hayes... I don't give a shit if you can give me zero kids or one hundred. What I care about is having you. If we decide later we want kids, then guess what? We can adopt. If we decide we're happy with just the three of us, that's how we'll stay. You are what matters to me, not some hypothetical future which may or may not exist."

The tears fell harder now. As much as I wanted to believe him, I understood the reality of the situation. Sure, he may feel that way now, but would it be the same in a year? Two years?

"What if you change your mind?"

"I won't." I tried to find a hint of hesitation or worry, but there was nothing in his face except utter honesty. "Cleo, I've waited seventeen years to have you again. There isn't a goddamn thing that could fuck that up, okay?" He leaned in, kissing me softly. I met him in earnest, giving back as good as I got.

"I love you," I whispered between languid kisses. "I love you so much."

He smiled against my lips. "That's the only time you've said it first."

"What?" I asked, pulling back. "Like ever?"

"Well, I don't know about that, but in the last few days, yeah. I wasn't going to say anything, because honestly, I didn't care who said it first. I just cared that you said it, but..." he trailed off, eyes twinkling. "I think I like the way it rolls off your tongue."

grady

. . .

"MISS CLEO, can we open the present now?" Charlie asked, staring outside as rain pelted the window like she was in an early 2000s music video. The weather had taken a turn over breakfast, and it looked like we were in for a Saturday indoors.

Cleo smiled over her cup of coffee. "Let me grab it, okay?"

"I'll help!" Charlie exclaimed. She jumped off the couch and snatched Cleo's hand, tugging her into the kitchen. All morning, my daughter had been staring longingly at the blue box on the table, sighing every five minutes as though it would speed up how fast we ate. So, naturally, I took my time.

If looks could kill, I would've been a goner.

I pushed to my feet, coffee in hand, as I wandered after them. Charlie was damn near vibrating with excitement as Cleo set the box in front of her. "Can I open it?" my daughter asked, not taking her eyes off the present.

Even I was intrigued. I had no idea what it was, but Cleo's thoughtfulness never failed to amaze me.

"Not yet," Cleo said. Her fingers tapped on the table, showing her nerves. "I wanted to say I know you didn't have the chance to meet your grandmother, but she was a truly amazing person. She would've loved you." Cleo glanced at me before continuing. "Before she passed, she gifted this to me, but I think she would've wanted you to have it."

That caught my attention. While Dad had told me Cleo saw Mom right before she passed, he hadn't said anything about a present. I hadn't noticed anything missing, so I wasn't sure what it could be.

Charlie nodded, glancing back at the present. "Can I open it?"

"Go ahead," Cleo said. She was wringing her fingers in front of her as she watched Charlie tear into the wrapping paper.

"Daddy, can you help me open this?" Charlie asked. "I can't do it."

"Sure, sunshine." Grabbing a knife from the holder, I walked over and

cut the taped edges. Charlie dug in the moment I stepped away, peeling away the flaps and standing on the seat to peer inside.

"What are these?" Charlie asked.

"They're mixing bowls," Cleo murmured, stepping forward to pull my mom's vintage Pyrex set from the box. "They've been passed down through the generations of women in your family, and I wanted you to have them."

I never paid much attention to family heirlooms because we didn't have much. Still, I'd heard her talk about those damn bowls more times than I could count, especially to Cleo. It never occurred to me to check and see where they were. I assumed Dad had hidden them somewhere like he did with most of Mom's stuff. But to know she'd given the set to Cleo before she passed? I don't know why it made me emotional. It was as if she were urging me to follow my heart, even from the grave. She loved Cleo, knew that Cleo would honor and cherish this set and the memories they'd made with it.

And what did it say about Cleo that, regardless of whether

we had gotten together or not, she would've given this to my daughter so it could stay in the family like Mom wanted? How did she not see she was family? Mom always considered her the daughter she never had, even after we had broken up.

"Can we use them today? When we make the cookies?" Charlie asked, lips curling into a wide grin.

"That's what I was hoping for," Cleo said. "And I think we'll start by making her favorite cookies ever."

"What's that?"

Cleo and I shared a knowing smile. "Homemade chewy oatmeal chocolate chip," we said at the same time.

Charlie scrunched up her nose. "Oatmeal?"

I laughed, coming up and lightly tugging on her unruly braid. "Don't knock it till you try it, kid. These are my favorites."

"Mine too," Cleo agreed. "Your grandmother is the one to thank for that."

Charlie perked up. "Maybe they'll be my favorite too!"

"Well, you already love her regular ones, so I'm sure you'll love these, too."

As I watched the two of them talk about what they needed, all I could think about was how lucky I was for the women in my life and how grateful I was my mom kept Cleo in her life when I had cut her out.

"OH MY GOSH, these are *so* good," Charlie cried, moaning into a freshly baked cookie. We'd had to fight her off the moment they came out of the oven because she was already foaming at the mouth. "I love all of your other cookies, but these are my favorite."

Cleo ducked her head, cheeks tinged with a bright flush. "I'm glad you loved them so much. You know, I think this is my best batch ever. It's probably because you made a great sous chef."

"A what?" Charlie asked, mouth stuffed full of a half-chewed dessert.

"Come on, sunshine. We don't talk with food in our mouths." In typical smartass fashion, my daughter grabbed the glass of milk and downed half of it in one go before mumbling a half-cocked, "Sorry."

"It's like second in command. I can't take all the credit for making them because you helped, too," Cleo explained.

I leaned back on the sofa, extending my arm along the back. My fingers brushed Cleo's shoulder, and I fought the urge to pull her close. Other than a few very discreet hand-holds, we'd avoided any kind of physical affection in front of Charlie. She wasn't blind. I was sure she could see how different I acted toward Cleo than her mom, but it didn't mean I was going to go around kissing and holding her as though Liv wasn't in the picture. "Did you have fun?" I asked, letting my finger skate along exposed skin.

I wasn't a saint, though. It was getting increasingly difficult to keep my hands to myself in entirety, especially when she was so goddamn good with my daughter. It was surprisingly hot. I could at least let myself have this.

"I had so much fun, Daddy. I think I like baking." Charlie turned toward Cleo. "Can we make other things, too?"

"We can make anything you want," she murmured.

"What about a cake?"

"Oh yeah, I love making cakes."

Charlie thought for a moment. "What about a really big cake?"

"Sure," Cleo said, laughing. "We could make a really big cake."

"Right now?"

"Nope, not right now," I said, cutting in. "The last thing I need is you running around on a never-ending sugar high. Maybe for your birthday, though."

"Wait, are we still going to be here for my birthday?" Charlie asked. I couldn't tell if there was excitement or worry in her voice. Now, I was kicking myself for opening not only one can of worms, but two.

Cleo and I still hadn't addressed the elephant in the room. Sure, it was easy enough to say she was mine and I was hers, but there were logistics we hadn't discussed. Where were we going to live? What about her job? What about Liv? Even though I knew we needed to figure them out, I didn't want to burst this bubble of happiness we had going on.

"When's your birthday?" Cleo asked, stepping in. She was likely thinking the same things as I was. After all, conversations were the whole reason we hadn't entirely given in to the sexual tension between us.

"February 22nd," she said proudly. "I'll be seven. Does that mean I can have seven layers?"

Cleo hesitated, glancing at me before answering. "You know, even if I'm not with you on your birthday, I can still make you a cake. Or I could send you a recipe you and your mom could make together."

"But I wanna make it with you," Charlie whined.

The room felt heavier than it had before, the playfulness of the day disappearing under the weight of uncertainty. Why did I have to bring up Charlie's birthday? It just seemed like the natural thing to do. In my mind, which was apparently a perfect alternate reality, there was no question whether Cleo would be with us or not. It was just a fact. She and Charlie would bake this big ass monstrosity of a cake while I watched and ate my fill. Liv would be there, sitting beside me, because the woman couldn't cook to save her life. It wasn't conventional by any means, but it felt right.

"We'll figure it out, sunshine," I murmured, saying it more to reassure myself than her.

Charlie shrugged, satisfied with my answer, and went back to munching on her cookie while Cleo stared at me. I was too much of a coward to see if she was pissed at my answer or if, maybe, she liked the idea of figuring it out.

I hoped it was the latter.

cleo

. . .

"UNO!" Charlie called as Grady and I stared at her behind our handful of cards. She laid a red two down on the pile, beaming at our misfortune.

"She's a swindler," I muttered, staring at my cards, which were woefully lacking in the ones I needed. The power had gone out over an hour ago, so we'd spent our time playing cards while hoping it would come back on, which didn't look like it would be anytime soon. Outside, the storm was still raging. You could barely see the road through the thick sheets of rain.

Grady shook his head. "I don't know where she gets it, honestly."

"Oh, come on. You're telling me you've never hustled anyone in a card game?" I drew three more cards before finally landing a red one.

"I didn't say that," he said with a wink. The simple move alone had my thighs clenching to stave off the way my stomach did a stupid little flip. "But I never taught her my tricks."

"What're you guys talking about?" she asked.

"Just how good you are," he said, sighing as she laid down her final card.

Charlie hopped up and danced around the table. "I win! I win!" she shouted as her dad and I set our hands down and watched her celebration. By the time she sat back down, she seemed settled. "I'm bored with this game."

"Thank god," Grady muttered.

She turned to me. "Have you ever heard my daddy play music? He's a professional."

One of the hardest things about talking to Charlie about her dad was knowing how much to tell her about our past. I was afraid of overstepping, but it wasn't like I wanted to keep things a secret from her. I wanted to share things with her, like the fact I was one of the first people to hear him sing live, and how, before the masses sang his praises, it was just me shouting from the front table in a dive bar.

"I have. He's excellent."

Beneath the table, Grady's hand covered mine, giving it a squeeze. "She was my first fan."

"Really?" Charlie's eyes grew wide.

"Really, really. Well, second, I guess. I even have a sweatshirt to prove it."

Grady burst out laughing, turning to me with a twinkle in his eye. "Oh my god, I forgot about that. You and my mom made those before my first show. Do you still have it?"

I nodded, ducking my head because I could feel the heat flush my face. "I do." Other than a picture of us as kids that I hid in my wallet, the shirt was one of the few things I kept after our breakup. Most of the time, it was tucked beneath piles of socks in my dresser, but on nights when the pain of loving and losing hit, I would pull it out in search of comfort.

Grady's eyes softened. "I want to see that."

"You should play for us, Daddy," Charlie said. "Can we bring the piano in here?"

I glanced at the spot along the wall where the old upright

piano once stood. It was empty, a glaring reminder of Marsha's death. "You still have it?"

"Dad moved it into my old closet. It was too hard to have it out here, apparently."

"When did he do that?"

Grady blew out a breath. "Not long after Mom passed. He tried to get rid of it, but I talked him into keeping it. Figured he would drag it out someday and put it back where it belonged, but so far, he's kept it locked away."

"Ah," I said, unable to find the words. While I didn't begrudge Robert for not wanting to stare at such a blatant reminder of Marsha, I wasn't sure I would have forgiven him if he'd sold it outright. Even if it was hers, there were so many of Grady's memories tied to it as well. To have just taken that away in a moment of grief would've been a travesty.

"Want to help me get it out? I don't even know if it's tuned."

"Guess there's only one way to find out."

Moving the piano was the least of our concerns. Once we got it out, we realized how terribly out of tune it was. It hadn't been cared for for years. Thankfully, Marsha kept a kit with it, so after an hour of watching instructional videos, Grady was able to tune it just enough so it wouldn't sound too twangy.

Charlie and I were nestled together on the couch, watching Grady set up. We'd spent part of the afternoon gathering all the candles we could find. Now that the sun was going down, I lit them to give the room a romantic glow.

"I'm a little rusty," he joked as he sat down, running his fingers along the keys. "I don't play nearly as much as I used to."

"It'll come to you," I promised. "I'm just excited to see you play."

"You should temper your expectations. I used to be much better." He played a few notes, settling into a classical rendition of

Somewhere Only We Know by Keane. Even though I had no idea what he would play, some parts of me were glad it was this song. I'd never been able to hear it without thinking of Grady and those sweet memories that felt like falling in love for the first time.

And when he started singing along, I felt myself melt into the familiarity of it. Though I'd heard him only a year ago at a concert in Ashwood, it was pretty different from this in-home concert he was treating Charlie and me to now. There were no bright lights, electric guitars, or drum kits. There was just Grady on his mother's out-of-tune piano, singing from his heart in front of his daughter and the woman he loved.

It was still weird to think of us like that—in love. I'd spent nearly half my life trying to convince myself otherwise. Yet, here I was trying to rewire my brain after two short weeks of being together again. What was weirder still was how right it felt falling into old habits after I stopped getting in my own way.

Loving Grady had never been hard, but letting him love me was another thing entirely. I could own that admission. I struggled with it in nearly every aspect of my life. But out of all the people who tried to break through, I'll admit Grady's determination and insistence had never made sense.

But was love supposed to?

As the song ended, Charlie and I both erupted with thunderous applause—at least, as much as we could, given we were only two people. Grady stood from the piano and bowed at the waist. "Thank you, thank you. What's next?"

Charlie tapped her finger against her chin. "What about the guitar, Daddy? Can you play that too?"

He glanced my way before clearing his throat and disappearing into his room with a mumbled, "Yeah, of course. One second."

When he came back, he was holding an old case that looked eerily like the one he had as a kid. It was covered in stickers, some from the places I guessed he had traveled to and bands he'd opened for. Surely it wasn't the same, though. He had all the money in the world to buy any guitar he wanted. It was crazy to assume he still had the old pawn shop one his mom had bought him.

As he pulled it free, I realized just how wrong I was. There, on the underside of the instrument, were our initials carved into the body. He'd done it shortly after we got together. I told him he was crazy, we didn't know what the future held for us, but he told me he was sure that no matter what, I was meant to be his girl. And then I saw the bluebird engraved at the bottom of the soundboard.

Be still, my fucking heart.

"I got it done shortly after, well, you know," he said sheepishly. "I've used it on every tour, at every show."

"Oh, Grady," I whispered. It took everything I had to stay in my seat and not walk over, crawl into his lap, and kiss him the way I wanted to. The way he and I both deserved.

It was disarming coming face-to-face with the fact that the man you thought had moved on and forgotten you had done everything but. He had held onto my memory so tightly, I wondered how he hadn't suffocated himself with it.

But then again, I had too, hadn't I? Even if I hadn't meant to, I'd held onto the idea I was too messed up to love again, that the men in my life—apart from my dad—would leave me or that I wasn't enough. The loss of Grady had followed me around, even through my relationship with Thomas. It had consumed me whether I'd been honest with myself or not.

Now we had a real chance to put the past behind us and right our wrongs, and that started with the way I looked back at our history.

If we hadn't broken up, who knows what our future would've looked like? We wouldn't have been the people we were today. He wouldn't have had Charlie or maybe even his career, and I don't know I would've been as close with my sisters. While we'd bonded over the years as my sisters reached adulthood, I hadn't ever felt the actual depth of our camaraderie until after Thomas and I divorced. Moving home had turned out to be one of the best things I'd ever done for our relationship.

"Now you know," Grady said gently, "that you've always been with me through all the years and shows and tours. I bring it out for every acoustic set."

I was up and out of my seat before I could stop myself, walking toward him with a sense of purpose. Grady tilted his head, staring up at me with parted lips, waiting to see what I would do. He didn't ask me what I was doing. He didn't tell me to stop, so I kissed him. Consequences be damned.

His arms wrapped around me, pulling me closer as he met each fevered stroke of my tongue with his own. We were lost in the other person for only a moment before Charlie's loud claps took us by surprise.

Turning around, we saw her smile as she jumped off the couch, did a little dance, and ran toward us. I knew she must have questions, but there was such a sense of relief I felt when her little body slammed into ours. Grady and I both opened our arms to welcome her into our embrace, the three of us laughing at the craziness of it all.

Charlie was the first to pull back. "Wait, does this mean you're gonna be my mom, too?"

I blinked, looking to Grady for some guidance because I had no idea what it meant. I didn't know what the future held for us, but I did know I wanted to be with them and I didn't care what it took or what I had to do.

"Well, I'm not sure what it means," I said honestly.

Her little brows furrowed together in confusion. "But Daddy says I'm not allowed to kiss anyone unless we're getting married…"

I glanced at him and narrowed my eyes. There was no way in hell she should grow up believing that, but we could cross that bridge later when the balance and fate of my complicated relationship with her father wasn't hanging in the balance.

Grady, to his credit, looked away sheepishly before focusing his attention on his daughter. "There's a lot Miss Cleo and I need to talk about, but." He paused to take a breath. "Would it be okay with you if she were, eventually, in that kind of role for you? No one, and I mean this, Charlie, no one will ever or could ever replace your mom. She loves you more than anything else in the world. But—"

"But you also love Miss Cleo?" she asked.

Grady didn't hesitate. He nodded, blue eyes shining as he said, "I do, very much. Is that okay with you?"

"Yes, because I love Miss Cleo, too! And so will Mommy. She'll be so happy."

I wasn't sure how I felt about that, but I would have time to analyze it later. Meeting Olivia was going to be one of the most nerve-wracking things I'd ever done. It would be worth it, but that didn't mean I was necessarily looking forward to it. She was gorgeous, talented, and had a multi-million-dollar business under her control. Though I knew there was nothing to worry about, I couldn't help but think about how she'd spent the last seventeen years by his side while I was trying my hardest to move on.

When our relationship became public, there would be criticisms, of course, both from the public and from my own mind. To be honest, it was strange to think about the reach of the announcement of his divorce and its impact on our relationship. I'm sure there would be rumors of infidelity on his side. It wouldn't matter what we said, people would draw their own conclusions about what happened and run with it.

The thought of it was terrifying, honestly. I'd never allowed myself to be in a position where I would be so openly hated and judged. Was I ready for that? Was I strong enough to handle the whispers of people around town?

Two weeks ago, I would've said not a chance. I would've counted myself out before ever testing my limits, but now that I had Grady back in my life, I knew the answer was a very loud, resounding yes. I would let myself be flayed apart and destroyed if it meant we could be together.

"Liv will love you, by the way," Grady said, giving my hand a reassuring squeeze. "She's heard me talk about you for years."

"Really?"

"Oh yeah," he chuckled. "She knows our whole story. Witnessed every moment I pined for the one I'd lost. She's your biggest supporter, other than me, obviously, and has been foaming at the mouth to meet you."

I didn't know why I was crying, but I felt the tears well up all the same. I'd spent so long feeling jealous of a woman I'd never met, and yet she was cheering Grady and me on the entire time. Was it silly to be thankful he had someone to fill his life with love, whether platonic or romantic, while we were both figuring our shit out? Maybe, but I was all the same. Besides, if they hadn't gotten together, they never would have had Charlie, who was becoming just as important to me as her father was.

"Hey, hey," Grady said, wiping away my tears. "No crying. I'm sorry. Was this too much?"

I couldn't help but laugh. "Why're you apologizing when I was the one who just outed us to your daughter?"

"I don't know that we were ever much of a secret," he chuckled. "I mean, I've been pretty obvious with how much I wanted you. It won't come as some big secret."

He had a point. There was no way anyone in my family would be surprised, except possibly my dad. That was just because I hadn't talked to him much in the past two weeks. I couldn't help but wonder what he would make of all this, especially when he hadn't remembered Grady to begin with. Would he think it was too soon? Was I rushing into things?

He hadn't said anything to Josie and Lennox, but he was

used to them making rash decisions where their hearts were concerned. I, on the other hand, was the exact opposite. I asked questions, overanalyzed, and spiraled before coming to an overly rational conclusion. When Mom asked me what was taking so long to marry Thomas, Dad offered his full support, allowing me all the time I needed.

I'd only ever seen a hint of concern when I came home from college the weekend after my birthday. I thought I'd hidden my despair over Grady and me breaking up well enough, but he'd seen right through me. We spent our days curled up in the living room, watching old movies as I eventually sobbed onto his chest.

"I know I'm wasting my breath, but try not to worry, okay?" Grady said, pulling me back to the present. "The only people whose opinions matter are the people we know love us and want the best for us."

He pulled me down onto his lap, patting the other open spot for Charlie, who immediately climbed up, and then he wrapped his arms around us both and squeezed us tight. It didn't alleviate my concerns or fear, but it brought me comfort, knowing we'd likely face a mess in our future, yet we would be able to get through it because we had each other.

I hoped that would be enough.

cleo

. . .

I WAS SITTING at the piano as Grady came back into the living room. He'd just put Charlie to sleep after a tearful bedtime. When they tried to call Olivia, which apparently, they did every night, she hadn't answered, which sent Charlie into a bit of a spiral. She was missing her mom something fierce, and my heart broke each time she wailed.

"Still nothing?" I asked, attempting to recall Chopsticks by memory, though not very well.

Grady collapsed on the couch, running his hand through his hair. "Nope. I texted her, too. It isn't like her to go silent like this. Her assistant said she hadn't spoken to her since before dinner, and she didn't have any scheduled meetings tonight."

"Maybe she fell asleep early?"

He snorted. "Liv is like a vampire. That woman doesn't understand the meaning of the word sleep. She survives on spite, ADHD medication, and Red Bull. Oh, and gin and tonics."

"And don't forget the blood of the innocent, apparently. I'm not sure Red Bull and meds are vampire staples," I teased, trying to lighten the mood. "The G and T's and spite seem on point, though."

"It's just weird, that's all. I don't know. I'm probably just overthinking."

I closed the fallboard, turning around to face him. "You don't think something happened to her, right? Like, she's okay?"

He waved me off. "Yeah, nothing like that. It's more like I'm worried she's laid up in bed, seriously sick, because she refuses to tell anyone she's hurting."

"Ah," I said, grimacing. "I know the feeling well."

"I'm well aware," Grady said with a roll of his eyes. "Do you remember when you got the flu right after we started college and you ended up getting the entire class sick because you refused to stay home?"

"It wasn't my finest moment," I confessed. "But I was worried I would fall behind!"

"Cleo, it'd been like three days, and we shared classes. I could've helped you with anything you needed."

"Blame it on my inability to let go," I said, raising my hands.

"Whatever you say," he chuckled, moving to the floor where the remnants of our card game littered the floor.

I almost moved to help him, but I hesitated, choosing instead to watch him as he worked. There was something utterly domestic about what we were doing. He'd tucked Charlie in, made sure she was asleep, and now here we were, talking about the past as he cleaned up after game night. It wasn't exciting or glamorous or over the top. It was easy, a glimpse into what I hoped the rest of my life would look like.

Plus, he was wearing a pair of grey, heathered sweatpants that had no reason being so sexy. How was I supposed to focus on cleaning up when I was so easily distracted?

When he finished, Grady turned to me, giving me a mocking smile. "Are you just going to gawk, or are you going to help?"

"I don't know," I said, crossing my legs. "I kind of like the look of you on your knees."

I meant it as a joke, but didn't miss the way his eyes flared with heat at my words. I'd never realized what a submissive side Grady had when we were younger. There wasn't much discussion about kinks or fantasies back then. I'd never even explored that side until I discovered romance novels that helped me explore parts of my desires I didn't know I had.

While I loved the thought of trusting someone enough to occasionally give up control of my body, I preferred to be the one calling the shots. I wanted to know I could stop at any time and be able to trust my partner to listen.

"And I like the look of you right there. My god," he whispered. There was something in the way he spoke, how his voice was full of both reverence and awe because of *me*. I found power in that. I was the one bringing him to his knees, the one who had him all tangled up in knots so severely he could barely breathe. "You're killing me."

I smiled. "You say that a lot."

"It's true. I look at you sometimes, and it nearly takes my breath away because this is real. You're here with me. I've dreamed about it for so many years, and now you're in front of me like the answer to a prayer. I'm not gonna take it for granted for even a second," he said. "And the sight of you sitting there on that bench like a goddamn queen on her throne? Well, it does something to me."

I glanced down, staring at the impressive bulge behind his sweatpants. Noticing my gaze, he let his hand slip down. My mouth went dry as he gripped his length through the fabric. "I see that," I murmured, licking my lips. This was too much and not enough. I hated the way my clothes felt on my body, the way I felt like I was burning up from the inside because of how badly I ached for his touch.

I'd never wanted anyone or anything the way I wanted Grady. It was more than just desire; it bordered on need. Like if he didn't touch me right now, then I might just die. Suddenly, I didn't care about all the things I said about waiting until we figured things out. That would come eventually, but there was no reason to deny myself something I wanted when it was right there in front of me.

"How badly do you want to touch me right now?" I asked, leaning forward.

His eyes tracked the movement, shifting on his knees as though trying to restrain himself. "So badly."

"Use your words."

His lips curled into a devious smirk as he glanced down the hall to make sure Charlie's door was still closed. When satisfied, he reached inside his pants and pulled himself free, stroking from root to tip. I could make it out through the candlelit glow around us, casting the obscene shadow of his ministrations on the wall. "I'm so fucking hard for you, bluebird. I'm literally fucking leaking."

I shuddered at the thought of his cock, throbbing and hard just from the idea of me. "Come here." He struggled to his feet, but I held up my hand to stop him. I wasn't sure what came over me. Maybe it'd always been my piqued curiosity at the way he used to play to my dominant side. "Crawl to me."

The smirk he gave me earlier grew into a full-blown, devious grin as he slowly dropped back to his knees and began crawling across the floor. There was something so hot about the way he did what I said without question. How this big, strong man would get on his hands and knees, slinking across the floor with his hard cock jutting out of the top of his pants because I told him to. He didn't care what it looked like; the possibility of being emasculated wasn't on his mind.

I gave him an order and he complied as if it were the simplest thing in the world.

Grady came to a stop in front of me, sitting back between my thighs. He ran one hand up my leg as the other gripped his length. "See what you do to me? You make me crazy. All the time, I can't stop thinking about all the ways I want you."

"And what're you thinking about right now?" I whispered.

He sucked in a breath, dropping his voice to a low purr that went straight to my core. "Pulling those shorts down and seeing if you're leaving a mess in your panties, if you're as soaked for me as I am hard for you."

Oh god, yes. He had no idea I was as pathetically weak for him as he was for me, but I wanted him to. I wanted to be the strong, confident woman he believed I was, so I leaned back, letting my elbows rest on the fallboard. "Take them off and find out."

"Yes, ma'am," he said, tongue darting out to wet his lips. They glistened in the low light as he reached forward, tucking his fingers into the waistband of my shorts and working them down. "Hips up, please."

I did as he asked, raising just enough for him to slip my shorts down my thighs. Then, his hands went to my knees, pushing them apart so he could see just how soaked I was.

"Oh, bluebird..." he groaned, trailing a finger delicately along the seam of my fabric-clad pussy. "Look at this. You must be hurting. Please let me help you. Please let me take the ache away."

We had joked about begging over the past few days, but I didn't think he was serious. Yet, here he was, gently stroking my soaked underwear like my pleasure was the only thing he was concerned about. It wasn't about how hard I made him, even though I could make out how painful it looked, the sheen of arousal around the head of his cock that was almost enough to make me say, "fuck it," and ease his pain first. Even if I did, I doubted Grady would let me. Not now that he'd seen just how needy I was.

"Yes," I breathed. The word had barely left my lips before he was dragging the fabric down my legs and bringing it to his mouth. I watched in rapture as he inhaled deeply, eyes closed and tongue sliding across the arousal left behind. My god. It probably shouldn't have been as hot as it was, but his obsession knew no bounds.

Before I could say anything, his eyes snapped open, honing in on the exposed flesh between my thighs. He surged forward, a groan rumbling in his chest as he feasted on me. My back arched against the piano, hands going to his hair to steady myself and pull him closer. There was nothing soft about the way he worked his tongue. He was starving, and I was the only thing that could satisfy his hunger.

"You like this, bluebird?" he murmured against my skin. Over the past few days, his stubble had grown thicker. Now it was rubbing against my inner thigh, the sensation strangely elevating the pleasure. "Am I making you feel good?"

"Holy shit, yes," I breathed, trying to keep my voice down. Charlie was just down the hall. The last thing either of us needed was to traumatize the poor kid with the sight of her father on his knees eating my pussy like it was the greatest thing he'd ever tasted. "So good, baby. Oh my god."

When he slid a single finger in, curling it up just a bit to hit a spot I wasn't even sure existed before now, I bit down on my lip to stop myself from crying out. Between that and the way he sucked my clit into his mouth, I could feel him pulling my orgasm to the surface.

"Grady, I'm going to—"

"Soak my face, bluebird. Fucking come on my tongue."

With a muffled cry, I let myself go. I basked in the toe-curling ecstasy that was my climax, and the way he prolonged it with languid strokes of his tongue. It was euphoric and all-consuming. I wanted nothing more than to float off into this bliss for the rest of my life.

With him, I knew I could.

When Grady pulled back, I surged forward, taking his chin between my fingers. My arousal coated his lips, glistening in the candlelight in a way that shouldn't be sexy, but was. "Did I do good?" he asked with a knowing smirk.

"So good, baby. Such a good boy," I said, kissing him. "But also, such a smartass."

He groaned against my mouth. "Don't call me that right now. I'm trying not to blow right here and now."

I pulled back, eyebrow raised. "Does someone have a little bit of a praise kink?"

"I have a *you* kink," he said earnestly. "Anything and everything that comes out of your mouth turns me on." I looked down, staring at the swollen head of his cock. "Don't look at me like that, either. I can't take it—"

"I don't want to wait," I murmured.

Grady paused, a crease forming between his furrowed brows. "What do you mean?"

I straightened my back, sitting tall. "I mean, there are a million different reasons why we should, don't get me wrong. There's a lot of shit we need to figure out, but I'm so fucking sick and tired of waiting for the things I want, Grady. Especially when they're right in front of me, and in this moment... All I want is you in every way I can have you."

Cupping my face with his strong, callous-laced hands, Grady kissed me. It was gentle at first, the kind of kiss we shared as kids because our love was sweet and simple, but then it grew into a sort of passion I'd never known. It was consuming. It was claiming.

It was us.

"I love you," I said between panting breaths. "I've always loved you."

Grady's hands moved down my body, gripping my waist as he hoisted me in the air. I thought he was going to take me to bed, but he didn't. He sat down on the piano bench and leaned against the fallboard, allowing me to gain back control as I straddled him.

"Lift up for me, bluebird," he said gently. I did as he asked, watching his cock spring free as he slipped his sweats down his thighs until nothing was separating us but space.

"Are you sure?" he asked, pulling his gaze from where his cock met my bare pussy. "I don't want to rush you."

"I've never been more sure of anything," I whispered. Reaching between us, I grabbed his cock and lined it with my entrance. Both of us stilled as I lowered my body, and the tip slipped in.

This was real. It was happening, and it felt right.

It'd been so long since I'd been with anyone, but I wasn't sure about Grady. We'd never talked much about his sex life. Obviously, he was married. They'd been intimate at least once, given Charlie's existence. She was gorgeous. I wouldn't have blamed him if it were more.

As if sensing my hesitation, he said, "I've got condoms in the bedroom, if you would feel more comfortable, but you should know I haven't been with anyone since the night Charlie was conceived."

I blinked back my shock. "That's been years—"

"Almost seven," he confirmed. "But the point is there's nothing you'd need to worry about."

"Neither do you. I've only been with two men in my life, and after I divorced Thomas, I was tested. All good." I kissed him. "If you're comfortable, I want to feel you, Grady. I don't want anything between us."

He nodded, and I slowly slid onto his length. Jesus Christ, the fit was tighter than I remembered. Had it always been like this? This angle had me feeling every agonizingly perfect inch of his cock, the way it stretched and filled me. I was struggling to contain my moans of pleasure and pain as he worked.

"Bite down on me if you need to scream, bluebird," he panted, pulling me closer. "Let me ease that pain."

Leaning forward, I bit down on his shoulder as he fully

seated himself inside of me. I felt changed. It was the knowledge that after tonight, nothing would be the same as it was before. It was me taking back control of my life and what I wanted while he claimed me in a way that soothed my fears.

"Holy fucking shit, Cleo," he breathed. I pulled back, admiring what I could see of the marks in his skin. His hand slid beneath the fabric of my T-shirt, pulling it up to reveal my lacy bra and hardened nipples. It would've been foolish for us to completely undress; we'd save that for when we knew we had complete and total privacy. What we were doing already had us both feeling a little reckless.

Grady leaned forward, moving the fabric aside, and took my nipple into his mouth. I leaned back, arms hooked around his neck in pure ecstasy as his tongue flicked across the hardened peak. Beneath me, he began to move. Slowly at first, but each shallow surge of his hips had excited pleasure coursing through my body.

"Holy shit," he murmured, switching to my other breast. "You feel so fucking good."

I met his movements with jerky ones of my own, but it'd been so long since I'd done this. I was clunky and out of practice. While it still felt good, nothing felt *right*. I wanted him to fuck me, to claim me, and this angle wasn't hitting it for me. "Wait, take me to the couch."

Without pulling out, he scooped me up and deposited me gently on my back. It was taking everything I had not to claw at his skin and beg him to destroy me because each shift and movement had him hitting a new spot that made me see stars. How had we let each other go? How had we lived so long without one another?

"I don't know if I can be gentle," he murmured, pulling out and looking down at the space where we were still connected. It was dark from my angle, but I could only imagine what he saw. How, just like his lips earlier, my arousal obscenely coated his bare cock. As he pushed back in, I squeezed myself around him. "Fuck," he groaned, the vibration going straight to my aching pussy. "Fuck, that feels so good. Holy shit."

"Please, baby," I pleaded. I didn't care that we'd traded places, didn't care that I was the one begging. Not if he gave in. "Please fuck me."

I wasn't sure what set him off. Maybe it was just the relief of not needing to hold back like before, or perhaps it was the way I begged. The moment the words left my lips, Grady let himself go. He pounded into me like a man possessed, driving me into the cushions with each thrust. It bordered on painful for a moment, stealing my breath, but then the pleasure surged. All I could think of was wanting more, more, more.

I hated not being able to scream, to thrash and cry and beg for more. I bit down so hard on my lip I thought it might bleed. Grady kissed me, swallowing my desperate whimpers. "You feel so good," he muttered. "You feel like mine."

"I am, I am," I cried, back bowing at the breath-stealing way he drove into me. "I'm all yours."

Grady unhooked my legs from his waist and set them on his shoulders before settling into a relentlessly torturous pace. The new angle was almost too much, too deep, but I loved it. Reveled in it.

I could feel the pleasure coursing through my body as I let my hand drift between our bodies to circle my clit, winding myself higher and higher like I was a time bomb waiting to explode. "Grady, I'm going to come."

"Yes," he whispered harshly. "Fucking come for me, baby. Fucking give me everything you have."

With one more thrust, Grady sent me over the edge. My orgasm slammed into me, stealing the air from my lungs. Every muscle in my body tensed up, wringing all the pleasure in one shuddering climax, and sending Grady hurtling for his own release.

"Shit, shit, shit," he groaned. "Cleo, baby, oh my god. Squeezing me so good."

He hid his face in the crook of my neck, movements faltering with his climax as he poured into me. I felt his hot breath on my neck, reveled in the way he stifled his cries on my skin. It was euphoric.

His arms gave out, and he collapsed on top of me with a chuckle, both of us sweaty messes. Normally, I'd hate the way my clothes stuck to my body and the dampness of his skin, but not now. Not after what we just did. Not when I was still craving him like I never had before.

Turning my head, I pressed a soft kiss to his cheek, earning a smile as he pulled me closer. "How does it keep getting better?" he mused. His voice was so low I wondered if I was meant to hear it, but then he continued. "Every day, I ask myself that, you know."

"And are you any closer to your answer?"

He shook his head. "No, but I look forward to spending the rest of my life trying to get there."

grady

. . .

LYING HERE with Cleo Hayes in my arms after a night full of the best sex of my life, there was only one thought on my mind: I was the luckiest man in the whole goddamn world.

Over the years, I'd thought that time and again, telling myself it couldn't possibly get better than the fame and family I'd procured through hard work and dedication. Even then, I knew I was lying to myself.

But no more.

After lying spent on the couch for a few minutes, we moved to the bedroom, taking our time to strip ourselves bare and take our time until we were utterly spent. I didn't think I'd ever come so much in a single night before. Just when I thought I was done, I'd catch a scent of her subtle vanilla scent, and it was over for me. By the time we finally called it quits, it was nearly 4:00 a.m. We had to force ourselves apart so we weren't complete zombies when Charlie inevitably came crashing through the door with the rising sun.

I looked down at the angel resting her head on my chest, her blonde hair fanned out against my tanned skin in a contrast that almost made it glow. Cleo was so beautiful it physically hurt—

her bare face and the light smattering of freckles across her nose and cheeks. Her pouty lips, a sweet pink that accentuated the sharp cupid's bow just above.

How lucky was I that we'd found our way back to one another?

Leaning down, I pressed a kiss to the top of her head. She stirred in my arms, blinking open her deep blue eyes and giving me a lazy smile. "Good morning," she said.

As she stretched, I remembered we were both naked, too lazy to put clothes back on after our little sex marathon. My cock stirred to life at the thought of being so close to her bare pussy. Honestly, I needed to get a hold of that. I was thirty-six, not sixteen. I couldn't be getting hard every time I was around her.

But right now, when we were in bed alone, I could make an exception.

I rolled her onto her back, relishing the way she immediately spread her legs and welcomed me between her thighs. There were faint marks along her neck, shoulders, and chest from where I'd licked and sucked and nipped at her skin all night, which I loved. The sight of them on her body, knowing I was the one who put them there, soothed the territorial beast in my chest.

I reached out and let my fingers trail along them. "So fucking beautiful."

Cleo glanced down, blushing. "Someone got carried away."

"Don't act like I'm the only one. If I walked into the bathroom, I'm sure I'd find some of my own."

"Maybe so," she said with a smirk. "I couldn't let you have all the fun, could I?"

"I wouldn't dream of it. I'll wear your hickeys with pride," I said, leaning in to kiss her. She met me halfway, wrapping her arms around my neck and pulling me closer. The head of my cock rubbed against her center, earning a soft gasp as I slowly slipped inside. "Are you sore, bluebird?"

"A little," she admitted. I moved to pull myself free because the last thing I wanted to do was hurt her, but she stopped me with a fierce look. "But don't you dare stop. Make love to me, Grady Wilde. Show me how much you love me."

Last night had been mostly dirty fucking. While we'd slowed it down a time or two, it was full of desperation and begging and frantic need. But as the early morning sun filtered through the curtains, bathing the room in a soft, golden glow, it felt different. It felt born of love and tenderness. Of whispered oaths and the promise of infinite tomorrows.

With our gazes locked, I dropped my forehead to hers. Cleo raised her leg, hooking it around my waist as I gripped her hip, securing her in place before I began to move. It sent currents of pleasure coursing through my body as I aimed to show her exactly how profound this moment felt.

Slipping my other hand beneath her back, I pulled her closer, digging into her skin with each powerful thrust. I couldn't get enough; I was gone for her. She had every bit of my heart, body, and soul. I didn't know what else I could offer her, but I knew I'd give her anything she asked for.

As her lips parted on a cry, I covered her mouth with my own, swallowing her moans of pleasure. "I love you," I said, picking up the pace, forcing myself deeper with each thrust. Each soft mewl she only made me want more. "I love you so much."

It wasn't long before her back bowed and sweet pussy tightened around me, sending me following her over the edge into toe-curling ecstasy before she could utter a single word. Nothing had ever felt so powerful, so meaningful before.

For the first time, I felt healed from the pain of our past. While I hated the time we lost, this may be how our story was meant to play out. When we were kids, I could understand what we shared was special, but I had taken her for granted nonetheless. I didn't realize how much I would miss the way she kissed me every time she left a room or placed her hand on my back when passing by. Or the way her smiles, the real ones at least, were so sporadic.

After a tender kiss, I sat back and looked down to where we were joined. The evidence of our climaxes coated my cock as I slipped out, and goddamn... It was so fucking hot seeing what was left of my cum leak out of her. Flicking my gaze up to meet hers, I reached forward and slowly pushed it back in. It didn't matter to me that it'd be wiped away when we dragged our spent bodies to the shower to clean up. I just wanted to lay claim to her in every way I could.

"That shouldn't be as hot as it is," she whispered, giving me a shy smile that I returned.

"When it comes to you and this pussy," I said, brushing my thumb over her clit, "everything is fucking sexy."

She laughed, the sound lightening the moment. "You're so crude."

"I can't help it. I'm in love."

Cleo's face softened at my words. "I know. I feel it." She placed her hand over her heart. "And it's terrifying, but I wouldn't have it any other way."

"I wouldn't either, baby." I grabbed her hand, bringing it up to my lips. "Now, let's get cleaned up before we get a wakeup call from a certain little girl who doesn't understand boundaries?"

TRUE TO FORM, Cleo and I had barely gotten dressed before we heard the pitter-patter of feet running down the hall toward our room. "Daddy, Miss Cleo!" she called before throwing open the door and storming inside. "I've been waiting on you guys forever. I'm so hungry." She patted her stomach for extra emphasis.

"Well, we can't have that, can we?" Cleo said, placing her hands on her hips. She'd thrown her hair up in a messy bun and donned one of my old band T-shirts that was so long it nearly swallowed the pair of cut-off shorts she was wearing.

Even though she had her own in the weekend bag Lennox packed, I love that Cleo wore my clothes. Whether it was out of a possessive need to show the world she was mine, or if it was just the familiarity of it all, it was so damn sexy.

Charlie shook her head. "Nope. We can't!"

"If you could have whatever you wanted for breakfast, what would you want?" Cleo asked, stooping to Charlie's height so they were level.

My daughter pursed her lips in thought. "I want something sweet, I think."

"You're gonna have to add something else in too, sunshine," I said, leaning against the doorframe.

"Bacon?" Charlie asked, perking up.

I laughed. "Sure. Bacon is fine. Eggs, too, though."

This time, Charlie's face scrunched up in disgust. "I really don't like eggs, Daddy."

"Then I guess you really don't want any sweets," I said, pushing off the wall and moving to stand behind Cleo. "And don't try to use those puppy-dog eyes on me. It's not gonna work."

Okay, so it almost always worked, but not when it came to food. My mom loved desserts more than anyone else I knew, but even she made sure to prioritize a somewhat balanced diet.

Charlie huffed, crossing her arms over her chest. "Fine." She turned to Cleo. "But can you make them all fluffy like you did the other day? I liked those."

"Anything for you, sunshine," she said, smiling as Charlie

held out her hand for her to take. Cleo hesitated for a moment before putting her hand into my daughter's, and then she was dragged off to the kitchen.

It was the first time I realized Cleo had ever used the nickname Liv and I did for Charlie. The fact that she was becoming comfortable enough not to overthink it made me smile. When she'd told me about her struggle with infertility, my heart had broken for her. Growing up, she'd talked about how much she wanted to be a mother, and that was taken away from her. She was so good with kids—the type of person who would've made an amazing parent. I hoped, though, she could come to think of Charlie as hers as much as she was Liv's and mine. I never wanted her to view herself as less than in that department.

I followed them down the hall and into the kitchen, laughing as Cleo instructed Charlie on what to pull from the fridge. "I'll get started on the coffee," I said, pressing a kiss to her cheek as I went by.

We were going to need it after the night we had. I was already feeling the exhaustion seep into my weary muscles.

After filling the pot and grinding down the beans, the aroma of fresh coffee filled the space. I nearly wept with relief as I turned around to face Charlie, who was currently attempting to whisk the eggs like Cleo had shown her. I thought she had it handled, but I was wrong. When I went to pour myself a cup of steaming liquid gold, Cleo called for her to bring the bowl over to the stove. I assumed she would've hopped off the chair first before grabbing the bowl, but apparently that wasn't how my daughter's mind worked.

Instead, she tried to climb off the chair while carrying the mixing bowl at the same time and tripped. I rushed forward to catch her, but instead, I felt the slimy sensation of egg yolks as they splashed all down the front of my clothes.

Cleo whipped around as the metal bowl crashed to the floor,

interrupting the peaceful silence we'd been enjoying moments ago.

Charlie's hands flew to her mouth. "I'm so sorry, Daddy! I didn't mean to."

"It's fine," I said, holding my hands up. "Just a little mess. Grab a wet towel, sunshine. Let's get this cleaned up."

"Here," Cleo said, rushing to my side. "Let me help. You go get changed."

"It's okay—" I began, but stopped the moment she narrowed her eyes and pointed toward the bedroom. "Yes, ma'am," I muttered, smirking as I padded into my bedroom to change.

Liv and I might've been married, but it didn't mean we did all the overly domestic things like making breakfast on Sunday mornings. In Nashville, we had a live-in chef who took care of most of the food prep and cooking for us. We didn't spend a lot of time at the house together, choosing instead to take Charlie to amusement parks or museums. I wanted her to experience all the things I never had as a kid, but maybe I was doing her a disservice by also forgetting about the things that made my childhood so wonderful. I mean, some of my best memories were spent in this very house with Mom and Dad doing mundane, everyday things.

As I slipped into the bathroom to change, I heard a knock at the door. I ordered groceries yesterday and was sure that it might be them. They were a little bit early, but that wasn't out of the ordinary.

"Can you grab that?" I called out, shrugging out of my clothes. "I think it's the groceries."

"Sure thing!" Cleo shouted back. She mumbled something to Charlie before heading to the door. The hinges creaked as she swung it open.

"Surprise!" I stilled at the familiar voice coming from the front, quickly pulling on a fresh shirt before hurrying out of the bedroom and hoping I was wrong.

Liv stood at the front door, wearing a smile as her eyes drifted from Cleo to me. She was overdressed, looking like she had just stepped off a photoshoot in a long, flowy skirt with knee-high cowboy boots and a frilly, lace tank top. Her hair was curled, and her makeup was perfect.

"Mommy!" Charlie screamed, running through the house. She moved past Cleo, nearly causing Liv to topple over as they collided. "I missed you so much!"

"Hey, sunshine! I missed you, too," she said, holding onto our daughter as though her life depended on it. She pulled back, holding Charlie back by her shoulders. "Let's look at you, huh? You've grown so much."

"I haven't grown that much," Charlie giggled. All her attention was stolen as she noticed the boxes in Liv's hand. "Are those for me?"

Liv laughed awkwardly, moving Charlie to the side. "They're for everyone. Though," she paused, looking at Cleo as she straightened up. "I'm so sorry. I wasn't sure if you'd be here, and I didn't know what you might want. I tried to get a variety, but the selection here is limited compared to what I'm used to." She held up two white boxes. "Grabbed some kolaches, too. Spicy and regular. Oh! And there are coffees in the car."

I came to a stop beside Cleo, glancing at her out of my periphery. She was still wearing a deer in the headlights look. I didn't think she'd moved this entire time. Oh god. This was a disaster.

"Hey," I said, moving in to give Liv a hug. "Uh, what're you doing here?"

"I was missing my girl something fierce," she said, giving Charlie a squeeze. "I know I should've called, but this seemed like more fun."

"Fun," I snorted. "You were feeling nosey."

"Yes, fun," Liv deadpanned. "Now, will you take these from me so I can introduce myself properly?" I did as she asked, watching carefully as she turned toward Cleo. Her lips spread in a wide grin as she held out her hand. "Hi! I'm Olivia, but please call me Liv. I don't really think there needs to be any kind of formality here amongst friends and lovers."

"Right," Cleo said slowly, reaching out to take Liv's hand. "I'm Cleo."

"It's so nice to officially meet you. I've heard so much about you. It's truly an honor."

Cleo's features softened a touch, but I could sense her walls going up. "You as well." Her gaze traveled from Liv to Charlie and finally to me. "I should go—"

"No!" Liv and I both said at the same time.

"Stay, please," I continued. "Have breakfast at least."

She shook her head. "I don't want to intrude—"

"Why not?" Liv asked. "I do it all the time."

I pinched the bridge of my nose, feeling any sense of control I had spiraling out of reach. "What she means is... You're not intruding. You were literally here, and we were in the middle of making breakfast. You should stay."

But she was already walking toward the bedroom to grab her overnight bag.

I turned to Liv, exasperated. "You couldn't have freaking called? Given me a heads up? Messenger pigeon?"

She gestured toward the bedroom. "Go get your girl and stop worrying about me! We can talk later," she whispered, shooing me off.

I jogged into my room, heart pounding as Cleo tossed the last of her clothes in the bag. I held up my hands as I got closer, scared the slightest movement would scare her off. "Please don't go, bluebird. I didn't know she was coming—"

"I'm not worried about that, Grady. I don't care. She seems lovely, but Charlie hasn't seen her mom in over two weeks, and you guys obviously have things to talk about."

"So do we," I said. My voice sounded desperate, which was precisely how I felt. "Please don't go."

"I have to," Cleo said, finally meeting my eyes.

"Let me drive you, at least." Maybe if I could get her alone, I could smooth things out. I could calm whatever fears were running through her head, so she'd come back here, and we could start the morning over.

"No, you should stay. I'm going to borrow your truck, if that's okay. And I'll have Lennox follow me out here later to bring it back. Don't worry."

"I'm not worried about the damn truck," I said as she zipped up the bag. I could feel her hesitation for only a moment before she walked past me, giving my hand a squeeze. I let her reach the door before I spoke. "Hey, don't go like this, *please.*"

We said things, we made promises, but I felt them slipping away the moment I heard Liv's voice. God. Out of all the things I thought to be worried about, this had never crossed my mind. Cleo knew I'd been married, knew that if we continued whatever this thing was, she'd end up meeting and having a relationship with my ex-wife. But knowing and seeing are two different things. When Liv was brought up in conversation, Cleo didn't have to see her standing in front of her.

"You're not. I just... I don't know. You guys deserve to spend the morning together after being apart for so long. I just want to make sure I'm not standing in the way of that."

"But you're not," I said, moving forward until I was standing right in front of her. Gently, I cupped her neck, feeling her pulse rapidly beating beneath my hands. "I've told you time and again. You belong here with us."

Cleo closed her eyes and leaned into my touch. I thought maybe it worked, that she would stay, but then she straightened up and stepped back. "I'll talk to you later, okay?"

I stood there in the doorway, watching her walk away until I heard the rumble of my old truck, and she pulled out onto the road, driving away.

"Well, that didn't really go as planned," Liv said, stepping up beside me with two steaming cups of coffee. She handed me one, which I took gratefully, taking a long sip to compose myself before I completely lost it.

"What the hell are you doing here?" I asked, heading into the kitchen where Charlie was already munching down on what had to have been her second donut, given the chocolatey mess she'd made on her hands and face. She gave me a small smile as I snatched a glazed concoction from the box.

She was hot on my heels, rounding the kitchen with the stubborn look she often got when preparing to bust some balls at work. "Look, in my defense, how was I supposed to know the one who got away was going to be here this morning? It's not like you told me. Which, in all actuality, I should be madder about since I've never met the woman. But I trust your judgement and all that."

"Liv," I growled, angrily taking a bite off the donut. "Don't do that."

"I'm just saying," she said, holding up her hands. "Besides, I already told you why I came in. I wanted to surprise Charlie. I missed her, Grady. Video calls weren't enough anymore. I missed you, too, you old grump. It's nice to see you, by the way."

Under different circumstances, I probably would've rolled my eyes and let things go, but I couldn't. Not when I didn't know what was going through Cleo's mind or if our relationship was already over before it'd ever begun again. "Why didn't you pick up last night? You could've at least told *me* you were planning on coming in. Hell, a text would've been better than nothing."

"What part of 'I wanted to surprise our daughter' do you not get?" She tapped my temple. "Did she fuck you stupid or something?"

"Very funny," I said dryly. "And don't talk about her like that."

"Ha! I knew it. God, you're so smitten. It's adorable." She beamed. "Listen, I know it didn't quite go as planned, but I didn't come out of malicious intent. You know that. I thought it would be nice for you to take a break for a bit. I know y'all haven't had any true alone time since you came down to Texas. Figured I could watch over Charlie while you go to get your girl."

"I had my girl. She was already here. Your plan clearly had flaws."

Liv rolled her eyes and sighed dramatically. "Yes, well, I see that now, Captain Obvious. But back when I concocted it, I really thought it was brilliant."

"You would," I said, stuffing my mouth and downing the sugary donut with the black coffee. It was hot as shit, but I hardly flinched.

"Come on," Liv said, tugging me toward the table. With a sigh, I followed her, dropping my ass in the seat across from my daughter. Charlie glanced at me and the box before nudging it over.

Fine. I guess another wouldn't hurt since I'm probably about to be single.

"Is Miss Cleo coming back?" Charlie asked, looking between Liv and me.

"Of course, she will," Liv said. "She just had to get some clean clothes."

Clean clothes? I mouthed, and Liv shrugged.

Charlie's brows furrowed. "But why can't she wear more of Daddy's like she was earlier?"

I nearly spat out my coffee all over the table, but I choked it down instead.

"You'd be much more comfortable in your own clothes over

someone else's, right?" Liv asked, and Charlie nodded. "Right. Miss Cleo feels the same."

Seemingly satisfied with the answer, Charlie reached for a kolache and took a big bite. I followed suit, grabbing a spicy one for me and a regular for Liv. We were silent for a minute, until I turned to her. "You're really okay with all of this?"

"Were the signed divorce papers not clear enough?" she snorted. "Yes, dummy. I'm very okay with it. I know you wouldn't bring anyone into our lives that would hurt our daughter. I trust your judgement. Plus, I've literally heard about her since the night she dumped your ass. Believe me when I tell you I'm not worried about Cleo's character for even a moment. And besides, Charlie loves her."

Our daughter beamed. "I do. Miss Cleo is great."

"See? She's great. I'm great. You're really a very lucky man, Mr. Wilde."

"You're such a smartass," I growled, though I couldn't help my smile.

Liv was right. I was fucking lucky. I was sitting here, surrounded by love, by two of the most important people in my life. I was blessed to not only have a daughter who lit up my world, but an amazing ex, who was both the mother of my child and my best friend. And finally, I had gotten Cleo Hayes back— the love of my fucking life.

cleo

. . .

I DROVE HOME IN SILENCE, letting only the creaking of the seat and rumble of the diesel engine fill the cab as I drove over the rough gravel road. Whatever happened back there wasn't my finest moment; I probably should have blasted something to drown out the overwhelming noise in my head, but for the first time in ages, I didn't want to.

Meeting Grady's ex-wife was inevitable. It was going to happen sooner rather than later. They had a kid, for crying out loud. So, why was I surprised when she showed up at Grady's door with a smile, arms laden with breakfast and coffee? Sure, it'd been unannounced, but she shouldn't need to make an announcement to visit her family.

After all, I was the one who was an outsider.

Except, I wasn't really, was I? I loved him first. He was mine before he was ever hers. Not that it was a competition. The thought was stupid, and I didn't really feel that way. If anything, I was glad he wasn't alone for the half of his life I wasn't a part of. I was grateful for the happiness he experienced, the success he'd achieved, and the life he'd built.

If it hadn't been for Liv and their relationship, regardless of what forces brought them together, they wouldn't have Charlie.

I wouldn't have Charlie.

Regardless of my relatively logical reasoning, for some reason, when I saw her standing there looking like a freaking supermodel, I panicked. My fight or flight response kicked in, and I was all flight. Suddenly, my clothes had felt too tight, and my skin itched with the need to get out of there. It was selfish, but I panicked. I just needed a moment to compose myself, and I'd be fine. I did hope Grady realized I wasn't running away, even though I gave him no indication otherwise.

As I pulled up to the house, I put the truck in park and let my head fall against the steering wheel. *God, Cleo. How do you have such a talent for complicating things?* It wasn't like I meant to, but sometimes I struggled to properly articulate what was going on in my head, which made matters worse. The only choice I had left was to retreat.

Rachel called it turtling. I called it spiraling.

The rumble of the engine centered me, and after a few minutes, I felt strong enough to step outside. I was sure either one or both of my parents would be waiting to jump on me the moment I walked through the door. And Lennox wouldn't be far behind. Maybe I could just take a shower, grab some fresh clothes, and drive back into town before anyone noticed I was here.

Yeah, fat chance.

Turning the ignition, I grabbed my bag and hopped out of the truck. It was quiet, which wasn't too unusual for a Sunday morning, seeing as most of the cowboys spent their Saturday nights in town at the Lone Star. I braced myself for an attack the moment I opened the door, but was met with the eerie silence of an empty room. Mom was usually at the table with her coffee, reading a book while Dad made breakfast. There wasn't even the lingering scent of coffee to comfort me.

As I crept to the back door and peeked outside, I was surprised to see Mom tending to her garden. For a moment, I wondered why she hadn't heard my truck and come running, but then it hit me. She wouldn't have batted an eye at the sound of a diesel engine. It was a necessity out here. Most, if not all, of our cowboys drove loud vehicles. She likely thought one of them was headed up to the barn and didn't realize I'd come home.

Maybe I could pull this off after all.

Heading back to my room, I was startled when I saw a figure sitting on the ottoman at the end of my bed. "Jesus, Dad! You scared me."

He turned over his shoulder, giving me a warm smile. "Last time I checked, I live here too, ya know."

"To be honest, I didn't realize anyone was in the house. It's too quiet," I said, setting my bag down.

"Different, huh?" he joked. "I'm not used to it myself, but I think I'll be able to get used to it eventually."

I padded across the floor to my bed, climbing on top and hugging one of the pillows to my chest. I didn't know how long he'd been here or why. Something about it was both comforting and made me uneasy at the same time.

"What're you doing in here?" I asked, drumming my fingers against my pillowcase.

He looked back toward the bookshelf that had pictures dating back to high school, and old academic trophies that probably should've been thrown out by now. "Don't mind me. I was just feeling a little nostalgic. It's been quite some time since your mother and I have been alone. Seems like it's gotten quiet overnight, especially with your sisters gone. They could fill a whole house with their noise, but sometimes you're so quiet I forget you're here."

"Well, I'll try to be as loud as possible from now on," I joked, still confused as to this sudden sense of sentimentality. "You're almost empty nesters."

That made his smile a little bit brighter. "Only took damn near forty years—"

"Hey! I'm not forty yet," I said, squeezing the pillow. "I still have four years to go before I get the distinction."

Dad shook his head. "Stop trying to age me, dammit. I already feel old as hell. I don't need the reminder that my baby girl is all grown up."

"Ah, Lennox has been grown, Daddy. For quite some time now."

His large, bushy eyebrows drew together. "She may be the baby of the family, but I'm not talkin' about your sister, Cleo. I'm talking about you. You're my baby girl. My firstborn."

I wasn't sure why his words had emotions clogging up my throat, but I couldn't speak. I'd just assumed he was talking about Lennox because, while he's always had a soft spot for all his daughters, I felt the bond between them had always been the strongest. She had him wrapped around her finger in a way neither Josie nor I ever had.

"Well, don't remind me of my age then," I muttered, not knowing what to say. "Seems rude to remind a woman of that kind of thing, you know?"

Dad looked around the room, and I wondered if he was judging the way I never redecorated when I came home. How my childhood bedroom and the one he was sitting in now would be nearly indistinguishable if you examined them side by side. "Your mom and I gave your sisters their own plots when they turned twenty-one. We offered the same to you once upon a time, and the offer still stands if you're looking to plant your roots. You know we'd love to have you nearby."

Once upon a time, I'd been happy for their offer. I'd been over the damn moon at the prospect of creating my own little haven right here where I grew up. But then Grady and I broke up, and it never felt right to live here with Thomas. I couldn't explain it, but I think some part of me subconsciously knew he would destroy any happy memories this land once held.

"I appreciate the offer, Dad. Really, I do, but—"

"But I think we both know your roots weren't meant to be planted here." I blinked back my shock, forcing my face to stay as neutral as possible. There was the smallest hint of sadness in his voice, but I couldn't focus on that. If I did, I'd have accepted the offer here and now, regardless of what I really wanted. But how could he know that? I hadn't even begun feeling that way until recently, until Grady. "I get it, and I want you to find the place that feels like home. After what you went through..." he trailed off, clearing his throat before continuing. "Well, you deserve to do whatever makes you happy. Just know your mom and I will support you no matter what."

Oh, my heart. My stupid, badly beaten, scared and cautious heart finally felt like it was breaking in two at the thought of upsetting my dad, even for a second. Before I could get up, he crossed the room and met me for a hug. He didn't hesitate to wrap his arms around me, squeezing tightly. The faint scent of his cologne still clung to his clothes from the morning, and I inhaled deeply, trying to keep the tears at bay.

"I love you, honey," he mumbled against my hair. "And I'm just so sorry."

Even if he didn't say it, I knew what his apology was for.

None of us had talked about Thomas since the night I told my family the truth about our relationship. It wasn't that anyone was purposely avoiding the topic, but we'd all been so busy I let it get swept under the rug. Part of me hoped that was where it would stay, but I think another part of me wanted to talk about it to someone other than Laura or Rachel. I wanted comfort from my sisters and safety from my parents. I wish I'd felt like I could turn to them sooner, that I could've confided in them the moment that first alarm bell rang. The first-time verbal spars turned black and blue.

But I'd been too stubborn, too afraid of being anything less than the perfect, dutiful daughter I tried to morph myself into. I worried I would be seen as too weak, too fragile, too damn pathetic. I heard the whispers of strangers when they gossiped, asking why victims of domestic violence didn't leave earlier. Their ignorance doused my fear and shame in gasoline while I lit the match and watched my life go up in flames.

"I am too, Daddy," I whispered. My words were muffled against his old cotton T-shirt, but I couldn't bring myself to move. It felt safe. It felt like home to be here with my father, letting him see a part of me I didn't let anyone else ever see.

"Oh, Cleo... You have nothing to be sorry about, honey. I should've known, I should've seen the signs. You've always been quiet. Much more reserved than your sisters," he said, rubbing small circles on my back. "But I should've known something was wrong."

"You couldn't have known."

Dad sucked in a breath, voice starting to crack as he spoke. "You're my baby, my daughter, my firstborn... I should have known, Cleo. And maybe I did on some level. Maybe that's why I've been so goddamn torn up about it since you told us."

I pulled back, looking up into his weary eyes. They were so consumed by regret that I couldn't bear it. "Dad..."

"You've always had this special light in your eyes. Even as a kid, and despite all the pressure and responsibility your mom and I put on you, it was there. And that light only grew as you got older and went off to college. That's why I didn't make you attend a small-town school, so you'd be close to us. I wanted you to go out there and feed that spark, even if it meant you leaving." He shook his head. "But when you came back from college, there was something different about you. I thought it was just about the breakup. I told myself it was normal, that it would've been strange if you hadn't been torn up about it because you and that boy were so tangled up in one another, but then it never came back. Each time I saw you, it was like looking at a damn ghost, and I—" Tears fell down his cheeks, but he didn't wipe them away. He let me see, and I forced myself to watch. It was the cruelest form of torture. "I was too stupid to speak up. To ask you if you were alright. I thought you'd come to me if you needed me, like you did when you were a little girl and believed there were monsters beneath your bed."

"It wasn't that simple," I whispered. "I wish it was."

"I know, and I've hated myself for my silence. I could've saved you so much pain if I'd just spoken up. If I'd just talked to you."

This time, I did reach up and wipe his tears away. "I get it. I really do. Sometimes I wish I'd spoken to someone sooner about what was happening behind closed doors. But if therapy has taught me anything, it's that I needed to learn how to save myself. I'd been saving others for so long I'd forgotten to advocate for myself, to be able to recognize that I stayed in situations that were not good for me just for the sake of someone else's comfort." I paused, blinking back tears. "Daddy, I needed to know I could rely on *myself* for once."

He gave me a watery smile. "I haven't told you this enough, but I'm proud of the woman you've become. Your mom and I made you grow up too fast. We relied on you too much."

I reached for his hand and gave it a squeeze. His skin was softer than it was a year ago, the byproduct of being forced into retirement earlier than he wanted. If it were his choice, he would've worked this land until the day he died. "You both did the best you could. I don't hold any grudges about that," I said honestly. "But I am finally at a point in my life where I need to focus on what's best for me versus what's best for this family."

"I know, and I want that for you, sugar. After so many years of looking defeated, I finally see a glimpse of your light again. Whatever, or whoever, is contributing to that, I want you to chase it," Dad said, voice breaking. "Even if it means your journey takes you off this ranch."

I didn't know what to say, so I just let him pull me into his arms and hold me like he used to when I was a little girl. Weeks ago, this kind of intimacy would've made me feel uncomfortable. It still did on some level. I would've batted Dad's concerns away and downplayed my past to appease whatever guilt he might have felt—whether it was warranted or not.

But as crazy as it sounded, I wasn't the same woman I was prior to Grady and Charlie showing up like a hellish tornado. They ripped the roof off my self-imposed martyrdom and forced me into a state of vulnerability I otherwise never would've experienced.

"I love you, Daddy," I whispered, letting the steady beat of his heart ground me.

He pressed a kiss to the top of my head. "I love you, too, sugar. You'll always be my little girl."

I wasn't sure how long we stayed like that. It was long enough I was nearly asleep when a knock sounded on the door. We both turned to look as Mom stood in the doorway, hand resting over her chest. "I hate to interrupt, but there is someone here asking to see you."

I groaned into Dad's chest. "Tell Lennox I'll deal with her later."

Mom rolled her eyes. "While I'm sure your sister would be thrilled to hear, she's not the one asking to see you."

"Who is it?" I asked with a yawn.

The soft cadence of boots on the hardwood floor caught my attention as a deep voice I knew better than my own said, "Me."

grady

. . .

I DIDN'T KNOW if I'd ever seen someone move as fast as Cleo did when I walked into her bedroom. One second, she was cuddling close with her father, and the next, she was standing in front of me, throwing her arms around my neck and pulling me close. Out of all the things I prepared for on the way over, her eagerness had not been on the list. I assumed I'd be met with resistance, that I'd have to drop to my knees and beg her not to leave me, to tell her I couldn't imagine my life without her.

After breakfast this morning, Liv had all but kicked me out of the house, telling me not to come back unless I got my girl. It seemed great until I was halfway here, realizing all the things that could go wrong. Then I panicked so severely I had to pull off on the side of the road so I didn't throw up all over my ex's rental car.

Cleo pulled back, staring up at me with silver-rimmed eyes. "What are you doing here?"

I opened my mouth to answer, but stopped at the sound of a throat clearing behind me. We turned to see her mother staring at us with amusement. She looked over my shoulder at her husband and jerked her chin. "Come on, Dougie. Let's leave the kids be."

Doug stood from the bed, grumbling under his breath about being comfortable, and moved to follow Ruby down the hall. He stopped at the threshold, rapping his knuckles against the frame. "Just remember this is still my house, son," he said, narrowing his eyes at me. I loved the fierce protective look, wondering if one day I'd be doing the same for my own daughter. *Abso-fucking-lutely, I would.* "No funny business."

Ruby gave an exasperated sigh. "Douglas Hayes! Don't make me tell you twice."

To his credit, Doug didn't balk. He held my gaze, waiting for a response. "Yes, sir," I said, giving him a little nod. "She's safe with me, I promise."

He held my gaze a moment longer before his expression softened a touch. "Good. Come find me before y'all head out."

"Love you, Daddy," Cleo whispered, clinging to my arm. We watched her parents disappear around the corner before she dragged me inside her bedroom and shut the door. It looked just like it did when she was a kid, a fact that made me so damn happy. It was so predictably Cleo. She wouldn't have wanted to put the time and effort into re-decorating a space just for the sake of it. The room was practical, so she left it alone.

"This takes me back," I said, perching on the edge of her bed. "The only thing missing are all the boy band posters. Are they hidden in your closet somewhere? We could drag them out and pretend we're sixteen again, making out in a rush while your parents were working in the barn."

Cleo leaned against the door, watching me with a dreamy smile. "Sorry to disappoint, but I trashed those the moment I got back from college."

"Damn. It won't feel the same, but I'm game if you are," I said with a wink.

She laughed, but it quickly died. "What're you doing here, Grady? I told you I would be back by."

There were a million things I wanted to say, but they were filled with flowery bullshit I just didn't have patience for. Might as well shoot straight and hope I hadn't misread her excitement at seeing me standing in her doorway as anything other than relief.

"I wasn't sure what you meant when you said that," I replied honestly, staring down at my hands in my lap. "I got scared, bluebird. I thought maybe you weren't going to come back, or if you did, it would just be to end things. Please know, I had no idea Liv was going to stop by. If I did, I would've told you—"

"I know that," she said, letting her head fall back against the wooden frame. "And honestly? Your fear is valid. I was scared, too. Scared of my own insecurities, of not being enough, of feeling like an outsider. I panicked and ran."

Hearing her admit that had me feeling like I'd failed her. Though I couldn't undo years of trauma in a matter of weeks, I was enamored by the idea that I'd done enough to reassure her of my feelings. That she had always been a part of me, of my life, even when we were apart. How my love for her was written into my music, immortalized in every song I'd sung across sold-out stadium tours. It hurt at first to put those feelings down on paper, but then it became solace.

Should I have gone to therapy somewhere along the way? Yeah, probably. But music had always been my way of working through even the toughest emotions. In the weeks after my mom passed, I became consumed with thoughts of grief and death, dealing with them the only way I knew how: by writing some of my most heartbreaking songs to date.

"The moment I pulled out of your driveway, I wanted to cut the engine and run back to your arms," she whispered. "I felt so stupid and silly, Grady. That wasn't the kind of first impression I wanted to make on Olivia, who, I'm sure, thinks I'm a complete basket case."

"Are you kidding? She kicked me out of my own house and told me not to come back unless you were with me," I chuckled.

"A woman after my own heart."

I held out my hands, elated when she pushed off the door and took them. "Your heart's already spoken for, bluebird. I claimed it twenty years ago when I asked you on our first date, and I'm here to claim it again if you'll let me."

Cleo blinked, letting a single tear fall down her cheek. "It's yours. It's always been yours." I widened my stance, inviting her to step even closer. "I don't really know what the future looks like, baby, but I know I want to figure it out by your side. No matter what is thrown our way."

I never considered myself a man in need of reassurance, but I realized I was different with her than with anyone else in my life. Cleo and I had hurt each other in the past, whether intentional or not, and things weren't always going to be a walk in the park. We'd need to feel comfortable checking in with one another, to be able to talk through situations that'd likely play upon our fears, especially once word got out about our relationship.

"I can't tell you how good it feels to hear you say that," I murmured, bringing her fingers to my lips. "Because once we walk out of this bedroom, there's no going back."

"You're mistaken if you ever thought we had a choice to begin with," she said. "Our past may have been riddled with storms, but we're still standing after the rain."

I smiled. "That sounds like a good line for a song."

Cleo leaned in, leaving only a fraction of space between our mouths as she whispered, "If you're good, I'll let you use it."

"I think you know exactly how good I can be, bluebird," I whispered, eliminating the space between us in a kiss. I meant for it to be quick, but Cleo deepened it before I had the chance to pull away. Winding her fingers into my hair, she pulled me closer and forced me to give her exactly what she wanted.

Who was I to tell her no?

I hauled her into my lap, and she immediately began grinding herself down on my growing cock. Gone was the shy girl I used to know. This dominant version of Cleo was quickly becoming one of my favorite sides to her. It wasn't even because of the sexual gratification I got out of it—which, don't get me wrong, was fucking fantastic. But it was more about the way she seemed utterly unapologetic and unashamed about the things she wanted. She could boss me around in the bedroom all she wanted, and I'd say, "Yes, ma'am," before obediently following orders.

My hands fell to her waist, feeling the roll of her hips as she moved. I couldn't help myself, couldn't stop the low groan I let slip free. She stopped, slamming her hand over my mouth before I had the chance to utter a muffled apology. "We gotta get out of here before we get caught," she said a little breathlessly.

I glanced down at my dick, which was straining against the zipper of my jeans. "Yeah, totally. Let me just walk into the living room with your dad while sporting a hard-on. That doesn't sound like a one-way ticket to getting my ass kicked or anything."

She giggled, climbing off my lap before yanking me to my feet. "Maybe that's the key. Think about all the *really* painful ways he'd torture you if he found out what we were just doing."

Suddenly, I was envisioning some kind of western-themed horror film where Doug chased me through the woods with a chainsaw, laughing maniacally. "Yup, there it goes," I said, quickly adjusting myself. "All good now."

"Good." Cleo leaned up to kiss my cheek. "Let me grab some more clothes, and we can get out of here."

"Can we pull over on a back road before we get home?" I asked, half-joking. When she gave me a wink before stepping into the bathroom, it took everything I had not to follow her in, consequences be damned, but I didn't.

I was a good boy and stayed put.

My phone vibrated, and I pulled it out to see a message from Liv.

LIV

Well???? Any update???

GRADY

Can you calm down with the question marks? They're obnoxious

LIV

Don't deflect

Did you get your girl????

I couldn't help but grin like an idiot as I typed out my response.

GRADY

I got her!

The following message was a picture of Charlie with her hands thrown up in the air in celebration.

"What're you smiling at?" Cleo asked, coming up to stand beside me.

"Liv texted me to see how it was going," I said, handing the device over so she could see for herself. She blushed as she read through the exchange before giving it back.

"She's really okay with this, huh?"

"She's probably a little too invested, if you ask me, but she's supportive. That's what matters." I tucked the phone in my pocket, reaching for Cleo's bag and throwing it over my shoulder. "Come on. Let's say bye to your dad so he doesn't bust down the door."

Cleo opened the door, but paused for a moment at the threshold, looking around her childhood bedroom. I said nothing, only squeezed her hand in a silent show of support and waited until she was ready. With a sigh, she led me out and down the hall toward the living room. Doug was reclining in the leather armchair while Ruby was crocheting something on the couch beside him. They both looked up as we entered, eyes wandering to where their daughter and I were holding hands.

Pushing to his feet, Doug ambled over and stood in front of us. "This mean you're moving out?" he asked, eyeing the bag over my shoulder.

"You can't get rid of me that easily," Cleo teased, stepping up to hug her father.

"Gettin' you outta the house has been anything but easy," he mumbled, glancing my direction.

She pulled back, brows furrowed as she asked, "What was that?"

"Nothing. I'm happy for you, sugar. That's all," he said, giving her a squeeze before stepping toward me with his hand outstretched. "You better not fuck this up, son."

"Daddy!" Cleo exclaimed at the exact moment her mother said, "Douglas!" but the man didn't flinch. He just stared at me, waiting for a response.

You'd think after thirty-six years, I wouldn't feel the need to cower before my girlfriend's dad, but here I was anyway. Not that I blamed him for whatever resentment he might have. I'd already broken his daughter's heart once. If I were in his shoes, I'd be just as wary.

Instead of making excuses, I gripped his hand and gave it a firm shake. "I'll protect her heart. You have my word, sir."

The skin around Doug's eyes crinkled as he cracked a smile. "Best see that you do. That's my little girl you got there. She's special."

"Okay, I need you both to stop," Cleo mumbled, wiping

beneath her eyes. "I'm going to stay at Grady's house for a few days, not shipping off to war. There doesn't need to be a teary-eyed farewell."

"A few days, my ass," Doug snorted. "Guess we'll see about that."

epilogue

· · ·

Cleo

one month later

"CLEO!"

I looked up at the sound of a slamming car door, watching Charlie run toward me at a dead sprint across the gravel driveway in front of my parents' house. "Hey sunshine!" I said, laughing as she slammed into me with the force of a freight train. If I hadn't braced for impact, we both would've crashed to the ground. "How was the drive?"

Charlie huffed, blowing a piece of loose hair out of her face. "Way too long. I got so bored. Daddy kept telling me to be patient, which I don't like, but then he told me he'd give me ten dollars for every hour I stayed quiet. I told him I'd do it for twenty, and he agreed." She looked around and lowered her voice. "I would've done it for some Sour Patch Kids."

This was where I probably should've told her that extorting her dad wasn't the best idea, but honestly, I couldn't fault her. She damn sure knew her worth. Who was I to tell her otherwise?

"Your secret's safe with me," I said, pantomiming zipping my lips tight.

"What secret would that be?" came a familiar voice. I looked up to find Liv ambling toward us, a knowing smile on her lips as she stood behind her daughter.

Charlie's eyes grew wide as she quickly blurted, "Nothing, Momma," before running toward the barn. Liv and I both turned around to watch her skip down the alley where Lennox was waiting with open arms.

"Did she extort Grady for cash again?" Liv asked, biting down on her lip.

I nodded, stifling my own laugh. "Yup. She sure did."

"I swear the kid is going to be the death of me," she sighed, turning back to give me a hug. Over the past month, she and I had grown close. Sometimes it felt strange confiding about my relationship with my boyfriend's ex-wife. Maybe it would've been different if Liv hadn't been so damn likeable. Our situation was anything but conventional, but we made it work all the same. "It's so good seeing you again, Cleo. Grady's been driving me crazy. The amount of sulking—"

At the mention of Grady's name, my gaze drifted over Liv's shoulder toward the man in question, who was shaking hands with Bishop and Lincoln. Whatever Liv had been saying faded into the background as all of my attention was focused straight ahead. He was wearing a tight black T-shirt that hugged his body like a second skin and a backward baseball cap. His sun-kissed skin seemed even more golden than it had last time I saw him.

It'd only been two weeks, but it might as well have been an eternity. According to Lennox, I'd grown to be quite the lovesick fool while Grady had been gone, which might have been true. She caught me doodling *Mrs. Grady Wilde* on one of the livestock invoices the other day. I wasn't sure I'd ever really live that down.

When all three guys headed our way and Grady's burning gaze locked on me, I took off at a run. I could hear the hoots and hollers around us as I jumped into his arms and kissed him. He slid his hand up my back, gripping my neck and holding me close until I'd completely melded my body to his.

Would I ever get used to this feeling? I hoped not. Every time he kissed me, touched me, or even looked in my direction, I felt a rush of excitement, reminiscent of when I was sixteen.

"God, I missed you," I mumbled against his lips.

"Never leave me like that again," he said back, setting me down on my feet. "I didn't sleep for shit without you in my bed."

"One," I said, swatting at his chest. I let my hand linger on his taut muscles just because I could. After all, I hadn't been able to gawk at him in weeks. A girl deserved a little eye candy. "You left me. I've been right here all along. And two—"

Grady captured my lips again in a bruising kiss. "Semantics," he said, cutting me off. "I don't ever want to be without you again."

"Pretty soon, that won't be a worry."

He looked over his shoulder at the moving truck parked in the driveway. Josie, Lennox, Lincoln, Bishop, and I had spent most of the day filling it with boxes of childhood memories and what little belongings I had left at the house.

Okay, in reality, my sisters and I mostly watched while the guys did the heavy lifting, but supervisors were important, too. Besides, I needed to soak up every minute I could with my niece while I could.

I wasn't sure I'd come to terms with the fact I was moving to Tennessee. In my head, Black Springs Ranch was still my home. This was the land that raised me, after all. It would continue to do so for my sisters and their growing families, too.

Josie and Lincoln were already talking about having another kid, and I reckoned Lennox and Bishop wouldn't take long to follow after their wedding next spring. Maybe sooner, given how often they were at it. Nothing would surprise me at this point.

Moving wasn't a choice I made lightly, but it felt right. Grady, Liv, and I talked about it extensively before they headed back to Tennessee. They were willing to do whatever it took to make our relationship a possibility, even talking about buying a home in Ashwood to live there part-time. But at the end of the day, I couldn't let them. They had made a life for themselves in Nashville. It was the only home Charlie had ever known. I wouldn't have felt right if Liv or Grady missed out on time with their daughter because I was unwilling to move.

As much as I loved the ranch and those who lived on it, it never felt like home to me. Try as I might, most of my life was spent attempting to change everything about myself so I was more like my sisters. All I wanted was a place to call my own. A place that was as comforting as it was exciting.

Color me surprised when I realized that the feeling came from a person, not a dot on the map.

With Grady, I didn't have to be anyone other than who I was. He knew every part of me—the good, the bad, and the particularly ugly—and loved them fiercely. My insecurities didn't bleed out as often. Instead of living life in my head, I could spend my days basking in his love and adoration.

"It won't be long at all." Grady put his hand in my back pocket and squeezed, letting loose a deep growl that sent goosebumps skittering across my skin. "Is it horrible that all I can think about is getting you into our brand new home and christening every single surface? Those countertops are just begging to have your bare ass imprinted on the marble, and the leather couches..."

"Maybe we could just leave now? I'm sure the others would understand," I murmured. After two weeks of nothing but a handful of phone calls and the random risqué text, I wasn't ashamed to admit I was just as ravenous for him as he was for me. He'd spent most of the past few weeks either talking with lawyers and his PR team about the divorce or house hunting.

Liv had offered to let us stay at their shared home in Nashville to make things easier, but Grady and I had both wanted our own space. As much as I was coming to adore his ex-wife, living with her permanently wasn't really something either of us was itching to do. She was nearly as bad as Charlie when it came to barging through a closed door without knocking. What if she walked in while we were having some alone time?

Thank you, but no thank you.

Grady and I both looked over at where our loved ones had gathered, each of them laughing and conversing like old friends. Seeing them all together tugged on my heart. I mean, it wasn't like I was moving to the other side of the world, but I wouldn't be able to walk through the door and seek their comfort either.

"We'll have our whole lives for that, but this?" Grady kissed my shoulder, gesturing toward our family. "We should soak this up while we can."

I nodded, letting him drag me over to join the fray. Liv had her arms draped over Charlie's shoulders as they watched Lennox and Bishop melt over Stella's high-pitched giggle. Josie and my mom had their heads bent together in conversation, as Lincoln and my dad looked out over the back pasture.

"Look who finally decided to grace us with their presence," Lincoln said. "Thought we were going to have to hide the kids in the house after that show of PDA. The barn is a great choice if you're looking for a quickie."

"Every damn day one of y'all says some shit that brings me one step closer to either the grave or a jail cell," Dad muttered, fighting a smile. Like most of us, he was well used to Lincoln's habit of saying whatever came to his mind, even if it was wildly inappropriate.

"We'll leave the barn to you two," Grady said, nodding toward my sisters. "The treehouse is ours."

"What about the treehouse?" Charlie squeaked. "Are the birds okay?"

"Yeah, the birds *and* the bees are safe up there," Lennox said, covering her mouth to stop from laughing. Bishop glanced up to the sky and pinched the bridge of his nose, muttering a curse beneath his breath.

"Oh, okay," Charlie said, looking up at her mom, confused. "Um, will the bees hurt the birds?"

"Only if they ask nicely," Lincoln quipped.

"You're not helping," Josie said.

He winced as she sent a quick jab into his ribs. "I don't understand why I'm the one in trouble. She started it."

"Well, I'm ending it," she said, crossing her arms over her chest.

"Whoa, okay, Mom," Lennox mocked. "Tell me, do you get some kind of handbook when you become parents that gives you these horrible comebacks?"

"You sure you wanna move away?" Dad joked, coming to stand next to me. "Look at all the fun you'll miss."

I rested my head on his shoulder, smiling as I watched my sisters playfully bicker. "I'm sure the family group chat will be enough to tide me over until you come visit."

"Yeah, yeah. Just leave your old man to fend for himself, then. Don't be surprised if I drop them on your doorstep at Christmas. I'm already dreading the drive. I might take Bishop and Josie in one car and leave your mom to fend for herself with Lennox and Lincoln."

"Doug, I'd be happy to send our private jet down for y'all," Liv said. "Might make the trip a little more bearable."

Dad pointed in her direction. "I knew I liked you."

"What do you think, Stella?" Lincoln asked, taking his daughter from Lennox's arms. He held her close before pressing a kiss to her forehead. "Wanna ride in a fancy private jet?"

"Would be better than listening to her scream for hours on end," Josie muttered.

"I don't know how you're keeping your shit together right now," Lincoln said, changing the subject. He clapped Dad on the shoulder, eyes locked on the moving truck. "Even the thought of Stella growing up and moving away makes my chest hurt."

All our eyes went to Dad as he started to laugh. "Are you kidding? I love my girls, but I've been trying to get rid of 'em for over a year now." He threw his thumb over his shoulder, gesturing toward the house. "Now, I don't have to worry about shit anymore. I can enjoy my retirement and walk around in my underwear if I want."

Had I just heard him right? "What do you mean by 'get rid of us'?" Lennox asked, stepping closer. "It's not like Josie and I are moving. We're still on the ranch."

"Yeah, but you're outta the house. That's all that matters."

"Why do I feel like you're hiding something?" she asked, crossing her arms.

"I'm not hiding anything. Y'all just don't pay attention." When none of us spoke, he continued. "Come on... You didn't really think this guy showed up by accident, did you?" he asked, pointing at Grady.

Grady's brows furrowed. "Wait, so you knew who I was when you booked me to play at your birthday?"

"No shit, Sherlock. Y'all really think I'm that dumb? Of course, I knew. I followed your career for years, just didn't say anything outta respect for my daughter," Dad said, jerking his chin my way.

Understanding dawned as I thought back to that day. Dad's memory had never been great, and I'd been too shocked to think straight, so when he said he didn't recognize Grady, I hadn't questioned it.

Of course, he knew.

Of course, he was the puppet-master pulling all our strings.

"When my buddy Frank wrote me that letter before he died last spring, I didn't realize the chain reaction it was gonna set off by inviting Lincoln down here," he continued, glancing at Josie. "Y'all getting together was a happy accident. I mean, I was hoping he'd run your piece of shit ex off, but I didn't expect all this. Seeing y'all got the wheels turning, though. I started paying closer attention to each of you girls." His gaze slid to Lennox and Bishop, who were both staring at Dad with wide eyes. "Don't give me that look. Y'all were about as subtle as a house on fire. It was easy to push you together."

"But how?" Bishop whispered, clearly confused.

"I needed to get y'all working together on the ranch without killing one another, but I didn't have a reason until I wound up in the hospital," he said with a grimace. "That wasn't part of my plan, but I worked with what I had, and, well, look at y'all now. You're welcome, by the way."

Lennox's jaw dropped. "Oh my god, you were playing *matchmaker* this whole time?"

"What? Like it's hard?" Dad asked. He turned toward me, hands braced on his hips. "You two were the biggest pains in my ass, though. At one point, I thought y'all were a lost cause, too damn stubborn to see what was right in front of you. Guess I was wrong."

I stood there, trying to wrap my mind around everything happening. "Let me get this straight... You paid for my ex-boyfriend and his band to play at your birthday party in an attempt to get us together?"

"Sure did."

"But you didn't even know about my divorce."

"You'd been in Texas for months, sugar. You wouldn't have stayed unless y'all were splittin' up. Plus, you stopped wearing your ring. I may be old, but I know damn well when a woman takes off her wedding ring, there's no going back."

"Douglas Hayes!" Mom exclaimed, smacking his arm. "I can't believe this. Why didn't you tell me? I could've helped!"

"Well, honey… I love you, but you would've meddled too much and scared everyone off." He shrugged, clearly not seeing any faults in his argument. Granted, neither did I. He was right; Mom really was the type to meddle. "Plus, you didn't ask. If you had—"

"I didn't know I needed to!" she shrieked.

"Oh, boy," Lincoln said, laughing. "Good thing you have that big, empty house, huh, Doug? Just you and Ruby. Alone. Forever."

Mom's lips twitched at the joke, but she quickly composed herself and continued staring at our dad like he'd just run over her garden with the lawnmower. She wasn't quick to forgive, either. Dad would likely be hearing about this for years to come.

"Well, shit." He rubbed the back of his neck. "Too late to ask you girls to move home? We've got plenty of room."

Bishop reached for Lennox, tugging her against his chest. "Sorry, Doug. This one is mine."

"Yeah," Lincoln agreed, following suit with Josie and Stella. He stared down at them like they were the only things that mattered. "Guess I should be thanking you for giving me these beautiful ladies."

"Kiss ass," Lennox muttered as Bishop kissed the top of her head.

I looked at Grady, whose bright blue eyes shone with unshed tears. He opened his arms, and I leaned into his embrace. "Thank you for meddling, Daddy," I whispered.

Dad turned to Mom. "You can't be too mad. Look at our girls." He held out a hand with a raised brow, practically begging for her to argue with him. She took it and let him pull her close. "And think about all the things we could do now that—"

"Nope! I've heard enough," Lennox said, breaking free of

Bishop's hold. "I draw the line at listening to y'all talk about your sex lives."

"Well, if that ain't the pot calling the kettle black," I murmured, stepping forward and glancing at everyone around me.

While I was making the best choice for myself, I couldn't deny I'd miss this—miss *them*. My chest ached, and eyes stung as I fought off tears. The sadness I felt wasn't tied to regret, but rather the knowledge that this road was one I had to walk alone. It was uncomfortable, but in an exciting way, knowing I was about to discover who I really was for the first time.

"Oh, Cleo," Mom said softly, opening her arms. "Come here, baby."

Quickly striding forward, I hugged her and let the tears fall as she stroked my back. It wasn't long before Dad joined in, and then both of my sisters. I was sure I felt Lincoln in the mix, and Bishop, too, though the bastard would likely never admit it.

"We're so proud of you," Dad whispered, giving me a squeeze. A chorus of agreements echoed his words. If they hadn't been supporting me, I likely would have fallen to the ground and wept.

And then I started crying harder, because how could he go and say something like that and expect me to be able to keep it together? I knew they were proud of me every day of my life, but it was strangely cathartic for him to show his pride at my leaving. "I'm going to miss you all so much."

"God, why am I crying?" Liv asked from the sidelines. I turned over my shoulder, smiling when I saw Grady with his arm resting over her shoulder. "Healthy family dynamics freak me out."

"You're getting rid of us for good," Lennox said, wiping beneath her eyes.

"Yeah, I'd like to show Stella where her mom and I met," Lincoln added.

Josie shook her head. "You can't take a baby into a bar."

"Why not?"

"Because it's a bar," she deadpanned.

"I don't see what the problem is."

Bishop clapped Lincoln on the shoulder. "You wouldn't."

Lincoln turned and flipped Bishop off, making our tears turn to laughter. As it died down, I realized there was nothing else to wait for. It was time to go.

"The driver will be by to get the truck later," Grady said, stepping up beside me and placing his hand on my back. "He said he'd be here this afternoon."

"Don't worry. We got it," Dad said, waving him off. Then he stuck his hand out for Grady to take. "Take care of my girl."

"I will, sir."

Dad's gaze shifted to me. "You're still my little girl, and you'll always have a place here, sugar. Don't forget that, okay?"

"I won't, Daddy," I mumbled, giving him one last hug. It lasted longer than the others, and I let his warmth ground me. "I'll let you know when we get there."

"You better," he said, giving me one last squeeze before letting me go. "Better get on the road or else these goodbyes are gonna keep going 'round in circles."

Everyone followed us as we walked to the car, where yet another round of hugs awaited us before we climbed inside. Grady reached over and squeezed my hand as he put the car in reverse. "You ready for this?"

I nodded, blowing out a breath as I stared out at my family. "Let's go."

THE HOUSE WAS dark as we pulled into the drive. It was surrounded by thick pine trees, hidden off the road from prying eyes. I'd seen it plenty of times in pictures, and when Grady FaceTimed me for a virtual tour.

It was the perfect secluded space for us.

The last half of the trip was spent in companionable silence, listening to Charlie snore in the backseat. Though she was keen, she didn't have the opportunity to lighten her dad's wallet this time. She didn't even wake up when we dropped Liv off at their house. She offered to take Charlie for the night, but Grady and I said no, wanting to make sure she didn't feel left out.

Quietly, we climbed out of Grady's truck and stared at our new home. "What do you think?"

I leaned into his warm presence. "I think we probably should've grabbed a hotel for the night so we don't have to sleep on air mattresses."

"Oh come on, we agreed it'd be fun. Kind of like a sleep-over," he pouted. "Where's your sense of adventure?"

"Probably packed away in one of the many boxes showing up tomorrow," I chuckled. "Come on, grab our girl so we can go inside."

He smiled at that, giving me a chaste kiss and tossing me the keys. "Go on in. I'll be there in a second."

Without waiting, I headed up the brick-paved walkway and unlocked the door. Grabbing my phone, I turned on the flash-light, scanning the wall for the switch. "There you are," I murmured.

The entryway was immediately bathed in light, illuminating a large portion of the living room ahead, where there were two large air mattresses already set up. Floor-to-ceiling steel paned windows sat on either side of the massive stone fireplace. They'd be beautiful during the day, but honestly, it was slightly creepy at night. Thankfully, our furniture was scheduled to arrive tomorrow. If Grady hadn't already grabbed them, curtains would be the first thing I'd order in the morning.

Soft footsteps had me turning around to see Grady carrying

Charlie into the house. He walked over and laid her down on one of the beds, tucking her in tightly before kissing her forehead.

"She didn't wake up?" I whispered, looking down at his daughter, whose mouth was hanging open.

Grady shook his head. "Nope. She's out." He pulled me close, brushing his lips over mine. "Why? Whatever could be on your mind?"

"I was just thinking about some promises you made back in Texas that involved christening all the rooms in the house."

Even though it was dark, I could see the glint of mischief in Grady's eyes. "I did say that, didn't I?"

"You sure did."

He looked around, gaze settling on the end of a long hallway. "The kitchen will have to wait, but," he paused, grabbing my head and tugging me down the darkened space, "we could always make use of our new bedroom."

I laughed as he kissed me deeply and passionately, my body relaxing in his arms as he trailed his mouth down my jaw to my neck. "Wait, there's something I need to do first," I said, stepping away and pulling my phone up. Pulling up the family text thread, I checked the time. 11:11 p.m. Then, I glanced at Grady before typing the words I had always longed to say.

CLEO

I'm home. 🩶

what's next?

Thank you so much for going on this wild ride. Y'all have been so wonderful that I couldn't resist giving you a little treat.

Keep reading for an exclusive sneak peek of *One More Round,* book one in the Pinecrest Ridge series.

olivia

. . .

One More Round Sneak Peek

I STARED down at the myriad of missed texts from my brother for what seemed like the hundredth time since I boarded the Hartstring's private jet just under four hours ago. The past three weeks had been spent in meetings with lawyers and board members as we navigated a merger that would triple our assets, securing some of the greatest independent artists I'd ever heard. My phone had been blowing up all morning, but I'd ignored everything for the sake of closing the deal.

If it hadn't been for my assistant flagging me down from outside the glass walls in our boardroom, I might not have checked it at all until I called my daughter this evening.

The stewardess came by, advising me to fasten my seatbelt as the pilot announced our descent to Nashville. I tucked my phone away and closed my eyes, gripping the armrest like I did every time I flew. You think I'd be used to it by now, but apparently not. I hated heights, and I hated flying even more. It didn't matter that the plane was private. It just meant there were fewer people to witness my panic attacks at the slightest hint of turbulence.

I gathered my things the moment the plane came to a stop, giving my thanks to the crew as they dropped the stairs. The Tennessee air was muggy, even though the sun had already gone down. Not that it made much of a difference either way. It stayed in a constant state of high humidity regardless of the time of day.

I scanned the tarmac and spotted the blacked-out SUV sitting just ahead. The headlights illuminated a tall figure standing just outside the door.

"Little ostentatious, don't you think?" my brother shouted as I descended the stairs. He met me at the bottom, wrapping me up in a warm hug. He smelled like home, like pine and sawdust. "Good to have you home, Livvy. Despite the circumstances."

"Yeah, those aren't great," I agreed, blowing out a breath. "How is John? Is there any news?"

Lukas inclined his head toward the vehicle. "Come on. We'll talk on the way." He grabbed my bags, heading to the open truck, while I slid into the passenger seat. As he settled behind the wheel, he looked over at me and smirked. "Sure you don't want to sit in the back? Isn't that what you're used to these days?"

"Fuck off," I muttered. "It isn't like I have much of a choice. You try taking conference calls and studying profit numbers while driving and tell me how that works for you."

My brother's laugh was deep and throaty. "Naw. I passed on that shit, remember? You're the prodigal daughter."

"Lucky me," I said, melting into the leather seat. We were silent as we drove away from the airport and merged onto the highway, heading toward our small hometown rather than the city. "Wait, we aren't staying in Nashville? I thought John was at the hospital."

A pause. "He was."

I turned in my seat to face him. *"Was?"*

Lukas sighed, drumming his fingers against the steering wheel. He looked so much older than I remembered. It hadn't been that long since I'd seen him, a couple of months at most, but there were deep bags beneath his eyes and a tiredness that seemed bone deep.

"He wanted to go home and spend whatever time he had left in the town he loved."

"And the doctors just let him? Can they do that?" I asked, pulling my brows together.

My brother shrugged. "They can't force him to stay against his will, Livvy. They advised against it, but he signed an AMA and wheeled himself out this morning."

I rubbed my temple. "So, what? He's just going home to die?"

Lukas's thrumming stopped, and the silence that took its place told me everything I needed to know.

"What the hell, Lukas? Isn't there anything we can do?"

"It's end-stage liver failure. We don't have a lot of options—"

"I mean, can someone get a medical power of attorney over him? Declare him unfit to make his own decisions?" I pulled up my phone and began scrolling. "Or what about a liver transplant? That has to be an option, right?"

He shook his head. "John refused all treatment, and he's been declared of sound mind."

"What did the doctors say? Did they give him some bullshit

about poor odds or something? Could we get a second opinion?"

"Jesus," Lukas mumbled. "I almost forgot how pushy you can be. I was there when the doctors told him a transplant was risky, given his age, just like any other procedure could be, but that there was a decent enough statistical rate of survival. They offered to set him up with other doctors for a secondary opinion, but John waived it all."

"He still said no?" My voice was barely above a whisper as I settled back into the leather.

Lukas reached over and gave my hand a slight squeeze. "I'm sorry, Livvy."

"What happens now?" I whispered, voice breaking. "I mean, how long?"

"We hired in-home care to make sure he's taken care of for however long he has left—"

I slammed my hand down on the dashboard. "Which is how long, Luke? Answer the question."

He ran a hand through his short, brown hair, mussing it slightly. "Three to six months if he's lucky."

Three to six months wouldn't even see John through to his next birthday. There'd be no more holiday celebrations, something that he always made a big fuss out of. No more fatherly advice followed by warm hugs and total understanding.

It would be gone. *Poof.* Just like dad.

"This is bullshit," I said as the first tear fell. I couldn't bring myself to wipe it away. The grief weighed too heavily on my heart.

"It is," he agreed. "But it's what he wanted. At the end of the day, all we can do is respect his wishes and hope he doesn't leave the world with unfinished business."

Lukas didn't let go of my hand as I cried. Not even when his emotions got the best of him, and he joined in as well. It was all too much to handle. We'd lost our dad at an early age, but Uncle

John had done his best to step up to the plate. He never had kids of his own, but Lukas and I were as good as.

We stayed like that in relative silence. The radio wasn't even loud enough to drown out the crunch of our tires against the asphalt. I focused on the noise, trying to push away the intrusive thoughts clamoring to be let in. It wasn't until I saw the "Welcome to Pinecrest" sign that I finally asked, "Does Mom know?"

Lukas blew out a long breath. "She does."

"How is she taking it?"

"About as well as could be expected," he said dryly. "She'll probably be two bottles of Chardonnay in by the time we reach the house."

I shifted in my seat. "Does she know I'm coming?"

"There wasn't really a way around that, Livvy. You've got to see her sometime."

"I know that. I just didn't think it'd be like *this*," I muttered. "But I guess nothing brings people together like an impending death in the family."

"Morbid but true," he chuckled. "If it makes you feel any better, I've put her in the main house with me while you get to escape to the cottage by yourself."

"Oh, thank god. I can lock the doors and never come out," I said.

Lukas laughed. "Yeah, I don't think sequestering yourself is gonna work. You know how persistent she can be. She'll probably camp outside your front door until you say something to her."

"The problem isn't speaking to her. It's saying what she wants to hear." I scoffed. "I can't give her what she wants, Luke. It's a nonstarter."

"Not even now?" he asked.

I shook my head. "Especially not now. It complicates things, sure, but the wheels are already in motion. I can't stop them. I don't *want* to stop them."

Lukas nodded but didn't say anything more. I could always count on him not to push me. He knew me better than that, knew I would shut down entirely if he did.

That courtesy was something Mom had never learned, though. She was often lost in her own world, indifferent to others' emotions until they somehow came back to affect her. Dad's death hadn't helped, either. If anything, she'd become more withdrawn over the years and quicker to adopt a victim-like mentality whenever she was met with opposition.

My brother called her selfish, and my therapist called it narcissism. Po-tay-to / po-tah-to, as far as I was concerned. Whatever it was had caused a rift between us that I didn't know how to mend.

Or if I even wanted to.

"Home sweet home," Lukas said, pulling up to the large wooden-framed gate at the front of our property. He rolled down the window and punched in the code as we waited for it to swing open slowly.

I looked at the empty hooks hanging from the worn cedar beam across the top. When I was a kid, Dad and I had come up with a name for the property. He said it hadn't mattered that it wasn't a working ranch; everything needed a name—something that set it apart from every other plot of land that people built on. So, we'd come up with Blue Moon Ranch, and he'd had a sign made the very next day.

After he died, it was the first thing our mother had taken down.

Lukas crept along the winding road that led past his home. It was a massive ranch-style house that looked like it had been plucked from the pages of a magazine. The exterior was made of rock and cedar, featuring huge windows that allowed for an unobstructed view of the sprawling acreage on each side. White pipe fencing gave the illusion of a fenced-in yard, but it was little more than decoration.

As we drove by, I noticed the darkened windows and curtains drawn. If it weren't for the single light illuminating the porch, it would've looked deserted.

"She's fucking subtle, isn't she?" Lukas asked. I followed his gaze to where a figure sat in a rocking chair adjacent to the front door. They were hidden behind a cloud of smoke, but I didn't need to see their face to know what lay behind it.

I turned away, feeling uneasy. Despite the dark tint, it felt as though our mother's gaze was burning a hole through the window. She might as well have put out her cigarette directly on my skin. "So much for quitting, huh?"

"Did you really think she was going to? She's like a fucking freight train," Lukas said, pulling up to my temporary home.

The cabin matched the exterior design of the main house, but it had a cozy feel that the other didn't have. It was small in comparison, but still had two bedrooms and bathrooms for guests. The living area was an open-concept space with tall ceilings that made the room feel larger than it was, and a small office was located just off the entrance.

I didn't bother with a response because neither of us had ever believed our mother when she said she was going to do anything. Smoking had been a hot-button topic growing up. It didn't matter that Lukas and I begged her to stop. She never did.

"So, you'll need to get groceries because I haven't had a chance to go to the store, but there should be plenty of drinks to choose from," Lukas said, hopping out of the SUV and grabbing my bags.

"Are we talking water, tea, and coffee? Or something stronger?" I asked, trailing slowly behind him up the cobblestone path that led to the front door.

Lukas keyed in the alarm code and flipped on the switch as

we stepped inside. He set my bags down in the entryway. "You know I always have a selection on hand," he said, smirking. "Especially when it comes to family reunions."

I came up behind him, wrapping my arms around his waist. "I love you," I mumbled into his back. "I knew I was your favorite sister."

He patted my hand, chuckling. "You're my only sister."

"Semantics," I said, stepping back and waving him off. "Still the favorite."

Lukas walked over and pulled two glasses from the bar cart in the living room. "Thirsty?"

I nodded vigorously before plopping down on the couch, letting out a big whoosh of air as I felt my body sink into the plush fabric. It'd been one hell of a day, and the prospect of the ones to come was already exhausting me.

The chime of ice cubes against crystal pulled me back as Lukas shook the glass above my face. "Bless you," I said, grabbing it with both hands and sitting up. The amber liquid burned as it landed on my tongue, but finished smooth as hell. "Oh, this is the good shit."

"Nothing but the best for you," Lukas said, raising his glass. He settled into the armchair across from me, crossing his ankle over his knee. "How long do you plan to stay?"

I looked down at the glass, tapping the outside three times. "I don't know."

He shifted, furrowing his brows. "What's that mean?"

"It means I don't know," I said, shrugging. "It means my life has felt like a shit show over the past few years. That this is the first time I've been able to disconnect and just exist in the silence."

Lukas hummed, swirling the liquor in his glass. "Pinecrest has been good to me, you know. Good place to raise a family—"

I snorted. "What do you know about that?"

"Hey! I have friends who aren't living the eternal bachelor life."

"Sure, you do," I said, downing the rest of my drink, shaking it in my brother's direction for a refill.

His gaze dropped to my hand and then back to my face. "You know where it is," he said, gesturing toward the bar cart.

I rolled my eyes, pushing off the couch. "You're the worst."

"Thought I was the best?"

"I've changed my mind," I said, snatching the decanter from the cart and setting it down in front of us.

Lukas watched as I refilled both glasses. "Speaking of family men... Does your ex-husband know you're in town?"

"Why do you say it like that? You make it sound so gross and horrible and miserable."

"Sorry... Baby daddy?"

I scrunched up my nose. "Ew, that's worse."

"Divorcée it is then," he said, leaning back.

"You know damn well we would still talk every day, even if Charlie wasn't in the picture," I said, pointing in his direction. "Grady's my best friend. It was never like that between us."

Lukas tented his fingers in front of his face. "And yet you have a kid."

I gave him a saccharine smile. "You, of all people, know you don't have to be in love to have a kid. We were lonely until we weren't. Honestly, I'm surprised you don't have any of your own, given your proclivity for practice."

My brother was many things, but an eternal bachelor would forever be at the top of the list. I could count on one hand the number of relationships he'd been in over his forty-two years, and at least two of them happened sometime between elementary and high school. He had quite the reputation around town as the kind to love'em and leave'em. Sometimes, I swore he tried to live up to the rumors instead of squashing them.

I leaned back, taking a sip. "And, of course, he knows. I

called him before I even boarded the plane. He offered to let me stay with them."

Lukas snorted. "Isn't that awkward? I mean, he's remarried."

"It's only weird to you because you're a forty-two-year-old man child who can't comprehend being in the same room with someone you slept with. I was the one who drew up the divorce papers. I was the one who told him to follow his dream." I shrugged. "She was it."

Not long after our divorce was final, Grady remarried his high school sweetheart. Cleo was wonderful. I absolutely adored her. It'd been a bumpy ride to get to where they were now, but I was so damn glad to see it worked out. If anyone deserved their fairytale ending, it was them.

Grady was my best friend. Except for the drunken, lonely night that resulted in Charlie's conception, it'd never been anything other than platonic for us. Our relationship was like one of those romantic comedies where two friends get married for some kind of mutual benefit. Except, instead of falling in love at the end, we got a divorce and shared custody. Our daughter may not have been planned, but I didn't realize how much I needed her until I held her in my arms. I'd always love him for that gift alone.

Grady helped me take over my company, and I helped him get the record deal he deserved. He'd given up so much of his life so that I could live out my dream. Even if he had benefited from it, too, it wasn't the same. The least I could do was finally set him free once I had it. When he'd found his forever, I didn't give him a choice. I had the divorce papers drawn up and signed my name before he could stop me.

"You were in the wedding," he deadpanned.

"Did you know it only takes five minutes to get ordained online?" His unamused stare remained absolute. "Anyway, I told him I was grateful for the offer but that I would much prefer to drive my big brother crazy."

Lukas snorted. "Charlie excited?"

"We haven't told her yet, but I'm gonna swing by tomorrow morning—apparently on my way to get groceries—and pick her up."

"And you're bringing her here? With mom so close?"

I let out a breath, deflating into the cushions. That was a great question. One I didn't want to answer but knew there was no use in avoiding. "I don't have a choice. I'm surprised she hasn't stormed over to Grady's house already and demanded to see her."

"This is so disappointing. I bet your daddy's rolling over in his grave right now."

It'd been two years since Mom had uttered those words before storming out of my door. They still stung like they did the day she said them. My divorce was just one of the many things my mother had never been able to move on from. The day I told her had been the last and final straw. Apparently, it had broken something in her brain that caused her to malfunction as a human being.

Neither Charlie nor I had seen her since. I'd wanted to keep it that way as long as I could, but that was going to come to an end.

It was almost ironic that John's health was the one thing that brought us back here. He'd tried to smooth it over countless times, but neither of us was willing to listen. I guess he'd get his wish in the end.

"Well," he drawled, downing the rest of his drink. "Here's to family reunions."

also by amber palmer

<u>The Darkness and Fire Trilogy</u>

Of Darkness and Fire

Of Truth and Traitors

Of Ashes and Crowns

<u>The Wicked Dark Duology</u>

The Night Runs Red

The Day Burns Bright

<u>Black Springs Ranch</u>

Between the Pines

Through the Dust

After the Rain

<u>Pinecrest Ridge</u>

One More Round

acknowledgments

It's baffling how many things can change in a year. At the end of 2024, I was ready to give up my dream and walk away from this career with a heavy heart. But then I was talked into something I never thought I would: Writing a contemporary, small-town, cowboy romance.

When I published Between the Pines, I never thought it would lead me to where I am today. Seeing my books end up in the hands of so many people is kind of wild. I mean, that's kind of the point, but I wasn't sure it was in the cards for me.

I fell in love with these characters, with their world, and now it's time for me to say, "See you later!"

It's bittersweet, but I know it isn't goodbye. Not by a long shot.

Wrapping up with Cleo and Grady just felt right. Honestly, this book was extremely difficult to write. Out of the three sisters, Cleo is most like me. It's kind of terrifying putting a huge part of myself out there to be criticized, but I am fiercely confident in the fact that people like Cleo and I deserve to have our moment in the sun.

But I also couldn't have done it on my own, and I'm grateful knowing I didn't have to.

To John: Thank you for keeping me fed and sane. For holding my hand and letting me cry and scream when the pressure became too much. For being the best assistant and helping (or trying to) keep me organized.

To Heather: I've said it once and I'll say it again… I couldn't do this without you. Thank you for being by my side from the beginning. For only giving me a little pushback when I said, "Hey, I think I'm going to write a book with cowboys." For making me a better and more confident writer with our editing-turned-yap sessions.

To Holly: Thank you for believing in me when I didn't believe in myself. For pushing me off the cliff into contemporary when I was terrified, and letting me ask a million questions. For being my biggest hype girl.

To Lauren: Thank you for making me read my first small-town romance and sending me down an inescapable rabbit hole that led me here. For giving me the room to feel all the emotions, and being ready to crawl into my shell with me when I wasn't ready to come out.

To Brittney: Thank you for championing these books. For always having my back and helping this series grow into everything I always dreamed it could be.

To Liz, Rose, Jill, Anna, and Ashley: Thank you for making Cleo and Grady's story exceptional. For giving me all the hype reactions and support and guidance to ensure these characters and this series ends in the best possible way.

To Viki: These books wouldn't be anything without the breathtaking covers you've created. Thank you for taking my very basic idea and creating the most amazing covers from it.

To my amazing readers: Thank you for shouting your love for this series from the mountaintops. For always hyping the characters up and spreading the word about Black Springs Ranch. I couldn't do any of this without you. Please know I love y'all so much!

Can't wait to see you again in Pinecrest.

XO,

Amber

meet amber

Amber Palmer is an American romance author specializing in paranormal and contemporary love stories. Born in Arizona and raised in Texas, she's the proud parent of three mischievous cats and one playful pup. When she's not devouring spicy romance novels, you can find her curating bookish Spotify playlists or jotting down ideas for her next project. A fierce advocate for mental health, Amber crafts characters who face and heal from deep traumas. She's unapologetically passionate about all things spicy—both in books and life—and loves gaming with her husband in her downtime.